VENDETTA

VENDETTA

A STORY OF ONE FORGOTTEN

Marie Corelli

Introduction by
Annik Valkanberg

Villainous Press
Denver, Colorado

ISBN-13: 978-1622254712

Published by
Villainous Press, an imprint of
The Publishing Consortium, LLC
PO Box 473190
Aurora, CO 80047

Villainous Press Trade Paperback Edition June 2014
Printed in the USA
www.VillainousPress.com

Introduction

Annik Valkanberg

MARIE Corelli. Have you ever heard of her? Perhaps you've read some of her contemporaries. Do the names Rudyard Kipling, H.G. Wells, and Sir Arthur Conan Doyle sound familiar?

The lovely and talented Ms. Corelli outsold them all—combined. She was the best-selling author of her time. British royals were very fond of her novels, as was Winston Churchill. Her books found their way to the strangest private libraries.

It's rumored Marie was a closeted lesbian with her best friend and long-time companion, Bertha Vyver. Indeed, she made sure Bertha was well cared for by leaving her estate to the one she loved.

Marie was an eccentric woman, and this gave rise to ugly reviews. Many of the male reviewers went out of their way to insult her instead of reviewing her work.

Typical of the times, unfortunately.

She developed a marked distaste for the press, holding

most of them in contempt. Even in the 1800's, the paparazzi went out of their way to get a story—any story—as long as it sold papers. She also felt that many of the articles were puff pieces designed to keep the socialites in the public eye.

Mark Twain had a distaste for her work and for her person, until he had the opportunity to travel to England and meet Marie. Perhaps because she was almost as eccentric as he was, Twain ended up changing his mind and appreciating the authoress.

Ms. Corelli appreciated history, particularly the local historical sites and buildings near Stratford-upon-Avon. She supported the restoration and preservation of the 1700's architecture, including donating time and funding to support the effort.

Unfortunately, during World War One, she was convicted of food hording, and her reputation suffered.

Despite outselling the authors whose names are recognized even today, Marie Corelli has been pushed to the background.

Thanks to Villainous Press, perhaps it is time to introduce her to a new, modern audience who can appreciate her work and the way she lived her life.

PREFACE

L EST those who read the following pages should deem this story at all improbable, it is perhaps necessary to say that its chief incidents are founded on an actual occurrence which took place in Naples during the last scathing visitation of the cholera in 1884. We know well enough, by the chronicle of daily journalism, that the infidelity of wives is, most unhappily, becoming common–far too common for the peace and good repute of society. Not so common is an outraged husband's vengeance–not often dare he take the law into his own hands–for in England, at least, such boldness on his part would doubtless be deemed a worse crime than that by which he personally is doomed to suffer. But in Italy things are on a different footing–the verbosity and red-tape of the law, and the hesitating verdict of special juries, are not there considered sufficiently efficacious to sooths a man's damaged honor and ruined name. And thus– whether right or wrong–it often happens that strange and awful deeds are perpetrated–deeds of which the world in general hears nothing, and which, when brought to light at last, are received with surprise and incredulity. Yet the romances planned by the brain of the novelist or dramatist are poor in comparison with the romances of real life-life wrongly termed commonplace, but which, in fact, teems with tragedies as great and dark and soul- torturing as any devised by Sophocles or Shakespeare. Nothing is more strange than truth–nothing, at times, more terrible!

MARIE CORELLI.
August, 1886.

1

I AM a dead man. Dead legally–dead by absolute proofs–
dead and buried! Ask for me in my native city and they
will tell you I was one of the victims of the cholera that
ravaged Naples in 1884, and that my mortal remains lie
moldering in the funeral vault of my ancestors. Yet–I live!
I feel the warm blood coursing through my veins–the blood of
thirty summers–the prime of early manhood invigorates me,
and makes these eyes of mine keen and bright–these muscles
strong as iron–this hand powerful of grip– this well-knit form
erect and proud of bearing. Yes!–I am alive, though declared to
be dead; alive in the fullness of manly force– and even sorrow
has left few distinguishing marks upon me, save one. My hair,
once ebony-black, is white as a wreath of Alpine snow, though
its clustering curls are thick as ever.

"A constitutional inheritance?" asks one physician,
observing my frosted locks.

"A sudden shock?" suggests another.

"Exposure to intense heat?" hints a third.

I answer none of them. I did so once. I told my story to a
man I met by chance–one renowned for medical skill and
kindliness. He heard me to the end in evident incredulity and
alarm, and hinted at the possibility of madness. Since then I
have never spoken.

But now I write. I am far from all persecution–I can set down the truth fearlessly. I can dip the pen in my own blood if I choose, and none shall gainsay me! For the green silence of a vast South American forest encompasses me–the grand and stately silence of a virginal nature, almost unbroken by the ruthless step of man's civilization–a haven of perfect calm, delicately disturbed by the fluttering wings and soft voices of birds, and the gentle or stormy murmur of the freeborn winds of heaven. Within this charmed circle of rest I dwell–here I lift up my overburdened heart like a brimming chalice, and empty it on the ground, to the last drop of gall contained therein. The world shall know my history.

Dead, and yet living! How can that be?–you ask. Ah, my friends! If you seek to be rid of your dead relations for a certainty, you should have their bodies cremated. Otherwise there is no knowing what may happen! Cremation is the best way–the only way. It is clean, and SAFE. Why should there be any prejudice against it? Surely it is better to give the remains of what we loved (or pretended to love) to cleansing fire and pure air than to lay them in a cold vault of stone, or down, down in the wet and clinging earth. For loathly things are hidden deep in the mold–things, foul and all unnamable–long worms–slimy creatures with blind eyes and useless wings–abortions and deformities of the insect tribe born of poisonous vapor– creatures the very sight of which would drive you, oh, delicate woman, into a fit of hysteria, and would provoke even you, oh, strong man, to a shudder of repulsion! But there is a worse thing than these merely physical horrors which come of so-called Christian burial–that is, the terrible uncertainty. What, if after we have lowered the narrow strong box containing our dear deceased relation into its vault or hollow in the ground– what, if after we have worn a seemly garb of woe, and tortured our faces into the fitting expression of gentle and patient melancholy–what, I say, if after all the reasonable precautions taken to insure safety, they should actually prove insufficient? What–if the prison to which we have consigned the deeply regretted one should not have such close doors as we fondly imagined? What, if the stout coffin should be wrenched apart by fierce and frenzied fingers—what, if our late dear friend should NOT be dead, but should, like Lazarus of old, come forth to challenge our affection anew? Should we not grieve sorely that we had failed to avail ourselves of the secure and classical method of cremation? Especially if we had benefited by worldly goods or money left to us by the so deservedly lamented! For we are self-deceiving hypocrites—few of us are really sorry for the dead—few of us remember them with any real tenderness or affection. And yet God knows! they may need more pity than we dream of!

But let me to my task. I, Fabio Romani, lately deceased, am about to chronicle the events of one short year—a year in which was compressed the agony of a long and tortured life-time! One little year!—one sharp thrust from the dagger of Time! It pierced my heart—the wound still gapes and bleeds, and every drop of blood is tainted as it falls!

One suffering, common to many, I have never known—that is—poverty. I was born rich. When my father, Count Filippo Romani, died, leaving me, then a lad of seventeen, sole heir to his enormous possessions— sole head of his powerful house— there were many candid friends who, with their usual kindness, prophesied the worst things of my future. Nay, there were even some who looked forward to my physical and mental destruction with a certain degree of malignant expectation— and they were estimable persons too. They were respectably connected—their words carried weight—and for a time I was an object of their maliciously pious fears. I was destined, according to their calculations, to be a gambler, a spendthrift, a drunkard, an incurable roue of the most abandoned character. Yet, strange to say, I became none of these things. Though a Neapolitan, with all the fiery passions and hot blood of my race, I had an innate scorn for the contemptible vices and low desires of the unthinking vulgar. Gambling seemed to me a delirious folly—drink, a destroyer of health and reason—and licentious extravagance an outrage on the poor. I chose my own way of life–a middle course between simplicity and luxury–a judicious mingling of home-like peace with the gayety of sympathetic social intercourse–an even tenor of intelligent existence which neither exhausted the mind nor injured the body.

I dwelt in my father's villa–a miniature palace of white marble, situated on a wooded height overlooking the Bay of Naples. My pleasure-grounds were fringed with fragrant groves of orange and myrtle, where hundreds of full-voiced nightingales warbled their love-melodies to the golden moon. Sparkling fountains rose and fell in huge stone basins carved with many a quaint design, and their cool murmurous splash refreshed the burning silence of the hottest summer air. In this retreat I lived at peace for some happy years, surrounded by books and pictures, and visited frequently by friends–young men whose tastes were more or less like my own, and who were capable of equally appreciating the merits of an antique volume, or the flavor of a rare vintage.

Of women I saw little or nothing. Truth to tell, I instinctively avoided them. Parents with marriageable daughters invited me frequently to their houses, but these invitations I generally refused. My best books warned me against feminine society–and I believed and accepted the warning. This tendency of mine exposed me to the ridicule of those among my companions who were amorously inclined, but their gay jests at what they termed my "weakness" never affected me. I trusted in friendship rather than love, and I had a friend–one for whom at that time I would gladly have laid down my life–one who inspired me with the most profound attachment. He, Guido Ferrari, also joined occasionally with others in the good-natured mockery I brought down upon myself by my shrinking dislike of women.

"Fie on thee, Fabio!" he would cry. "Thou wilt not taste life till thou hast sipped the nectar from a pair of rose-red lips–thou shalt not guess the riddle of the stars till thou hast gazed deep down into the fathomless glory of a maiden's eyes—thou canst not know delight till thou hast clasped eager arms round a coy waist and heard the beating of a passionate heart against thine own! A truce to thy musty volumes! Believe it, those ancient and sorrowful philosophers had no manhood in them—their blood was water—and their slanders against women were but the pettish utterances of their own deserved disappointments. Those who miss the chief prize of life would fain persuade others that it is not worth having. What, man! Thou, with a ready wit, a glancing eye, a gay smile, a supple form, thou wilt not enter the lists of love? What says Voltaire of the blind god?

"Qui que tu sois voila ton maitre, Il fut—il est—ou il doit etre !"

When my friend spoke thus I smiled, but answered nothing. His arguments failed to convince me. Yet I loved to hear him talk—his voice was mellow as the note of a thrush, and his eyes had an eloquence greater than all speech. I loved him—God knows! unselfishly, sincerely—with that rare tenderness sometimes felt by schoolboys for one another, but seldom experienced by grown men. I was happy in his society, as he, indeed, appeared to be in mine. We passed most of our time together, he, like myself, having been bereaved of his parents in early youth, and therefore left to shape out his own course of life as suited his particular fancy. He chose art as a profession, and, though a fairly successful painter, was as poor as I was rich. I remedied this neglect of fortune for him in various ways with due forethought and delicacy—and gave him as many commissions as I possibly could without rousing his suspicion or wounding his pride. For he possessed a strong attraction for me—we had much the same tastes, we shared the same sympathies, in short, I desired nothing better than his confidence and companionship.

In this world no one, however harmless, is allowed to continue happy. Fate—or caprice—cannot endure to see us monotonously at rest. Something perfectly trivial—a look, a word, a touch, and lo! a long chain of old associations is broken asunder, and the peace we deemed so deep and lasting in finally interrupted. This change came to me, as surely as it comes to all. One day—how well I remember it!—one sultry evening toward the end of May, 1881, I was in Naples. I had passed the afternoon in my yacht, idly and slowly sailing over the bay, availing myself of what little wind there was. Guido's absence (he had gone to Rome on a visit of some weeks' duration) rendered me somewhat of a solitary, and as my light craft ran into harbor, I found myself in a pensive, half-uncertain mood, which brought with it its own depression. The few sailors who manned my vessel dispersed right and left as soon as they were landed—each to his own favorite haunts of pleasure or dissipation—but I was in no humor to be easily amused. Though I had plenty of acquaintance in the city, I cared little for such entertainment as they could offer me. As I strolled along through one of the principal streets, considering whether or not I should return on foot to my own dwelling on the heights, I heard a sound of singing, and perceived in the distance a glimmer of white robes. It was the Month of Mary, and I at once concluded that this must be an approaching Procession of the Virgin. Half in idleness, half in curiosity, I stood still and waited. The singing voices came nearer and nearer—I saw the priests, the acolytes, the swinging gold censers heavy with fragrance, the flaring candles, the snowy veils of children and girls—and then all suddenly the picturesque beauty of the scene danced before my eyes in a whirling blur of brilliancy and color from which looked forth—one face! One face beaming out like a star from a cloud of amber tresses—one face of rose-tinted, childlike loveliness—a loveliness absolutely perfect, lighted up by two luminous eyes, large and black as night—one face in which the small, curved mouth smiled half provokingly, half sweetly! I gazed and gazed again, dazzled and excited, beauty makes such fools of us all! This was a woman—one of the sex I mistrusted and avoided—a woman in the earliest spring of her youth, a girl of fifteen or sixteen at the utmost. Her veil had been thrown back by accident or design, and for one brief moment I drank in that soul-tempting glance, that witch-like smile! The procession passed–the vision faded– but in that breath of time one epoch of my life had closed forever, and another had begun!

* * *

Of course I married her. We Neapolitans lose no time in such matters. We are not prudent. Unlike the calm blood of Englishmen, ours rushes swiftly through our veins–it is warm as wine and sunlight, and needs no fictitious stimulant. We love, we desire, we possess; and then? We tire, you say? These southern races are so fickle! All wrong–we are less tired than you deem. And do not Englishmen tire? Have they no secret ennui at times when sitting in the chimney nook of "home, sweet home," with their fat wives and ever-spreading families? Truly, yes! But they are too cautious to say so.

I need not relate the story of my courtship–it was brief and sweet as a song sung perfectly. There were no obstacles. The girl I sought was the only daughter of a ruined Florentine noble of dissolute character, who gained a bare subsistence by frequenting the gaming- tables. His child had been brought up in a convent renowned for strict discipline–she knew nothing of the world. She was, he assured me, with maudlin tears in his eyes, "as innocent as a flower on the altar of the Madonna." I believed him–for what could this lovely, youthful, low-voiced maiden know of even the shadow of evil? I was eager to gather so fair a lily for my own proud wearing–and her father gladly gave her to me, no doubt inwardly congratulating himself on the wealthy match that had fallen to the lot of his dowerless daughter.

We were married at the end of June, and Guido Ferrari graced our bridal with his handsome and gallant presence.

"By the body of Bacchus!" he exclaimed to me when the nuptial ceremony was over, "thou hast profited by my teaching, Fabio! A quiet rogue is often most cunning! Thou hast rifled the casket of Venus, and stolen her fairest jewel–thou hast secured the loveliest maiden in the two Sicilies!"

I pressed his hand, and a touch of remorse stole over me, for he was no longer first in my affection. Almost I regretted it–yes, on my very wedding-morn I looked back to the old days–old now though so recent–and sighed to think they were ended. I glanced at Nina, my wife. It was enough! Her beauty dazzled and overcame me. The melting languor of her large limpid eyes stole into my veins–I forgot all but her. I was in that high delirium of passion in which love, and love only, seems the keynote of creation. I touched the topmost peak of the height of joy–the days were feasts of fairy-land, the nights dreams of rapture! No; I never tired! My wife's beauty never paled upon me; she grew fairer with each day of possession. I never saw her otherwise than attractive, and within a few months she had probed all the depths of my nature. She discovered how certain sweet looks of hers could draw me to her side, a willing and devoted slave; she measured my weakness with her own power; she knew–what did she not know? I torture myself with these foolish memories. All men past the age of twenty have learned somewhat of the tricks of women–the pretty playful nothings that weaken the will and sap the force of the strongest hero. She loved me? Oh, yes, I suppose so! Looking back on those days, I can frankly say I believe she loved me–as nine hundred wives out of a thousand love their husbands, namely–for what they can get. And I grudged her nothing. If I chose to idolize her, and raise her to the stature of an angel when she was but on the low level of mere womanhood, that was my folly, not her fault.

We kept open house. Our villa was a place of rendezvous for the leading members of the best society in and around Naples. My wife was universally admired; her lovely face and graceful manners were themes of conversation throughout the whole neighborhood. Guido Ferrari, my friend, was one of those who were loudest in her praise, and the chivalrous homage he displayed toward her doubly endeared him to me. I trusted him as a brother; he came and went as pleased him; he brought Nina gifts of flowers and fanciful trifles adapted to her taste, and treated her with fraternal and delicate kindness. I deemed my happiness perfect—with love, wealth, and friendship, what more could a man desire?

Yet another drop of honey was added to my cup of sweetness. On the first morning of May, 1882, our child was born—a girl-babe, fair as one of the white anemones which at that season grew thickly in the woods surrounding out home. They brought the little one to me in the shaded veranda where I sat at breakfast with Guido—a tiny, almost shapeless bundle, wrapped in soft cashmere and old lace. I took the fragile thing in my arms with a tender reverence; it opened its eyes; they were large and dark like Nina's, and the light of a recent heaven seemed still to linger in their pure depths. I kissed the little face; Guido did the same; and those clear, quiet eyes regarded us both with a strange half-inquiring solemnity. A bird perched on a bough of jasmine broke into a low, sweet song, the soft wind blew and scattered the petals of a white rose at our feet. I gave the infant back to the nurse, who waited to receive it, and said, with a smile, "Tell my wife we have welcomed her May-blossom."

Guido laid his hand on my shoulder as the servant retired; his face was unusually pale.

"Thou art a good fellow, Fabio!" he said, abruptly.

"Indeed! How so?" I asked, half laughingly; "I am no better than other men."

"You are less suspicious than the majority," he returned, turning away from me and playing idly with a spray of clematis that trailed on one of the pillars of the veranda.

I glanced at him in surprise. "What do you mean, *amico*? Have I reason to suspect any one?"

He laughed and resumed his seat at the breakfast-table.

"Why, no!" he answered, with a frank look. "But in Naples the air is pregnant with suspicion—jealousy's dagger is ever ready to strike, justly or unjustly—the very children are learned in the ways of vice. Penitents confess to priests who are worse than penitents, and by Heaven! in such a state of society, where conjugal fidelity is a farce"–he paused a moment, and then went on–"is it not wonderful to know a man like you, Fabio? A man happy in home affections, without a cloud on the sky of his confidence?"

"I have no cause for distrust," I said. "Nina is as innocent as the little child of whom she is to-day the mother."

"True!" exclaimed Ferrari. "Perfectly true!" and he looked me full in the eyes, with a smile. "White as the virgin snow on the summit of Mont Blanc–purer than the flawless diamond–and unapproachable as the furthest star! Is it not so?"

I assented with a certain gravity; something in his manner puzzled me. Our conversation soon turned on different topics, and I thought no more of the matter. But a time came–and that speedily–when I had stern reason to remember every word he had uttered.

2

EVERYONE knows what kind of summer we had in Naples in 1884. The newspapers of all lands teemed with the story of its horrors. The cholera walked abroad like a destroying demon; under its withering touch scores of people, young and old, dropped down in the streets to die. The fell disease, born of dirt and criminal neglect of sanitary precautions, gained on the city with awful rapidity, and worse even than the plague was the unreasoning but universal panic. The never-to-be-forgotten heroism of King Humbert had its effect on the more educated classes, but among the low Neapolitan populace, abject fear, vulgar superstition, and utter selfishness reigned supreme. One case may serve as an example of many others. A fisherman, well known in the place, a handsome and popular young fellow, was seized, while working in his boat, with the first symptoms of cholera. He was carried to his mother's house. The old woman, a villainous-looking hag, watched the little procession as it approached her dwelling, and taking in the situation at once, she shut and barricaded her door.

"*Santissima Madonna!*" she yelled, shrilly, through a half-opened window. "Leave him in the street, the abandoned, miserable one! The ungrateful pig! He would bring the plague to his own hard-working, honest mother! Holy Joseph! who would have children? Leave him in the street, I tell you!"

It was useless to expostulate with this feminine scarecrow; her son was, happily for himself, unconscious, and after some more wrangling he was laid down on her doorstep, where he shortly afterward expired, his body being afterward carted away like so much rubbish by the *beccamorti*.

The heat in the city was intense. The sky was a burning dome of brilliancy, the bay was still as a glittering sheet of glass. A thin column of smoke issuing from the crater of Vesuvius increased the impression of an all-pervading, though imperceptible ring of fire, that seemed to surround the place. No birds sung save in the late evening, when the nightingales in my gardens broke out in a bubbling torrent of melody, half joyous, half melancholy. Up on that wooded height where I dwelt it was comparatively cool. I took all precautions necessary to prevent the contagion from attacking our household; In fact, I would have left the neighborhood altogether, had I not known that hasty flight from an infected district often carries with it the possibility of closer contact with the disease. My wife, besides, was not nervous—I think very beautiful women seldom are. Their superb vanity is an excellent shield to repel pestilence; it does away with the principal element of danger—fear. As for our Stella, a toddling mite of two years old, she was a healthy child, for whom neither her mother nor myself entertained the least anxiety.

Guido Ferrari came and stayed with us, and while the cholera, like a sharp scythe put into a field of ripe corn, mowed down the dirt- loving Neapolitans by hundreds, we three, with a small retinue of servants, none of whom were ever permitted to visit the city, lived on farinaceous food and distilled water, bathed regularly, rose and retired early, and enjoyed the most perfect health.

Among her many other attractions my wife was gifted with a beautiful and well-trained voice. She sung with exquisite expression, and many an evening when Guido and myself sat smoking in the garden, after little Stella had gone to bed, Nina would ravish our ears with the music of her nightingale notes, singing song after song, quaint *stornelli* and *ritornelli*–songs of the people, full of wild and passionate beauty. In these Guido would often join her, his full baritone chiming in with her delicate and clear soprano as deliciously as the fall of a fountain with the trill of a bird. I can hear those two voices now; their united melody still rings mockingly in my ears; the heavy perfume of orange-blossom, mingled with myrtle, floats toward me on the air; the yellow moon burns round and full in the dense blue sky, like the King of Thule's goblet of gold flung into a deep sea, and again I behold those two heads leaning together, the one fair, the other dark; my wife, my friend–those two whose lives were a million times dearer to me than my own. Ah! they were happy days–days of self-delusion always are. We are never grateful enough to the candid persons who wake us from our dream–yet such are in truth our best friends, could we but realize it.

August was the most terrible of all the summer months in Naples. The cholera increased with frightful steadiness, and the people seemed to be literally mad with terror. Some of them, seized with a wild spirit of defiance, plunged into orgies of vice and intemperance with a reckless disregard of consequences. One of these frantic revels took place at a well-known cafe. Eight young men, accompanied by eight girls of remarkable beauty, arrived, and ordered a private room, where they were served with a sumptuous repast. At its close one of the party raised his glass and proposed, "Success to the cholera!" The toast was received with riotous shouts of applause, and all drank it with delirious laughter. That very night every single one of the revelers died in horrible agony; their bodies, as usual, were thrust into flimsy coffins and buried one on top of another in a hole hastily dug for the purpose. Dismal stories like these reached us every day, but we were not morbidly impressed by them. Stella was a living charm against pestilence; her innocent playfulness and prattle kept us amused and employed, and surrounded us with an atmosphere that was physically and mentally wholesome.

One morning–one of the very hottest mornings of that scorching month–I woke at an earlier hour than usual. A suggestion of possible coolness in the air tempted me to rise and stroll through the garden. My wife slept soundly at my side. I dressed softly, without disturbing her. As I was about to leave the room some instinct made me turn back to look at her once more. How lovely she was! she smiled in her sleep! My heart beat as I gazed–she had been mine for three years–mine only!–and my passionate admiration and love of her had increased in proportion to that length of time. I raised one of the scattered golden locks that lay shining like a sunbeam on the pillow, and kissed it tenderly. Then–all unconscious of my fate–I left her.

A faint breeze greeted me as I sauntered slowly along the garden walks–a breath of wind scarce strong enough to flutter the leaves, yet it had a salt savor in it that was refreshing after the tropical heat of the past night. I was at that time absorbed in the study of Plato, and as I walked, my mind occupied itself with many high problems and deep questions suggested by that great teacher. Lost in a train of profound yet pleasant thought, I strayed on further than I intended, and found myself at last in a by-path, long disused by our household–a winding footway leading downward in the direction of the harbor. It was shady and cool, and I followed the road almost unconsciously, till I caught a glimpse of masts and white sails gleaming through the leafage of the overarching trees. I was then about to retrace my steps, when I was startled by a sudden sound. It was a low moan of intense pain–a smothered cry that seemed to be wrung from some animal in torture. I turned in the direction whence it came, and saw, lying face downward on the grass, a boy–a little fruit-seller of eleven or twelve years of age. His basket of wares stood beside him, a tempting pile of peaches, grapes, pomegranates, and melons–lovely but dangerous eating in cholera times. I touched the lad on the shoulder."

"What ails you?" I asked. He twisted himself convulsively

and turned his face toward me–a beautiful face, though livid with anguish.

"The plague, signor!" he moaned; "the plague! Keep away from me, for the love of God! I am dying!"

I hesitated. For myself I had no fear. But my wife–my child–for their sakes it was necessary to be prudent. Yet I could not leave this poor boy unassisted. I resolved to go to the harbor in search of medical aid. With this idea in my mind I spoke cheerfully.

"Courage, my boy," I said; "do not lose heart! All illness is not the plague. Rest here till I return; I am going to fetch a doctor."

The little fellow looked at me with wondering, pathetic eyes, and tried to smile. He pointed to his throat, and made an effort to speak, but vainly. Then he crouched down in the grass and writhed in torture like a hunted animal wounded to the death. I left him and walked on rapidly; reaching the harbor, where the heat was sulphurous and intense, I found a few scared-looking men standing aimlessly about, to whom I explained the boy's case, and appealed for assistance. They all hung back–none of them would accompany me, not even for the gold I offered. Cursing their cowardice, I hurried on in search of a physician, and found one at last, a sallow Frenchman, who listened with obvious reluctance to my account of the condition in which I had left the little fruit-seller, and at the end shook his head decisively, and refused to move.

"He is as good as dead," he observed, with cold brevity. "Better call at the house of the *Misericordia*; the brethren will fetch his body."

"What!" I cried; "you will not try to see if you can save him?"

The Frenchman bowed with satirical suavity.

"Monsieur must pardon me! My own health would be seriously endangered by touching a cholera corpse. Allow me to wish monsieur the good-day!"

And he disappeared, shutting his door in my face. I was thoroughly exasperated, and though the heat and the fetid odor of the sunbaked streets made me feel faint and sick, I forgot all danger for myself as I stood in the plague-stricken city, wondering what I should do next to obtain succor. A grave, kind voice saluted my ear.

"You seek aid, my son?"

I looked up. A tall monk, whose cowl partly concealed his pale, but resolute features, stood at my side—one of those heroes who, for the love of Christ, came forth at that terrible time and faced the pestilence fearlessly, where the blatant boasters of no-religion scurried away like frightened hares from the very scent of danger. I greeted him with an obeisance, and explained my errand.

"I will go at once," he said, with an accent of pity in his voice. "But I fear the worst. I have remedies with me; I may not be too late."

"I will accompany you," I said, eagerly. "One would not let a dog die unaided; much less this poor lad, who seems friendless."

The monk looked at me attentively as we walked on together.

"You are not residing in Naples?" he asked.

I gave him my name, which he knew by repute, and described the position of my villa.

"Up on that height we enjoy perfect health," I added. "I cannot understand the panic that prevails in the city. The plague is fostered by such cowardice."

"Of course!" he answered, calmly. "But what will you? The people here love pleasure. Their hearts are set solely on this life. When death, common to all, enters their midst, they are like babes scared by a dark shadow. Religion itself"—here he sighed deeply—"has no hold upon them."

"But you, my father," I began, and stopped abruptly, conscious of a sharp throbbing pain in my temples.

"I," he answered, gravely, "am the servant of Christ. As

such, the plague has no terrors for me. Unworthy as I am, for my Master's sake I am ready—nay, willing—to face all deaths."

He spoke firmly, yet without arrogance. I looked at him in a certain admiration, and was about to speak, when a curious dizziness overcame me, and I caught at his arm to save myself from falling. The street rocked like a ship at sea, and the skies whirled round me in circles of blue fire. The feeling slowly passed, and I heard the monk's voice, as though it were a long way off, asking me anxiously what was the matter. I forced a smile.

"It is the heat, I think," I said, in feeble tones like those of a very aged man. "I am faint—giddy. You had best leave me here—see to the boy. Oh, my God!"

This last exclamation was wrung out of me by sheer anguish. My limbs refused to support me, and a pang, cold and bitter as though naked steel had been thrust through my body, caused me to sink down upon the pavement in a kind of convulsion. The tall and sinewy monk, without a moment's hesitation, dragged me up and half carried, half led me into a kind of *auberge*, or restaurant for the poorer classes. Here he placed me in a recumbent position on one of the wooden benches, and called up the proprietor of the place, a man to whom he seemed to be well known. Though suffering acutely I was conscious, and could hear and see everything that passed.

"Attend to him well, Pietro—it is the rich Count Fabio Romani. Thou wilt not lose by thy pains. I will return within an hour."

"The Count Romani! *Santissima Madonna!* He has caught the plague!"

"Thou fool!" exclaimed the monk, fiercely. "How canst thou tell? A stroke of the sun is not the plague, thou coward! See to him, or by St. Peter and the keys there shall be no place for thee in heaven!"

The trembling innkeeper looked terrified at this menace, and submissively approached me with pillows, which he placed under my head. The monk, meanwhile, held a glass to my lips containing some medicinal mixture, which I swallowed mechanically.

"Rest here, my son," he said, addressing me in soothing tones. "These people are good-natured. I will but hasten to the boy for whom you sought assistance–in less than an hour I will be with you again."

I laid a detaining hand on his arm.

"Stay," I murmured, feebly, "let me know the worst. Is this the plague?"

"I hope not!" he replied, compassionately. "But what if it be? You are young and strong enough to fight against it without fear."

"I have no fear," I said. "But, father, promise me one thing–send no word of my illness to my wife–swear it! Even if I am unconscious–dead–swear that I shall not be taken to the villa. Swear it! I cannot rest till I have your word."

"I swear it most willingly, my son," he answered, solemnly. "By all I hold sacred, I will respect your wishes."

I was infinitely relieved–the safety of those I loved was assured– and I thanked him by a mute gesture. I was too weak to say more. He disappeared, and my brain wandered into a chaos of strange fancies. Let me try to resolve these delusions. I plainly see the interior of the common room where I lie. There is the timid innkeeper–he polishes his glasses and bottles, casting ever and anon a scared glance in my direction. Groups of men look in at the door, and, seeing me, hurry away. I observe all this–I know where I am–yet I am also climbing the steep passes of an Alpine gorge–the cold snow is at my feet–I hear the rush and roar of a thousand torrents. A crimson cloud floats above the summit of a white glacier–it parts asunder gradually, and in its bright center a face smiles forth! "Nina! my love, my wife, my soul!" I cry aloud. I stretch out my arms–I clasp her!–bah! it is this good rogue of an innkeeper who holds me in his musty embrace! I struggle with him fiercely–pantingly.

"Fool!" I shriek in his ear. "Let me go to her–her lips pout for kisses–let me go!"

Another man advances and seizes me; he and the innkeeper force me back on the pillows–they overcome me, and the utter incapacity of a terrible exhaustion steals away my strength. I cease to struggle. Pietro and his assistant look down upon me.

"*E morto!*" they whisper one to the other.

I hear them and smile. Dead? Not I! The scorching sunlight streams through the open door of the inn–the thirsty flies buzz with persistent loudness–some voices are singing "*La Fata di Amalfi*"–I can distinguish the words–

"*Chiagnaro la mia sventura Si non tuorne chiu, Rosella! Tu d' Amalfi la chiu bella, Tu na Fata si pe me! Viene, vie, regina mie, Viene curre a chisto core, Ca non c'e non c'e sciore, Non c'e Stella comm'a te!*"

That is a true song, Nina mia! "*Non c'e Stella comm' a te!*" What did Guido say? "Purer than the flawless diamond– unapproachable as the furthest star!" That foolish Pietro still polishes his wine-bottles. I see him–his meek round face is greasy with heat and dust; but I cannot understand how he comes to be here at all, for I am on the banks of a tropical river where huge palms grow wild, and drowsy alligators lie asleep in the sun. Their large jaws are open–their small eyes glitter greenly. A light boat glides over the silent water–in it I behold the erect lithe figure of an Indian. His features are strangely similar to those of Guido. He draws a long thin shining blade of steel as he approaches. Brave fellow!–he means to attack single-handed the cruel creatures who lie in wait for him on the sultry shore. He springs to land–I watch him with a weird fascination. He passes the alligators–he seems not to be aware of their presence–he comes with swift, unhesitating step to ME–it is I whom he seeks–it is in MY heart that he plunges the cold steel dagger, and draws it out again dripping with blood! Once–twice–thrice!–and yet I cannot die! I writhe–I moan in bitter anguish! Then something dark comes between me and the glaring sun– something cool and shadowy, against which I fling myself despairingly. Two dark eyes look steadily into mine, and a voice speaks:

"Be calm, my son, be calm. Commend thyself to Christ!"

It is my friend the monk. I recognize him gladly. He has returned from his errand of mercy. Though I can scarcely speak, I hear myself asking for news of the boy. The holy man crosses himself devoutly.

"May his young soul rest in peace! I found him dead."

I am dreamily astonished at this. Dead–so soon! I cannot understand it; and I drift off again into a state of confused imaginings. As I look back now to that time, I find I have no specially distinct recollection of what afterward happened to me. I know I suffered intense, intolerable pain–that I was literally tortured on a rack of excruciating anguish–and that through all the delirium of my senses I heard a muffled, melancholy sound like a chant or prayer. I have an idea that I also heard the tinkle of the bell that accompanies the Host, but my brain reeled more wildly with each moment, and I cannot be certain of this. I remember shrieking out after what seemed an eternity of pain, "Not to the villa! no, no, not there! You shall not take me–my curse on him who disobeys me!"

I remember then a fearful sensation, as of being dragged into a deep whirlpool, from whence I stretched up appealing hands and eyes to the monk who stood above me–I caught a drowning glimpse of a silver crucifix glittering before my gaze, and at last, with one loud cry for help, I sunk–down–down! into an abyss of black night and nothingness!

3

THERE followed a long drowsy time of stillness and shadow. I seemed to have fallen in some deep well of delicious oblivion and obscurity. Dream-like images still flitted before my fancy–these were at first undefinable, but after a while they took more certain shapes. Strange fluttering creatures hovered about me– lonely eyes stared at me from a visible deep gloom; long white bony fingers grasping at nothing made signs to me of warning or menace. Then– very gradually, there dawned upon my sense of vision a cloudy red mist like a stormy sunset, and from the middle of the blood-like haze a huge black hand descended toward me. It pounced upon my chest–it grasped my throat in its monstrous clutch, and held me down with a weight of iron. I struggled violently–I strove to cry out, but that terrific pressure took from me all power of utterance. I twisted myself to right and left in an endeavor to escape–but my tyrant of the sable hand had bound me in on all sides. Yet I continued to wrestle with the cruel opposing force that strove to overwhelm me–little by little–inch by inch–so! At last! One more struggle– victory! I woke! Merciful God! Where was I? In what horrible atmosphere–in what dense darkness? Slowly, as my senses returned to me, I remembered my recent illness. The monk– the man Pietro–where were they? What had they done to me?

By degrees, I realized that I was lying straight down upon my back—the couch was surely very hard? Why had they taken the pillows from under my head? A pricking sensation darted through my veins—I felt my own hands curiously—they were warm, and my pulse beat strongly, though fitfully. But what was this that hindered my breathing? Air—air! I must have air! I put up my hands—horror! They struck against a hard opposing substance above me. Quick as lightning then the truth flashed upon my mind! I had been buried—buried alive; this wooden prison that enclosed me was a coffin! A frenzy surpassing that of an infuriated tiger took swift possession of me—with hands and nails I tore and scratched at the accursed boards—with all the force of my shoulders and arms I toiled to wrench open the closed lid! My efforts were fruitless! I grew more ferociously mad with rage and terror. How easy were all deaths compared to one like this! I was suffocating—I felt my eyes start from their sockets—blood sprung from my mouth and nostrils—and icy drops of sweat trickled from my forehead. I paused, gasping for breath. Then, suddenly nerving myself for one more wild effort, I hurled my limbs with all the force of agony and desperation against one side of my narrow prison. It cracked—it split asunder!—and then—a new and horrid fear beset me, and I crouched back, panting heavily. If—if I were buried in the ground—so ran my ghastly thoughts—of what use to break open the coffin and let in the mold—the damp wormy mold, rich with the bones of the dead—the penetrating mold that would choke up my mouth and eyes, and seal me into silence forever! My mind quailed at this idea—my brain tottered on the verge of madness! I laughed—think of it!—and my laugh sounded in my ears like the last rattle in the throat of a dying man. But I could breathe more easily—even in the stupefaction of my fears—I was conscious of air. Yes!—the blessed air had rushed in somehow. Revived and encouraged as I recognized this fact, I felt with both hands till I found the crevice I had made, and then with frantic haste and strength I pulled and dragged at the wood, till suddenly the whole side of the coffin gave way, and I was able to force up the lid. I stretched out my arms–no weight of earth impeded their movements–I felt nothing but air– empty air. Yielding to my first strong impulse, I leaped out of the hateful box, and fell–fell some little distance, bruising my hands and knees on what seemed to be a stone pavement. Something weighty fell also, with a dull crashing thud close to me. The darkness was impenetrable. But there was breathing room, and the atmosphere was cool and refreshing. With some pain and difficulty I raised myself to a sitting position where I had fallen. My limbs were stiff and cramped as well as wounded, and I shivered as with strong ague. But my senses were clear–the tangled chain of my disordered thoughts became even and connected–my previous mad excitement gradually calmed, and I began to consider my condition. I had certainly been buried alive–there was no doubt of that. Intense pain had, I suppose, resolved itself into a long trance of unconsciousness–the people of the inn where I had been taken ill had at once believed me to be dead of cholera, and with the panic-stricken, indecent haste common in all Italy, especially at a time of plague, had thrust me into one of those flimsy coffins which were then being manufactured by scores in Naples–mere shells of thin deal, nailed together with clumsy hurry and fear. But how I blessed their wretched construction! Had I been laid in a stronger casket, who knows if even the most desperate frenzy of my strength might not have proved unavailing! I shuddered at the thought. Yet the question remained– Where was I? I reviewed my case from all points, and for some time could arrive at no satisfactory conclusion. Stay, though! I remembered that I had told the monk my name; he knew that I was the only descendant of the rich Romani family. What followed? Why, naturally, the good father had only done what his duty called upon him to do. He had seen me laid in the vault of my ancestors–the great Romani vault that had never been opened since my father's body was carried to its last resting-place with all the solemn pomp and magnificence of a wealthy nobleman's funeral obsequies. The more I thought of this the more probable it seemed. The Romani vault! Its forbidding gloom had terrified me as a lad when I followed my father's coffin to the stone niche assigned to it, and I had turned my eyes away in shuddering pain when I was told to look at the heavy oaken casket hung with tattered velvet and ornamented with tarnished silver, which contained all that was left of my mother, who died young. I had felt sick and faint and cold, and had only recovered myself when I stood out again in the free air with the blue dome of heaven high above me. And now I was shut in the same vault—a prisoner—with what hope of escape? I reflected. The entrance to the vault, I remembered, was barred by a heavy door of closely twisted iron—from thence a flight of steep steps led downward—downward to where in all probability I now was. Suppose I could in the dense darkness feel my way to those steps and climb up to that door—of what avail? It was locked—nay, barred—and as it was situated in a remote part of the burial-ground, there was no likelihood of even the keeper of the cemetery passing by it for days—perhaps not for weeks. Then must I starve? Or die of thirst? Tortured by these imaginings, I rose up from the pavement and stood erect. My feet were bare, and the cold stone on which I stood chilled me to the marrow. It was fortunate for me, I thought, that they had buried me as a cholera corpse—they had left me half-clothed for fear of infection. That is, I had my flannel shirt on and my usual walking trousers. Something there was, too, round my neck; I felt it, and as I did so a flood of sweet and sorrowful memories rushed over me. It was a slight gold chain, and on it hung a locket containing the portraits of my wife and child. I drew it out in the darkness; I covered it with passionate kisses and tears—the first I had shed since my death-like trance—tears scalding and bitter welled into my eyes. Life was worth living while Nina's smile lightened the world! I resolved to fight for existence, no matter what dire horrors should be yet in store for me. Nina—my love—my beautiful one! Her face gleamed out upon me in the pestilent gloom of the charnel-house; her eyes beckoned me–her young faithful eyes that were now, I felt sure, drowned in weeping for my supposed death. I seemed to see my tender-hearted darling sobbing alone in the empty silence of the room that had witnessed a thousand embraces between herself and me; her lovely hair disheveled; her sweet face pale and haggard with the bitterness of grief! Baby Stella, too, no doubt she would wonder, poor innocent! why I did not come to swing her as usual under the orange boughs. And Guido–brave and true friend! I thought of him with tenderness. I felt I knew how deep and lasting would be his honest regret for my loss. Oh, I would leave no means of escape untried; I would find some way out of this grim vault! How overjoyed they would all be to see me again–to know that I was not dead after all! What a welcome I should receive! How Nina would nestle into my arms; how my little child would cling to me; how Guido would clasp me by the hand! I smiled as I pictured the scene of rejoicing at the dear old villa–the happy home sanctified by perfect friendship and faithful love!

A deep hollow sound booming suddenly on my ears startled me–one! two! three! I counted the strokes up to twelve. It was some church bell tolling the hour. My pleasing fancies dispersed–I again faced the drear reality of my position. Twelve o'clock! Midday or midnight? I could not tell. I began to calculate. It was early morning when I had been taken ill–not much past eight when I had met the monk and sought his assistance for the poor little fruit- seller who had after all perished alone in his sufferings. Now supposing my illness had lasted some hours, I might have fallen into a trance–died–as those around me had thought, somewhere about noon. In that case they would certainly have buried me with as little delay as possible–before sunset at all events. Thinking these points over one by one, I came to the conclusion that the bell I had just heard must have struck midnight–the midnight of the very day of my burial. I shivered; a kind of nervous dread stole over me. I have always been physically courageous, but at the same time, in spite of my education, I am somewhat superstitious–what

Neapolitan is not? it runs in the southern blood. And there was something unutterably fearful in the sound of that midnight bell clanging harshly on the ears of a man pent up alive in a funeral vault with the decaying bodies of his ancestors close within reach of his hand! I tried to conquer my feelings—to summon up my fortitude. I endeavored to reason out the best method of escape. I resolved to feel my way, if possible, to the steps of the vault, and with this idea in my mind I put out my hands and began to move along slowly and with the utmost care. What was that? I stopped; I listened; the blood curdled in my veins! A shrill cry, piercing, prolonged, and melancholy, echoed through the hollow arches of my tomb. A cold perspiration broke out all over my body—my heart beat so loudly that I could hear it thumping against my ribs. Again—again—that weird shriek, followed by a whir and flap of wings. I breathed again.

"It is an owl," I said to myself, ashamed of my fears; "a poor innocent bird—a companion and watcher of the dead, and therefore its voice is full of sorrowful lamentation—but it is harmless," and I crept on with increased caution. Suddenly out of the dense darkness there stared two large yellow eyes, glittering with fiendish hunger and cruelty. For a moment I was startled, and stepped back; the creature flew at me with the ferocity of a tiger- cat! I fought with the horrible thing in all directions; it wheeled round my head, it pounced toward my face, it beat me with its large wings—wings that I could feel but not see; the yellow eyes alone shone in the thick gloom like the eyes of some vindictive demon! I struck at it right and left—the revolting combat lasted some moments—I grew sick and dizzy, yet I battled on recklessly. At last, thank Heaven! the huge owl was vanquished; it fluttered backward and downward, apparently exhausted, giving one wild screech of baffled fury, as its lamp-like eyes disappeared in the darkness. Breathless, but not subdued—every nerve in my body quivering with excitement—I pursued my way, as I thought, toward the stone staircase. feeling the air with my outstretched hands as I groped along. In a little while I met with an obstruction–it was hard and cold–a stone wall, surely? I felt it up and down and found a hollow in it–was this the first step of the stair? I wondered; it seemed very high. I touched it cautiously–suddenly I came in contact with something soft and clammy to the touch like moss or wet velvet. Fingering this with a kind of repulsion, I soon traced out the oblong shape of a coffin Curiously enough, I was not affected much by the discovery. I found myself monotonously counting the bits of raised metal which served, as I judged, for its ornamentation. Eight bits lengthwise–and the soft wet stuff between–four bits across; then a pang shot through me, and I drew my hand away quickly, as I considered–WHOSE coffin was this? My father's? Or was I thus plucking, like a man in delirium, at the fragments of velvet on that cumbrous oaken casket wherein lay the sacred ashes of my mother's perished beauty? I roused myself from the apathy into which I had fallen. All the pains I had taken to find my way through the vault were wasted; I was lost in the profound gloom, and knew not where to turn. The horror of my situation presented itself to me with redoubled force. I began to be tormented with thirst. I fell on my knees and groaned aloud.

"God of infinite mercy!" I cried. "Savior of the world! By the souls of the sacred dead whom Thou hast in Thy holy keeping, have pity upon me! Oh, my mother! if indeed thine earthly remains are near me–think of me, sweet angel in that heaven where thy spirit dwells at rest–plead for me and save me, or let me die now and be tortured no more!"

I uttered these words aloud, and the sound of my wailing voice ringing through the somber arches of the vault was strange and full of fantastic terror to my own ears. I knew that were my agony much further prolonged I should go mad. And I dared not picture to myself the frightful things which a maniac might be capable of, shut up in such a place of death and darkness, with moldering corpses for companions! I remained on my knees, my face buried in my hands. I forced myself into comparative calmness, and strove to preserve the equilibrium of my distracted mind. Hush! What exquisite far-off floating voice of cheer was that? I raised my head and listened, entranced!

"Jug, jug, Jug! lodola, lodola! trill-lil-lil! sweet, sweet, sweet!"

It was a nightingale. Familiar, delicious, angel-throated bird! How I blessed thee in that dark hour of despair! How I praised God for thine innocent existence! How I sprung up and laughed and wept for joy, as, all unconscious of me, thou didst shake out a shower of pearly warblings on the breast of the soothed air! Heavenly messenger of consolation!–even now I think of thee with tenderness–for thy sweet sake all birds possess me as their worshiper; humanity has grown hideous in my sight, but the singing-life of the woods and hills–how pure, how fresh!–the nearest thing to happiness on this side heaven!

A rush of strength and courage invigorated me. A new idea entered my brain. I determined to follow the voice of the nightingale. It sung on sweetly, encouragingly–and I began afresh my journeying through the darkness. I fancied that the bird was perched on one of the trees outside the entrance of the vault, and that if I tried to get within closer hearing of its voice, I should most likely be thus guided to the very staircase I had been so painfully seeking. I stumbled along slowly. I felt feeble, and my limbs shook under me. This time nothing impeded my progress; the nightingale's liquid notes floated nearer and nearer, and hope, almost exhausted, sprung up again in my heart. I was scarcely conscious of my own movements. I seemed to be drawn along like one in a dream by the golden thread of the bird's sweet singing. All at once I caught my foot against a stone and fell forward with some force, but I felt no pain–my limbs were too numb to be sensible of any fresh suffering. I raised my heavy, aching eyes in the darkness; as I did so I uttered an exclamation of thanksgiving. A slender stream of moonlight, no thicker than the stem of an arrow, slanted downward toward me, and showed me that I had at last reached the spot I sought–in fact, I had fallen upon the lowest step of the stone stairway. I could not distinguish the entrance door of the vault, but I knew that it must be at the summit of the steep ascent. I was too weary to move further just then. I lay still where I was, staring at the solitary moon-ray, and listening to the nightingale, whose rapturous melodies now rang out upon my ears with full distinctness. ONE! The harsh- toned bell I had heard before clanged forth the hour. It would soon be morning; I resolved to rest till then. Utterly worn out in body and mind, I laid down my head upon the cold stones as readily as if they had been the softest cushions, and in a few moments forgot all my miseries in a profound sleep.

* * *

I must have slumbered for some time, when I was suddenly awakened by a suffocating sensation of faintness and nausea, accompanied by a sharp pain on my neck as though some creatures were stinging me. I put my hand up to the place– God! shall I ever forget the feel of the THING my trembling fingers closed upon! It was fastened in my flesh–a winged, clammy, breathing horror! It clung to me with a loathly persistency that nearly drove me frantic, and wild with disgust and terror I screamed aloud! I closed both hands convulsively upon its fat, soft body–I literally tore it from my flesh and flung it as far back as I could into the interior blackness of the vault. For a time I believe I was indeed mad–the echoes rang with the piercing shrieks I could not restrain! Silent at last through sheer exhaustion I glared about me. The moonbeam had vanished, in its place lay a shaft of pale gray light, by which I could easily distinguish the whole length of the staircase and the closed gateway it its summit. I rushed up the ascent with the feverish haste of a madman–I grasped the iron grating with both hands and shook it fiercely It was firm as a rock, locked fast. I called for help. Utter silence answered me. I peered through the closely twisted bars. I saw the grass, the drooping boughs of trees, and straight before my line of vision a little piece of the blessed sky, opal tinted and faintly blushing with the consciousness of the approaching sunrise I drank in the sweet fresh air, a long trailing branch of the wild grape vine hung near me; its leaves were covered thickly with dew. I squeezed one hand through the grating and gathered a few of these green morsels of coolness–I ate them greedily. They seemed to me more delicious than anything I had ever tasted, they relieved the burning fever of my parched throat and tongue. The glimpse of the trees and sky soothed and calmed me. There was a gentle twittering of awaking birds, my nightingale had ceased singing.

I began to recover slowly from my nervous terrors, and leaning against the gloomy arch of my charnel house I took courage to glance backward down the steep stairway up which I had sprung with such furious precipitation. Something white lay in a corner on the seventh step from the top. Curious to see what it was, I descended cautiously and with some reluctance; it was the half of a thick waxen taper, such as are used in the Catholic ritual at the burial of the dead. No doubt it had been thrown down there by some careless acolyte, to save himself the trouble of carrying it after the service had ended. I looked at it meditatively. If I only had a light! I plunged my hands half abstractedly into the pockets of my trousers–something jingled! Truly they had buried me in haste. My purse, a small bunch of keys, my card-case–one by one I drew them out and examined them surprisedly–they looked so familiar, and withal so strange! I searched again; and this time found something of real value to one in my condition–a small box of wax vestas. Now, had they left me my cigar-case? No, that was gone. It was a valuable silver one–no doubt the monk, who attended my supposed last moments, had taken it, together with my watch and chain, to my wife.

Well, I could not smoke, but I could strike a light. And there was the funeral taper ready for use. The sun had not yet risen. I must certainly wait till broad day before I could hope to attract by my shouts any stray person who might pass through the cemetery. Meanwhile, a fantastic idea suggested itself. I would go and look at my own coffin! Why not? It would be a novel experience. The sense of fear had entirely deserted me; the possession of that box of matches was sufficient to endow me with absolute hardihood. I picked up the church-candle and lighted it; it gave at first a feeble flicker, but afterward burned with a clear and steady flame. Shading it with one hand from the draught, I gave a parting glance at the fair daylight that peeped smilingly in through my prison door, and then went down—down again into the dismal place where I had passed the night in such indescribable agony.

4

NUMBERS of lizards glided away from my feet as I descended the steps, and when the flare of my torch penetrated the darkness I heard a scurrying of wings mingled with various hissing sounds and wild cries. I knew now—none better—what weird and abominable things had habitation in this storehouse of the dead, but I felt I could defy them all, armed with the light I carried. The way that had seemed so long in the dense gloom was brief and easy, and I soon found myself at the scene of my unexpected awakening from sleep. The actual body of the vault was square-shaped, like a small room enclosed within high walls—walls which were scooped out in various places so as to form niches in which the narrow caskets containing the bones of all the departed members of the Romani family were placed one above the other like so many bales of goods arranged evenly on the shelves of an ordinary warehouse. I held the candle high above my head and looked about me with a morbid interest. I soon perceived what I sought—my own coffin.

There it was in a niche some five feet from the ground, its splintered portions bearing decided witness to the dreadful struggle I had made to obtain my freedom. I advanced and examined it closely. It was a frail shell enough—unlined, unornamented–a wretched sample of the undertaker's art, though God knows I had no fault to find with its workmanship, nor with the haste of him who fashioned it. Something shone at the bottom of it–it was a crucifix of ebony and silver. That good monk again! His conscience had not allowed him to see me buried without this sacred symbol; he had perhaps laid it on my breast as the last service he could render me; it had fallen from thence, no doubt, when I had wrenched my way through the boards that enclosed me. I took it and kissed it reverently–I resolved that if ever I met the holy father again, I would tell him my story, and, as a proof of its truth, restore to him this cross, which he would be sure to recognize. Had they put my name on the coffin-lid? I wondered. Yes, there it was–painted on the wood in coarse, black letters, "FABIO ROMANI"–then followed the date of my birth; then a short Latin inscription, stating that I had died of cholera on August 15, 1884. That was yesterday–only yesterday! I seemed to have lived a century since then.

I turned to look at my father's resting-place. The velvet on his coffin hung from its sides in moldering remnants–but it was not so utterly damp-destroyed and worm-eaten as the soaked and indistinguishable material that still clung to the massive oaken chest in the next niche, where SHE lay–she from whose tender arms I had received my first embrace–she in whose loving eyes I had first beheld the world! I knew by a sort of instinct that it must have been with the frayed fragments on her coffin that my fingers had idly played in the darkness. I counted as before the bits of metal– eight bits length-wise, and four bits across–and on my father's close casket there were ten silver plates lengthwise and five across. My poor little mother! I thought of her picture–it hung in my library at home; the picture of a young, smiling, dark-haired beauty, whose delicate tint was as that of a peach ripening in the summer sun. All that loveliness had decayed into–what? I shuddered involuntarily–then I knelt humbly before those two sad hollows in the cold stone, and implored the blessing of the dead and gone beloved ones to whom, while they lived, my welfare had been dear. While I occupied this kneeling position the flame of my torch fell directly on some small object that glittered with remarkable luster. I went to examine it; it was a jeweled pendant composed of one large pear-shaped pearl, set round with fine rose brilliants! Surprised at this discovery, I looked about to see where such a valuable gem could possibly have come from I then noticed an unusually large coffin lying sideways on the ground; it appeared as if it had fallen suddenly and with force, for a number of loose stones and mortar were sprinkled near it. Holding the light close to the ground, I observed that a niche exactly below the one in which I had been laid was empty, and that a considerable portion of the wall there was broken away. I then remembered that when I had sprung so desperately out of my narrow box I had heard something fall with a crash beside me, This was the thing, then–this long coffin, big enough to contain a man seven feet high and broad in proportion. What gigantic ancestor had I irreverently dislodged?–and was it from a skeleton throat that the rare jewel which I held in my hand had been accidentally shaken?

My curiosity was excited, and I bent close to examine the lid of this funeral chest. There was no name on it–no mark of any sort, save one–a dagger roughly painted in red. Here was a mystery! I resolved to penetrate it. I set up my candle in a little crevice of one of the empty niches, and laid the pearl and diamond pendant beside it, thus disembarrassing myself of all encumbrance. The huge coffin lay on its side, as I have said; its uppermost corner was splintered; I applied both hands to the work of breaking further asunder these already split portions. As I did so a leather pouch or bag rolled out and fell at my feet. I picked it up and opened it–it was full of gold pieces! More excited than ever, I seized a large pointed stone, and by the aid of this extemporized instrument, together with the force of my own arms, hands, and feet, I managed, after some ten minutes' hard labor, to break open the mysterious casket.

When I had accomplished this deed I stared at the result like a man stupefied. No moldering horror met my gaze—no blanched or decaying bones; no grinning skull mocked me with its hollow eye-sockets. I looked upon a treasure worthy of an emperor's envy! The big coffin was literally lined and packed with incalculable wealth. Fifty large leathern bags tied with coarse cord lay uppermost; more than half of these were crammed with gold coins, the rest were full of priceless gems—necklaces, tiaras, bracelets, watches, chains, and other articles of feminine adornment were mingled with loose precious stones—diamonds, rubies, emeralds, and opals, some of unusual size and luster, some uncut, and some all ready for the jeweler's setting. Beneath these bags were packed a number of pieces of silk, velvet, and cloth of gold, each piece being wrapped by itself in a sort of oil-skin, strongly perfumed with camphor and other spices. There were also three lengths of old lace, fine as gossamer, of matchless artistic design, in perfect condition. Among these materials lay two large trays of solid gold workmanship, most exquisitely engraved and ornamented, also four gold drinking-cups, of quaint and massive construction. Other valuables and curious trifles there were, such as an ivory statuette of Psyche on a silver pedestal, a waistband of coins linked together, a painted fan with a handle set in amber and turquois, a fine steel dagger in a jeweled sheath, and a mirror framed in old pearls. Last, but not least, at the very bottom of the chest lay rolls upon rolls of paper money amounting to some millions of francs—in all far surpassing what I had myself formerly enjoyed from my own revenues. I plunged my hands deep in the leathern bags; I fingered the rich materials; all this treasure was mine! I had found it in my own burial vault! I had surely the right to consider it as my property? I began to consider—how could it have been placed there without my knowledge? The answer to this question occurred to me at once. Brigands! Of course!—what a fool I was not to have thought of them before; the dagger painted on the lid of the chest should have guided me to the solution of the mystery. A red dagger was the recognized sign-manual of a bold and dangerous brigand named Carmelo Neri, who, with his reckless gang, haunted the vicinity of Palermo.

"So!" I thought, "this is one of your bright ideas, my cut-throat Carmelo! Cunning rogue! you calculated well—you thought that none would disturb the dead, much less break open a coffin in search of gold. Admirably planned, my Carmelo! But this time you must play a losing game! A supposed dead man coming to life again deserves something for his trouble, and I should be a fool not to accept the goods the gods and the robbers provide. An ill-gotten hoard of wealth, no doubt; but better in my hands than in yours friend Carmelo!"

And I meditated for some minutes on this strange affair If, indeed— and I saw no reason to doubt it—I had chanced to find some of the spoils of the redoubtable Neri, this great chest must have been brought over by sea from Palermo. Probably four stout rascals had carried the supposed coffin in a mock solemn procession, under the pretense of its containing the body of a comrade. These thieves have a high sense of humor. Yet the question remained to be solved—How had they gained access to MY ancestral vault, unless by means of a false key? All at once I was left in darkness, My candle went out as though blown upon by a gust of air. I had my matches, and of course could easily light it again, but I was puzzled to imagine the cause of its sudden extinction. I looked about me in the temporary gloom and saw, to my surprise, a ray of light proceeding from a corner of the very niche where I had fixed the candle between two stones. I approached and put my hand to the place; a strong draught blew through a hole large enough to admit the passage of three fingers. I quickly relighted my torch, and examining this hole and the back of the niche attentively, found that four blocks of granite in the wall had been removed and their places supplied by thick square logs cut from the trunks of trees. These logs were quite loosely fitted. I took them out easily one by one, and then came upon a close pile of brushwood. As I gradually cleared this away a large aperture disclosed itself wide enough for any man to pass through without trouble. My heart beat with the rapture of expected liberty; I clambered up–I looked–thank God! I saw the landscape–the sky! In two minutes I stood outside the vault on the soft grass, with the high arch of heaven above me, and the broad Bay of Naples glittering deliciously before my eyes! I clapped my hands and shouted for pure joy! I was free! Free to return to life, to love, to the arms of my beautiful Nina–free to resume the pleasant course of existence on the gladsome earth–free to forget, if I could, the gloomy horrors of my premature burial. If Carmelo Neri had heard the blessings I heaped upon his head–he would for once have deemed himself a saint rather than a brigand. What did I not owe to the glorious ruffian! Fortune and freedom! for it was evident that this secret passage into the Romani vault had been cunningly contrived by himself or his followers for their own private purposes. Seldom has any man been more grateful to his best benefactor than I was to the famous thief upon whose grim head, as I knew, a price had been set for many months. The poor wretch was in hiding. Well! the authorities should get no aid from me, I resolved; even if I were to discover his whereabouts. Why should I betray him? He had unconsciously done more for me than my best friend. Nay, what friends will you find at all in the world when you need substantial good? Few, or none. Touch the purse–test the heart!

What castles in the air I built as I stood rejoicing in the morning light and my newly acquired liberty–what dreams of perfect happiness flitted radiantly before my fancy! Nina and I would love each other more fondly than before, I thought–our separation had been brief, but terrible–and the idea of what it might have been would endear us to one another with tenfold fervor. And little Stella! Why–this very evening I would swing her again under the orange boughs and listen to her sweet shrill laughter! This very evening I would clasp Guido's hand in a gladness too great for words! This very night my wife's fair head would lie pillowed on my breast in an ecstatic silence broken only by the music of kisses. Ah! my brain grew dizzy with the joyful visions that crowded thickly and dazzlingly upon me! The sun had risen–his long straight beams, like golden spears, touched the tops of the green trees, and roused little flashes as of red and blue fire on the shining surface of the bay. I heard the rippling of water and the measured soft dash of oars; and somewhere from a distant boat the mellifluous voice of a sailor sung a verse of the popular ritornello–

"Sciore d'amenta Sta parolella mia tieul' ammento Zompa llari llira! Sciore limone! Le voglio fa mori de passione Zompa llari llira!"

I smiled–*"Mori de passione!"* Nina and I would know the meaning of those sweet words when the moon rose and the nightingales sung their love-songs to the dreaming flowers! Full of these happy fancies, I inhaled the pure morning air for some minutes, and then re-entered the vault.

5

THE FIRST thing I did was to repack all the treasures I had discovered. This work was easily accomplished. For the present I contented myself with taking two of the leathern bags for my own use, one full of gold pieces, the other of jewels. The chest had been strongly made, and was not much injured by being forced open. I closed its lid as tightly as possible, and dragged it to a remote and dark corner of the vault, where I placed three heavy stones upon it. I then took the two leathern pouches I had selected, and stuffed one in each of the pockets of my trousers. The action reminded me of the scantiness of attire in which I stood arrayed. Could I be seen in the public roads in such a plight? I examined my purse, which, as I before stated, had been left to me, together with my keys and card-case, by the terrified persons who had huddled me into my coffin with such scant ceremony. It contained two twenty-franc pieces and some loose silver. Enough to buy a decent costume of some sort. But where could I make the purchase, and how? Must I wait till evening and slink out of this charnel-house like the ghost of a wretched criminal? No! come what would, I made up my mind not to linger a moment longer in the vault. The swarms of beggars that infest Naples exhibit themselves in every condition of rags, dirt, and misery; at the very worst I could only be taken for one of them. And whatever difficulties I might encounter, no matter!–they would soon be over.

Satisfied that I had placed the brigand coffin in a safe position, I secured the pearl and diamond pendant I had first found, to the chain round my neck. I intended this ornament as a gift for my wife. Then, once more climbing through the aperture, I closed it completely with the logs and brushwood as it was before, and examining it narrowly from the outside, I saw that it was utterly impossible to discern the smallest hint of any entrance to a subterranean passage, so well and cunningly had it been contrived. Now, nothing more remained for me to do but to make the best of my way to the city, there to declare my identity, obtain food and clothes, and then to hasten with all possible speed to my own residence.

Standing on a little hillock, I looked about me to see which direction I should take. The cemetery was situated on the outskirts of Naples–Naples itself lay on my left hand. I perceived a sloping road winding in that direction, and judged that if I followed it it would lead me to the city suburbs. Without further hesitation I commenced my walk. It was now full day. My bare feet sunk deep in the dust that was hot as desert sand–the blazing sun beat down fiercely on my uncovered head, but I felt none of these discomforts; my heart was too full of gladness. I could have sung aloud for delight as I stepped swiftly along toward home–and Nina! I was aware of a great weakness in my limbs–my eyes and head ached with the strong dazzling light; occasionally, too, an icy shiver ran through me that made my teeth chatter. But I recognized these symptoms as the after effects of my so nearly fatal illness, and I paid no heed to them. A few weeks' rest under my wife's loving care, and I knew I should be as well as ever. I stepped on bravely. For some time I met no one, but at last I overtook a small cart laden with freshly gathered grapes. The driver lay on his seat asleep; his pony meanwhile cropped the green herbage by the roadside, and every now and then shook the jingling bells on his harness as though expressing the satisfaction he felt at being left to his own devices. The piled-up grapes looked tempting, and I was both hungry and thirsty, I laid a hand on the sleeping man's shoulder; he awoke with a start. Seeing me, his face assumed an expression of the wildest terror; he jumped from his cart and sunk down on his knees in the dust, imploring me by the Madonna, St. Joseph, and all the saints to spare his life. I laughed; his fears seemed to me ludicrous. Surely there was nothing alarming about me beyond my paucity of clothing.

"Get up, man!" I said. "I want nothing of you but a few grapes, and for them I will pay." And I held out to him a couple of francs. He rose from the dust, still trembling and eying me askance with evident suspicion, took several bunches of the purple fruit, and gave them to me without saying a word. Then, pocketing the money I proffered, he sprung into his cart, and lashing his pony till the unfortunate animal plunged and reared with pain and fury, rattled off down the road at such a break-neck speed that I saw nothing but a whirling blot of wheels disappearing in the distance. I was amused at the absurdity of this man's terror. What did he take me for, I wondered? A ghost or a brigand? I ate my grapes leisurely as I walked along—they were deliciously cool and refreshing—food and wine in one. I met several other persons as I neared the city, market people and venders of ices—but they took no note of me—in fact, I avoided them all as much as possible. On reaching the suburbs I turned into the first street I saw that seemed likely to contain a few shops. It was close and dark and foul-smelling, but I had not gone far down it when I came upon the sort of place I sought—a wretched tumble-down hovel, with a partly broken window, through which a shabby array of second-hand garments were to be dimly perceived, strung up for show on pieces of coarse twine. It was one of those dirty dens where sailors, returning from long voyages, frequently go to dispose of the various trifles they have picked up in foreign countries, so that among the forlorn specimens of second-hand wearing apparel many quaint and curious objects were to be seen, such as shells, branches of rough coral, strings of beads, cups and dishes carved out of cocoa-nut, dried gourds, horns of animals, fans, stuffed parakeets, and old coins—while a grotesque wooden idol peered hideously forth from between the stretched-out portions of a pair of old nankeen trousers, as though surveying the miscellaneous collection in idiotic amazement. An aged man sat smoking at the open door of this promising habitation—a true specimen of a Neapolitan grown old. The skin of his face was like a piece of brown parchment scored all over with deep furrows and wrinkles, as though Time, disapproving of the history he had himself penned upon it, had scratched over and blotted out all records, so that no one should henceforth be able to read what had once been clear writing. The only animation left in him seemed to have concentrated itself in his eyes, which were black and bead- like, and roved hither and thither with a glance of ever-restless and ever-suspicious inquiry. He saw me coming toward him, but he pretended to be absorbed in a profound study of the patch of blue sky that gleamed between the closely leaning houses of the narrow street. I accosted him—and he brought his gaze swiftly down to my level, and stared at me with keen inquisitiveness.

"I have had a long tramp," I said, briefly, for he was not the kind of man to whom I could explain my recent terrible adventure, "and I have lost some of my clothes by an accident on the way. Can you sell me a suit? Anything will do—I am not particular."

The old man took his pipe from his mouth.

"Do you fear the plague?" he asked.

"I have just recovered from an attack of it," I replied, coolly.

He looked at me attentively from head to foot, and then broke into a low chuckling laugh.

"Ha! ha!" he muttered, half to himself, half to me. "Good— good! Here is one like myself—not afraid—not afraid! We are not cowards. We do not find fault with the blessed saints—they send the plague. The beautiful plague!–I love it! I buy all the clothes I can get that are taken from the corpses–they are nearly always excellent clothes. I never clean them–I sell them again at once–yes–yes! Why not? The people must die–the sooner the better! I help the good God as much as I can." And the old blasphemer crossed himself devoutly.

I looked down upon him from where I stood drawn up to my full height, with a glance of disgust. He filled me with something of the same repulsion I had felt when I touched the unnamable Thing that fastened on my neck while I slept in the vault.

"Come!" I said, somewhat roughly, "will you sell me a suit or no?"

"Yes, yes!" and he rose stiffly from his seat; he was very short of stature, and so bent with age and infirmity that he looked more like the crooked bough of a tree than a man, as he hobbled before me into his dark shop. "Come inside, come inside! Take your choice; there is enough here to suit all tastes. See now, what would you? Behold here the dress of a gentleman, ah! what beautiful cloth, what strong wool! English make? Yes, yes! He was English that wore it; a big, strong milord, that drank beer and brandy like water–and rich–just heaven!–how rich! But the plague took him; he died cursing God, and calling bravely for more brandy. Ha, ha! a fine death– a splendid death! His landlord sold me his clothes for three francs–one, two, three–but you must give me six; that is fair profit, is it not? And I am old and poor. I must make something to live upon."

I threw aside the tweed suit he displayed for my inspection. "Nay," I said, "I care nothing for the plague, but find me something better than the cast-off clothing of a brandy-soaked Englishman. I would rather wear the motley garb of a fellow who played the fool in carnival."

The old dealer laughed with a crackling sound in his withered throat, like the rattling of stones in a tin pot.

"Good, good!" he croaked. "I like that, I like that! Thou art old, but thou art merry. That pleases me; one should laugh always. Why not? Death laughs; you never see a solemn skull; it laughs always!"

And he plunged his long lean fingers into a deep drawer full of miscellaneous garments, mumbling to himself all the while. I stood beside him in silence, pondering on his words, "Thou art OLD, but merry." What did he mean by calling ME old? He must be blind, I thought, or in his dotage. Suddenly he looked up.

"Talking of the plague," he said, "it is not always wise. It did a foolish thing yesterday–a very foolish thing. It took one of the richest men in the neighborhood, young too, strong and brave; looked as if he would never die. The plague touched him in the morning– before sunset he was nailed up and put down in his big family vault–a cold lodging, and less handsomely furnished than his grand marble villa on the heights yonder. When I heard the news I told the Madonna she was wicked. Oh, yes! I rated her soundly; she is a woman, and capricious; a good scolding brings her to reason. Look you! I am a friend to God and the plague, but they both did a stupid thing when they took Count Fabio Romani."

I started, but quickly controlled myself into an appearance of indifference.

"Indeed!" I said, carelessly. "And pray who was he that he should not deserve to die as well as other people?"

The old man raised himself from his stooping attitude, and stared at me with his keen black eyes.

"Who was he? who was he?" he cried, in a shrill tone. "Oh, he! One can see you know nothing of Naples. You have not heard of the rich Romani? See you, I wished him to live. He was clever and bold, but I did not grudge him that–no, he was good to the poor; he gave away hundreds of francs in charity. I have seen him often–I saw him married." And here his parchment face screwed itself into an expression of the most malignant cruelty. "Pah! I hate his wife–a fair, soft thing, like a white snake! I used to watch them both from the corners of the streets as they drove along in their fine carriage, and I wondered how it would all end, whether he or she would gain the victory first. I wanted HIM to win; I would have helped him to kill her, yes! But the saints have made a mistake this time, for he is dead, and that she-devil has all. Oh, yes! God and the plague have done a foolish thing for once."

I listened to the old wretch with deepening aversion, yet with some curiosity too. Why should he hate my wife? I thought, unless, indeed, he hated all youth and beauty, as was probably the case. And if he had seen me as often as he averred he must know me by sight. How was it then that he did not recognize me now? Following out this thought, I said aloud:

"What sort of looking man was this Count Romani? You say he was handsome—was he tall or short—dark or fair?"

Putting back his straggling gray locks from his forehead, the dealer stretched out a yellow, claw-like hand, as though pointing to some distant vision.

"A beautiful man!" he exclaimed; "a man good for the eyes to see! As straight as you are!—as tall as you are!—as broad as you are! But your eyes are sunken and dim—his were full and large and sparkling. Your face is drawn and pale—his was of a clear olive tint, round and flushed with health; and his hair was glossy black—ah! as jet- black, my friend, as yours is snow-white!"

I recoiled from these last words in a sort of terror; they were like an electric shock! Was I indeed so changed? Was it possible that the horrors of a night in the vault had made such a dire impression upon me? My hair white?—mine! I could hardly believe it. If so, perhaps Nina would not recognize me— she might be terrified at my aspect— Guido himself might have doubts of my identity. Though, for that matter, I could easily prove myself to be indeed Fabio Romani—even if I had to show the vault and my own sundered coffin. While I revolved all this in my mind the old man, unconscious of my emotion, went on with his mumbling chatter.

"Ah, yes, yes! He was a fine fellow—a strong fellow. I used

to rejoice that he was so strong. He could have taken the little throat of his wife between finger and thumb and nipped it–so! and she would have told no more lies. I wanted him to do it–I waited for it. He would have done it surely, had he lived. That is why I am sorry he died."

Mastering my feelings by a violent effort, I forced myself to speak calmly to this malignant old brute.

"Why do you hate the Countess Romani so much?" I asked him with sternness. "Has she done you any harm?"

He straightened himself as much as he was able and looked me full in the eyes.

"See you!" he answered, with a sort of leering laugh about the corners of his wicked mouth. "I will tell you why I hate her–yes–I will tell you, because you are a man and strong. I like strong men– they are sometimes fooled by women, it is true– but then they can take revenge. I was strong myself once. And you–you are old–but you love a jest–you will understand. The Romani woman has done me no harm. She laughed–once. That was when her horses knocked me down in the street. I was hurt–but I saw her red lips widen and her white teeth glitter–she has a baby smile–the people will tell you–so innocent! I was picked up–her carriage drove on–her husband was not with her–he would have acted differently. But it is no matter–I tell you she laughed–and then I saw at once the likeness."

"The likeness!" I exclaimed impatiently, for his story annoyed me. "What likeness?"

"Between her and my wife," the dealer replied, fixing his cruel eyes upon me with increasing intensity of regard. "Oh, yes! I know what love is. I know too that God had very little to do with the making of women. It was a long time before even He could find the Madonna. Yes–yes, I know! I tell you I married a thing as beautiful as a morning in spring-time–with a little head that seemed to droop like a flower under its weight of sunbeam hair–and eyes! ah–like those of a tiny child when it looks up and asks you for kisses. I was absent once–I returned and found her sleeping tranquilly–yes! on the breast of a black-browed street-singer from Venice–a handsome lad enough and brave as a young lion. He saw me and sprung at my throat–I held him down and knelt upon his chest–she woke and gazed upon us, too terrified to speak or scream–she only shivered and made a little moaning sound like that of a spoiled baby. I looked down into her prostrate lover's eyes and smiled. 'I will not hurt you,' I said. 'Had she not consented, you could not have gained the victory. All I ask of you is to remain here for a few moments longer.' He stared, but was mute. I bound him hand and foot so that he could not stir. Then I took my knife and went to her. Her blue eyes glared wide–imploringly she turned them upon me–and ever she wrung her small hands and shivered and moaned. I plunged the keen bright blade deep through her soft white flesh–her lover cried out in agony–her heart's blood welled up in a crimson tide, staining with a bright hue the white garments she wore; she flung up her arms–she sank back on her pillows–dead. I drew the knife from her body, and with it cut the bonds of the Venetian boy. I then gave it to him.

"'Take it as a remembrance of her,' I said. 'In a month she would have betrayed you as she betrayed me.'"

"He raged like a madman. He rushed out and called the gendarmes. Of course I was tried for murder–but it was not murder–it was justice. The judge found extenuating circumstances. Naturally! He had a wife of his own. He understood my case. Now you know why I hate that dainty jeweled woman up at the Villa Romani. She is just like that other one–that creature I slew–she has just the same slow smile and the same child-like eyes. I tell you again, I am sorry her husband is dead–it vexes me sorely to think of it. For he would have killed her in time–yes!–of that I am quite sure!"

6

I LISTENED to his narrative with a pained feeling at my heart, and a shuddering sensation as of icy cold ran through my veins. Why, I had fancied that all who beheld Nina must, perforce, love and admire her. True, when this old man was accidentally knocked down by her horses (a circumstance she had never mentioned to me), it was careless of her not to stop and make inquiry as to the extent of his injuries, but she was young and thoughtless; she could not be intentionally heartless. I was horrified to think that she should have made such an enemy as even this aged and poverty-stricken wretch; but I said nothing. I had no wish to betray myself. He waited for me to speak and grew impatient at my silence.

"Say now, my friend!" he queried, with a sort of childish eagerness, "did I not take a good vengeance? God himself could not have done better!"

"I think your wife deserved her fate," I said, curtly, "but I cannot say I admire you for being her murderer."

He turned upon me rapidly, throwing both hands above his head with a frantic gesticulation. His voice rose to a kind of muffled shriek.

"Murderer you call me—ha! ha! that is good. No, no! She murdered me! I tell you I died when I saw her asleep in her lover's arms–she killed me at one blow. A devil rose up in my body and took swift revenge; that devil is in me now, a brave devil, a strong devil! That is why I do not fear the plague; the devil in me frightens away death. Someday it will leave me"– here his smothered yell sunk gradually to a feeble, weary tone; "yes, it will leave me and I shall find a dark place where I can sleep; I do not sleep much now." He eyed me half wistfully.

"You see," he explained, almost gently, "my memory is very good, and when one thinks of many things one cannot sleep. It is many years ago, but every night I see HER; she comes to me wringing her little white hands, her blue eyes stare, I hear short moans of terror. Every night, every night!" He paused, and passed his hands in a bewildered way across his forehead. Then, like a man suddenly waking from sleep, he stared as though he saw me now for the first time, and broke into a low chuckling laugh.

"What a thing, what a thing it is, the memory!" he muttered. "Strange–strange! See, I remembered all that, and forgot you! But I know what you want–a suit of clothes–yes, you need them badly, and I also need the money for them. Ha, ha! And you will not have the fine coat of Milord Inglese! No, no! I understand. I will find you something–patience, patience!"

And he began to grope among a number of things that were thrown in a confused heap at the back of the shop. While in this attitude he looked so gaunt and grim that he reminded me of an aged vulture stooping over carrion, and yet there was something pitiable about him too. In a way I was sorry for him; a poor half-witted wretch, whose life had been full of such gall and wormwood. What a different fate was his to mine, I thought. I had endured but one short night of agony; how trifling it seemed compared to HIS hourly remorse and suffering! He hated Nina for an act of thoughtlessness; well, no doubt she was not the only woman whose existence annoyed him; it was most probably that he was at enmity with all women. I watched him pityingly as he searched among the worn-out garments which were his stock-in-trade, and wondered why Death, so active in smiting down the strongest in the city, should have thus cruelly passed by this forlorn wreck of human misery, for whom the grave would have surely been a most welcome release and rest. He turned round at last with an exulting gesture.

"I have found it!" he exclaimed. "The very thing to suit you. You are perhaps a coral-fisher? You will like a fisherman's dress. Here is one, red sash, cap and all, in beautiful condition! He that wore it was about your height it will fit you as well as it fitted him, and, look you! the plague is not in it, the sea has soaked through and through it; it smells of the sand and weed."

He spread out the rough garb before me. I glanced at it carelessly.

"Did the former wearer kill HIS wife?" I asked, with a slight smile.

The old rag-picker shook his head and made a sign with his outspread fingers expressive of contempt.

"Not he!–He was a fool–He killed himself"

"How was that? By accident or design?"

"Che! Che! He knew very well what he was doing. It happened only two months since. It was for the sake of a black-eyed jade, she lives and laughs all day long up at Sorrento. He had been on a long voyage, he brought her pearls for her throat and coral pins for her hair. She had promised to marry him. He had just landed, he met her on the quay, he offered her the pearl and coral trinkets. She threw them back and told him she was tired of him. Just that–nothing more. He tried to soften her; she raged at him like a tiger-cat. Yes, I was one of the little crowd that stood round them on the quay, I saw it all. Her black eyes flashed, she stamped and bit her lips at him, her full bosom heaved as though it would burst her laced bodice. She was only a market-girl, but she gave herself the airs of a queen. 'I am tired of you!' she said to him. 'Go! I wish to see you no more.' He was tall and well-made, a powerful fellow; but he staggered, his face grew pale, his lips quivered. He bent his head a little–turned–and before any hand could stop him he sprung from the edge of the quay into the waves, they closed over his head, for he did not try to swim; he just sunk down, down, like a stone. Next day his body came ashore, and I bought his clothes for two francs; you shall have them for four."

"And what became of the girl?" I asked.

"Oh, SHE! She laughs all day long, as I told you. She has a new lover every week. What should SHE care?"

I drew out my purse. "I will take this suit," I said. "You ask four francs, here are six, but for the extra two you must show me some private corner where I can dress."

"Yes, yes. But certainly!" and the old fellow trembled all over with avaricious eagerness as I counted the silver pieces into his withered palm. "Anything to oblige a generous stranger! There is the place I sleep in; it is not much, but there is a mirror–HER mirror–the only thing I keep of hers; come this way, come this way!"

And stumbling hastily along, almost falling over the disordered bundles of clothing that lay about in all directions, he opened a little door that seemed to be cut in the wall, and led me into a kind of close cupboard, smelling most vilely, and furnished with a miserable pallet bed and one broken chair. A small square pane of glass admitted light enough to see all that there was to be seen, and close to this extemporized window hung the mirror alluded to, a beautiful thing set in silver of antique workmanship, the costliness of which I at once recognized, though into the glass itself I dared not for the moment look. The old man showed me with some pride that the door to this narrow den of his locked from within.

"I made the lock and key, and fitted it all myself," he said. "Look how neat and strong! Yes; I was clever once at all that work–it was my trade–till that morning when I found her with the singer from Venice; then I forgot all I used to know–it went away somehow, I could never understand why. Here is the fisherman's suit; you can take your time to put it on; fasten

58

the door; the room is at your service."

And he nodded several times in a manner that was meant to be friendly, and left me. I followed his advice at once and locked myself in. Then I stepped steadily to the mirror hanging on the wall, and looked at my own reflection. A bitter pang shot through me. The dealer's sight was good, he had said truly. I was old! If twenty years of suffering had passed over my head, they could hardly have changed me more terribly. My illness had thinned my face and marked it with deep lines of pain; my eyes had retreated far back into my head, while a certain wildness of expression in them bore witness to the terrors I had suffered in the vault, and to crown all, my hair was indeed perfectly white. I understood now the alarm of the man who had sold me grapes on the highway that morning; my appearance was strange enough to startle any one. Indeed, I scarcely recognized myself. Would my wife, would Guido recognize me? Almost I doubted it. This thought was so painful to me that the tears sprung to my eyes. I brushed them away in haste.

"Fy on thee, Fabio! Be a man!" I said, addressing myself angrily. "Of what matter after all whether hairs are black or white? What matter how the face changes, so long as the heart is true? For a moment, perhaps, thy love may grow pale at sight of thee; but when she knows of thy sufferings, wilt thou not be dearer to her than ever? Will not one of her soft embraces recompense thee for all thy past anguish, and suffice to make thee young again?"

And thus encouraging my sinking spirits, I quickly arrayed myself in the Neapolitan coral-fisher's garb. The trousers were very loose, and were provided with two long deep pockets, convenient receptacles, which easily contained the leathern bags of gold and jewels I had taken from the brigand's coffin. When my hasty toilet was completed I took another glance at the mirror, this time with a half-smile. True, I was greatly altered; but after all I did not look so bad. The fisherman's picturesque costume became me well; the scarlet cap sat jauntily on the snow-white curls that clustered so thickly over my forehead, and the consciousness I had of approaching happiness sent a little of the old fearless luster back into my sunken eyes. Besides, I knew I should not always have this care-worn and wasted appearance; rest, and perhaps a change of air, would infallibly restore the roundness to my face and the freshness to my complexion; even my white locks might return to their pristine color, such things had been; and supposing they remained white? well!–there were many who would admire the peculiar contrast between a young man's face and an old man's hair.

Having finished dressing, I unlocked the door of the stuffy little cabin and called the old rag-picker. He came shuffling along with his head bent, but raising his eyes as he approached me, he threw up his hands in astonishment, exclaiming,

"*Santissima Madonna!* But you are a fine man–a fine man! Eh, eh! Holy Joseph! What height and breadth! A pity–a pity you are old; you must have been strong when you were young!"

Half in joke, and half to humor him in his fancy for mere muscular force, I rolled up the sleeve of my jacket to the shoulder, saying, lightly,

"Oh, as for being strong! There is plenty of strength in me still, you see."

He stared; laid his yellow fingers on my bared arm with a kind of ghoul-like interest and wonder, and felt the muscles of it with childish, almost maudlin admiration.

"Beautiful, beautiful!" he mumbled. "Like iron–just think of it! Yes, yes. You could kill anything easily. Ah! I used to be like that once. I was clever at sword-play. I could, with well-tempered steel, cut asunder a seven-times-folded piece of silk at one blow without fraying out a thread. Yes, as neatly as one cuts butter! You could do that too if you liked. It all lies in the arm–the brave arm that kills at a single stroke."

And he gazed at me intently with his small blear eyes as though anxious to know more of my character and temperament. I turned abruptly from him, and called his attention to my own discarded garments.

"See," I said, carelessly; "you can have these, though they are not of much value. And, stay, here are another three francs for some socks and shoes, which I dare say you can find to suit me."

He clasped his hands ecstatically, and poured out a torrent of thanks and praises for this additional and unexpected sum, and protesting by all the saints that he and the entire contents of his shop were at the service of so generous a stranger, he at once produced the articles I asked for. I put them on—and then stood up thoroughly equipped and ready to make my way back to my own home when I chose. But I had resolved on one thing. Seeing that I was so greatly changed, I determined not to go to the Villa Romani by daylight, lest I should startle my wife too suddenly. Women are delicate; my unexpected appearance might give her a nervous shock which perhaps would have serious results. I would wait till the sun had set, and then go up to the house by a back way I knew of, and try to get speech with one of the servants. I might even meet my friend Guido Ferrari, and he would break the joyful news of my return from death to Nina by degrees, and also prepare her for my altered looks. While these thoughts flitted rapidly through my brain, the old ragpicker stood near me with his head on one side like a meditative raven, and regarded me intently.

"Are you going far?" he asked at last, with a kind of timidity.

"Yes," I answered him, abruptly; "very far."

He laid a detaining hand on my sleeve, and his eyes glittered—with a malignant expression.

"Tell me," he muttered, eagerly, "tell me—I will keep the secret. Are you going to a woman?"

I looked down upon him, half in disdain, half in amusement.

"Yes!" I said, quietly, "I am going to a woman."

He broke into silent laughter—hideous laughter that

contorted his visage and twisted his body in convulsive writhings.

I glanced at him in disgust, and shaking off his hand from my arm, I made my way to the door of the shop He hobbled quickly after me, wiping away the moisture that his inward merriment had brought into his eyes.

"Going to a woman!" he croaked "Ha, ha! You are not the first, nor will you be the last, that has gone so! Going to a woman! that is well–that is good! Go to her, go! You are strong, you have a brave arm! Go to her, find her out, and– KILL HER! Yes, yes–you will be able to do it easily–quite easily! Go and kill her'"

He stood at his low door mouthing and pointing, his stunted figure and evil face reminding me of one of Heinrich Heine's dwarf devils who are depicted as piling fire on the heads of the saints. I bade him "Good day" in an indifferent tone, but he made me no answer I walked slowly away. Looking back once I saw him still standing on the threshold of his wretched dwelling, his wicked mouth working itself into all manner of grimaces, while with his crooked fingers he made signs in the air as if he caught an invisible something and throttled it. I went on down the street and out of it into the broader thoroughfares, with his last words ringing in my ears, "go and kill her!"

7

THAT day seemed very long to me. I wandered aimlessly about the city, seeing few faces that I knew, for the wealthier inhabitants, afraid of the cholera, had either left the place together or remained closely shut within their own houses. Everywhere I went something bore witness to the terrible ravages of the plague. At almost every corner I met a funeral procession. Once I came upon a group of men who were standing in an open door way packing a dead body into a coffin too small for it. There was something truly revolting in the way they doubled up the arms and legs and squeezed in the shoulders of the deceased man—one could hear the bones crack. I watched the brutal proceedings for a minute or so, and then I said aloud:

"You had better make sure he is quite dead,"

The *beccamorti* looked at me in surprise; one laughed grimly and swore. "By the body of God, if I thought he were not I would twist his accursed neck for him! But the cholera never fails, he is dead for certain—see!" And he knocked the head of the corpse to and fro against the sides of the coffin with no more compunction than if it had been a block of wood. Sickened at the sight, I turned away and said no more. On reaching one of the more important thoroughfares I perceived several knots of people collected, who glanced at one another with eager yet shamed faces, and spoke in low voices. A whisper reached my ears, "The king! the king!" All heads were turned in one direction; I paused and looked also. Walking at a leisurely pace, accompanied by a few gentlemen of earnest mien and grave deportment, I saw the fearless monarch, Humbert of Italy–he whom his subjects delight to honor. He was making a round of visits to all the vilest holes and corners of the city, where the plague raged most terribly–he had not so much as a cigarette in his mouth to ward off infection. He walked with the easy and assured step of a hero; his face was somewhat sad, as though the sufferings of his people had pressed heavily upon his sympathetic heart. I bared my head reverently as he passed, his keen kind eyes lighted on me with a smile.

"A subject for a painting, yon white-haired fisherman!" I heard him say to one of his attendants. Almost I betrayed myself. I was on the point of springing forward and throwing myself at his feet to tell him my story. It seemed to me both cruel and unnatural that he, my beloved sovereign, should pass me without recognition–me, to whom he had spoken so often and so cordially. For when I visited Rome, as I was accustomed to do annually, there were few more welcome guests at the balls of the Quirinal Palace than Count Fabio Romani. I began to wonder stupidly who Fabio Romani was; the gay gallant known as such seemed no longer to have any existence–a "white-haired fisherman" usurped his place. But though I thought these things I refrained from addressing the king. Some impulse, however, led me to follow him at a respectful distance, as did also many others. His majesty strolled through the most pestilential streets with as much unconcern as though he wore taking his pleasure in a garden of roses; he stepped quietly into the dirtiest hovels where lay both dead and dying; he spoke words of kindly encouragement to the grief- stricken and terrified mourners, who stared through their tears at the monarch with astonishment and gratitude; silver and gold were gently dropped into the hands of the suffering poor, and the very pressing cases received the royal benefactor's personal attention and immediate relief. Mothers with infants in their arms knelt to implore the king's blessing–which to pacify them he gave with a modest hesitation, as though he thought himself unworthy, and yet with a parental tenderness that was infinitely touching. One wild- eyed, black-haired girl flung herself down on the ground right in the king's path; she kissed his feet, and then sprung erect with a gesture of triumph.

"I am saved!" she cried; "the plague cannot walk in the same road with the king!"

Humbert smiled, and regarded her somewhat as an indulgent father might regard a spoiled daughter; but he said nothing, and passed on. A cluster of men and women standing at the open door of one of the poorest-looking houses in the street next attracted the monarch's attention. There was some noisy argument going on; two or three *beccamorti* were loudly discussing together and swearing profusely–some women were crying bitterly, and in the center of the excited group a coffin stood on end as though waiting for an occupant. One of the gentlemen in attendance on the king preceded him and announced his approach, whereupon the loud clamor of tongues ceased, the men bared their heads, and the women checked their sobs.

"What is wrong here, my friends?" the monarch asked with exceeding gentleness.

There was silence for a moment; the *beccamorti* looked sullen and ashamed. Then one of the women, with a fat good-natured face and eyes rimmed redly round with weeping, elbowed her way through the little throng to the front and spoke.

"May the Holy Virgin and saints bless your majesty!" she cried, in shrill accents. "And as for what is wrong, it would soon be right if those shameless pigs," pointing to the *beccamorti*, "would let us alone. They would kill a man rather than wait an hour–one little hour! The girl is dead, your majesty–and Giovanni, poor lad! will not leave her; he has his two arms round her tight–Holy Virgin!– think of it! and she a cholera corpse–and do what we can, he will not be parted from her, and they seek her body for the burial. And if we force him away, *poverino*, he will lose his head for certain. One little hour, your majesty, just one, and the reverend father will come and persuade Giovanni better than we can."

The king raised his hand with a slight gesture of command–the little crowd parted before him–and he entered the miserable dwelling wherein lay the corpse that was the cause of all the argument. His attendants followed; I, too, availed myself of a corner in the doorway. The scene disclosed was so terribly pathetic that few could look upon it without emotion–Humbert of Italy himself uncovered his head and stood silent. On a poor pallet bed lay the fair body of a girl in her first youth, her tender loveliness as yet untouched even by the disfiguring marks of the death that had overtaken her. One would have thought she slept, had it not been for the rigidity of her stiffened limbs, and the wax- like pallor of her face and hands. Right across her form, almost covering it from view, a man lay prone, as though he had fallen there lifeless–indeed he might have been dead also for any sign he showed to the contrary. His arms were closed firmly round the girl's corpse– his face was hidden from view on the cold breast that would no more respond to the warmth of his caresses. A straight beam of sunlight shot like a golden spear into the dark little room and lighted up the whole scene–the prostrate figures on the bed–the erect form of the compassionate king, and the grave and anxious faces of the little crowd of people who stood around him.

"See! that is the way he has been ever since last night when she died," whispered the woman who had before spoken; "and his hands are clinched round her like iron–one cannot move a finger!"

The king advanced. He touched the shoulder of the unhappy lover. His voice, modulated to an exquisite softness, struck on the ears of the listeners like a note of cheerful music.

"*Figlio mio!*"

There was no answer. The women, touched by the simple endearing words of the monarch, began to sob though gently, and even the men brushed a few drops from their eyes. Again the king spoke.

"*Figlio mio!* I am your king. Have you no greeting for me?"

The man raised his head from its pillow on the breast of the beloved corpse and stared vacantly at the royal speaker. His haggard face, tangled hair, and wild eyes gave him the appearance of one who had long wandered in a labyrinth of frightful visions from which there was no escape but self-murder.

"Your hand, my son!" resumed the king in a tone of soldier-like authority.

Very slowly–very reluctantly–as though he were forced to the action by some strange magnetic influence which he had no power to withstand, he loosened his right arm from the dead form it clasped so pertinaciously, and stretched forth the hand as commanded. Humbert caught it firmly within his own and held it fast–then looking the poor fellow full in the face, he said with grave steadiness and simplicity,

"There is no death in love, my friend!"

The young man's eyes met his–his set mouth softened–and wresting his hand passionately from that of the king, he broke into a passion of weeping. Humbert at once placed a protecting arm around him, and with the assistance of one of his attendants raised him from the bed, and led him unresistingly away, as passively obedient as a child, though sobbing convulsively as he went. The rush of tears had saved his reason, and most probably his life. A murmur of enthusiastic applause greeted the good king as he passed through the little throng of persons who had witnessed what had taken place. Acknowledging it with a quiet unaffected bow, he left the house, and signed to the *beccamorti*, who still waited outside, that they were now free to perform their melancholy office. He then went on his way attended by more heart-felt blessings and praises than ever fell to the lot of the proudest conqueror returning with the spoils of a hundred battles. I looked after his retreating figure till I could see it no more—I felt that I had grown stronger for the mere presence of a hero—a man who indeed was "every inch a king." I am a royalist—yes. Governed by such a sovereign, few men of calm reason would be otherwise. But royalist though I am, I would assist in bringing about the dethronement and death of a mean tyrant, were he crowned king a hundred times over! Few monarchs are like Humbert of Italy—even now my heart warms when I think of him—in all the distraction of my sufferings, his figure stands out like a supreme embodied Beneficent Force surrounded by the clear light of unselfish goodness—a light in which Italia suns her fair face and smiles again with the old sweet smile of her happiest days of high achievement—days in which he children were great, simply because they were EARNEST. The fault of all modern labor lies in the fact that there is no heart in anything we do—we seldom love our work for work's sake—we perform it solely for what we can get by it. Therein lies the secret of failure. Friends will scarcely serve each other unless they can also serve their own interests—true, there are exceptions to this rule, but they are deemed fools for their pains.

As soon as the king disappeared I also left the scene of the foregoing incident. I had a fancy to visit the little restaurant where I had been taken ill, and after some trouble I found it. The door stood open. I saw the fat landlord, Pietro, polishing his glasses as though he had never left off; and there in the same corner was the very wooden bench on which I had lain—where I had— as was generally supposed—died. I stepped in. The landlord looked up and bade me good-day. I returned his salutation, and ordered some coffee and rolls of bread. Seating myself carelessly at one of the little tables I turned over the newspaper, while he bustled about in haste to serve me. As he dusted and rubbed up a cup and saucer for my use, he said, briskly,

"You have had a long voyage, *amico*? And successful fishing?"

For a moment I was confused and knew not what to answer, but gathering my wits together I smiled and answered readily in the affirmative.

"And you?" I said, gaily. "How goes the cholera?"

The landlord shook his head dolefully.

"Holy Joseph! do not speak of it. The people die like flies in a honey-pot. Only yesterday—body of Bacchus!—who would have thought it?"

And he sighed deeply as he poured out the steaming coffee, and shook his head more sorrowfully than before.

"Why, what happened yesterday?" I asked, though I knew perfectly well what he was going to say; "I am a stranger in Naples, and empty of news."

The perspiring Pietro laid a fat thumb on the marble top of the table, and with it traced a pattern meditatively.

"You never heard of the rich Count Romani?" he inquired.

I made a sign in the negative, and bent my face over my coffee-cup.

"Ah, well!" he went on with a half groan, "it does not matter—there is no Count Romani any more. It is all gone—finished! But he was rich—as rich as the king, they say—yet see how low the saints brought him! Fra Cipriano of the Benedictines carried him in here yesterday morning—he was struck by the plague—in five hours he was dead," here the landlord caught a mosquito and killed it—"ah! as dead as that *zinzara*! Yes, he lay dead on that very wooden bench opposite to you. They buried him before sunset. It is like a bad dream!"

I affected to be deeply engrossed with the cutting and Spreading of my roll and butter.

"I see nothing particular about it," I said, indifferently. "That he was rich is nothing—rich and poor must die alike."

"And that is true, very true," assented Pietro, with another groan, "for not all his property could save the blessed Cipriano."

I started, but quickly controlled myself.

"What do you mean?" I asked, as carelessly as I could. "Are you talking of some saint?"

"Well, if he were not canonized he deserves to be," replied the landlord; "I speak of the holy Benedictine father who brought hither the Count Romani in a dying condition. Ah! little he knew how soon the good God would call him himself!"

I felt a sickening sensation at my heart.

"Is he dead?" I exclaimed.

"Dead as the martyrs!" answered Pietro. "He caught the plague, I suppose, from the count, for he was bending over him to the last. Ay, and he sprinkled holy water over the corpse, and laid his own crucifix upon it in the coffin. Then up he went to the Villa Romani, taking with him the count's trinkets, his watch, ring, and cigar- case–and nothing would satisfy him but that he should deliver them himself to the young contessa, telling her how her husband died."

My poor Nina!–I thought. "Was she much grieved?" I inquired, with a vague curiosity.

"How do I know?" said the landlord, shrugging his bulky shoulders. "The reverend father said nothing, save that she swooned away. But what of that? Women swoon at everything–from a mouse to a corpse. As I said, the good Cipriano attended the count's burial–and he had scarce returned from it when he was seized with the illness. And this morning he died at the monastery–may his soul rest in peace! I heard the news only an hour ago. Ah! he was a holy man! He has promised me a warm corner in Paradise, and I know he will keep his word as truly as St. Peter himself."

I pushed away the rest of my meal untasted. The food choked me. I could have shed tears for the noble, patient life thus self- sacrificed. One hero the less in this world of unheroic, uninspired persons! I sat silent, lost in sorrowful thought. The landlord looked at me curiously.

"The coffee does not please you?" he said at last. "You

have no appetite?" I forced a smile.

"Nay–your words would take the edge off the keenest appetite ever born of the breath of the sea. Truly Naples affords but sorry entertainment to a stranger; is there naught to hear but stories of the dying and the dead?"

Pietro put on an air that was almost apologetic.

"Well, truly!" he answered, resignedly–"very little else. But what would you, *amico*? It is the plague and the will of God."

As he said the last words my gaze was caught and riveted by the figure of a man strolling leisurely past the door of the cafe. It was Guido Ferrari–my friend! I would have rushed out to speak to him–but something in his look and manner checked the impulse as it rose in me. He was walking very slowly, smoking a cigar as he went; there was a smile on his face, and in his coat he wore a freshly- gathered rose La Gloire de France, similar to those that grew in such profusion on the upper terrace of my villa. I stared at him as he passed–my feelings underwent a kind of shock. He looked perfectly happy and tranquil, happier indeed than ever I remembered to have seen him, and yet–and yet, according to HIS knowledge, I, his best friend, had died only yesterday! With this sorrow fresh upon him, he could smile like a man going to a *festa*, and wear a coral-pink rose, which surely was no sign of mourning! For one moment I felt hurt, the next, I laughed at my own sensitiveness. After all, what of the smile, what of the rose! A man could not always be answerable for the expression of his countenance, and as for the flower, he might have gathered it *en passent*, without thinking, or what was still more likely, the child Stella might have given it to him, in which case he would have worn it to please her. He displayed no badge of mourning? True!–but then consider–I had only died yesterday! There had been no time to procure all those outward appurtenances of woe which social customs rendered necessary, but which were no infallible sign of the heart's sincerity. Satisfied with my own self-reasoning I made no attempt to follow Guido in his walk–I let him go on his way unconscious of my existence. I would wait, I thought, till the evening–then everything would be explained.

I turned to the landlord. "How much to pay?" I asked.

"What you will, *amico*" he replied–"I am never hard on the fisher folk–but times are bad, or you would be welcome to a breakfast for nothing. Many and many a day have I done as much for men of your craft, and the blessed Cipriano who is gone used to say that St. Peter would remember me for it. It is true the Madonna gives a special blessing if one looks after the fishers, because all the holy apostles were of the trade; and I would be loath to lose her protection–yet-"

I laughed and tossed him a franc. He pocketed it at once and his eyes twinkled.

"Though you have not taken half a franc's worth," he admitted, with an honesty very unusual in a Neapolitan–"but the saints will make it up to you, never fear!"

"I am sure of that!" I said, gaily. "Addio, my friend! Prosperity to you and our Lady's favor!"

This salutation, which I knew to be a common one with Sicilian mariners, the good Pietro responded to with amiable heartiness, wishing me luck on my next voyage. He then betook himself anew to the polishing of his glasses–and I passed the rest of the day in strolling about the least frequented streets of the city, and longing impatiently for the crimson glory of the sunset, which, like a wide flag of triumph, was to be the signal of my safe return to love and happiness.

8

IT CAME at last, the blessed, the longed-for evening. A soft breeze sprung up, cooling the burning air after the heat of the day, and bringing with it the odors of a thousand flowers. A regal glory of shifting colors blazed on the breast of heaven–the bay, motionless as a mirror, reflected all the splendid tints with a sheeny luster that redoubled their magnificence. Pricked in every vein by the stinging of my own desires, I yet restrained myself; I waited till the sun sunk below the glassy waters–till the pomp and glow attending its departure had paled into those dim, ethereal hues which are like delicate draperies fallen from the flying forms of angels–till the yellow rim of the round full moon rose languidly on the edge of the horizon–and then keeping back my eagerness no longer, I took the well-known road ascending to the Villa Romani, My heart beat high–my limbs trembled with excitement–my steps were impatient and precipitate–never had the way seemed so long. At last I reached the great gate-way–it was locked fast–its sculptured lions looked upon me frowningly. I heard the splash and tinkle of the fountains within, the scents of the roses and myrtle were wafted toward me with every breath I drew. Home at last! I smiled–my whole frame quivered with expectancy and delight. It was not my intention to seek admission by the principal entrance–I contented myself with one long, loving look, and turned to the left, where there was a small private gate leading into an avenue of ilex and pine, interspersed with orange-trees. This was a favorite walk of mine, partly on account of its pleasant shade even in the hottest noon– partly because it was seldom frequented by any member of the household save myself. Guido occasionally took a turn with me there, but I was more often alone, and I was fond of pacing up and down in the shadow of the trees, reading some favorite book, or giving myself up to the *dolcefar niente* of my own imaginings. The avenue led round to the back of the villa, and as I now entered it, I thought I would approach the house cautiously by this means and get private speech with Assunta, the nurse who had charge of little Stella, and who was moreover an old and tried family servant, in whose arms my mother had breathed her last.

The dark trees rustled solemnly as I stepped quickly yet softly along the familiar moss-grown path. The place was very still– sometimes the nightingales broke into a bubbling torrent of melody, and then were suddenly silent, as though overawed by the shadows of the heavy interlacing boughs, through which the moonlight flickered, casting strange and fantastic patterns on the ground. A cloud of *lucciole* broke from a thicket of laurel, and sparkled in the air like gems loosened from a queen's crown. Faint odors floated about me, shaken from orange boughs and trailing branches of white jasmine. I hastened on, my spirits rising higher the nearer I approached my destination. I was full of sweet anticipation and passionate longing–I yearned to clasp my beloved Nina in my arms– to see her lovely lustrous eyes looking fondly into mine–I was eager to shake Guido by the hand–and as for Stella, I knew the child would be in bed at that hour, but still, I thought, I must have her wakened to see me. I felt that my happiness would not be complete till I had kissed her little cherub face, and caressed those clustering curls of hers that were like spun gold. Hush–hush! What was that? I stopped in my rapid progress as though suddenly checked by an invisible hand. I listened with strained ears. That sound—was it not a rippling peal of gay sweet laughter? A shiver shook me from head to foot. It was my wife's laugh—I knew the silvery chime of it well! My heart sunk coldly—I paused irresolute. She could laugh then like that, while she thought me lying dead— dead and out of her reach forever! All at once I perceived the glimmer of a white robe through the trees; obeying my own impulse, I stepped softly aside—I hid behind a dense screen of foliage through which I could see without being seen. The clear laugh rang out once again on the stillness—its brightness pierced my brain like a sharp sword! She was happy—she was even merry—she wandered here in the moonlight joyous-hearted, while I—I had expected to find her close shut within her room, or else kneeling before the Mater Dolorosa in the little chapel, praying for my soul's rest, and mingling her prayers with her tears! Yes—I had expected this— we men are such fools when we love women! Suddenly a terrible thought struck me. Had she gone mad? Had the shock and grief of my so unexpected death turned her delicate brain? Was she roaming about, poor child, like Ophelia, knowing not whither she went, and was her apparent gayety the fantastic mirth of a disordered brain? I shuddered at the idea— and bending slightly apart the boughs behind which I was secreted, I looked out anxiously. Two figures were slowly approaching— my wife and my friend, Guido Ferrari. Well—there was nothing in that—it was as it should be—was not Guido as my brother? It was almost his duty to console and cheer Nina as much as lay in his power. But stay! stay! did I see aright—was she simply leaning on his arm for support—or—a fierce oath, that was almost a cry of torture, broke from my lips! Oh, would to God I had died! Would to God I had never broken open the coffin in which I lay at peace! What was death—what were the horrors of the vault—what was anything I had suffered to the anguish that racked me now? The memory of it to this day burns in my brain like inextinguishable fire, and my hand involuntarily clinches itself in an effort to beat back the furious bitterness of that moment! I know not how I restrained the murderous ferocity that awoke within me—how I forced myself to remain motionless and silent in my hiding-place. But I did. I watched the miserable comedy out to its end. I looked dumbly on at my own betrayal! I saw my honor stabbed to the death by those whom I most trusted, and yet I gave no sign! They—Guido Ferrari and my wife—came so close to my hiding- place that I could note every gesture and hear every word they uttered. They paused within three steps of me—his arm encircled her waist—hers was thrown carelessly around his neck—her head rested on his shoulder. Even so had she walked with me a thousand times! She was dressed in pure white save for one spot of deep color near her heart—a red rose, as red as blood. It was pinned there with a diamond pin that flashed in the moonlight. I thought wildly, that instead of that rose, there should be blood indeed—instead of a diamond pin there should be the good steel of a straight dagger! But I had no weapon—I stared at her, dry-eyed and mute. She looked lovely—exquisitely lovely! No trace of grief marred the fairness of her face—her eyes were as languidly limpid and tender as ever—her lips were parted in the child-like smile that was so sweet—so innocently trustful! She spoke—ah, Heaven! the old bewitching music of her low voice made my heart leap and my brain reel.

"You foolish Guido!" she said, in dreamily amused accents. "What would have happened, I wonder, if Fabio had not died so opportunely."

I waited eagerly for the answer. Guido laughed lightly.

"He would never have discovered anything. You were too clever for him, *piccinina*! Besides, his conceit saved him—he had so good an opinion of himself that he would not have deemed it possible for you to care for any other man."

My wife—flawless diamond-pearl of pure womanhood!—sighed half restlessly.

"I am glad he is dead!" she murmured; "but, Guido mio, you are imprudent. You cannot visit me now so often—the servants will talk! Then I must go into mourning for at least six months—and there are many other things to consider."

Guido's hand played with the jeweled necklace she wore—be bent and kissed the place where its central pendant rested. Again–again, good sir, I pray you! Let no faint scruples interfere with your rightful enjoyment! Cover the white flesh with caresses–it is public property! a dozen kisses more or less will not signify! So I madly thought as I crouched among the trees–the tigerish wrath within me making the blood beat in my head like a hundred hammer- strokes.

"Nay then, my love," he replied to her, "it is almost a pity Fabio is dead! While he lived he played an excellent part as a screen–he was an unconscious, but veritable duenna of propriety for both of us, as no one else could be!"

The boughs that covered me creaked and rustled. My wife started, and looked uneasily round her.

"Hush!" she said, nervously. "He was buried only yesterday–and they say there are ghosts sometimes. This avenue, too–I wish we had not come here–it was his favorite walk. Besides," she added, with a slight accent of regret, "after all he was the father of my child– you must think of that."

"By Heaven!" exclaimed Guido, fiercely, "do I not think of it? Ay– and I curse him for every kiss he stole from your lips!"

I listened half stupefied. Here was a new phase of the marriage law! Husbands were thieves then–they "stole" kisses; only lovers were honest in their embraces! Oh, my dear friend–my more than brother– how near you were to death at that moment! Had you but seen my face peering pallidly through the dusky leaves–could you have known the force of the fury pent up within me–you would not have valued your life at one *baiocco*!

"Why did you marry him?" he asked, after a little pause, during which he toyed with the fair curls that floated against his breast.

She looked up with a little mutinous pout, and shrugged her shoulders.

"Why? Because I was tired of the convent, and all the stupid, solemn ways of the nuns; also because he was rich, and

I was horribly poor. I cannot bear to be poor! Then he loved me"–here her eyes glimmered with malicious triumph–"yes–he was mad for me–and–"

"You loved him?" demanded Guido, almost fiercely.

"*Ma che!*" she answered, with an expressive gesture. "I suppose I did–for a week or two. As much as one ever loves a husband! What does one marry for at all? For convenience–money–position–he gave me these things, as you know."

"You will gain nothing by marrying me, then," he said, jealously.

She laughed, and laid her little white hand, glittering with rings, lightly against his lips.

"Of course not! Besides–have I said I will marry you? You are very agreeable as a lover–but otherwise–I am not sure! And I am free now–I can do as I like; I want to enjoy my liberty, and–"

She was not allowed to complete her sentence, for Ferrari snatched her close to his breast and held her there as in a vise. His face was aflame with passion.

"Look you, Nina," he said, hoarsely, "you shall not fool me, by Heaven! you shall not! I have endured enough at your hands, God knows! When I saw you for the first time on the day of your marriage with that poor fool, Fabio–I loved you, madly–ay, wickedly as I then thought, but not for the sin of it did I repent. I knew you were woman, not angel, and I waited my time. It came–I sought you– I told you my story of love ere three months of wedded life had passed ever your head. I found you willing–ready–nay, eager to hear me! You led me on; you know you did! You tempted me by touch, word and look; you gave me all I sought! Why try to excuse it now? You are as much my wife as ever you were Fabio's–nay–you are more so, for you love me–at least you say so–and though you lied to your husband, you dare not lie to me. I tell you, you DARE NOT! I never pitied Fabio, never–he was too easily duped, and a married man has no right to be otherwise than suspicious and ever on his guard; if he relaxes in his vigilance he has only himself to blame when his honor is flung like a ball from hand to hand, as one plays with a child's toy. I repeat to you, Nina, you are mine, and I swear you shall never escape me!"

The impetuous words coursed rapidly from his lips, and his deep musical voice had a defiant ring as it fell on the stillness of the evening air. I smiled bitterly as I heard! She struggled in his arms half angrily.

"Let me go," she said. "You are rough, you hurt me!"

He released her instantly. The violence of his embrace had crushed the rose she wore, and its crimson leaves fluttered slowly down one by one on the ground at her feet. Her eyes flashed resentfully, and an impatient frown contracted her fair level brows. She looked away from him in silence, the silence of a cold disdain. Something in her attitude pained him, for he sprung forward and caught her hand, covering it with kisses.

"Forgive me, carina mia" he cried, repentantly. "I did not mean to reproach you. You cannot help being beautiful–it is the fault of God or the devil that you are so, and that your beauty maddens me! You are the heart of my heart, the soul of my soul! Oh, Nina mia, let us not waste words in useless anger. Think of it, we are free– free! Free to make life a long dream of delight–delight more perfect than angels can know! The greatest blessing that could have befallen us is the death of Fabio, and now that we are all in all to each other, do not harden yourself against me! Nina, be gentle with me–of all things in the world, surely love is best!"

She smiled, with the pretty superior smile of a young empress pardoning a recreant subject, and suffered him to draw her again, but with more gentleness, into his embrace. She put up her lips to meet his–I looked on like a man in a dream! I saw them cling together–each kiss they exchanged was a fresh stab to my tortured soul.

"You are so foolish, Guido mio" she pouted, passing her little jeweled fingers through his clustering hair with a light caress–"so impetuous–so jealous! I have told you over and over again that I love you! Do you not remember that night when Fabio sat out on the balcony reading his Plato, poor fellow!"–here she laughed musically–"and we were trying over some songs in the drawing–room–did I not say then that I loved you best of any one in the world? You know I did! You ought to be satisfied!"

Guido smiled, and stroked her shining golden curls.

"I AM satisfied," he said, without any trace of his former heated impatience–"perfectly satisfied. But do not expect to find love without jealousy. Fabio was never jealous–I know–he trusted you too implicitly–he was nothing of a lover, believe me! He thought more of himself than of you. A man who will go away for days at a time on solitary yachting and rambling excursions, leaving his wife to her own devices–a man who reads Plato in preference to looking after HER, decides his own fate, and deserves to be ranked with those so-called wise but most ignorant philosophers to whom Woman has always remained an unguessed riddle. As for me–I am jealous of the ground you tread upon–of the air that touches you–I was jealous of Fabio while he lived–and–by heaven!"–his eyes darkened with a somber wrath–"if any other man dared now to dispute your love with me I would not rest till his body had served my sword as a sheath!"

Nina raised her head from his breast with an air of petulant weariness.

"Again!" she murmured, reproachfully, "you are going to be angry AGAIN!"

He kissed her.

"Not I, sweet one! I will be as gentle as you wish, so long as you love me and only me. Come–this avenue is damp and chilly for you– shall we go in?"

My wife–nay, I should say OUR wife, as we had both shared her impartial favors–assented. With arms interlaced and walking slowly, they began to retrace their steps toward the house. Once they paused.

"Do you hear the nightingales?" asked Guido.

Hear them! Who could not hear them? A shower of

melody rained from the trees on every side—the pure, sweet, passionate tones pierced the ear like the repeated chime of little golden bells—the beautiful, the tender, the God-inspired birds sung their love- stories simply and with perfect rapture—love-stories untainted by hypocrisy—unsullied by crime—different, ah! so very different from the love-stones of selfish humanity! The exquisite poetic idyl of a bird's life and love—is it not a thing to put us inferior creatures to shame—for are we ever as true to our vows as the lark to his mate?—are we as sincere in our thanksgivings for the sunlight as the merry robin who sings as blithely in the winter snow as in the flower-filled mornings of spring? Nay—not we! Our existence is but one long impotent protest against God, combined with an insatiate desire to get the better of one another in the struggle for base coin!

Nina listened—and shivered, drawing her light scarf more closely about her shoulders.

"I hate them" she said, pettishly; "their noise is enough to pierce one's ears. And HE used to be so fond of them! he used to sing—what was it?

'Ti salute, Rosignuolo, *Nel tuo duolo, il saluto! Sei l'amante delta rosa Che morendo si fa sposa!*"

Her rich voice rippled out on the air, rivaling the songs of the nightingales themselves. She broke off with a little laugh—

"Poor Fabio! there was always a false note somewhere when he sung. Come, Guido!"

And they paced on quietly, as though their consciences were clean— as though no just retribution dogged their steps—as though no shadow of a terrible vengeance loomed in the heaven of their pilfered happiness! I watched them steadily as they disappeared in the distance—I stretched my head eagerly out from between the dark boughs and gazed after their retreating figures till the last glimmer of my wife's white robe had vanished behind the thick foliage. They were gone—they would return no more that night.

I sprung out from my hiding-place. I stood on the spot where they had stood. I tried to bring home to myself the actual truth of what I had witnessed. My brain whirled—circles of light swam giddily before me in the air—the moon looked blood-red. The solid earth seemed unsteady beneath my feet—almost I doubted whether I was indeed alive, or whether I was not rather the wretched ghost of my past self, doomed to return from the grave to look helplessly upon the loss and ruin of all the fair, once precious things of by-gone days. The splendid universe around me seemed no more upheld by the hand of God—no more a majestic marvel; it was to me but an inflated bubble of emptiness—a mere ball for devils to kick and spurn through space! Of what avail these twinkling stars—these stately leaf-laden trees—these cups of fragrance we know as flowers—this round wonder of the eyes called Nature? of what avail was God Himself, I widely mused, since even He could not keep one woman true? She whom I loved—she as delicate of form, as angel-like in face as the child-bride of Christ, St. Agnes—she, even she was— what? A thing lower than the beasts, a thing as vile as the vilest wretch in female form that sells herself for a gold piece—a thing— great Heaven!—for all men to despise and make light of—for the finger of Scorn to point out—for the foul hissing tongue of Scandal to mock at! This creature was my wife—the mother of my child—she had cast mud on her soul by her own free will and choice—she had selected evil as her good—she had crowned herself with shame willingly, nay—joyfully; she had preferred it to honor. What should be done? I tortured myself occasionally with this question. I stared blankly on the ground—would some demon spring from it and give me the answer I sought? What should be done with HER—with HIM, my treacherous friend, my smiling betrayer? Suddenly my eyes lighted on the fallen rose-leaves—those that had dropped when Guido's embrace had crushed the flower she wore. There they lay on the path, curled softly at the edges like little crimson shells. I stooped and picked them up—I placed them all in the hollow of my hand and looked at them. They had a sweet odor—almost I kissed them—nay, nay, I could not—they had too recently lain on the breast of an embodied Lie! Yes;

she was that, a Lie, a living, lovely, but accursed Lie! "Go and kill her" Stay! where had I heard that? Painfully I considered, and at last remembered–and then I thought moodily that the starved and miserable rag-picker was more of a man than I. He had taken his revenge at once; while I, like a fool, had let occasion slip. Yes, but not forever! There were different ways of vengeance; one must decide the best, the keenest way–and, above all, the way that shall inflict the longest, the cruelest agony upon those by whom honor is wronged. True–it would be sweet to slay sin in the act of sinning, but then–must a Romani brand himself as a murderer in the sight of men? Not so; there were other means–other roads, leading to the same end if the tired brain could only plan them out. Slowly I dragged my aching limbs to the fallen trunk of a tree and sat down, still holding the dying rose-leaves in my clinched palm. There was a surging noise in my ears–my mouth tasted of blood, my lips were parched and burning as with fever. "A white-haired fisherman." That was me! The king had said so. Mechanically I looked down at the clothes I wore–the former property of a suicide. "He was a fool," the vender of them had said, "he killed himself."

Yes, there was no doubt of it–he was a fool. I would not follow his example, or at least not yet. I had something to do first–something that must be done if I could only see my way clear to it. Yes–if I could only see my way and follow it straightly, resolutely, remorselessly! My thoughts were confused, like the thoughts of a fever-stricken man in delirium–the scent of the rose-leaves I held sickened me strangely–yet I would not throw them from me; no, I would keep them to remind me of the embraces I had witnessed! I felt for my purse! I found and opened it, and placed the withering red petals carefully within it. As I slipped it again in my pocket I remembered the two leathern pouches I carried– the one filled with gold, the other with the jewels I had intended for–HER. My adventures in the vault recurred to me; I smiled as I recollected the dire struggle I had made for life and liberty. Life and liberty!–of what use were they to me now, save for one thing– revenge? I was not wanted; I was not expected back to refill my former place on earth–the large fortune I had possessed was now my wife's by the decree of my own last will and testament, which she would have no difficulty in proving. But still, wealth was mine–the hidden stores of the brigands were sufficient to make any man more than rich for the term of his natural life. As I considered this, a sort of dull pleasure throbbed in my veins. Money! Anything could be done for money–gold would purchase even vengeance. But what sort of vengeance? Such a one as I sought must be unique–refined, relentless, and complete. I pondered deeply. The evening wind blew freshly up from the sea; the leaves of the swaying trees whispered mysteriously together; the nightingales warbled on with untired sweetness; and the moon, like the round shield of an angel warrior, shone brightly against the dense blue background of the sky. Heedless of the passing of hours, I sat still, lost in a bewildered reverie. "There was always a false note somewhere when he sung!" So she had said, laughing that little laugh of hers as cold and sharp as the clash of steel. True, true; by all the majesty of Heaven, most true! There was indeed a false note–jarring, not so much the voice as the music of life itself. There is stuff in all of us that will weave, as we desire it, into a web of stately or simple harmony; but let the meteor-like brilliancy of a woman's smile– a woman's touch–a woman's LIE–intermingle itself with the strain, and lo! the false note is struck, discord declares itself, and God Himself, the great Composer, can do nothing in this life to restore the old calm tune of peaceful, unspoiled days! So I have found; so all of you must find, long before you and sorrow grow old together.

"A white-haired fisherman!"

The words of the king repeated themselves over and over again in my tortured brain. Yes–I was greatly changed, I looked worn and old– no one would recognize me for my former self. All at once, with this thought, an idea occurred to me–a plan of vengeance, so bold, so new, and withal so terrible, that I started from my seat as though stung by an adder. I paced up and down restlessly, with this lurid light of fearful revenge pouring in on every nook and cranny of my darkened mind. From whence had come this daring scheme? What devil, or rather what angel of retribution, had whispered it to my soul? Dimly I wondered–but amid all my wonder I began practically to arrange the details of my plot. I calculated every small circumstance that was likely to occur in the process of carrying it out. My stupefied senses became aroused from the lethargy of despair, and stood up like soldiers on the alert armed to the teeth. Past love, pity, pardon, patience–pooh! what were all these resources of the world's weakness to ME? What was it to me that the bleeding Christ forgave His enemies in death? He never loved a woman! Strength and resolution returned to me. Let common sailors and rag-pickers resort to murder and suicide as fit outlets for their unreasoning brute wrath when wronged; but as for me, why should I blot my family escutcheon with a merely vulgar crime? Nay, the vengeance of a Romani must be taken with assured calmness and easy deliberation–no haste, no plebeian fury, no effeminate fuss, no excitement. I walked up and down slowly, meditating on every point of the bitter drama in which I had resolved to enact the chief part, from the rise to the fall of the black curtain. The mists cleared from my brain–I breathed more easily–my nerves steadied themselves by degrees–the prospect of what I purposed doing satisfied me and calmed the fever in my blood. I became perfectly cool and collected. I indulged in no more futile regrets for the past–why should I mourn the loss of a love I never possessed? It was not as if they had waited till my supposed sudden death–no! within three months of my marriage they had fooled me; for three whole years they had indulged in their criminal amour, while I, blind dreamer, had suspected nothing. NOW I knew the extent of my injury; I was a man bitterly wronged, vilely duped. Justice, reason, and self-respect demanded that I should punish to the utmost the miserable tricksters who had played me false. The passionate tenderness I had felt for my wife was gone–I plucked it from my heart as I would have torn a thorn from my flesh–I flung it from me with disgust as I had flung away the unseen reptile that had fastened on my neck in the vault. The deep warm friendship of years I had felt for Guido Ferrari froze to its very foundations–and in its place there rose up, not hate, but pitiless, immeasurable contempt. A stern disdain of myself also awoke in me, as I remembered the unreasoning joy with which, I had hastened–as I thought–home, full of eager anticipation and Romeo-like ardor. An idiot leaping merrily to his death over a mountain chasm was not more fool than I! But the dream was over–the delusion of my life was passed. I was strong to avenge–I would be swift to accomplish. So, darkly musing for an hour or more, I decided on the course I had to pursue, and to make the decision final I drew from my breast the crucifix that the dead monk Cipriano had laid with me in my coffin, and kissing it, I raised it aloft, and swore by that sacred symbol never to relent, never to relax, never to rest, till I had brought my vow of just vengeance to its utmost fulfillment. The stars, calm witnesses of my oath, eyed me earnestly from their judgment thrones in the quiet sky–there was a brief pause in the singing of the nightingales, as though they too listened–the wind sighed plaintively, and scattered a shower of jasmine blossoms like snow at my feet. Even so, I thought, fall the last leaves of my white days– days of pleasure, days of sweet illusion, days of dear remembrance; even so let them wither and perish utterly forever! For from henceforth my life must be something other than a mere garland of flowers–it must be a chain of finely tempered steel, hard, cold, and unbreakable–formed into links strong enough to wind round and round two false lives and imprison them so closely as to leave no means of escape. This was what must be done– and I resolved to do it. With a firm, quiet step I turned to leave the avenue. I opened the little private wicket, and passed into the dusty road. A clanging noise caused me to look up as I went by the principal entrance of the Villa Romani. A man servant–my own man-servant by the by–was barring the great gates for the night. I listened as he slid the bolts into their places, and turned the key. I remembered that those gates had been thoroughly fastened before, when I came up the road from Naples–why then had they been opened since? To let out a visitor? Of course! I smiled grimly at my wife's cunning! She evidently knew what she was about. Appearances must be kept up–the Signor Ferrari must be decorously shown out by a servant at the chief entrance of the house. Naturally!–all very unsuspicious– looking and quite in keeping with the proprieties! Guido had just left her then? I walked steadily, without hurrying my pace, down the hill toward the city, and on the way I overtook him. He was strolling lazily along, smoking as usual, and he held a spray of stephanotis in his hand–well I knew who had given it to him! I passed him–he glanced up carelessly, his handsome face clearly visible in the bright moonlight–but there was nothing about a common fisherman to attract his attention–his look only rested upon me for a second and was withdrawn immediately. An insane desire possessed me to turn upon him–to spring at his throat–to wrestle with him and throw him in the dust at my feet–to spit at him and trample upon him–but I repressed those fierce and dangerous emotions. I had a better game to play–I had an exquisite torture in store for him, compared to which a hand-to-hand fight was mere vulgar fooling. Vengeance ought to ripen slowly in the strong heat of intense wrath, till of itself it falls–hastily snatched before its time it is like unmellowed fruit, sour and ungrateful to the palate. So I let my dear friend–my wife's consoler–saunter on his heedless way without interference–I passed, leaving him to indulge in amorous musings to his false heart's content. I entered Naples, and found a night's lodging at one of the usual resorts for men of my supposed craft, and, strange to say, I slept soundly and dreamlessly. Recent illness, fatigue, fear, and sorrow, all aided to throw me like an exhausted child upon the quiet bosom of slumber, but perhaps the most powerfully soothing opiate to my brain was the consciousness I had of a practical plan of retribution–more terrible perhaps than any human creature had yet devised, so far as I knew. Unchristian you call me? I tell you again, Christ never loved a woman! Had He done so, He would have left us some special code of justice.

9

I ROSE very early the next morning—I was more than ever strengthened in my resolutions of the past night—my projects were entirely formed, and nothing remained now but for me to carry them out. Unobserved of any one I took my way again to the vault. I carried with me a small lantern, a hammer, and some strong nails. Arrived at the cemetery I looked carefully everywhere about me, lest some stray mourner or curious stranger might possibly be in the neighborhood. Not a soul was in sight. Making use of the secret passage, I soon found myself on the scene of my recent terrors and sufferings, all of which seemed now so slight in comparison with, the mental torture of my present condition. I went straight to the spot where I had left the coffined treasure— I possessed myself of all the rolls of paper money, and disposed them in various small packages about my person and in the lining of my clothes till, as I stood, I was worth many thousands of francs. Then with the help of the tools I had brought, I mended the huge chest in the split places where I had forced it open, and nailed it up fast so that it looked as if it had never been touched. I lost no time over my task, for I was in haste. It was my intention to leave Naples for a fortnight or more, and I purposed taking my departure that very day. Before leaving the vault I glanced at the coffin I myself had occupied. Should I mend that and nail it up as though my body were still inside? No—better leave it as it was—roughly broken open—it would serve my purpose better so. As soon as I had finished all I had to do, I clambered through the private passage, closing it after me with extra care and caution, and then I betook myself directly to the Molo. On making inquiries among the sailors who were gathered there, I heard that a small coasting brig was on the point of leaving for Palermo. Palermo would suit me as well as any other place; I sought out the captain of the vessel. He was a brown-faced, merry-eyed mariner—he showed his glittering white teeth in the most amiable of smiles when I expressed my desire to take passage with him, and consented to the arrangement at once for a sum which I thought extremely moderate, but which I afterward discovered to be about treble his rightful due. But the handsome rogue cheated me with such grace and exquisite courtesy, that I would scarcely have had him act otherwise than he did. I hear a good deal of the "plain blunt honesty" of the English. I dare say there is some truth in it, but for my own part I would rather be cheated by a friendly fellow who gives you a cheery word and a bright look than receive exact value for my money from the "plain blunt" boor who seldom has the common politeness to wish you a good-day.

We got under way at about nine o'clock—the morning was bright, and the air, for Naples, was almost cool. The water rippling against the sides of our little vessel had a gurgling, chatty murmur, as though it were talking vivaciously of all the pleasant things it experienced between the rising and the setting of the sun; of the corals and trailing sea-weed that grew in its blue depths, of the lithe glittering fish that darted hither and thither between its little waves, of the delicate shells in which dwelt still more delicate inhabitants, fantastic small creatures as fine as filmy lace, that peeped from the white and pink doors of their transparent habitations, and looked as enjoyingly on the shimmering blue-green of their ever-moving element as we look on the vast dome of our sky, bespangled thickly with stars. Of all these things, and many more as strange and sweet, the gossiping water babbled unceasingly; it had even something to say to me concerning woman and woman's love. It told me gleefully how many fair female bodies it had seen sunk in the cold embrace of the conquering sea, bodies, dainty and soft as the sylphs of a poet's dream, yet which, despite their exquisite beauty, had been flung to and fro in cruel sport by the raging billows, and tossed among pebbles for the monsters of the deep to feed upon.

As I sat idly on the vessel's edge and looked down, down into the clear Mediterranean, brilliantly blue as a lake of melted sapphires, I fancied I could see her the Delilah of my life, lying prone on the golden sand, her rich hair floating straightly around her like yellow weed, her hands clinched in the death agony, her laughing lips blue with the piercing chilliness of the washing tide— powerless to move or smile again. She would look well so, I thought—better to my mind than she looked in the arms of her lover last night. I fell into a train of profound meditation—a touch on my shoulder startled me. I looked up, the captain of the brig stood beside me. He smiled and held out a cigarette.

"The signor will smoke?" he said courteously.

I accepted the little roll of fragrant Havanna half mechanically.

"Why do you call me signor?" I inquired brusquely. "I am a coral- fisher."

The little man shrugged his shoulders and bowed deferentially, yet with the smile still dancing gaily in his eyes and dimpling his olive cheeks.

"Oh, certainly! As the signor pleases—ma—" And he ended with another expressive shrug and bow.

I looked at him fixedly. "What do you mean?" I asked with some sternness.

With that birdlike lightness and swiftness which were part of his manner, the Sicilian skipper bent forward and laid a brown finger on my wrist.

"*Scusa, vi prego!* But the hands are not those of a fisher of coral."

I glanced down at them. True enough, their smoothness and pliant shape betrayed my disguise–the gay little captain was sharp-witted enough to note the contrast between them and the rough garb I wore, though no one else with whom I had come in contact had been as keen of observation as he. At first I was slightly embarrassed by his remark–but after a moment's pause I met his gaze frankly, and lighting my cigarette I said, carelessly:

"Ebbene! And what then, my friend?"

He made a deprecatory gesture with his hands.

"Nay, nay, nothing–but only this. The signor must understand he is perfectly safe with me. My tongue is discreet– I talk of things only that concern myself. The signor has good reasons for what he does– of that I am sure. He has suffered; it is enough to look in his face to see that. Ah, Dio if there are so many sorrows in life; there is love," he enumerated rapidly on his fingers–"there is revenge– there are quarrels–there is loss of money; any of these will drive a man from place to place at all hours and in all weathers. Yes; it is so, indeed–I know it! The signor has trusted himself in my boat–I desire to assure him of my best services."

And he raised his red cap with so charming a candor that in my lonely and morose condition I was touched to the heart. Silently I extended my hand–he caught it with an air in which respect, sympathy, and entire friendliness were mingled. And yet he overcharged me for my passage, you exclaim! Ay–but he would not have made me the object of impertinent curiosity for twenty times the money! You cannot understand the existence of such conflicting elements in the Italian character? No–I dare say not. The tendency of the calculating northerner under the same circumstances would have been to make as much out of me as possible by means of various small and contemptible items, and then to go with broadly honest countenance to the nearest police-station and describe my suspicious appearance and manner, thus exposing me to fresh expense besides personal annoyance. With the rare tact that distinguishes the southern races the captain changed the conversation by a reference to the tobacco we were both enjoying.

"It is good, is it not?" he asked.

"Excellent!" I answered, as indeed it was.

His white teeth glittered in a smile of amusement.

"It should be of the finest quality—for it is a present from one who will smoke nothing but the choice brands. Ah, Dio! what a fine gentleman spoiled is Carmelo Neri!"

I could not repress a slight start of surprise. What caprice of Fate associated me with this famous brigand? I was actually smoking his tobacco, and I owed all my present wealth to his stolen treasures secreted in my family vault!

"You know the man, then?" I inquired with some curiosity.

"Know him? As well as I know myself. Let me see, it is two months— yes—two months to-day since he was with me on board this very vessel. It happened in this way—I was at Gaeta— he came to me and told me the gendarmes were after him. He offered me more gold than I ever had in my life to take him to Termini, from whence he could get to one of his hiding-places in the Montemaggiore. He brought Teresa with him; he found me alone on the brig, my men had gone ashore. He said, 'Take us to Termini and I will give you so much; refuse and I will slit your throat.' Ha! ha! ha! That was good. I laughed at him. I put a chair for Teresa on deck, and gave her some big peaches. I said, 'See, my Carmelo! what use is there in threats? You will not kill me, and I shall not betray you. You are a thief, and a bad thief—by all the saints you are—but I dare say you would not be much worse than the hotel-keepers, if you could only keep your hand off your knife.' (For you know, signor, if you once enter a hotel you must pay almost a ransom before you can get out again!) Yes—and I reasoned with Carmelo in this manner: I told him, 'I do not want a large fortune for carrying you and Teresa across to Termini—pay me the just passage and we shall part friends, if only for Teresa's sake.' Well, he was surprised. He smiled that dark smile of his, which may mean gratitude or murder. He looked at Teresa. She sprung up from her seat, and let her peaches fall from her lap on the deck. She put her little hands on mine–the tears were in her pretty blue eyes. 'You are a good man,' she said. 'Some woman must love you very much!' Yes–she said that. And she was right. Our Lady be praised for it!"

And his dark eyes glanced upward with a devout gesture of thanksgiving. I looked at him with a sort of jealous hunger gnawing at my heart. Here was another self-deluded fool–a fond wretch feasting on the unsubstantial food of a pleasant dream–a poor dupe who believed in the truth of woman!

"You are a happy man," I said with a forced smile; "you have a guiding star for your life as well as for your boat–a woman that loves you and is faithful? is it so?"

He answered me directly and simply, raising his cap slightly as he did so.

"Yes, signor–my mother."

I was deeply touched by his naive and unexpected reply– more deeply than I cared to show. A bitter regret stirred in my soul–why, oh, why had my mother died so young! Why had I never known the sacred joy that seemed to vibrate through the frame, and sparkle in the eyes of this common sailor! Why must I be forever alone, with a curse of a woman's lie on my life, weighing me down to the dust and ashes of a desolate despair! Something in my face must have spoken my thoughts, for the captain said, gently:

"The signor has no mother?"

"She died when I was but a child," I answered, briefly.

The Sicilian puffed lightly at his cigarette in silence–the silence of an evident compassion. To relieve him of his friendly embarrassment, I said:

"You spoke of Teresa? Who is Teresa?"

"Ah, you may well ask, signor! No one knows who she is; she loves Carmelo Neri, and there all is said. Such a little thing she is—so delicate! like a foam-bell on the waves; and Carmelo—You have seen Carmelo, signor?"

I shook my head in the negative.

"Ebbene! Carmelo is big and rough and black like a wolf of the forests, all hair and fangs; Teresa is, well! you have seen a little cloud in the sky at night, wandering past the moon all flecked with pale gold?—that is Teresa. She is, small and slight as a child; she has rippling curls, and soft praying eyes, and tiny, weak, white hands, not strong enough to snap a twig in two. Yet she can do anything with Carmelo—she is the one soft spot in his life."

"I wonder if she is true to him," I muttered, half to myself and half aloud.

The captain caught up my words with an accent of surprise.

"True to him? Ah, Dio! but the signor does not know her. There was one of Carmelo's own band, as bold and handsome a cut-throat as ever lived—he was mad for Teresa—he followed her everywhere like a beaten cur. One day he found her alone; he tried to embrace her—she snatched a knife from his own girdle and stabbed him with it, like a little fury! She did not kill him then, but Carmelo did afterward. To think of a little woman like that with such a devil in her! It is her boast that no man, save Carmelo, has ever touched so much as a ringlet of her hair. Ay; she is true to him—more's the pity."

"Why—you would not have her false?" I asked.

"Nay, nay—for a false woman deserves death—but still it is a pity Teresa should have fixed her love on Carmelo. Such a man! One day the gendarmes will have him, then he will be in the galleys for life, and she will die. Yes—you may be sure of that! If grief does not kill her quickly enough, then she will kill herself, that is certain! She is slight and frail to look at as a flower, but her soul is strong as iron. She, will have her own way in death as well as in love—some women are made so, and it is generally the weakest- looking among them who have the most courage."

Our conversation was here interrupted by one of the sailors who came for his master's orders. The talkative skipper, with an apologetic smile and bow, placed his box of cigarettes beside me where I sat, and left me to my own reflections.

I was not sorry to be alone. I needed a little breathing time—a rest in which to think, though my thoughts, like a new solar system, revolved round the red planet of one central idea, VENGENCE. "A false woman deserves death." Even this simple Sicilian mariner said so. "Go and kill her, go and kill her!" These words reiterated themselves over and over again in my ears, till I found myself almost uttering them aloud. My soul sickened at the contemplation of the woman Teresa—the mistress of a wretched brigand whose name was fraught with horror—whose looks were terrific—she, even SHE could keep herself sacred from the profaning touch of other men's caresses—she was proud of being faithful to her wolf of the mountains, whose temper was uncertain and treacherous—she could make lawful boast of her fidelity to her blood-stained lover—while Nina—the wedded wife of a noble whose descent was lofty and unsullied, could tear off the fair crown of honorable marriage and cast it in the dust—could take the dignity of an ancient family and trample upon it—could make herself so low and vile that even this common Teresa, knowing all, might and most probably would, refuse to touch her hand, considering it polluted. Just God! what had Carmelo Neri done to deserve the priceless jewel of a true woman's heart? what had I done to merit such foul deception as that which I was now called upon to avenge? Suddenly I thought of my child. Her memory came upon me like a ray of light—I had almost forgotten her. Poor little blossom!—the slow hot tears forced themselves between my eyelids, as I called up before my fancy the picture of the soft baby face—the young untroubled eyes—the little coaxing mouth always budding into innocent kisses! What should I do with her? When the plan of punishment I had matured in my brain was carried out to its utmost, should I take her with me far, far away into some quiet corner of the world, and devote my life to hers? Alas! alas! she, too, would be a woman and beautiful–she was a flower born of a poisoned tree, who could say that there might not be a canker-worm hidden even in her heart, which waited but for the touch of maturity to commence its work of destruction! Oh, men! you that have serpents coiled round your lives in the shape of fair false women–if God has given you children by them, the curse descends upon you doubly! Hide it as you will under the society masks we are all forced to wear, you know there is nothing more keenly torturing than to see innocent babes look trustingly in the deceitful eyes of an unfaithful wife, and call her by the sacred name of "Mother." Eat ashes and drink wormwood, you shall find them sweet in comparison to that nauseating bitterness! For the rest of the day I was very much alone. The captain of the brig spoke cheerily to me now and then, but we were met by light contrary winds that necessitated his giving most of his attention to the management of his vessel, so that he could not permit himself to yield to the love of gossip that was inherent in him. The weather was perfect, and notwithstanding our constant shifting and tacking about to catch the erratic breeze, the gay little brig made merry and rapid way over the sparkling Mediterranean, at a rate that promised our arrival at Palermo by the sunset of the following day. As the evening came on the wind freshened, and by the time the moon soared like a large blight bird into the sky, we were scudding along sideways, the edge of our vessel leaning over to kiss the waves that gleamed like silver and gold, flecked here and there with phosphorescent flame. We skimmed almost under the bows of a magnificent yacht–the English flag floated from her mast–her sails glittered purely white in the moonbeams, and she sprung over the water like a sea-gull. A man, whose tall athletic figure was shown off to advantage by the yachting costume he wore, stood on deck, his arm thrown round the waist of a girl beside him. We were but a minute or two passing the stately vessel, yet I saw plainly this loving group of two, and–I pitied the man! Why? He was English undoubtedly–the son of a country where the very soil is supposed to be odorous of virtue– therefore the woman beside him must be a perfect pearl of purity; an Englishman never makes a mistake in these things! Never? Are you sure? Ah, believe me, there is not much difference nowadays between women of opposite nations. Once there was–I am willing to admit that possibility. Once, from all accounts received, the English rose was the fitting emblem of the English woman, but now, since the world has grown so wise and made such progress in the art of running rapidly downhill, is even the aristocratic British peer quite easy in his mind regarding his fair peeress? Can he leave her to her own devices with safety? Are there not men, boastful too of their "blue blood," who are perhaps ready to stoop to the thief's trick of entering his house during his absence by means of private keys, and stealing away his wife's affections?–and is not she, though a mother of three or four children, ready to receive with favor the mean robber of her husband's rights and honor? Read the London newspapers any day and you will find that once "moral" England is running a neck and neck race with other less hypocritical nations in pursuit of social vice. The barriers that once existed are broken down; "professional beauties" are received in circles where their presence formerly would have been the signal for all respectable women instantly to retire; ladies of title are satisfied to caper on the boards of the theatrical stage, in costumes that display their shape as undisguisedly as possible to the eyes of the grinning public, or they sing in concert halls for the pleasure of showing themselves off, and actually accept the vulgar applause of unwashed crowds with a smile and a bow of gratitude! Ye gods! what has become of the superb pride of the old regime– the pride which disdained all ostentation and clung to honor more closely than life! What a striking sign of the times too, is this: let a woman taint her virtue BEFORE marriage, she is never forgiven–her sin is never forgotten; but let her do what she will when she has a husband's name to screen her, and society winks its eyes at her crimes. Couple this fact with the general spirit of mockery that prevails in fashionable circles—mockery of religion, mockery of sentiment, mockery of all that is best and noblest in the human heart—add to it the general spread of "free-thought," and THEREFORE of conflicting and unstable opinions—let all these things together go on for a few years longer and England will stare at her sister nations like a bold woman in a domino—her features partly concealed from a pretense at shame, but her eyes glittering coldly through the mask, betraying to all who look at her how she secretly revels in her new code of lawlessness coupled with greed. For she will always be avaricious—and the worst of it is, that her nature being prosaic, there will be no redeeming grace to cast a glamour about her. France is unvirtuous enough, God knows, yet there is a sunshiny smile on her lips that cheers the heart. Italy is also unvirtuous, yet her voice is full of bird-like melody, and her face is a dream of perfect poetry! But England unvirtuous will be like a cautiously calculating, somewhat shrewish matron, possessed of unnatural and unbecoming friskiness, without either laugh, or song, or smile—her one god, Gold, and her one commandment, the suggested eleventh, "Thou shall not be found out!"

I slept that night on deck. The captain offered me the use of his little cabin, and was, in his kind-hearted manner, truly distressed at my persistent refusal to occupy it.

"It is bad to sleep in the moonlight, signor," he said, anxiously. "It makes men mad, they say."

I smiled. Had madness been my destiny, I should have gone mad last night, I thought!

"Have no fear!" I answered him, gently. "The moonlight is a joy to me—it has no impression on my mind save that of peace. I shall rest well here, my friend—do not trouble yourself about me."

He hesitated and then abruptly left me, to return in the space of two or three minutes with a thick rug of sheepskin. He insisted so earnestly on my accepting this covering as a protection from the night air, that, to please him, I yielded to his entreaties and lay down, wrapped in its warm folds. The good-natured fellow then wished me a "*Buon riposo, signor!*" and descended to his own resting-place, humming a gay tune as he went. From my recumbent posture on the deck I stared upward at the myriad stars that twinkled softly in the warm violet skies—stared long and fixedly till it seemed to me that our ship had also become a star, and was sailing through space with its glittering companions. What inhabitants peopled those fair planets, I wondered? Mere men and women who lived and loved and lied to one another as bravely as we do? or superior beings to whom the least falsehood is unknown? Was there one world among them where no women were born? Vague fancies—odd theories—flitted through my brain, I lived over again the agony of my imprisonment in the vaults—again I forced myself to contemplate the scene I had witnessed between my wife and her lover—again I meditated on every small detail requisite to the fulfillment of the terrible vengeance I had designed. I have often wondered how, in countries where divorce is allowed, a wronged husband can satisfy himself with so meager a compensation for his injuries as the mere getting rid of the woman who has deceived him. It is no punishment to her—it is what she wishes. There is not even any very special disgrace in it according to the present standard of social observances. Were public whipping the recognized penalty for the crime of a married woman's infidelity, there would be fewer of the like scandals—the divorce might follow the scourging. A daintily brought-up feminine creature would think twice, nay, fifty times, before she would run the risk of allowing her delicate body to be lashed by whips wielded by the merciless hands of a couple of her own sex—such a prospect of degradation, pain, shame, and outraged vanity would be more effectual to kill the brute in her than all the imposing ceremonials of courts of law and special juries. Think of it, kings, lords, and commons! Whipping at the cart's tail was once a legal punishment—if you would stop the growing immorality and reckless vice of women you had best revive it again–only apply it to rich as well as to poor, for it is most probable that the gay duchesses and countesses of your lands will need its sharp services more frequently than the work-worn wives of your laboring men. Luxury, idleness, and love of dress are hot-beds for sin–look for it, therefore, not so much in the hovels of the starving and naked as in the rose-tinted, musk- scented boudoirs of the aristocracy–look for it, as your brave physicians would search out the seeds of a pestilence that threatens to depopulate a great city, and trample it out if you CAN and WILL– if you desire to keep the name of your countries glorious in the eyes of future history. Spare not the rod because "my lady" forsooth! with her rich hair falling around her in beauteous dishevelment and her eyes bathed in tears, implores your mercy–for by very reason of her wealth and station she deserves less pity than the painted outcast who knows not where to turn for bread. A high post demands high duty! But I talk wildly. Whipping is done away with, for women at least–we give a well-bred shudder of disgust at the thought of it. When do we shudder with equal disgust at our own social enormities? Seldom or never. Meanwhile, in cases of infidelity, husbands and wives can separate and go on their different ways in comparative peace. Yes–some can and some do; but I am not one of these. No law in all the world can mend the torn flag of MY honor; therefore I must be a law to myself–a counsel, a jury, a judge, all in one and from my decision there can be no appeal! Then I must act as executioner–and what torture was ever so perfectly unique as the one I have devised? So I mused, lying broadly awake, with face upturned to the heavens, watching the light of the moon pouring itself out on the ocean like a shower of gold, while the water rushed gurgling softly against the sides of the brig, and broke into the laughter of white foam as we scudded along.

10

ALL THE next day the wind was in our favor, and we arrived at Palermo an hour before sunset. We had scarcely run into harbor when a small party of officers and gendarmes, heavily laden with pistols and carbines, came on board and showed a document authorizing them to search the brig for Carmelo Neri. I was somewhat anxious for the safety of my good friend the captain—but he was in nowise dismayed; he smiled and welcomed the armed emissaries of the government as though they were his dearest friends.

"To give you my opinion frankly," he said to them, as he opened a flask of line Chianti for their behalf, "I believe the villain Carmelo is somewhere about Gaeta. I would not tell you a lie—why should I? Is there not a reward offered, and am not I poor? Look you, I would do my best to assist you!"

One of the men looked at him dubiously.

"We received information," he said, in precise, business-like tones, "that Neri escaped from Gaeta two months since, and was aided and abetted in his escape by one Andrea Luziani, owner of the coasting brig 'Laura,' journeying for purposes of trade between Naples and Palermo. You are Andrea Luziani, and this is the brig 'Laura,'—we are right in this; is it not so?"

"As if you could ever be wrong, caro!" cried the captain

with undiminished gayety, clapping him on the shoulder. "Nay, if St. Peter should have the bad taste to shut you out of heaven, you would be cunning enough to find another and better entrance! Ah, Dio! I believe it! Yes, you are right about my name and the name of my brig, but in the other things,"–here he shook his fingers with an expressive sign of denial–"you are wrong–wrong–all wrong!" He broke into a gay laugh. "Yes, wrong–but we will not quarrel about it! Have some more Chianti! Searching for brigands is thirsty work. Fill your glasses, amici–spare not the flask–there are twenty more below stairs!"

The officers smiled in spite of themselves, as they drank the proffered wine, and the youngest-looking of the party, a brisk, handsome fellow, entered into the spirit of the captain with ardor, though he evidently thought he should trap him into a confession unawares, by the apparent carelessness and bonhomie of his manner."

"Bravo, Andrea!" he cried, merrily. "So! let us all be friends together! Besides, what harm is there in taking a brigand for a passenger–no doubt he would pay you better than most cargoes!"

But Andrea was not to be so caught. On the contrary; he raised his hands and eyes with an admirably feigned expression of shocked alarm.

"Our Lady and the saints forgive you!" he exclaimed, piously, "for thinking that I, an honest *marinaro*, would accept one *baiocco* from an accursed brigand! Ill-luck would follow me ever after! Nay, nay– there has been a mistake; I know nothing of Carmelo Neri, and I hope the saints will grant that I may never meet him!"

He spoke with so much apparent sincerity that the officers in command were evidently puzzled, though the fact of their being so did not deter them from searching the brig thoroughly. Disappointed in their expectations, they questioned all on board, including myself, but were of course unable to obtain any satisfactory replies. Fortunately they accepted my costume as a sign of my trade, and though they glanced curiously at my white hair, they seemed to think there was nothing suspicious about me. After a few more effusive compliments and civilities on the part of the captain, they took their departure, completely baffled, and quite convinced that the information they had received had been somehow incorrect. As soon as they were out of sight, the merry Andrea capered on his deck like a child in a play-ground, and snapped his fingers defiantly.

"Per Bacco!" he cried, ecstatically, "they should as soon make a priest tell confessional secrets, as force me, honest Andrea Luziani, to betray a man who has given me good cigars! Let them run back to Gaeta and hunt in every hole and corner! Carmelo may rest comfortably in the Montemaggiore without the shadow of a gendarme to disturb him! Ah, signor!" for I had advanced to bid him farewell–"I am truly sorry to part company with you! You do not blame me for helping away a poor devil who trusts me?"

"Not I!" I answered him heartily. "On the contrary, I would there were more like you. Addio I and with this," here I gave him the passage-money we had agreed upon, "accept my thanks. I shall not forget your kindness; if you ever need a friend, send to me."

"But," he said, with a naive mingling of curiosity and timidity, "how can I do that if the signor does not tell me his name?"

I had thought of this during the past night. I knew it would be necessary to take a different name, and I had resolved on adopting that of a school-friend, a boy to whom I had been profoundly attached in my earliest youth, and who had been drowned before my eyes while bathing in the Venetian Lido. So I answered Andrea's question at once and without effort.

"Ask for the Count Cesare Oliva," I said. "I shall return to Naples shortly, and should you seek me, you will find me there."

The Sicilian doffed his cap and saluted me profoundly.

"I guessed well," he remarked, smilingly, "that the Signor

Conte's hands were not those of a coral-fisher. Oh, yes! I know a gentleman when I see him–though we Sicilians say we are all gentlemen. It is a good boast, but alas! not always true! *A rivederci, signor!* Command me when you will–I am your servant!"

Pressing his hand, I sprung lightly from the brig on to the quay.

"*A rivederci!*" I called to him. "Again, and yet again, a thousand thanks!"

"Oh! *tropp' onore, signor–tropp' onore!*" and thus I left him, standing still bareheaded on the deck of his little vessel, with a kindly light on his brown face like the reflection of a fadeless sunbeam. Good-hearted, merry rogue! His ideas of right and wrong were oddly mixed–yet his lies were better than many truths told us by our candid friends–and you may be certain the great Recording Angel knows the difference between a lie that saves and a truth that kills, and metes out Heaven's reward or punishment accordingly.

My first care, when I found myself in the streets of Palermo, was to purchase clothes of the best material and make adapted to a gentleman's wear. I explained to the tailor whose shop I entered for this purpose that I had joined a party of coral-fishers for mere amusement, and had for the time adopted their costume. He believed my story the more readily as I ordered him to make several more suits for me immediately, giving him the name of Count Cesare Oliva, and the address of the best hotel in the city. He served me with obsequious humility, and allowed me the use of his private back- room, where I discarded my fisher garb for the dress of a gentleman–a ready-made suit that happened to fit me passably well. Thus arrayed as became my station, I engaged rooms at the chief hotel of Palermo for some weeks–weeks that were for me full of careful preparation for the task of vengeful retribution that lay before me. One of my principal objects was to place the money I had with me in safe hands. I sought out the leading banker in Palermo, and introducing myself under my adopted name, I stated that I had newly returned to Sicily after some years' absence. He received me well, and though he appeared astonished at the large amount of wealth I had brought, he was eager and willing enough to make satisfactory arrangements with me for its safe keeping, including the bag of jewels, some of which, from their unusual size and luster, excited his genuine admiration. Seeing this, I pressed on his acceptance a fine emerald and two large brilliants, all unset, and requested him to have a ring made of them for his own wear. Surprised at my generosity, he at first refused—but his natural wish to possess such rare gems finally prevailed, and he took them, overpowering me with thanks—while I was perfectly satisfied to see that I had secured his services so thoroughly by my jeweled bribe, that he either forgot, or else saw no necessity to ask me for personal references, which in my position would have been exceeding difficult, if not impossible, to obtain. When this business transaction was entirely completed, I devoted myself to my next consideration—which was to disguise myself so utterly that no one should possibly be able to recognize the smallest resemblance in me to the late Fabio Romani, either by look, voice, or trick of manner. I had always worn a mustache—it had turned white in company with my hair. I now allowed my beard to grow—it came out white also. But in contrast with these contemporary signs of age, my face began to fill up and look young again; my eyes, always large and dark, resumed their old flashing, half-defiant look—a look, which it seemed to me, would make some familiar suggestion to those who had once known me as I was before I died. Yes—they spoke of things that must be forgotten and unuttered; what should I do with these tell-tale eyes of mine?

I thought, and soon decided. Nothing was easier than to feign weak sight-sight that was dazzled by the heat and brilliancy of the southern sunshine, I would wear smoke-colored glasses. I bought them as soon as the idea occurred to me, and alone in my room before the mirror I tried their effect. I was satisfied; they perfectly completed the disguise of my face. With them and my white hair and beard, I looked like a well-preserved man of fifty-five or so, whose only physical ailment was a slight affection of the eyes.

The next thing to alter was my voice. I had, naturally, a peculiarly soft voice and a rapid, yet clear, enunciation, and it was my habit, as it is the habit of almost every Italian, to accompany my words with the expressive pantomime of gesture. I took myself in training as an actor studies for a particular part. I cultivated a harsh accent, and spoke with deliberation and coldness–occasionally with a sort of sarcastic brusquerie, carefully avoiding the least movement of hands or head during converse. This was exceedingly difficult of attainment to me, and took me an infinite deal of time and trouble; but I had for my model a middle-aged Englishman who was staying in the same hotel as myself, and whose starched stolidity never relaxed for a single instant. He was a human iceberg– perfectly respectable, with that air of decent gloom about him which is generally worn by all the sons of Britain while sojourning in a foreign clime. I copied his manners as closely as possible; I kept my mouth shut with the same precise air of not-to-be-enlightened obstinacy–I walked with the same upright drill demeanor–and I surveyed the scenery with the same superior contempt. I knew I had succeeded at last, for I overheard a waiter speaking of me to his companion as "the white bear!"

One other thing I did. I wrote a courteous note to the editor of the principal newspaper published in Naples–a newspaper that I knew always found its way to the Villa Romani–and inclosing fifty francs, I requested him to insert a paragraph for me in his next issue, This paragraph was worded somewhat as follows:

"The Signor Conte Cesare Oliva, a nobleman who has been for many years absent from his native country, has, we understand, just returned, possessed of almost fabulous wealth, and is about to arrive in Naples, where he purposes making his home for the future. The leaders of society here will no doubt welcome with enthusiasm so distinguished an addition to the brilliant circles commanded by their influence."

The editor obeyed my wishes, and inserted what I sent him, word for word as it was written. He sent me the paper containing it "with a million compliments," but was discreetly silent concerning the fifty francs, though I am certain he pocketed them with unaffected joy. Had I sent him double the money, he might have been induced to announce me as a king or emperor in disguise. Editors of newspapers lay claim to be honorable men; they may be so in England, but in Italy most of them would do anything for money. Poor devils! who can blame them, considering how little they get by their limited dealings in pen and ink! In fact, I am not at all certain but that a few English newspaper editors might be found capable of accepting a bribe, if large enough, and if offered with due delicacy. There are surely one or two magazines, for instance, in London, that would not altogether refuse to insert an indifferently, even badly written article, if paid a thousand pounds down for doing it!

On the last day but one of my sojourn in Palermo I was reclining in an easy-chair at the window of the hotel smoking-room, looking out on the shimmering waters of the gulf. It was nearly eight o'clock, and though the gorgeous colors of the sunset still lingered in the sky, the breeze blew in from the sea somewhat coldly, giving warning of an approaching chilly night. The character I had adopted, namely that of a somewhat harsh and cynical man who had seen life and did not like it, had by constant hourly practice become with me almost second nature—indeed, I should have had some difficulty in returning to the easy and thoughtless abandon of my former self. I had studied the art of being churlish till I really WAS churlish; I had to act the chief character in a drama, and I knew my part thoroughly well. I sat quietly puffing at my cigar and thinking of nothing in particular—for, as far as my plans went, I had done with thought, and all my energies were strung up to action—when I was startled by a loud and increasing clamor, as of the shouting of a large crowd coming onward like an overflowing tide. I leaned out of the window, but could see nothing, and I was wondering what the noise could mean, when an excited waiter threw open the door of the smoking-room and cried, breathlessly:

"Carmelo Neri, signor! Carmelo Neri! They have him, *poverino*! they have him at last!"

Though almost as strongly interested in this news as the waiter himself, I did not permit my interest to become manifest. I never forgot for a second the character I had assumed, and drawing the cigar slowly from my lips I merely said:

"Then they have caught a great rascal. I congratulate the Government! Where is the fellow?"

"In the great square," returned the garcon, eagerly. "If the signor would walk round the corner he would see Carmelo, bound and fettered. The saints have mercy upon him! The crowds there are thick as flies round a honeycomb! I must go thither myself–I would not miss the sight for a thousand francs!"

And he ran off, as full of the anticipated delight of looking at a brigand as a child going to its first fair. I put on my hat and strolled leisurely round to the scene of excitement. It was a picturesque sight enough; the square was black with a sea of eager heads, and restless, gesticulating figures, and the center of this swaying, muttering crowd was occupied by a compact band of mounted gendarmes with drawn swords flashing in the pale evening light–both horses and men nearly as motionless as though cast in bronze. They were stationed opposite the head-quarters of the Carabinieri, where the chief officer of the party had dismounted to make his formal report respecting the details of the capture before proceeding further. Between these armed and watchful guards, with his legs strapped to a sturdy mule, his arms tied fast behind him, and his hands heavily manacled, was the notorious Neri, as dark and fierce as a mountain thunder-storm. His head was uncovered–his thick hair, long and unkempt, hung in matted locks upon his shoulders–his heavy mustachios and beard were so black and bushy that they almost concealed his coarse and forbidding features–though I could see the tiger-like glitter of his sharp white teeth as he bit and gnawed his under lip in impotent fury and despair–and his eyes, like leaping flames, blazed with a wrathful ferocity from under his shaggy brows. He was a huge, heavy man, broad and muscular; his two hands clinched, tied and manacled behind him, looked like formidable hammers capable of striking a man down dead at one blow; his whole aspect was repulsive and terrible–there was no redeeming point about him–for even the apparent fortitude he assumed was mere bravado–meretricious courage–which the first week of the galleys would crush out of him as easily as one crushes the juice out of a ripe grape. He wore a nondescript costume of vari-colored linen, arranged in folds that would have been the admiration of an artist. It was gathered about him by means of a brilliant scarlet sash negligently tied. His brawny arms were bare to the shoulder–his vest was open, and displayed his strong brown throat and chest heaving with the pent-up anger and fear that raged within him. His dark grim figure was set off by a curious effect of color in the sky–a long wide band of crimson cloud, as though the sun-god had thrown down a goblet of ruby wine and left it to trickle along the smooth blue fairness of his palace floor–a deep after-glow, which burned redly on the olive-tinted eager faces of the multitude that were everywhere upturned in wonder and ill-judged admiration to the brutal black face of the notorious murderer and thief, whose name had for years been the terror of Sicily. I pressed through the crowd to obtain a nearer view, and as I did so a sudden savage movement of Neri's bound body caused the gendarmes to cross their swords in front of his eyes with a warning clash. The brigand laughed hoarsely.

"*Corpo di Cristo!*" he muttered–"think you a man tied hand and foot can run like a deer? I am trapped–I know it! But tell HIM," and he indicated some person in the throng by a nod of

111

his head "tell him to come hither–I have a message for him."

The gendarmes looked at one another, and then at the swaying crowd about them in perplexity–they did not understand.

Carmelo, without wasting more words upon them, raised himself as uprightly as he could in his strained and bound position, and called aloud:

"Luigi Biscardi! *Capitano!* Oh he–you thought I could not see you! Dio! I should know you in hell! Come near, I have a parting word for you."

At the sound of his strong harsh voice, a silence half of terror, half of awe, fell upon the chattering multitude. There was a sudden stir as the people made way for a young man to pass through their ranks–a slight, tall, rather handsome fellow, with a pale face and cold, sneering eyes. He was dressed with fastidious care and neatness in the uniform of the Bersagliere– and he elbowed his way along with the easy audacity of a privileged dandy. He came close up to the brigand and spoke carelessly, with a slightly mocking smile playing round the corners of his mouth.

"Ebbene!" he said, "you are caught at last, Carmelo! You called me– here I am. What do you want with me, rascal?"

Neri uttered a ferocious curse between his teeth, and looked for an instant like a wild beast ready to spring.

"You betrayed me," he said in fierce yet smothered accents–"you followed me–you hunted me down! Teresa told me all. Yes–she belongs to you now–you have got your wish. Go and take her–she waits for you–make her speak and tell you how she loves you–IF YOU CAN!"

Something jeering and withal threatening in the ruffian's look, evidently startled the young officer, for he exclaimed hastily:

"What do you mean, wretch? You have not–my God! you have not KILLED her?"

Carmelo broke into a loud savage laugh.

"She has killed herself!" he cried, exultingly. "Ha, ha, I

thought you would wince at that! She snatched my knife and stabbed herself with it! Yes–rather than see your lying white face again–rather than feel your accursed touch! Find her–she lies dead and smiling up there in the mountains and her last kiss was for ME–for ME–you understand! Now go! and may the devil curse you!"

Again the gendarmes clashed their swords suggestively–and the brigand resumed his sullen attitude of suppressed wrath and feigned indifference. But the man to whom he had spoken staggered and seemed about to fall–his pale face grew paler–he moved away through the curious open-eyed by-standers with the mechanical air of one who knows not whether he be alive or dead. He had evidently received an unexpected shock–a wound that pierced deeply and would be a long time healing.

I approached the nearest gendarme and slipped a five-franc piece into his hand.

"May one speak?" I asked, carelessly. The man hesitated.

"For one instant, signor. But be brief."

I addressed the brigand in a low clear-tone.

"Have you any message for one Andrea Luziani? I am a friend of his."

He looked at me and a dark smile crossed his features.

"Andrea is a good soul. Tell him if you will that Teresa is dead. I am worse than dead. He will know that I did not kill Teresa. I could not! She had the knife in her breast before I could prevent her. It is better so."

"She did that rather than become the property of another man?" I queried.

Carmelo Neri nodded in acquiescence. Either my sight deceived me, or else this abandoned villain had tears glittering in the depth of his wicked eyes.

The gendarme made me a sign, and I withdrew. Almost at the same moment the officer in command of the little detachment appeared, his spurs clinking with measured metallic music on the hard stones of the pavement–he sprung into his saddle and gave the word–the crowd dispersed to the right and left–the horses were put to a quick trot, and in a few moments the whole party with the bulky frowning form of the brigand in their midst had disappeared. The people broke up into little groups talking excitedly of what had occurred, and scattered here and there, returning to their homes and occupations– and more swiftly than one could have imagined possible, the great square was left almost empty. I paced up and down for a while thinking deeply; I had before my mind's eye the picture of the slight fair Teresa as described by the Sicilian captain, lying dead in the solitudes of the Montemaggiore with that self-inflicted wound in her breast which had set her free of all men's love and persecution. There WERE some women then who preferred death to infidelity? Strange! very strange! common women of course they must be–such as this brigand's mistress; your daintily fed, silk-robed duchess would find a dagger somewhat a vulgar consoler–she would rather choose a lover, or better still a score of lovers. It is only brute ignorance that selects a grave instead of dishonor–modern education instructs us more wisely, and teaches us not to be over- squeamish about such a trifle as breaking a given word or promise. Blessed age of progress! Age of steady advancement when the apple of vice is so cunningly disguised and so prettily painted that we can actually set it on a porcelain dish and hand it about among our friends as a valuable and choice fruit of virtue–and no one finds out the fraud we are practicing, nay, we scarcely perceive it ourselves, it is such an excellent counterfeit!

As I walked to and fro, I found myself continually passing the head office of the Carabinieri, and, acting on a sudden impulse of curiosity, I at last entered the building, determined to ask for a few particulars concerning the brigand's capture. I was received by a handsome and intelligent-looking man, who glanced at the card with which I presented myself, and saluted me with courteous affability.

"Oh, yes!" he said, in answer to my inquiries, "Neri has given us a great deal of trouble. But we had our suspicions that he had left Gaeta, where he was for a time in hiding. A few stray bits of information gleaned here and there put us on the right track."

"Was he caught easily, or did he show fight?"

"He gave himself up like a lamb, signor! It happened in this way. One of our men followed the woman who lived with Neri, one Teresa, and traced her up to a certain point, the corner of a narrow mountain pass—where she disappeared. He reported this, and thereupon we sent out an armed party. These crept at midnight two by two, till they were formed in a close ring round the place where Neri was judged to be. With the first beam of morning they rushed in upon him and took him prisoner. It appears that he showed no surprise—he merely said, 'I expected you!' He was found sitting by the dead body of his mistress; she was stabbed and newly bleeding. No doubt he killed her, though he swears the contrary—lies are as easy to him as breathing."

"But where were his comrades? I thought he commanded a large band?"

"So he did, signor; and we caught three of the principals only a fortnight ago, but of the others no trace can be found. I suppose Carmelo himself dismissed them and sent them far and wide through the country. At any rate, they are disbanded, and with these sort of fellows, where there is no union there is no danger."

"And Neri's sentence?" I asked.

"Oh, the galleys for life of course; there is no possible alternative."

I thanked my informant, and left the office. I was glad to have learned these few particulars, for the treasure I had discovered in my own family vault was now more mine than ever. There was not the remotest chance of any one of the Neri band venturing so close to Naples in search of it, and I thought with a grim smile that had the brigand chief himself known the story of my wrongs, he would most probably have rejoiced to think that his buried wealth was destined to aid me in carrying out so elaborate a plan of vengeance. All difficulties smoothed themselves before me—obstacles were taken out of my path— my way was made perfectly clear—each trifling incident was a new finger-post pointing out the direct road that led me to the one desired end. God himself seemed on my side, as He is surely ever on the side of justice! Let not the unfaithful think that because they say long prayers or go regularly and devoutly to church with meek faces and piously folded hands that the Eternal Wisdom is deceived thereby. My wife could pray—she could kneel like a lovely saint in the dim religious light of the sacred altars, her deep eyes upturned to the blameless, infinitely reproachful Christ—and look you! each word she uttered was a blasphemy, destined to come back upon herself as a curse. Prayer is dangerous for liars—it is like falling willfully on an upright naked sword. Used as an honorable weapon the sword defends—snatched up as the last resource of a coward it kills.

11

THE THIRD week of September was drawing to its close when I returned to Naples. The weather had grown cooler, and favorable reports of the gradual decrease of the cholera began to gain ground with the suffering and terrified population. Business was resumed as usual, pleasure had again her votaries, and society whirled round once more in its giddy waltz as though it had never left off dancing. I arrived in the city somewhat early in the day, and had time to make some preliminary arrangements for my plan of action. I secured the most splendid suite of apartments in the best hotel, impressing the whole establishment with a vast idea of my wealth and importance. I casually mentioned to the landlord that I desired to purchase a carriage and horses–that I needed a first-class valet, and a few other trifles of the like sort, and added that I relied on his good advice and recommendation as to the places where I should best obtain all that I sought. Needless to say, he became my slave–never was monarch better served than I–the very waiters hustled each other in a race to attend upon me, and reports of my princely fortune, generosity, and lavish expenditure, began to flit from month to month–which was the result I desired to obtain.

And now the evening of my first day in Naples came, and

I, the supposed Conte Cesare Oliva, the envied and flattered noble, took the first step toward my vengeance. It was one of the loveliest evenings possible, even in that lovely land–a soft breeze blew in from the sea–the sky was pearl-like and pure as an opal, yet bright with delicate shifting clouds of crimson and pale mauve–small, fleecy flecks of Radiance, that looked like a shower of blossoms fallen from some far invisible flower-land. The waters of the bay were slightly ruffled by the wind, and curled into tender little dark-blue waves tipped with light forges of foam. After my dinner I went out and took my way to a well-known and popular cafe which used to be a favorite haunt of mine in the days when I was known as Fabio Romani, Guido Ferrari was a constant habitue of the place, and I felt that I should find him there. The brilliant rose-white and gold saloons were crowded, and owing to the pleasant coolness of the air there were hundreds of little tables pushed far out into the street, at which groups of persons were seated, enjoying ices, wine, or coffee, and congratulating each other on the agreeable news of the steady decrease of the pestilence that had ravaged the city. I glanced covertly yet quickly round. Yes! I was not mistaken–there was my quondam friend, my traitorous foe, sitting at his ease, leaning comfortably back in one chair, his feet put up on another. He was smoking, and glancing now and then through the columns of the Paris "Figaro." He was dressed entirely in black–a hypocritical livery, the somber hue of which suited his fine complexion and perfectly handsome features to admiration. On the little finger of the shapely hand that every now and then was raised to adjust his cigar, sparkled a diamond that gave out a myriad scintillations as it flashed in the evening light–it was of exceptional size and brilliancy, and even at a distance I recognized it as my own property!

So!–a love-gift, signor, or an in memoriam of the dear and valued friend you have lost? I wondered–watching him in dark scorn the while–then recollecting myself, I sauntered slowly toward him, and perceiving a disengaged table next to his, I drew a chair to it and sat down He looked at me in differently

118

over the top of his newspaper—but there was nothing especially attractive in the sight of a white-haired man wearing smoke-colored spectacles, and he resumed his perusal of the "Figaro" immediately. I rapped the end of my walking-cane on the table and summoned a waiter from whom I ordered coffee. I then lighted a cigar, and imitating Ferrari's easy posture, smoked also. Something in my attitude then appeared to strike him, for he laid down his paper and again looked at me, this time with more interest and something of uneasiness. "*Ca commence, mon ami!*" I thought, but I turned my head slightly aside and feigned to be absorbed in the view. My coffee was brought—I paid for it and tossed the waiter an unusually large gratuity—he naturally found it incumbent upon him to polish my table with extra zeal, and to secure all the newspapers, pictorial or otherwise, that were lying about, for the purpose of obsequiously depositing them in a heap at my right hand. I addressed this amiable garcon in the harsh and deliberate accents of my carefully disguised voice.

"By the way, I suppose you know Naples well?"

"Oh, si, signor!"

"Ebbene, can you tell me the way to the house of one Count Fabio Romani, a wealthy nobleman of this city?"

Ha! a good hit this time! Though apparently not looking at him I saw Ferrari start as though he had been stung, and then compose himself in his seat with an air of attention. The waiter meanwhile, in answer to my question, raised his hands, eyes and shoulders all together with a shrug expressive of resigned melancholy.

"*Ah, gran Dio! e morto!*"

"Dead!" I exclaimed, with a pretended start of shocked surprise. "So young? Impossible!"

"Eh! what will you, signor? It was la pesta; there was no remedy. La pesta cares nothing for youth or age, and spares neither rich nor poor."

For a moment I leaned my head on my hand, affecting to be overcome by the suddenness of the news. Then looking up,

119

I said, regretfully:

"Alas! I am too late! I was a friend of his father's. I have been away for many years, and I had a great wish to meet the young Romani whom I last saw as a child. Are there any relations of his living– was he married?"

The waiter, whose countenance had assumed a fitting lugubriousness in accordance with what he imagined were my feelings, brightened up immediately as he replied eagerly:

"Oh, si, signor! The Contessa Romani lives up at the villa, though I believe she receives no one since her husband's death. She is young and beautiful as an angel. There is a little child too."

A hasty movement on the part of Ferrari caused me to turn my eyes, or rather my spectacles, in his direction. He leaned forward, and raising his hat with the old courteous grace I knew so well, said politely:

"Pardon me, signor, for interrupting you! I knew the late young Count Romani well–perhaps better than any man in Naples. I shall be delighted to afford you any information you may seek concerning him."

Oh, the old mellow music of his voice–how it struck on my heart and pierced it like the refrain of a familiar song loved in the days of our youth. For an instant I could not speak–wrath and sorrow choked my utterance. Fortunately this feeling was but momentary–slowly I raised my hat in response to his salutation, and answered stiffly:

"I am your servant, signor. You will oblige me indeed if you can place me in communication with the relatives of this unfortunate young nobleman. The elder Count Romani was dearer to me than a brother–men have such attachments occasionally. Permit me to introduce myself," and I handed him my visiting-card with a slight and formal bow. He accepted it, and as he read the name it bore he gave me a quick glance of respect mingled with pleased surprise.

"The Conte Cesare Oliva!" he exclaimed. "I esteem myself most fortunate to have met you! Your arrival has already been notified to us by the avant-courier of the fashionable intelligence, so that we are well aware," here laughing lightly, "of the distinctive right you have to a hearty welcome in Naples. I am only sorry that any distressing news should have darkened the occasion of your return here after so long an absence. Permit me to express the hope that it may at least be the only cloud for you on our southern sunshine!"

And he extended his hand with that ready frankness and bonhomie which are always a part of the Italian temperament, and were especially so of his. A cold shudder ran through my veins. God! could I take his hand in mine? I must—if I would act my part thoroughly—for should I refuse he would think it strange—even rude—I should lose the game by one false move. With a forced smile I hesitatingly held out my hand also—it was gloved, yet as he clasped it heartily in his own the warm pressure burned through the glove like fire. I could have cried out in agony, so excruciating was the mental torture which I endured at that moment. But it passed, the ordeal was over, and I knew that from henceforth I should be able to shake hands with him as often and as indifferently as with any other man. It was only this FIRST time that it galled me to the quick. Ferrari noticed nothing of my emotion—he was in excellent spirits, and turning to the waiter, who had lingered to watch us make each other's acquaintance, he exclaimed:

"More coffee, garcon, and a couple of glorias." Then looking toward me, "You do not object to a gloria, conte? No? That is well. And here is MY card," taking one from his pocket and laying it on the table. "Guido Ferrari, at your service, an artist and a very poor one. We shall celebrate our meeting by drinking each other's health!"

I bowed. The waiter vanished to execute his orders and Ferrari drew his chair closer to mine.

"I see you smoke," he said, gaily. "Can I offer you one of my cigars? They are unusually choice. Permit me," and he proffered roe a richly embossed and emblazoned silver cigar-case, with the Romani arms and coronet and MY OWN

INITIALS engraved thereon. It was mine, of course—I took it with a sensation of grim amusement—I had not seen it since the day I died!

"A fine antique," I remarked, carelessly, turning it over and over in my hand, "curious and valuable. A gift or an heirloom?"

"It belonged to my late friend, Count Fabio," he answered, puffing a light cloud of smoke in the air as he drew his cigar from his lips to speak. "It was found in his pocket by the priest who saw him die. That and other trifles which he wore on his person were delivered to his wife, and—"

"She naturally gave YOU the cigar-case as a memento of your friend," I said, interrupting him.

"Just so. You have guessed it exactly. Thanks," and he took the case from me as I returned it to him with a frank smile.

"Is the Countess Romani young?" I forced myself to inquire.

"Young and beautiful as a midsummer morning!" replied Ferrari, with enthusiasm. "I doubt if sunlight ever fell on a more enchanting woman! If you were a young man, conte, I should be silent regarding her charms—but your white hairs inspire one with confidence. I assure you solemnly, though Fabio was my friend, and an excellent fellow in his ways, he was never worthy of the woman he married!"

"Indeed!" I said, coldly, as this dagger-thrust struck home to my heart. "I only knew him when he was quite a boy. He seemed to me then of a warm and loving temperament, generous to a fault, perhaps over-credulous, yet he promised well. His father thought so, I confess I thought so too. Reports have reached me from time to time of the care with which he managed the immense fortune left to him. He gave large sums away in charity, did he not? and was he not a lover of books and simple pleasures?"

"Oh, I grant you all that!" returned Ferrari, with some impatience. "He was the most moral man in immoral Naples, if you care for that sort of thing. Studious—philosophic—parfait gentilhomme–proud as the devil, virtuous, unsuspecting, and–withal–a fool!"

My temper rose dangerously–but I controlled it, and remembering my part in the drama I had constructed, I broke into violent, harsh laughter.

"Bravo!" I exclaimed. "One can easily see what a first-rate young fellow YOU are! You have no liking for moral men–ha, ha! excellent! I agree with you. A virtuous man and a fool are synonyms nowadays. Yes–I have lived long enough to know that! And here is our coffee– behold also the glorias! I drink your health with pleasure, Signor Ferrari–you and I must be friends!"

For one moment he seemed startled by my sudden outburst of mirth– the next, he laughed heartily himself, and as the waiter appeared with the coffee and cognac, inspired by the occasion, he made an equivocal, slightly indelicate joke concerning the personal charms of a certain Antoinetta whom the garcon was supposed to favor with an eye to matrimony. The fellow grinned, in nowise offended–and pocketing fresh gratuities from both Ferrari and myself, departed on new errands for other customers, apparently in high good humor with himself, Antoinetta, and the world in general. Resuming the interrupted conversation I said:

"And this poor weak-minded Romani–was his death sudden?"

"Remarkably so," answered Ferrari, leaning back in his chair, and turning his handsome flushed face up to the sky where the stars were beginning to twinkle out one by ones "it appears from all accounts that he rose early and went out for a walk on one of those insufferably hot August mornings, and at the furthest limit of the villa grounds he came upon a fruit-seller dying of cholera. Of course, with his quixotic ideas, he must needs stay and talk to the boy, and then run like a madman through the heat into Naples, to find a doctor for him. Instead of a physician he met a priest, and he was taking this priest to the assistance of the fruit-seller (who by the bye died in the meantime and was past all caring for) when he himself was struck down by the plague. He was carried then and there to a common inn, where in about five hours he died–all the time shrieking curses on any one who should dare to take him alive or dead inside his own house. He showed good sense in that at least– naturally he was anxious not to bring the contagion to his wife and child."

"Is the child a boy or a girl?" I asked, carelessly.

"A girl. A mere baby–an uninteresting old-fashioned little thing, very like her father."

My poor little Stella.

Every pulse of my being thrilled with indignation at the indifferently chill way in which he, the man who had fondled her and pretended to love her, now spoke of the child. She was, as far as he knew, fatherless; he, no doubt, had good reason to suspect that her mother cared little for her, and, I saw plainly that she was, or soon would be, a slighted and friendless thing in the household. But I made no remark–I sipped my cognac with an abstracted air for a few seconds–then I asked:

"How was the count buried? Your narrative interests me greatly."

"Oh, the priest who was with him saw to his burial, and I believe, was able to administer the last sacraments. At any rate, he had him laid with all proper respect in his family vault–I myself was present at the funeral."

I started involuntarily, but quickly repressed myself.

"YOU were present–YOU–YOU–" and my voice almost failed me.

Ferrari raised his eyebrows with a look of surprised inquiry.

"Of course! You are astonished at that? But perhaps you do not understand. I was the count's very closest friend, closer than a brother, I may say. It was natural, even necessary, that I should attend his body to its last resting place."

By this time I had recovered myself.

"I see–I see!" I muttered, hastily. "Pray excuse me–my age

renders me nervous of disease in any form, and I should have thought the fear of contagion might have weighed with you."

"With ME!" and he laughed lightly. "I was never ill in my life, and I have no dread whatever of cholera. I suppose I ran some risk, though I never thought about it at the time–but the priest–one of the Benedictine order–died the very next day."

"Shocking!" I murmured over my coffee-cup. "Very shocking. And you actually entertained no alarm for yourself?"

"None in the least. To tell you the truth, I am armed against contagious illnesses, by a conviction I have that I am not doomed to die of any disease. A prophecy"–and here a cloud crossed his features–"an odd prophecy was made about me when I was born, which, whether it comes true or not, prevents me from panic in days of plague."

"Indeed!" I said, with interest, for this was news to me. "And may one ask what this prophecy is?"

"Oh, certainly. It is to the effect that I shall die a violent death by the hand of a once familiar friend. It was always an absurd statement–an old nurse's tale–but it is now more absurd than ever, considering that the only friend of the kind I ever had or am likely to have is dead and buried–namely, Fabio Romani."

And he sighed slightly. I raised my head and looked at him steadily.

12

THE SHELTERING darkness of the spectacles I wore prevented him from noticing the searching scrutiny of my fixed gaze. His face was shadowed by a faint twinge of melancholy; his eyes were thoughtful and almost sad.

"You loved him well then in spite of his foolishness?" I said.

He roused himself from the pensive mood into which he had fallen, and smiled.

"Loved him? No! Certainly not–nothing so strong as that! I liked him fairly–he bought several pictures of me–a poor artist has always some sort of regard for the man who buys his work. Yes, I liked him well enough–till he married."

"Ha! I suppose his wife came between you?" He flushed slightly, and drank off the remainder of his cognac in haste.

"Yes," he replied, briefly, "she came between us. A man is never quite the same after marriage. But we have been sitting a long time here–shall we walk?"

He was evidently anxious to change the subject I rose slowly as though my joints were stiff with age, and drew out my watch, a finely jeweled one, to see the time. It was past nine o'clock.

"Perhaps," I said, addressing him, "you will accompany me

as far as my hotel. I am compelled to retire early as a rule–I suffer much from a chronic complaint of the eyes as you perceive," here touching my spectacles, "and I cannot endure much artificial light. We can talk further on our way. Will you give me a chance of seeing your pictures? I shall esteem myself happy to be one of your patrons."

"A thousand thanks!" he answered, gaily. "I will show you my poor attempts with pleasure. Should you find anything among them to gratify your taste, I shall of course be honored. But, thank Heaven! I am not as greedy of patronage as I used to be–in fact I intended resigning the profession altogether in about six months or so."

"Indeed! Are you coming into a fortune?" I asked, carelessly.

"Well–not exactly," he answered, lightly. "I am going to marry one–that is almost the same thing, is it not?"

"Precisely! I congratulate you!" I said, in a studiously indifferent and slightly bored tone, though my heart pulsed fiercely with the torrent of wrath pent up within it. I understood his meaning well. In six months he proposed marrying my wife. Six months was the shortest possible interval that could be observed, according to social etiquette, between the death of one husband and the wedding of another, and even that was so short as to be barely decent. Six months– yet in that space of time much might happen–things undreamed of and undesired–slow tortures carefully measured out, punishment sudden and heavy! Wrapped in these somber musings I walked beside him in profound silence. The moon shone brilliantly; groups of girls danced on the shore with their lovers, to the sound of a flute and mandolin–far off across the bay the sound of sweet and plaintive singing floated from some boat in the distance, to our ears–the evening breathed of beauty, peace and love. But I–my fingers quivered with restrained longing to be at the throat of the graceful liar who sauntered so easily and confidently beside me. Ah! Heaven, if he only knew! If he could have realized the truth, would his face have worn quite so careless a smile—would his manner have been quite so free and dauntless? Stealthily I glanced at him; he was humming a tune softly under his breath, but feeling instinctively, I suppose, that my eyes were upon him, he interrupted the melody and turned to me with the question:

"You have traveled far and seen much, conte!"

"I have."

"And in what country have you found the most beautiful women!"

"Pardon me, young sir," I answered, coldly, "the business of life has separated me almost entirely from feminine society. I have devoted myself exclusively to the amassing of wealth, understanding thoroughly that gold is the key to all things, even to woman's love; if I desired that latter commodity, which I do not. I fear that I scarcely know a fair face from a plain one—I never was attracted by women, and now at my age, with my settled habits, I am not likely to alter my opinion concerning them—and I frankly confess those opinions are the reverse of favorable."

Ferrari laughed. "You remind me of Fabio!" he said. "He used to talk in that strain before he was married—though he was young and had none of the experiences which may have made you cynical, conte! But he altered his ideas very rapidly—and no wonder!"

"Is his wife so very lovely then?" I asked.

"Very! Delicately, daintily beautiful. But no doubt you will see her for yourself—as a friend of her late husband's father, you will call upon her, will you not?"

"Why should I?" I said, gruffly—"I have no wish to meet her! Besides, an inconsolable widow seldom cares to receive visitors—I shall not intrude upon her sorrows!"

Never was there a better move than this show of utter indifference I affected. The less I appeared to care about seeing the Countess Romani, the more anxious Ferrari was to introduce me—(introduce me!—to my wife!)—and he set to work preparing his own doom with assiduous ardor.

"Oh, but you must see her!" he exclaimed, eagerly. "She will receive you, I am sure, as a special guest. Your age and your former acquaintance with her late husband's family will win from her the utmost courtesy, believe me! Besides, she is not really inconsolable—" He paused suddenly. We had arrived at the entrance of my hotel. I looked at him steadily.

"Not really inconsolable?" I repeated, in a tone of inquiry Ferrari broke into a forced laugh,

"Why no!" he said, "What would you? She is young and light-hearted— perfectly lovely and in the fullness of youth and health. One cannot expect her to weep long, especially for a man she did not care for."

I ascended the hotel steps. "Pray come in!" I said, with an inviting movement of my hand. "You must take a glass of wine before you leave. And so—she did not care for him, you say?"

Encouraged by my friendly invitation and manner, Ferrari became more at this ease than ever, and hooking his arm through mine as we crossed the broad passage of the hotel together, he replied in a confidential tone:

"My dear conte, how CAN a woman love a man who is forced upon her by her father for the sake of the money he gives her? As I told you before, my late friend was utterly insensible to the beauty of his wife—he was cold as a stone, and preferred his books. Then naturally she had no love for him!"

By this time we had reached my apartments, and as I threw open the door, I saw that Ferrari was taking in with a critical eye the costly fittings and luxurious furniture. In answer to this last remark, I said with a chilly smile:

"And as I told YOU before, my dear Signor Ferarri, I know nothing whatever about women, and care less than nothing for their loves or hatreds! I have always thought of them more or less as playful kittens, who purr when they are stroked the right way, and scream and scratch when their tails are trodden on. Try this Montepulciano!"

He accepted the glass I proffered him, and tasted the wine with the air of a connoisseur.

"Exquisite!" he murmured, sipping it lazily. "You are lodged en prince here, conte! I envy you!"

"You need not," I answered. "You have youth and health, and—as you have hinted to me—love; all these things are better than wealth, so people say. At any rate, youth and health are good things—love I have no belief in. As for me, I am a mere luxurious animal, loving comfort and ease beyond anything. I have had many trials—I now take my rest in my own fashion."

"A very excellent and sensible fashion!" smiled Ferrari, leaning his head easily back on the satin cushions of the easy-chair into which he had thrown himself.

"Do you know, conte, now I look at you well, I think you must have been very handsome when you were young! You have a superb figure."

I bowed stiffly. "You flatter me, signor! I believe I never was specially hideous—but looks in a man always rank second to strength, and of strength I have plenty yet remaining."

"I do not doubt it," he returned, still regarding me attentively with an expression in which there was the faintest shadow of uneasiness.

"It is an odd coincidence, you will say, but I find a most extraordinary resemblance in the height and carriage of your figure to that of my late friend Romani."

I poured some wine out for myself with a steady hand, and drank it.

"Really?" I answered. "I am glad that I remind you of him—if the reminder is agreeable! But all tall men are much alike so far as figure goes, providing they are well made."

Ferrari's brow was contracted in a musing frown and he answered not. He still looked at me, and I returned his look without embarrassment. Finally he roused himself, smiled, and finished drinking his glass of Montepulciano. Then he rose to go.

"You will permit me to mention your name to the Countess Romani, I hope?" he said, cordially. "I am certain she will receive you, should you desire it."

I feigned a sort of vexation, and made an abrupt movement of impatience.

"The fact is," I said, at last, "I very much dislike talking to women. They are always illogical, and their frivolity wearies me. But you have been so friendly that I will give you a message for the countess–if you have no objection to deliver it. I should be sorry to trouble you unnecessarily–and you perhaps will not have an opportunity of seeing her for some days?"

He colored slightly and moved uneasily. Then with a kind of effort, he replied:

"On the contrary, I am going to see her this very evening. I assure you it will be a pleasure to me to convey to her any greeting you may desire to send."

Oh, it is no greeting," I continued, calmly, noting the various signs of embarrassment in his manner with a careful eye. "It is a mere message, which, however, may enable you to understand why I was anxious to see the young man who is dead. In my very early manhood the elder Count Romani did me an inestimable service. I never forgot his kindness–my memory is extraordinarily tenacious of both benefits and injuries–and I have always desired to repay it in some suitable manner. I have with me a few jewels of almost priceless value– I have myself collected them, and I reserved them as a present to the son of my old friend, simply as a trifling souvenir or expression of gratitude for past favors received from his family. His sudden death has deprived me of the pleasure of fulfilling this intention–but as the jewels are quite useless to me, I am perfectly willing to hand them over to the Countess Romani, should she care to have them. They would have been hers had her husband lived–they should be hers now. If you, signor, will report these facts to her and learn her wishes with respect to the matter, I shall be much indebted to you."

"I shall be delighted to obey you," replied Ferrari, courteously, rising at the same time to take his leave. "I am proud to be the bearer of so pleasing an errand. Beautiful women love jewels, and who shall blame them? Bright eyes and diamonds go well together! *A rivederci, Signor Conte!* I trust we shall meet often."

"I have no doubt we shall," I answered, quietly.

He shook hands cordially–I responded to his farewell salutations with the brief coldness which was now my habitual manner, and we parted. From the window of my saloon I could see him sauntering easily down the hotel steps and from thence along the street. How I cursed him as he stepped jauntily on–how I hated his debonair grace and easy manner! I watched the even poise of his handsome head and shoulders, I noted the assured tread, the air of conscious vanity– the whole demeanor of the man bespoke his perfect self-satisfaction and his absolute confidence in the brightness of the future that awaited him when that stipulated six months of pretended mourning for my untimely death should have expired. Once, as he walked on his way, he turned and paused–looking back–he raised his hat to enjoy the coolness of the breeze on his forehead and hair. The light of the moon fell full on his features and showed them in profile, like a finely-cut cameo against the dense dark-blue background of the evening sky. I gazed at him with a sort of grim fascination–the fascination of a hunter for the stag when it stands at bay, just before he draws his knife across its throat. He was in my power–he had deliberately thrown himself in the trap I had set for him. He lay at the mercy of one in whom there was no mercy. He had said and done nothing to deter me from my settled plans. Had he shown the least tenderness of recollection for me as Fabio Romani, his friend and benefactor–had he hallowed my memory by one generous word–had he expressed one regret for my loss–I might have hesitated, I might have somewhat changed my course of action so that punishment should have fallen more lightly on him than on her. For I knew well enough that she, my wife, was the worst sinner of the two. Had SHE chosen to respect herself, not all the forbidden love in the world could have touched her honor. Therefore, the least sign of compunction or affection from Ferrari for me, his supposed dead friend, would have turned the scale in his favor, and in spite of his treachery, remembering how SHE must have encouraged him, I would at least have spared him torture. But no sign had been given, no word had been spoken, there was no need for hesitation or pity, and I was glad of it! All this I thought as I watched him standing bareheaded in the moonlight, on his way to–whom? To my wife, of course. I knew that well enough. He was going to console her widow's tears–to soothe her aching heart–a good Samaritan in very earnest! He moved, he passed slowly out of my sight. I waited till I had seen the last glimpse of his retreating figure, and then I left the window satisfied with my day's work. Vengeance had begun.

13

QUITE early in the next day Ferrari called to see me. I was at breakfast–he apologized for disturbing me at the meal.

"But," he explained, frankly, "the Countess Romani laid such urgent commands upon me that I was compelled to obey. We men are the slaves of women!"

"Not always," I said, dryly, as I motioned him to take a seat– "there are exceptions–myself for instance. Will you have some coffee?"

"Thanks, I have already breakfasted. Pray do not let me be in your way, my errand is soon done. The countess wishes me to say–"

"You saw her last night?" I interrupted him.

He flushed slightly. "Yes–that is–for a few minutes only. I gave her your message. She thanks you, and desires me to tell you that she cannot think of receiving the jewels unless you will first honor her by a visit. She is not at home to ordinary callers in consequence of her recent bereavement–but to you, so old a friend of her husband's family, a hearty welcome will be accorded."

I bowed stiffly. "I am extremely flattered!" I said, in a somewhat sarcastic tone, "it is seldom I receive so tempting an invitation! I regret that I cannot accept it–at least, not at present. Make my compliments to the lady, and tell her so in whatever sugared form of words you may think best fitted to please her ears."

He looked surprised and puzzled.

"Do you really mean," he said, with a twinge of hauteur in his accents, "that you will not visit her—that you refuse her request?"

I smiled. "I really mean, my dear Signor Ferrari, that, being always accustomed to have my own way, I can make no exception in favor of ladies, however fascinating they may be. I have business in Naples— it claims my first and best attention. When it is transacted I may possibly try a few frivolities for a change—at present I am unfit for the society of the fair sex—an old battered traveler as you see, brusque, and unaccustomed to polite lying. But I promise you I will practice suave manners and a court bow for the countess when I can spare time to call upon her. In the meanwhile I trust to you to make her a suitable and graceful apology for my non-appearance."

Ferrari's puzzled and vexed expression gave way to a smile—finally he laughed aloud. "Upon my word!" he exclaimed, gaily, "you are really a remarkable man, conte! You are extremely cynical! I am almost inclined to believe that you positively hate women."

"Oh, by no means! Nothing so strong as hatred," I said, coolly, as I peeled and divided a fine peach as a finish to my morning's meal. "Hatred is a strong passion—to hate well one must first have loved. No, no—I do not find women worth hating—I am simply indifferent to them. They seem to me merely one of the burdens imposed on man's existence— graceful, neatly packed, light burdens in appearance, but in truth, terribly heavy and soul-crushing."

"Yet many accept such burdens gaily!" interrupted Ferrari, with a smile. I glanced at him keenly.

"Men seldom attain the mastery over their own passions," I replied; "they are in haste to seize every apparent pleasure that comes in their way, Led by a hot animal impulse which they call love, they snatch at a woman's beauty as a greedy school-boy snatches ripe fruit–and when possessed, what is it worth? Here is its emblem"– and I held up the stone of the peach I had just eaten–"the fruit is devoured–what remains? A stone with a bitter kernel."

Ferrari shrugged his shoulders.

"I cannot agree with you, count," he said; "but I will not argue with you. From your point of view you may be right–but when one is young, and life stretches before you like a fair pleasure-ground, love and the smile of woman are like sunlight falling on flowers! You too must have felt this–in spite of what you say, there must have been a time in your life when you also loved!"

"Oh, I have had my fancies, of course!" I answered, with an indifferent laugh. "The woman I fancied turned out to be a saint–I was not worthy of her–at least, so I was told. At any rate, I was so convinced of her virtue and my own unworthiness–that–I left her."

He looked surprised. "An odd reason, surely, for resigning her, was it not?"

"Very odd–very unusual–but a sufficient one for me. Pray let us talk of something more interesting–your pictures, for instance. When may I see them?"

"When you please," he answered, readily–"though I fear they are scarcely worth a visit. I have not worked much lately. I really doubt whether I have any that will merit your notice."

"You underrate your powers, signor," I said with formal politeness. "Allow me to call at your studio this afternoon. I have a few minutes to spare between three and four o'clock, if that time will suit you."

"It will suit me admirably," he said, with a look of gratification; "but I fear you will be disappointed. I assure you I am no artist."

I smiled. I knew that well enough. But I made no reply to his remark–I said, "Regarding the matter of the jewels for the Countess Romani–would you care to see them?"

"I should indeed," he answered; "they are unique specimens, I think?"

"I believe so," I answered, and going to an escritoire in the corner of the room, I unlocked it and took out a massive carved oaken jewel-chest of square shape, which I had had made in Palermo. It contained a necklace of large rubies and diamonds, with bracelets to match, and pins of their hair–also a sapphire ring–a cross of fine rose-brilliants, and the pearl pendant I had first found in the vault. All the gems, with the exception of this pendant, had been reset by a skillful jeweler in Palermo, who had acted under my superintendence–and Ferrari uttered an exclamation of astonishment and admiration as he lifted the glittering toys out one by one and noted the size and brilliancy of the precious stones.

"They are trifles," I said, carelessly–"but they may please a woman's taste–and they amount to a certain fixed value. You would do me a great service if you consented to take them to the Contessa Romani for me–tell her to accept them as heralds of my forthcoming visit. I am sure you will know how to persuade her to take what would unquestionably have been hers had her husband lived. They are really her property–she must not refuse to receive what is her own."

Ferrari hesitated and looked at me earnestly.

"You–WILL visit her–she may rely on your coming for a certainty, I hope?"

I smiled. "You seem very anxious about it. May I ask why?"

"I think," he replied at once, "that it would embarrass the countess very much if you gave her no opportunity to thank you for so munificent and splendid a gift–and unless she knew she could do so, I am certain she would not accept it."

"Make yourself quite easy," I answered. "She shall thank me to her heart's content. I give you my word that within a few days I will call upon the lady–in fact you said you would introduce me–I accept your offer!"

He seemed delighted, and seizing my hand, shook it

cordially.

"Then in that case I will gladly take the jewels to her," he exclaimed. "And I may say, count, that had you searched the whole world over, you could not have found one whose beauty was more fitted to show them off to advantage. I assure you her loveliness is of a most exquisite character!"

"No doubt!" I said, dryly. "I take your word for it. I am no judge of a fair face or form. And now, my good friend, do not think me churlish if I request you leave me in solitude for the present. Between three and four o'clock I shall be at your studio."

He rose at once to take his leave. I placed the oaken box of jewels in the leathern case which had been made to contain it, strapped and locked it, and handed it to him together with its key. He was profuse in his compliments and thanks—almost obsequious, in truth— and I discovered another defect in his character—a defect which, as his friend in former days, I had guessed nothing of. I saw that very little encouragement would make him a toady—a fawning servitor on the wealthy—and in our old time of friendship I had believed him to be far above all such meanness, but rather of a manly, independent nature that scorned hypocrisy. Thus we are deluded even by our nearest and dearest—and is it well or ill for us, I wonder, when we are at last undeceived? Is not the destruction of illusion worse than illusion itself? I thought so, as my quondam friend clasped my hand in farewell that morning. What would I not have given to believe in him as I once did! I held open the door of my room as he passed out, carrying the box of jewels for my wife, and as I bade him a brief adieu, the well-worn story of Tristram and Kind Mark came to my mind. He, Guido, like Tristram, would in a short space clasp the gemmed necklace round the throat of one as fair and false as the fabled Iseulte, and I—should I figure as the wronged king? How does the English laureate put it in his idyll on the subject?

"'Mark's way,' said Mark, and clove him through the brain."

Too sudden and sweet a death by far for such a traitor! The Cornish king should have known how to torture his betrayer! I knew—and I meditated deeply on every point of my design, as I sat alone for an hour after Ferrari had left me. I had many things to do—I had resolved on making myself a personage of importance in Naples, and I wrote several letters and sent out visiting-cards to certain well- established families of distinction as necessary preliminaries to the result I had in view. That day, too, I engaged a valet—a silent and discreet Tuscan named Vincenzo Flamma. He was an admirably trained servant—he never asked questions—was too dignified to gossip, and rendered me instant and implicit obedience—in fact he was a gentleman in his way, with far better manners than many who lay claim to that title. He entered upon his duties at once, and never did I know him to neglect the most trifling thing that could add to my satisfaction or comfort. In making arrangements with him, and in attending to various little matters of business, the hours slipped rapidly away, and in the afternoon, at the time appointed, I made my way to Ferrari's studio. I knew it of old—I had no need to consult the card he had left with me on which the address was written. It was a queer, quaintly built little place, situated at the top of an ascending road—its windows commanded an extensive view of the bay and the surrounding scenery. Many and many a happy hour had I passed there before my marriage reading some favorite book or watching Ferrari as he painted his crude landscapes and figures, most of which I good-naturedly purchased as soon as completed. The little porch over-grown with star-jasmine looked strangely and sorrowfully familiar to my eyes, and my heart experienced a sickening pang of regret for the past, as I pulled the bell and heard the little tinkling sound to which I was so well accustomed. Ferrari himself opened the door to me with eager rapidity—he looked excited and radiant.

"Come in, come in!" he cried with effusive cordiality. "You will find everything in confusion, but pray excuse it. It is some time since I had any visitors. Mind the steps, conte!—the place is rather dark just here—Everyone stumbles at this particular corner."

So talking, and laughing as he talked, he escorted me up the short narrow flight of stairs to the light airy room where he usually worked. Glancing round it, I saw at once the evidences of neglect and disorder—he had certainly not been there for many days, though he had made an attempt to arrange it tastefully for my reception. On the table stood a large vase of flowers grouped with artistic elegance—I felt instinctively that my wife had put them there. I noticed that Ferrari had begun nothing new—all the finished and unfinished studies I saw I recognized directly. I seated myself in an easy-chair and looked at my betrayer with a calmly critical eye. He was what the English would call "got up for effect." Though in black, he had donned a velvet coat instead of the cloth one he had worn in the morning—he had a single white japonica in his buttonhole—his face was pale and his eyes unusually brilliant. He looked his best—I admitted it, and could readily understand how an idle, pleasure-seeking feminine animal might be easily attracted by the purely physical beauty of his form and features. I spoke a part of my thoughts aloud.

"You are not only an artist by profession, Signer Ferrari—you are one also in appearance."

He flushed slightly and smiled.

"You are very amiable to say so," he replied, his pleased vanity displaying itself at once in the expression of his face. "But I am well aware that you flatter me. By the way, before I forget it, I must tell you that I fulfilled your commission."

"To the Countess Romani?"

"Exactly. I cannot describe to you her astonishment and delight at the splendor and brilliancy of those jewels you sent her. It was really pretty to watch her innocent satisfaction."

I laughed.

"Marguerite and the jewel song in 'Faust,' I suppose, with new scenery and effects?" I asked, with a slight sneer. He bit his lip and looked annoyed. But he answered, quietly:

"I see you must have your joke, conte; but remember that if you place the countess in the position of Marguerite, you, as the giver of the jewels, naturally play the part of Mephistopheles."

"And you will be Faust, of course!" I said, gaily. "Why, we might mount the opera with a few supernumeraries and astonish Naples by our performance! What say you? But let us come to business. I like the picture you have on the easel there—may I see it more closely?"

He drew it nearer; it was a showy landscape with the light of the sunset upon it. It was badly done, but I praised it warmly, and purchased it for five hundred francs. Four other sketches of a similar nature were then produced. I bought these also. By the time we got through these matters, Ferrari was in the best of humors. He offered me some excellent wine and partook of it himself; he talked incessantly, and diverted me extremely, though my inward amusement was not caused by the witty brilliancy of his conversation. No, I was only excited to a sense of savage humor by the novelty of the position in which we two men stood. Therefore I listened to him attentively, applauded his anecdotes—all of which I had heard before—admired his jokes, and fooled his egotistical soul till he had no shred of self-respect remaining. He laid his nature bare before me—and I knew what it was at last—a mixture of selfishness, avarice, sensuality, and heartlessness, tempered now and then by a flash of good-nature and sympathetic attraction which were the mere outcomes of youth and physical health—no more. This was the man I had loved—this fellow who told coarse stories only worthy of a common pot-house, and who reveled in a wit of a high and questionable flavor; this conceited, empty-headed, muscular piece of humanity was the same being for whom I had cherished so chivalrous and loyal a tenderness! Our conversation was broken in upon at last by the sound of approaching wheels. A carriage was heard ascending the road—it came nearer—it stopped at the door. I set down the glass of wine I had just raised to my lips, and looked at Ferrari steadily.

"You expect other visitors?" I inquired.

He seemed embarrassed, smiled, and hesitated.

"Well–I am not sure–but–" The bell rang. With a word of apology Ferrari hurried away to answer it. I sprung from my chair–I knew–I felt who was coming. I steadied my nerves by a strong effort. I controlled the rapid beating of my heart; and fixing my dark glasses more closely over my eyes, I drew myself up erect and waited calmly. I heard Ferrari ascending the stairs–a light step accompanied his heavier footfall–he spoke to his companion in whispers. Another instant–and he flung the door of the studio wide open with the haste and reverence due for the entrance of a queen. There was a soft rustle of silk–a delicate breath of perfume on the air–and then–I stood face to face with my wife!

14

OW DAZZLINGLY lovely she was! I gazed at her with the same bewildered fascination that had stupefied my reason and judgment when I beheld her for the first time. The black robes she wore, the long crape veil thrown back from her clustering hair and *mignonne* face, all the somber shadows of her mourning garb only served to heighten and display her beauty to greater advantage. A fair widow truly! I, her lately deceased husband, freely admitted the magnetic power of her charms! She paused for an instant on the threshold, a winning smile on her lips; she looked at me, hesitated, and finally spoke in courteous accents:

"I think I cannot be mistaken! Do I address the noble Conte Cesare Oliva?"

I tried to speak, but could not. My mouth was dry and parched with excitement, my throat swelled and ached with the pent-up wrath and despair of my emotions. I answered her question silently by a formal bow. She at once advanced, extending both her hands with the coaxing grace of manner I had so often admired.

"I am the Countess Romani," she said, still smiling. "I heard from Signor Ferrari that you purposed visiting his studio this afternoon, and I could not resist the temptation of coming to express my personal acknowledgments for the almost regal gift you sent me. The jewels are really magnificent. Permit me to offer you my sincere thanks!"

I caught her outstretched hands and wrung them hard–so hard that the rings she wore must have dug into her flesh and hurt her, though she was too well-bred to utter any exclamation. I had fully recovered myself, and was prepared to act out my part.

"On the contrary, *madame*," I said in a strong harsh voice, "the thanks must come entirely from me for the honor you have conferred upon me by accepting trifles so insignificant– especially at a time when the cold brilliancy of mere diamonds must jar upon the sensitive feelings of your recent widowhood. Believe me, I sympathize deeply with your bereavement. Had your husband lived, the jewels would have been his gift to you, and how much more acceptable they would then have appeared in your eyes! I am proud to think you have condescended so far as to receive them from so unworthy a hand as mine."

As I spoke her face paled–she seemed startled, and regarded me earnestly. Sheltered behind my smoked spectacles, I met the gaze of her large dark eyes without embarrassment. Slowly she withdrew her slight fingers from my clasp. I placed an easy chair for her, she sunk softly into it with her old air of indolent ease, the ease of a spoiled empress or sultan's favorite, while she still continued to look up at me thoughtfully Ferrari, meanwhile, busied himself in bringing out more wine, he also produced a dish of fruit and some sweet cakes, and while occupied in these duties as our host he began to laugh.

"Ha, ha! you are caught!" he exclaimed to me gaily. "You must know we planned this together, *madame* and I, just to take you by surprise. There was no knowing when you would be persuaded to visit the contessa, and she could not rest till she had thanked you, so we arranged this meeting. Could anything be better? Come, conte, confess that you are charmed!"

"Of course I am!" I answered with a slight touch of satire in my tone. "Who would not be charmed in the presence of such youth and beauty! And I am also flattered—for I know what exceptional favor the Contessa Romani extends toward me in allowing me to make her acquaintance at a time which must naturally be for her a secluded season of sorrow."

At these words my wife's face suddenly assumed an expression of wistful sadness and appealing gentleness

"Ah, poor unfortunate Fabio," she sighed. "How terrible it seems that he is not here to greet you! How gladly he would have welcomed any friend of his father's—he adored his father, poor fellow! I cannot realize that he is dead. It was too sudden, too dreadful! I do not think I shall ever recover the shock of his loss!"

And her eyes actually filled with tears; though the fact did not surprise me in the least, for many women can weep at will. Very little practice is necessary—and we men are such fools, we never know how it is done; we take all the pretty feigned piteousness for real grief, and torture ourselves to find methods of consolation for the feminine sorrows which have no root save in vanity and selfishness. I glanced quickly from my wife to Ferrari: he coughed, and appeared embarrassed—he was not so good an actor as she was an actress. Studying them both, I know not which feeling gained the mastery in my mind—contempt or disgust.

"Console yourself, *madame*," I said, coldly. "Time should be quick to heal the wounds of one so young and beautiful as you are! Personally speaking, I much regret your husband's death, but I would entreat YOU not to give way to grief, which, however sincere, must unhappily be useless. Your life lies before you—and may happy days and as fair a future await you as you deserve!"

She smiled, her tear-drops vanished like morning dew disappearing in the heat.

"I thank you for your good wishes, conte," she said "but it rests with you to commence my happy days by honoring me with a visit. You will come, will you not? My house and all that it contains are at your service!"

I hesitated. Ferrari looked amused.

"Madame is not aware of your dislike to the society of ladies, conte," he said, and there was a touch of mockery in his tone. I glanced at him coldly, and addressed my answer to my wife.

"Signor Ferrari is perfectly right," I said, bending over her, and speaking in a low tone; "I am often ungallant enough to avoid the society of mere women, but, alas! I have no armor of defense against the smile of an angel."

And I bowed with a deep and courtly reverence. Her face brightened– she adored her own loveliness, and the desire of conquest awoke in her immediately. She took a glass of wine from my hand with a languid grace, and fixed her glorious eyes full on me with a smile.

"That is a very pretty speech," she said, sweetly, "and it means, of course, that you will come to-morrow. Angels exact obedience! Gui–, I mean Signor Ferrari, you will accompany the conte and show him the way to the villa?"

Ferrari bent his head with some stiffness. He looked slightly sullen.

"I am glad to see," he observed, with some petulance, "that your persuasions have carried more conviction to the Conte Oliva than mine. To me he was apparently inflexible."

She laughed gaily. "Of course! It is only a woman who can always win her own way–am I not right, conte?" And she glanced up at me with an arch expression of mingled mirth and malice. What a love of mischief she had! She saw that Guido was piqued, and she took intense delight in teasing him still further.

"I cannot tell, *madame*," I answered her. "I know so little of your charming sex that I need to be instructed. But I instinctively feel that YOU must be right, whatever you say. Your eyes would convert an infidel!"

Again she looked at me with one of those wonderfully brilliant, seductive, arrow-like glances–then she rose to take her leave.

"An angel's visit truly," I said, lightly, "sweet, but brief!"

"We shall meet to-morrow," she replied, smiling. "I consider I have your promise; you must not fail me! Come as early as you like in the afternoon, then you will see my little girl Stella. She is very like poor Fabio. Till tomorrow, adieu!"

She extended her hand. I raised it to my lips. She smiled as she withdrew it, and looking at me, or rather at the glasses I wore, she inquired:

"You suffer with your eyes?"

"Ah, *madame*, a terrible infirmity! I cannot endure the light. But I should not complain–it is a weakness common to age."

You do not seem to be old," she said, thoughtfully. With a woman's quick eye she had noted, I suppose, the unwrinkled smoothness of my skin, which no disguise could alter. But I exclaimed with affected surprise:

"Not old! With these white hairs!"

"Many young men have them," she said. "At any rate, they often accompany middle age, or what is called the prime of life. And really, in your case, they are very becoming!"

And with a courteous gesture of farewell she moved to leave the room. Both Ferrari and myself hastened to escort her downstairs to her carriage, which stood in waiting at the door– the very carriage and pair of chestnut ponies which I myself had given her as a birthday present. Ferrari offered to assist her in mounting the step of the vehicle; she put his arm aside with a light jesting word and accepted mine instead. I helped her in, and arranged her embroidered wraps about her feet, and she nodded to us both as we stood bareheaded in the afternoon sunlight watching her departure. The horses started at a brisk canter, and in a couple of minutes the dainty equipage was out of sight. When nothing more of it could be seen than the cloud of dust stirred up by its rolling wheels, I turned to look at my companion. His face was stern, and his brows were drawn together in a frown. Stung already! I thought. Already the little asp of jealousy commenced its bitter work! The trifling favor HIS light-o'-love and MY wife had extended to me in choosing

MY arm instead of HIS as a momentary support had evidently been sufficient to pique his pride. God! what blind bats men are! With all their high capabilities and immortal destinies, with all the world before them to conquer, they can sink unnerved and beaten down to impotent weakness before the slighting word or insolent gesture of a frivolous feminine creature, whose best devotions are paid to the mirror that reflects her in the most becoming light! How easy would be my vengeance, I mused, as I watched Ferrari. I touched him on the shoulder; he started from his uncomfortable reverie and forced a smile. I held out a cigar-case.

"What are you dreaming of?" I asked him, laughingly. "Hebe as she waited on the gods, or Venus as she rose in bare beauty from the waves? Either, neither, or both? I assure you a comfortable smoke is as pleasant in its way as the smile of a woman."

He took a cigar and lighted it, but made no answer.

"You are dull, my friend," I continued, hooking my arm through his and pacing him up and down on the turf in front of his studio. "Wit, they say, should be sharpened by the glance of a bright eye; how comes it that the edge of your converse seems blunted? Perhaps your feelings are too deep for words? If so, I do not wonder at it, for the lady is extremely lovely."

He glanced quickly at me.

"Did I not say so?" he exclaimed. "Of all creatures under heaven she is surely the most perfect! Even you, conte, with your cynical ideas about women, even you were quite subdued and influenced by her; I could see it!"

I puffed slowly at my cigar and pretended to meditate.

"Was I?" I said at last, with an air of well-acted surprise. "Really subdued and influenced? I do not think so. But I admit I have never seen a woman so entirely beautiful."

He stopped in his walk, loosened his arm from mine, and regarded me fixedly.

"I told you so," he said, deliberately. "You must remember that I told you so. And now perhaps I ought to warn you."

"Warn me!" I exclaimed, in feigned alarm. "Of what? against whom? Surely not the Contessa Romani, to whom you were so anxious to introduce me? She has no illness, no infectious disorder? She is not dangerous to life or limb, is she?"

Ferrari laughed at the anxiety I displayed for my own bodily safety–an anxiety which I managed to render almost comic–but he looked somewhat relieved too.

"Oh, no," he said, "I meant nothing of that kind. I only think it fair to tell you that she has very seductive manners, and she may pay you little attentions which would flatter any man who was not aware that they are only a part of her childlike, pretty ways; in short, they might lead him erroneously to suppose himself the object of her particular preference, and–"

I broke into a violent fit of laughter, and clapped him roughly on the shoulder.

"Your warning is quite unnecessary, my good young friend," I said. "Come now, do I look a likely man to attract the attention of an adored and capricious beauty? Besides, at my age the idea is monstrous! I could figure as her father, as yours, if you like, but in the capacity of a lover–impossible!"

He eyed me attentively

"She said you did not seem old," he murmured, half to himself and half to me.

"Oh, I grant you she made me that little compliment, certainly," I answered, amused at the suspicions that evidently tortured his mind; "and I accepted it as it was meant–in kindness. I am well aware what a battered and unsightly wreck of a man I must appear in her eyes when contrasted with YOU, Sir Antinous!"

He flushed warmly. Then, with a half-apologetic air, he said:

"Well, you must forgive me if I have seemed over-scrupulous. The contessa is like a–a sister to me; in fact, my late friend Fabio encouraged a fraternal affection between us, and now he is gone I feel it more than ever my duty to protect her, as it were, from herself. She is so young and light-hearted and thoughtless that–but you understand me, do you not?"

I bowed. I understood him perfectly. He wanted no more poachers on the land he himself had pilfered. Quite right, from his point of view! But I was the rightful owner of the land after all, and I naturally had a different opinion of the matter. However, I made no remark, and feigned to be rather bored by the turn the conversation was taking. Seeing this, Ferrari exerted himself to be agreeable; he became a gay and entertaining companion once more, and after he had fixed the hour for our visit to the Villa Romani the next afternoon, our talk turned upon various matters connected with Naples and its inhabitants and their mode of life. I hazarded a few remarks on the general immorality and loose principles that prevailed among the people, just to draw my companion out and sound his character more thoroughly–though I thought I knew his opinions well.

"Pooh, my dear conte," he exclaimed, with a light laugh, as he threw away the end of his cigar, and watched it as it burned dully like a little red lamp among the green grass where it had fallen, "what is immorality after all? Merely a matter of opinion. Take the hackneyed virtue of conjugal fidelity. When followed out to the better end what is the good of it–where does it lead? Why should a man be tied to one woman when he has love enough for twenty? The pretty slender girl whom he chose as a partner in his impulsive youth may become a fat, coarse, red-faced female horror by the time he has attained to the full vigor of manhood–and yet, as long as she lives, the law insists that the full tide of passion shall flow always in one direction– always to the same dull, level, unprofitable shore! The law is absurd, but it exists; and the natural consequence is that we break it. Society pretends to be horrified when we do–yes, I know; but it is all pretense. And the thing is no worse in Naples than it is in London, the capital of the moral British race, only here we are perfectly frank, and make no effort to hide our little sins, while there, they cover them up carefully and make believe to be virtuous. It is the veriest humbug–the parable of Pharisee and Publican over again.

"Not quite," I observed, "for the Publican was repentant, and Naples is not."

"Why should she be?" demanded Ferrari. "What, in the name of Heaven, is the good of being penitent about anything? Will it mend matters? Who is to be pacified or pleased by our contrition? God? My dear conte, there are very few of us nowadays who believe in a Deity. Creation is a mere caprice of the natural elements. The best thing we can do is to enjoy ourselves while we live; we have a very short time of it, and when we die there is an end of all things so far as we are concerned."

"That is your creed?" I asked.

"That is my creed, certainly. It was Solomon's in his heart of hearts. 'Eat, drink and be merry, for to-morrow we die.' It is the creed of Naples, and of nearly all Italy. Of course the vulgar still cling to exploded theories of superstitious belief, but the educated classes are far beyond the old-world notions."

"I believe you," I answered, composedly. I had no wish to argue with him; I only sought to read his shallow soul through and through that I might be convinced of his utter worthlessness. "According to modern civilization there is really no special need to be virtuous unless it suits us. The only thing necessary for pleasant living is to avoid public scandal."

"Just so!" agreed Ferrari; "and that can always be easily managed. Take a woman's reputation–nothing is so easily lost, we all know, before she is actually married; but marry her well, and she is free. She can have a dozen lovers if she likes, and if she is a good manager her husband need never be the wiser. He has HIS amours, of course–why should she not have hers also? Only some women are clumsy, they are over-sensitive and betray themselves too easily; then the injured husband (carefully concealing his little peccadilloes) finds everything out and there is a devil of a row–a moral row, which is the worst kind of row. But a really clever woman can always steer clear of slander if she likes."

Contemptible ruffian! I thought, glancing at his handsome face and figure with scarcely veiled contempt. With all his advantages of education and his well-bred air he was yet ruffian to the core—as low in nature, if not lower, than the half-savage tramp for whom no social law has ever existed or ever will exist. But I merely observed:

"It is easy to see that you have a thorough knowledge of the world and its ways. I admire your perception! From your remarks I judge that you have no sympathy with marital wrongs?"

"Not the least," he replied, dryly; "they are too common and too ludicrous. The 'wronged husband,' as he considers himself in such cases, always cuts such an absurd figure."

"Always?" I inquired, with apparent curiosity.

"Well, generally speaking, he does. How can he remedy the matter? He can only challenge his wife's lover. A duel is fought in which neither of the opponents are killed, they wound each other slightly, embrace, weep, have coffee together, and for the future consent to share the lady's affections amicably."

"*Veramente!*" I exclaimed, with a forced laugh, inwardly cursing his detestable flippancy; "that is the fashionable mode of taking vengeance?"

"Absolutely the one respectable way of doing it," he replied; "it is only the canaille who draw heart's blood in earnest."

Only the canaille! I looked at him fixedly. His smiling eyes met mine with a frank and fearless candor. Evidently he was not ashamed of his opinions, he rather gloried in them. As he stood there with the warm sunlight playing upon his features he seemed the very type of youthful and splendid manhood; an Apollo in exterior—in mind a Silenus. My soul sickened at the sight of him. I felt that the sooner this strong treacherous life was crushed the better; there would be one traitor less in the world at any rate. The thought of my dread but just purpose passed over me like the breath of a bitter wind—a tremor shook my nerves. My face must have betrayed some sign of my inward emotion, for Ferrari exclaimed:

"You are fatigued, conte? You are ill! Pray take my arm!"

He extended it as he spoke. I put it gently but firmly aside.

"It is nothing," I said, coldly; "a mere faintness which often overcomes me, the remains of a recent illness." Here I glanced at my watch; the afternoon was waning rapidly.

"If you will excuse me," I continued, "I will now take leave of you. Regarding the pictures you have permitted me to select, my servant shall call for them this evening to save you the trouble of sending them."

"It is no trouble—" began Ferrari.

"Pardon me," I interrupted him; "you must allow me to arrange the matter in my own way. I am somewhat self-willed, as you know."

He bowed and smiled—the smile of a courtier and sycophant—a smile I hated. He eagerly proposed to accompany me back to my hotel, but I declined this offer somewhat peremptorily, though at the same time thanking him for his courtesy. The truth was I had had almost too much of his society; the strain on my nerves began to tell; I craved to be alone. I felt that if I were much longer with him I should be tempted to spring at him and throttle the life out of him. As it was, I bade him adieu with friendly though constrained politeness; he was profuse in his acknowledgments of the favor I had done him by purchasing his pictures. I waived all thanks aside, assuring him that my satisfaction in the matter far exceeded his, and that I was proud to be the possessor of such valuable proofs of his genius. He swallowed my flattery as eagerly as a fish swallows bait, and we parted on excellent terms. He watched me from his door as I walked down the hilly road with the slow and careful step of an elderly man; once out of his sight, however, I quickened my pace, for the tempest of conflicting sensations within me made it difficult for me to maintain even the appearance of composure. On entering my apartment at the hotel the first thing that met my eyes was a large gilt osier basket, filled with fine fruit and flowers, placed conspicuously on the center-table.

I summoned my valet. "Who sent this?" I demanded.

"Madame the Contessa Romani," replied Vincenzo. with discreet gravity. "There is a card attached, if the *eccelenza* will be pleased to look."

I did look. It was my wife's visiting-card, and on it was written in her own delicate penmanship–

"To remind the conte of his promised visit tomorrow."

A sudden anger possessed me. I crumpled up the dainty glossy bit of pasteboard and flung it aside. The mingled odors of the fruit and flowers offended my senses.

"I care nothing for these trifles," I said, addressing Vincenzo almost impatiently. "Take them to the little daughter of the hotel- keeper; she is a child, she will appreciate them. Take them away at once."

Obediently Vincenzo lifted the basket and bore it out of the room. I was relieved when its fragrance and color had vanished. I, to receive as a gift, the product of my own garden! Half vexed, half sore at heart, I threw myself into an easy chair–anon I laughed aloud! So! Madame commences the game early, I thought. Already paying these marked attentions to a man she knows nothing of beyond that he is reported to be fabulously wealthy. Gold, gold forever! What will it not do! It will bring the proud to their knees, it will force the obstinate to servile compliance, it will conquer aversion and prejudice. The world is a slave to its yellow glitter, and the love of woman, that perishable article of commerce, is ever at its command. Would you obtain a kiss from a pair of ripe-red lips that seem the very abode of honeyed sweetness? Pay for it then with a lustrous diamond; the larger the gem the longer the kiss! The more diamonds you give, the more caresses you will get. The *jeunesse doree* who ruin themselves and their ancestral homes for the sake of the newest and prettiest female puppet on the stage know this well enough. I smiled bitterly as I thought of the languid witching look my wife had given me when she said,

"You do not seem to be old!" I knew the meaning of her eyes; I had not studied their liquid lights and shadows so long for nothing. My road to revenge was a straight and perfectly smooth line–almost too smooth. I could have wished for some difficulty, some obstruction; but there was none– absolutely none. The traitors walked deliberately into the trap set for them. Over and over again I asked myself quietly and in cold blood–was there any reason why I should have pity on them? Had they shown one redeeming point in their characters? Was there any nobleness, any honesty, any real sterling good quality in either of them to justify my consideration? And always the answer came, NO! Hollow to the heart's core, hypocrites both, liars both–even the guilty passion they cherished for one another had no real earnestness in it save the pursuit of present pleasure; for she, Nina, in that fatal interview in the avenue where I had been a tortured listener, had hinted at the possibility of tiring of her lover, and HE had frankly declared to me that very day that it was absurd to suppose a man could be true to one woman all his life. In brief, they deserved their approaching fate. Such men as Guido and such women as my wife, are, I know, common enough in all classes of society, but they are not the less pernicious animals, meriting extermination as much, if not more, than the less harmful beasts of prey. The poor beasts at any rate tell no lies, and after death their skins are of some value; but who shall measure the mischief done by a false tongue–and of what use is the corpse of a liar save to infect the air with pestilence? I used to wonder at the superiority of men over the rest of the animal creation, but I see now that it is chiefly gained by excess of selfish cunning. The bulky, good-natured, ignorant lion who has only one honest way of defending himself, namely with tooth and claw, is no match for the jumping two-legged little rascal who hides himself behind a bush and fires a gun aimed direct at the bigger brute's heart. Yet the lion's mode of battle is the braver of the two, and the cannons, torpedoes and other implements of modern warfare are proofs of man's cowardice and cruelty as much as they are of his diabolical ingenuity. Calmly comparing the ordinary lives of men and beasts–judging them by their abstract virtues merely–I am inclined to think the beasts the more respectable of the two!

15

WELCOME to Villa Romani!"

The words fell strangely on my ears. Was I dreaming, or was I actually standing on the smooth green lawn of my own garden, mechanically saluting my own wife, who, smiling sweetly, uttered this cordial greeting? For a moment or two my brain became confused; the familiar veranda with its clustering roses and jasmine swayed unsteadily before my eyes; the stately house, the home of my childhood, the scene of my past happiness, rocked in the air as though it were about to fall. A choking sensation affected my throat. Even the sternest men shed tears sometimes. Such tears too! wrung like drops of blood from the heart. And I–I could have wept thus. Oh, the dear old home! and how fair and yet how sad it seemed to my anguished gaze! It should have been in ruins surely–broken and cast down in the dust like its master's peace and honor. Its master, did I say? Who was its master? Involuntarily I glanced at Ferrari, who stood beside me. Not he–not he; by Heaven he should never be master! But where was MY authority? I came to the place as a stranger and an alien. The starving beggar who knows not where to lay his head has no emptier or more desolate heart than I had as I looked wistfully on the home which was mine before I died! I noticed some slight changes here and there; for instance, my deep easy-chair that had always occupied one particular corner of the veranda was gone; a little tame bird that I had loved, whose cage used to hang up among the white roses on the wall, was also gone. My old butler, the servant who admitted Ferrari and myself within the gates, had an expression of weariness and injury on his aged features which he had not worn in my time, and which I was sorry to see. And my dog, the noble black Scotch collie, what had become of him, I wondered? He had been presented to me by a young Highlander who had passed one winter with me in Rome, and who, on returning to his native mountains, had sent me the dog, a perfect specimen of its kind, as a souvenir of our friendly intercourse. Poor Wyvis! I thought. Had they made away with him? Formerly he had always been visible about the house or garden; his favorite place was on the lowest veranda step, where he loved to bask in the heat of the sun. And now he was nowhere visible. I was mutely indignant at his disappearance, but I kept strict watch over my feelings, and remembered in time the part I had to play.

"Welcome to Villa Romani!" so said my wife. Then, remarking my silence as I looked about me, she added with a pretty coaxing air,

"I am afraid after all you are sorry you have come to see me!"

I smiled. It served my purpose now to be as gallant and agreeable as I could; therefore I answered:

"Sorry, *madame*! If I were, then should I be the most ungrateful of all men! Was Dante sorry, think you, when he was permitted to behold Paradise?"

She blushed; her eyes drooped softly under their long curling lashes. Ferrari frowned impatiently–but was silent. She led the way into the house–into the lofty cool drawing-room, whose wide windows opened out to the garden. Here all was the same as ever with the exception of one thing–a marble bust of myself as a boy had been removed. The grand piano was open, the mandolin lay on a side- table, looking as though it had been recently used; there were fresh flowers and ferns in all the tall Venetian glass vases. I seated myself and remarked on the beauty of the house and its surroundings.

"I remember it very well," I added, quietly.

"You remember it!" exclaimed Ferrari, quickly, as though surprised.

"Certainly. I omitted to tell you, my friend, that I used to visit this spot often when a boy. The elder Conte Romani and myself played about these grounds together. The scene is quite familiar to me."

Nina listened with an appearance of interest.

"Did you ever see my late husband?" she asked.

"Once," I answered her, gravely. "He was a mere child at the time, and, as far as I could discern, a very promising one. His father seemed greatly attached to him. I knew his mother also."

"Indeed," she exclaimed, settling herself on a low ottoman and fixing her eyes upon me; "what was she like?"

I paused a moment before replying. Could I speak of that unstained sacred life of wifehood and motherhood to this polluted though lovely creature?

"She was a beautiful woman unconscious of her beauty," I answered at last. "There, all is said. Her sole aim seemed to be to forget herself in making others happy, and to surround her home with an atmosphere of goodness and virtue. She died young."

Ferrari glanced at me with an evil sneer in his eyes.

"That was fortunate," he said. "She had no time to tire of her husband, else—who knows?"

My blood rose rapidly to an astonishing heat, but I controlled myself.

"I do not understand you," I said, with marked frigidity. "The lady I speak of lived and died under the old regime of noblesse oblige. I am not so well versed in modern social forms of morality as yourself."

Nina hastily interposed. "Oh, my dear conte," she said,

laughingly, "pay no attention to Signor Ferrari! He is rash sometimes, and says very foolish things, but he really does not mean them. It is only his way! My poor dear husband used to be quite vexed with him sometimes, though he WAS so fond of him. But, conte, as you know so much about the family, I am sure you will like to see my little Stella. Shall I send for her, or are you bored by children?"

"On the contrary, *madame*, I am fond of them," I answered, with forced composure, though my heart throbbed with mingled delight and agony at the thought of seeing my little one again. "And the child of my old friend's son must needs have a double interest for me."

My wife rang the bell, and gave orders to the maid who answered it to send her little girl to her at once. Ferrari meanwhile engaged me in conversation, and strove, I could see, by entire deference to my opinions, to make up for any offense his previous remark might have given. A few moments passed–and then the handle of the drawing-room door was timidly turned by an evidently faltering and unpracticed hand. Nina called out impatiently–"Come in, baby! Do not be afraid– come in!" With that the door slowly opened and my little daughter entered. Though I had been so short a time absent from her it was easy to see the child had changed very much. Her face looked pinched and woebegone, its expression was one of fear and distrust. The laughter had faded out of her young eyes, and was replaced by a serious look of pained resignation that was pitiful to see in one of her tender years. Her mouth drooped plaintively at the corners–her whole demeanor had an appealing anxiety in it that spoke plainly to my soul and enlightened me as to the way she had evidently been forgotten and neglected. She approached us hesitatingly, but stopped half-way and looked doubtfully at Ferrari. He met her alarmed gaze with a mocking smile.

"Come along, Stella!" he said. "You need not be frightened! I will not scold you unless you are naughty. Silly child! you look as if I were the giant in the fairy tale, going to eat you up for dinner. Come and speak to this gentleman—he knew your papa."

At this word her eyes brightened, her small steps grew more assured and steady—she advanced and put her tiny hand in mine. The touch of the soft, uncertain little fingers almost unmanned me. I drew her toward me and lifted her on my knee. Under pretense of kissing her I hid my face for a second or two in her clustering fair curls, while I forced back the womanish tears that involuntarily filled my eyes. My poor little darling! I wonder now how I maintained my set composure before the innocent thoughtfulness of her gravely questioning gaze! I had fancied she might possibly be scared by the black spectacles I wore—children are frightened by such things sometimes—but she was not. No; she sat on my knee with an air of perfect satisfaction, though she looked at me so earnestly as almost to disturb my self-possession. Nina and Ferrari watched her with some amusement, but she paid no heed to them—she persisted in staring at me. Suddenly a slow sweet smile—the tranquil smile of a contented baby, dawned all over her face; she extended her little arms, and, of her own accord, put up her lips to kiss me! Half startled at this manifestation of affection, I hurriedly caught her to my heart and returned her caress, then I looked furtively at my wife and Guido. Had they any suspicion? No! why should they have any? Had not Ferrari himself seen me BURIED? Reassured by this thought I addressed myself to Stella, making my voice as gratingly harsh as I could, for I dreaded the child's quick instinct.

"You are a very charming little lady!" I said, playfully. "And so your name is Stella? That is because you are a little star, I suppose?"

She became meditative. "Papa said I was," she answered, softly and shyly.

"Papa spoiled you!" interposed Nina, pressing a filmy black-bordered handkerchief to her eyes. "Poor papa! You were not so naughty to him as you are to me."

The child's lip quivered, but she was silent.

"Oh, fie!" I murmured, half chidingly. "Are you ever naughty? Surely not! All little stars are good–they never cry–they are always bright and calm."

Still she remained mute–a sigh, deep enough for an older sufferer, heaved her tiny breast. She leaned her head against my arm and raised her eyes appealingly.

"Have you seen my papa?" she asked, timidly. "Will he come back soon?"

For a moment I did not answer her. Ferrari took it upon himself to reply roughly. "Don't talk nonsense, baby! You know your papa has gone away–you were too naughty for him, and he will never come back again. He has gone to a place where there are no tiresome little girls to tease him."

Thoughtless and cruel words! I at once understood the secret grief that weighed on the child's mind. Whenever she was fretful or petulant, they evidently impressed it upon her that her father had left her because of her naughtiness. She had taken this deeply to heart; no doubt she had brooded upon it in her own vague childish fashion, and had puzzled her little brain as to what she could possibly have done to displease her father so greatly that he had actually gone away never to return. Whatever her thoughts were, she did not on this occasion give vent to them by tears or words. She only turned her eyes on Ferrari with a look of intense pride and scorn, strange to see in so little a creature–a true Romani look, such as I had often noticed in my father's eyes, and such as I knew must be frequently visible in my own. Ferrari saw it, and burst out laughing loudly.

"There!" he exclaimed. "Like that she exactly resembles her father! It is positively ludicrous! Fabio, all over! She only wants one thing to make the portrait perfect." And approaching her, he snatched one of her long curls and endeavored to twist it over her mouth in the form of a mustache. The child struggled angrily, and hid her face against my coat. The more she tried to defend herself the greater the malice with which Ferrari tormented her. Her mother did not interfere–she only laughed.

I held the little thing closely sheltered in my embrace, and steadying down the quiver of indignation in my voice, I said with quiet firmness:

"Fair play, signor! Fair play! Strength becomes mere bullying when it is employed against absolute weakness."

Ferrari laughed again, but this time uneasily, and ceasing his monkish pranks, walked to the window. Smoothing Stella's tumbled hair, I added with a sarcastic smile:

"This little *donzella*, will have her revenge when she grows up. Recollecting how one man teased her in childhood, she, in return, will consider herself justified in teasing all men. Do you not agree with me, *madame?*" I said, turning to my wife, who gave me a sweetly coquettish look as she answered:

"Well, really, conte, I do not know! For with the remembrance of one man who teased her, must come also the thought of another who was kind to her–yourself–she will find it difficult to decide the *juste milieu.*"

A subtle compliment was meant to be conveyed in these words. I acknowledged it by a silent gesture of admiration, which she quickly understood and accepted. Was ever a man in the position of being delicately flattered by his own wife before? I think not! Generally married persons are like candid friends–fond of telling each other very unpleasant truths, and altogether avoiding the least soupcon of flattery. Though I was not so much flattered as amused–considering the position of affairs. Just then a servant threw open the door and announced dinner. I set my child very gently down from my knee and whisperingly told her that I would come and see her soon again. She smiled trustfully, and then in obedience to her mother's imperative gesture, slipped quietly out of the room. As soon as she had gone I praised her beauty warmly, for she was really a lovely little thing–but I could see my admiration of her was not very acceptable to either my wife or her lover. We all went in to dinner–I, as guest, having the privilege of escorting my fair and spotless spouse! On our reaching the dining-room Nina said–

"You are such an old friend of the family, conte, that perhaps you will not mind sitting at the head of the table?"

"*Tropp' onore, signora!*" I answered, bowing gallantly, as I at once resumed my rightful place at my own table, Ferrari placing himself on my right hand, Nina on my left. The butler, my father's servant and mine, stood as of old behind my chair, and I noticed that each time he supplied me with wine he eyed me with a certain timid curiosity—but I knew I had a singular and conspicuous appearance, which easily accounted for his inquisitiveness. Opposite to where I sat, hung my father's portrait—the character I personated permitted me to look at it fixedly and give full vent to the deep sigh which in very earnest broke from my heart. The eyes of the picture seemed to gaze into mine with a sorrowful compassion—almost I fancied the firm-set lips trembled and moved to echo my sigh.

"Is that a good likeness?" Ferrari asked, suddenly.

I started, and recollecting myself, answered: "Excellent! So true a resemblance that it arouses along train of memories in my mind— memories both bitter and sweet. Ah! what a proud fellow he was!"

"Fabio was also very proud," chimed in my wife's sweet voice. "Very cold and haughty."

Little liar! How dared she utter this libel on my memory! Haughty, I might have been to others, but never to her—and coldness was no part of my nature. Would that it were! Would that I had been a pillar of ice, incapable of thawing in the sunlight of her witching smile! Had she forgotten what a slave I was to her? what a poor, adoring, passionate fool I became under the influence of her hypocritical caresses! I thought this to myself, but I answered aloud:

"Indeed! I am surprised to hear that. The Romani hauteur had ever to my mind something genial and yielding about it—I know my friend was always most gentle to his dependents."

The butler here coughed apologetically behind his hand—an old trick of his, and one which signified his intense desire to speak.

Ferrari laughed, as he held out his glass for more wine.

"Here is old Giacomo," he said, nodding to him lightly. "He remembers both the Romanis—ask him HIS opinion of Fabio—he worshiped his master."

I turned to my servant, and with a benignant air addressed him:

"Your face is not familiar to me, my friend," I said. "Perhaps you were not here when I visited the elder Count Romani?"

"No, *eccellenza*," replied Giacomo, rubbing his withered hands nervously together, and speaking with a sort of suppressed eagerness, "I came into my lord's service only a year before the countess died—I mean the mother of the young count."

"Ah! then I missed making your acquaintance," I said, kindly, pitying the poor old fellow, as I noticed how his lips trembled, and how altogether broken he looked. "You knew the last count from childhood, then?"

"I did, *eccellenza*!" And his bleared eyes roved over me with a sort of alarmed inquiry.

"You loved him well?" I said, composedly, observing him with embarrassment.

"*Eccellenza*, I never wish to serve a better master. He was goodness itself—a fine, handsome, generous lad—the saints have his soul in their keeping! Though sometimes I cannot believe he is dead—my old heart almost broke when I heard it. I have never been the same since—my lady will tell you so—she is often displeased with me."

And he looked wistfully at her; there was a note of pleading in his hesitating accents. My wife's delicate brows drew together in a frown, a frown that I had once thought came from mere petulance, but which I was now inclined to accept as a sign of temper. "Yes, indeed, Giacomo," she said, in hard tones, altogether unlike her usual musical voice. "You are growing so forgetful that it is positively annoying. You know I have often to tell you the same thing several times. One command ought to be sufficient for you."

Giacomo passed his hand over his forehead in a troubled way, sighed, and was silent. Then, as if suddenly recollecting his duty, he refilled my glass, and shrinking aside, resumed his former position behind my chair.

The conversation now turned on desultory and indifferent matters. I knew my wife was an excellent talker, but on that particular evening I think she surpassed herself. She had resolved to fascinate me, THAT I saw at once, and she spared no pains to succeed in her ambition. Graceful sallies, witty bon-mots tipped with the pungent sparkle of satire, gay stories well and briskly told, all came easily from her lips, so that though I knew her so well, she almost surprised me by her variety and fluency. Yet this gift of good conversation in a woman is apt to mislead the judgment of those who listen, for it is seldom the result of thought, and still more seldom is it a proof of intellectual capacity. A woman talks as a brook babbles; pleasantly, but without depth. Her information is generally of the most surface kind—she skims the cream off each item of news, and serves it up to you in her own fashion, caring little whether it be correct or the reverse. And the more vivaciously she talks, the more likely she is to be dangerously insincere and cold-hearted, for the very sharpness of her wit is apt to spoil the more delicate perceptions of her nature. Show me a brilliant woman noted for turning an epigram or pointing a satire, and I will show you a creature whose life is a masquerade, full of vanity, sensuality and pride. The man who marries such a one must be content to take the second place in his household, and play the character of the henpecked husband with what meekness he best may. Answer me, ye long suffering spouses of "society women" how much would you give to win back your freedom and self-respect? to be able to hold your head up unabashed before your own servants? to feel that you can actually give an order without its being instantly countermanded? Ah, my poor friends! millions will not purchase you such joy; as long as your fascinating fair ones are like Caesar's wife, "above suspicion" (and they are generally prudent managers), so long must you dance in their chains like the good-natured clumsy bears that you are, only giving vent to a growl now and then; a growl which at best only excites ridicule. My wife was of the true world worldly; never had I seen her real character so plainly as now, when she exerted herself to entertain and charm me. I had thought her *spirituelle*, ethereal, angelic! never was there less of an angel than she! While she talked, I was quick to observe the changes on Ferrari's countenance. He became more silent and sullen as her brightness and cordiality increased. I would not appear aware of the growing stiffness in his demeanor; I continued to draw him into the conversation, forcing him to give opinions on various subjects connected with the art of which he was professedly a follower. He was very reluctant to speak at all; and when compelled to do so, his remarks were curt and almost snappish, so much so that my wife made a laughing comment on his behavior.

"You are positively ill-tempered, Guido!" she exclaimed, then remembering she had addressed him by his Christian name, she turned to me and added—"I always call him Guido, *en famille*; you know he is just like a brother to me."

He looked at her and his eyes flashed dangerously, but he was mute. Nina was evidently pleased to see him in such a vexed mood; she delighted to pique his pride, and as he steadily gazed at her in a sort of reproachful wonder, she laughed joyously. Then rising from the table, she made us a coquettish courtesy.

"I will leave you two gentlemen to finish your wine together," she said, "I know all men love to talk a little scandal, and they must be alone to enjoy it. Afterward, will you join me in the veranda? You will find coffee ready."

I hastened to open the door for her as she passed out smiling; then, returning to the table, I poured out more wine for myself and Ferrari, who sat gloomily eying his own reflection in the broad polished rim of a silver fruit-dish that stood near him. Giacomo, the butler, had long ago left the room; we were entirely alone. I thought over my plans for a moment or two; the game was as interesting as a problem in chess. With the deliberation of a prudent player I made my next move.

"A lovely woman!" I murmured, meditatively, sipping my wine, "and intelligent also. I admire your taste, *signor!*"

He started violently. "What—what do you mean?" he demanded, half fiercely. I stroked my mustache and smiled at him benevolently.

"Ah, young blood! young blood!" I sighed, shaking my head, "it will have its way! My good sir, why be ashamed of your feelings? I heartily sympathize with you; if the lady does not appreciate the affection of so ardent and gallant an admirer, then she is foolish indeed! It is not every woman who has such a chance of happiness."

"You think—you imagine that—that—I—"

"That you are in love with her?" I said, composedly. "*Ma—certamente!* And why not? It is as it should be. Even the late conte could wish no fairer fate for his beautiful widow than that she should become the wife of his chosen friend. Permit me to drink your health! Success to your love!" And I drained my glass as I finished speaking. Unfortunate fool! He was completely disarmed; his suspicions of me melted away like mist before the morning light. His face cleared—he seized my hand and pressed it warmly.

"Forgive me, conte," he said, with remorseful fervor; "I fear I have been rude and unsociable. Your kind words have put me right again. You will think me a jealous madman, but I really fancied that you were beginning to feel an attraction for her yourself, and actually—(pardon me, I entreat of you!) actually I was making up my mind to—to kill you!"

I laughed quietly. "*Veramente!* How very amiable of you! It was a good intention, but you know what place is paved with similar designs?"

"Ah, conte, it is like your generosity to take my confession so lightly; but I assure you, for the last hour I have been absolutely wretched!"

"After the fashion of all lovers, I suppose," I answered "torturing yourself without necessity! Well, well, it is very amusing! My young friend, when you come to my time of life, you will prefer the chink of gold to the laughter and kisses of women. How often must I repeat to you that I am a man absolutely indifferent to the tender passion? Believe it or not, it is true."

He drank off his wine at one gulp and spoke with some excitement.

"Then I will frankly confide in you. I DO love the contessa. Love! it is too weak a word to describe what I feel. The touch of her hand thrills me, her very voice seems to shake my soul, her eyes burn through me! Ah! YOU cannot know–YOU could not understand the joy, the pain–"

"Calm yourself," I said, in a cold tone, watching my victim as his pent-up emotion betrayed itself, "The great thing is to keep the head cool when the blood burns. You think she loves you?"

"Think! Gran Dio! She has–" here he paused and his face flushed deeply–"nay! I have no right to say anything on that score. I know she never cared for her husband."

"I know that too!" I answered, steadily. "The most casual observer cannot fail to notice it."

"Well, and no wonder!" he exclaimed, warmly. "He was such an undemonstrative fool! What business had such a fellow as that to marry so exquisite a creature!"

My heart leaped with a sudden impulse of fury, but I controlled my voice and answered calmly:

"*Requiescat in pace!* He is dead–let him rest. Whatever his faults, his wife of course was true to him while he lived; she considered him worthy of fidelity–is it not so?"

He lowered his eyes as he replied in an indistinct tone:

"Oh, certainly!"

"And you–you were a most loyal and faithful friend to him,

in spite of the tempting bright eyes of his lady?"

Again he answered huskily, "Why, of course!" But the shapely hand that rested on the table so near to mine trembled.

"Well, then," I continued, quietly, "the love you bear now to his fair widow is, I imagine, precisely what he would approve. Being, as you say, perfectly pure and blameless, what can I wish otherwise than this—may it meet with the reward it deserves!"

While I spoke he moved uneasily in his chair, and his eyes roved to my father's picture with restless annoyance. I suppose he saw in it the likeness to his dead friend. After a moment or two of silence he turned to me with a forced smile—

"And so you really entertain no admiration for the contessa?"

"Oh, pardon me, I DO entertain a very strong admiration for her, but not of the kind you seem to suspect. If it will please you, I can guarantee that I shall never make love to the lady unless—"

"Unless what?" he asked, eagerly.

"Unless she happens to make love to me, In which case it would be ungallant not to reciprocate!"

And I laughed harshly. He stared at me in blank surprise. "SHE make love to YOU!" he exclaimed, "You jest. She would never do such a thing."

"Of course not!" I answered, rising and clapping him heavily on the shoulder. "Women never court men, it is quite unheard of; a reverse of the order of nature! You are perfectly safe, my friend; you will certainly win the recompense you so richly merit. Come, let us go and drink coffee with the fair one."

And arm-in-arm we sauntered out to the veranda in the most friendly way possible. Ferrari was completely restored to good humor, and Nina, I thought, was rather relieved to see it. She was evidently afraid of Ferrari—a good point for me to remember. She smiled a welcome to us as we approached, and began to pour out the fragrant coffee. It was a glorious evening; the moon was already high in the heavens, and the nightingales' voices echoed softly from the distant woods. As I seated myself in a low chair that was placed invitingly near that of my hostess, my ears were startled by a long melancholy howl, which changed every now and then to an impatient whine.

"What is that?" I asked, though the question was needless, for I knew the sound.

"Oh, it is that tiresome dog Wyvis," answered Nina, in a vexed tone. "He belonged to Fabio. He makes the evening quite miserable with his moaning."

"Where is he?"

"Well, after my husband's death he became so troublesome, roaming all over the house and wailing; and then he would insist on sleeping in Stella's room close to her bedside. He really worried me both day and night, so I was compelled to chain him up."

Poor Wyvis! He was sorely punished for his fidelity.

"I am very fond of dogs," I said, slowly, "and they generally take to me with extraordinary devotion. May I see this one of yours?"

"Oh, certainly! Guido, will you go and unfasten him?"

Guido did not move; he leaned easily back in his chair sipping his coffee.

"Many thanks," he answered, with a half laugh; "perhaps you forget that last time I did so he nearly tore me to pieces. If you do not object, I would rather Giacomo undertook the task."

"After such an account of the animal's conduct, perhaps the conte will not care to see him. It is true enough," turning to me as she spoke, "Wyvis has taken a great dislike to Signor Ferrari—and yet he is a good-natured dog, and plays with my little girl all day if she goes to him. Do you feel inclined to see him? Yes?" And, as I bowed in the affirmative, she rang a little bell twice, and the butler appeared.

"Giacomo," she continued, "unloose Wyvis and send him

here."

Giacomo gave me another of those timid questioning glances, and departed to execute his order. In another five minutes, the howling had suddenly ceased, a long, lithe, black, shadowy creature came leaping wildly across the moonlighted lawn–Wyvis was racing at full speed. He paid no heed to his mistress or Ferrari; he rushed straight to me with a yelp of joy. His huge tail wagged incessantly, he panted thirstily with excitement, he frisked round and round my chair, he abased himself and kissed my feet and hands, he rubbed his stately head fondly against my knee. His frantic demonstrations of delight were watched by my wife and Ferrari with utter astonishment. I observed their surprise, and said lightly:

"I told you how it would be! It is nothing remarkable, I assure you. All dogs treat me in the same way."

And I laid my hand on the animal's neck with a commanding pressure; he lay down at once, only now and then raising his large wistful brown eyes to my face as though he wondered what had changed it so greatly. But no disguise could deceive his intelligence–the faithful creature knew his master. Meantime I thought Nina looked pale; certainly the little jeweled white hand nearest to me shook slightly.

"Are you afraid of this noble animal, *madame*?" I asked, watching her closely. She laughed, a little forcedly.

"Oh, no! But Wyvis is usually so shy with strangers, and I never saw him greet any one so rapturously except my late husband. It is really very odd!"

Ferrari, by his looks, agreed with her, and appeared to be uneasily considering the circumstance.

"Strange to say," he remarked, "Wyvis has for once forgotten me. He never fails to give me a passing snarl."

Hearing his voice, the dog did indeed commence growling discontentedly; but a touch from me silenced him. The animal's declared enmity toward Ferrari surprised me–it was quite a new thing, as before my burial his behavior to him had been perfectly friendly.

174

"I have had a great deal to do with dogs in my time," I said, speaking in a deliberately composed voice. "I have found their instinct marvelous; they generally seem to recognize at once the persons who are fond of their society. This Wyvis of yours, contessa, has no doubt discovered that I have had many friends among his brethren, so that there is nothing strange in his making so much of me."

The air of studied indifference with which I spoke, and the fact of my taking the exuberant delight of Wyvis as a matter of course, gradually reassured the plainly disturbed feelings of my two betrayers, for after a little pause the incident was passed over, and our conversation went on with pleasant and satisfactory smoothness. Before my departure that evening, however, I offered to chain up the dog—"as, if I do this," I added, "I guarantee he will not disturb your night's rest by his howling."

This suggestion met with approval, and Ferrari walked with me to show me where the kennel stood. I chained Wyvis, and stroked him tenderly; he appeared to understand, and he accepted his fate with perfect resignation, lying down upon his bed of straw without a sign of opposition, save for one imploring look out of his intelligent eyes as I turned away and left him.

On making my adieus to Nina, I firmly refused Ferrari's offered companionship in the walk back to my hotel.

"I am fond of a solitary moonlight stroll," I said. "Permit me to have my own way in the matter."

After some friendly argument they yielded to my wishes. I bade them both a civil "good-night," bending low over my wife's hand and kissing it, coldly enough, God knows, and yet the action was sufficient to make her flush and sparkle with pleasure. Then I left them, Ferrari himself escorting me to the villa gates, and watching me pass out on the open road. As long as he stood there, I walked with a slow and meditative pace toward the city, but the instant I heard the gate clang heavily as it closed, I hurried back with a cautious and noiseless step. Avoiding the great entrance, I slipped round to the western side of the grounds, where there was a close thicket of laurel that extended almost up to the veranda I had just left. Entering this and bending the boughs softly aside as I pushed my way through, I gradually reached a position from whence I could see the veranda plainly, and also hear anything that passed. Guido was sitting on the low chair I had just vacated, leaning his head back against my wife's breast; he had reached up one arm so that it encircled her neck, and drew her head down toward his. In this half embrace they rested absolutely silent for some moments. Suddenly Ferrari spoke:

"You are very cruel, Nina! You actually made me think you admired that rich old conte."

She laughed. "So I do! He would be really handsome if he did not wear those ugly spectacles. And his jewels are lovely. I wish he would give me some more!"

"And supposing he were to do so, would you care for him, Nina?" he demanded, jealously. "Surely not. Besides, you have no idea how conceited he is. He says he will never make love to a woman unless she first makes love to him; what do you think of that?"

She laughed again, more merrily than before.

"Think! Why, that he is very original–charmingly so! Are you coming in, Guido?"

He rose, and standing erect, almost lifted her from her chair and folded her in his arms.

"Yes, I AM coming in," he answered; "and I will have a hundred kisses for every look and smile you bestowed on the conte! You little coquette! You would flirt with your grandfather!"

She rested against him with apparent tenderness, one hand playing with the flower in his buttonhole, and then she said, with a slight accent of fear in her voice–

"Tell me, Guido, do you not think he is a little like–like FABIO? Is there not a something in his manner that seems familiar?"

"I confess I have fancied so once or twice," he returned, musingly; "there is rather a disagreeable resemblance. But what of that? many men are almost counterparts of each other. But I tell you what I think. I am almost positive he is some long-lost relation of the family–Fabio's uncle for all we know, who does not wish to declare his actual relationship. He is a good old fellow enough, I believe, and is certainly rich as Croesus; he will be a valuable friend to us both. Come, *sposina mia*, it is time to go to rest."

And they disappeared within the house, and shut the windows after them. I immediately left my hiding-place, and resumed my way toward Naples. I was satisfied they had no suspicion of the truth. After all, it was absurd of me to fancy they might have, for people in general do not imagine it possible for a buried man to come back to life again. The game was in my own hands, and I now resolved to play it out with as little delay as possible.

16

TIME FLEW swiftly on—a month, six weeks, passed, and during that short space I had established myself in Naples as a great personage—great, because of my wealth and the style in which I lived. No one in all the numerous families of distinction that eagerly sought my acquaintance cared whether I had intellect or intrinsic personal worth; it sufficed to them that I kept a carriage and pair, an elegant and costly equipage, softly lined with satin and drawn by two Arabian mares as black as polished ebony. The value of my friendship was measured by the luxuriousness of my box at the opera, and by the dainty fittings of my yacht, a swift trim vessel furnished with every luxury, and having on board a band of stringed instruments which discoursed sweet music when the moon emptied her horn of silver radiance on the rippling water. In a little while I knew everybody who was worth knowing in Naples; everywhere my name was talked of, my doings were chronicled in the fashionable newspapers; stories of my lavish generosity were repeated from mouth to mouth, and the most highly colored reports of my immense revenues were whispered with a kind of breathless awe at every cafe and street corner. Tradesmen waylaid my reticent valet, Vincenzo, and gave him douceurs in the hope he would obtain my custom for them—

"tips" which he pocketed in his usual reserved and discreet manner, but which he was always honest enough to tell me of afterward. He would most faithfully give me the name and address of this or that particular tempter of his fidelity, always adding–"As to whether the rascal sells good things or bad our Lady only knows, but truly he gave me thirty francs to secure your Excellency's good-will. Though for all that I would not recommend him if your excellency knows of a more honest man!"

Among other distinctions which my wealth forced upon me, were the lavish attentions of match-making mothers. The black spectacles which I always wore, were not repulsive to these diplomatic dames– on the contrary, some of them assured me they were most becoming, so anxious were they to secure me as a son-in-law. Fair girls in their teens, blushing and ingenuous, were artfully introduced to me–or, I SHOULD say, thrust forward like slaves in a market for my inspection– though, to do them justice, they were remarkably shrewd and sharp-witted for their tender years. Young as they were, they were keenly alive to the importance of making a good match– and no doubt the pretty innocents laid many dainty schemes in their own minds for liberty and enjoyment when one or the other of them should become the Countess Oliva and fool the old black-spectacled husband to her heart's content. Needless to say their plans were not destined to be fulfilled, though I rather enjoyed studying the many devices they employed to fascinate me. What pretty ogling glances I received!–what whispered admiration of my "beautiful white hair! so distingue"–what tricks of manner, alternating from grave to gay, from rippling mirth to witching languor! Many an evening I sat at ease on board my yacht, watching with a satirical inward amusement, one, perhaps two or three of these fair schemers ransacking their youthful brains for new methods to entrap the old millionaire, as they thought me, into the matrimonial net. I used to see their eyes–sparkling with light in the sunshine– grow liquid and dreamy in the mellow radiance of the October moon, and turn upon me with a vague wistfulness most lovely to behold, and—most admirably feigned! I could lay my hand on a bare round white arm and not be repulsed—I could hold little clinging fingers in my own as long as I liked without giving offense such are some of the privileges of wealth!

In all the parties of pleasure I formed, and these were many—my wife and Ferrari were included as a matter of course. At first Nina demurred, with some plaintive excuse concerning her "recent terrible bereavement," but I easily persuaded her out of this. I even told some ladies I knew to visit her and add their entreaties to mine, as I said, with the benignant air of an elderly man, that it was not good for one so young to waste her time and injure her health by useless grieving. She saw the force of this, I must admit, with admirable readiness, and speedily yielded to the united invitations she received, though always with a well-acted reluctance, and saying that she did so merely "because the Count Oliva was such an old friend of the family and knew my poor dear husband as a child."

On Ferrari I heaped all manner of benefits. Certain debts of his contracted at play I paid privately to surprise him—his gratitude was extreme. I humored him in many of his small extravagances—I played with his follies as an angler plays the fish at the end of his line, and I succeeded in winning his confidence. Not that I ever could surprise him into a confession of his guilty amour—but he kept me well informed as to what he was pleased to call "the progress of his attachment," and supplied me with many small details which, while they fired my blood and brain to wrath, steadied me more surely in my plan of vengeance. Little did he dream in whom he was trusting!—little did he know into whose hands he was playing! Sometimes a kind of awful astonishment would come over me as I listened to his trivial talk, and heard him make plans for a future that was never to be. He seemed so certain of his happiness—so absolutely sure that nothing could or would intervene to mar it. Traitor as he was he was unable to foresee punishment—materialist to the heart's core, he had no knowledge of the divine law of compensation. Now and then a dangerous impulse stirred me–a desire to say to him point-blank:

"You are a condemned criminal–a doomed man on the brink of the grave. Leave this light converse and frivolous jesting–and, while there is time, prepare for death!"

But I bit my lips and kept stern silence. Often, too, I felt disposed to seize him by the throat, and, declaring my identity, accuse him of his treachery to his face, but I always remembered and controlled myself. One point in his character I knew well–I had known it of old–this was his excessive love of good wine. I aided and abetted him in this weakness, and whenever he visited me I took care that he should have his choice of the finest vintages. Often after a convivial evening spent in my apartments with a few other young men of his class and caliber, he reeled out of my presence, his deeply flushed face and thick voice bearing plain testimony as to his condition. On these occasions I used to consider with a sort of fierce humor how Nina would receive him–for though she saw no offense in the one kind of vice she herself practiced, she had a particular horror of vulgarity in any form, and drunkenness was one of those low failings she specially abhorred.

"Go to your lady-love, *mon beau* Silenus!" I would think, as I watched him leaving my hotel with a couple of his boon companions, staggering and laughing loudly as he went, or singing the last questionable street-song of the Neapolitan *bas-peuple*. "You are in a would-be riotous and savage mood–her finer animal instincts will revolt from you, as a lithe gazelle would fly from the hideous gambols of a rhinoceros. She is already afraid of you–in a little while she will look upon you with loathing and disgust–*tant pis pour vous, tant mieux pour moi!*"

I had of course attained the position of *ami intime* at the Villa Romani. I was welcome there at any hour–I could examine and read my own books in my own library at leisure (what a privilege was mine); I could saunter freely through the beautiful gardens accompanied by Wyvis, who attended me as a matter of course; in short, the house was almost at my disposal, though I never passed a night under its roof. I carefully kept up my character as a prematurely elderly man, slightly invalided by a long and arduous career in far-off foreign lands, and I was particularly prudent in my behavior toward my wife before Ferrari. Never did I permit the least word or action on my part that could arouse his jealousy or suspicion. I treated her with a sort of parental kindness and reserve, but she—trust a woman for intrigue!—she was quick to perceive my reasons for so doing. Directly Ferrari's back was turned she would look at me with a glance of coquettish intelligence, and smile—a little mocking, half-petulant smile—or she would utter some disparaging remark about him, combining with it a covert compliment to me. It was not for me to betray her secrets—I saw no occasion to tell Ferrari that nearly every morning she sent her maid to my hotel with fruit and flowers and inquiries after my health—nor was my valet Vincenzo the man to say that he carried gifts and similar messages from me to her. But at the commencement of November things were so far advanced that I was in the unusual position of being secretly courted by my own wife!—I reciprocating her attentions with equal secrecy! The fact of my being often in the company of other ladies piqued her vanity—she knew that I was considered a desirable party—and—she resolved to win me. In this case I also resolved—to be won! A grim courtship truly—between a dead man and his own widow! Ferrari never suspected what was going on; he had spoken of me as "that poor fool Fabio, he was too easily duped;" yet never was there one more "easily duped" than himself, or to whom the epithet "poor fool" more thoroughly applied. As I said before, he was SURE—too sure of his own good fortune. I wished to excite his distrust and enmity sometimes, but this I found I could not do. He trusted me—yes! as much as in the old days I had trusted HIM. Therefore, the catastrophe for him must be sudden as well as fatal—perhaps, after all, it was better so.

During my frequent visits to the villa I saw much of my child Stella. She became passionately attached to me–poor little thing!– her love was a mere natural instinct, had she but known it. Often, too, her nurse, Assunta, would bring her to my hotel to pass an hour or so with me. This was a great treat to her, and her delight reached its climax when I took her on my knee and told her a fairy story–her favorite one being that of a good little girl whose papa suddenly went away, and how the little girl grieved for him till at last some kind fairies helped her to find him again. I was at first somewhat afraid of old Assunta– she had been MY nurse–was it possible that she would not recognize me? The first time I met her in my new character I almost held my breath in a sort of suspense– but the good old woman was nearly blind, and I think she could scarce make out my lineaments. She was of an entirely different nature to Giacomo the butler–she thoroughly believed her master to be dead, as indeed she had every reason to do, but strange to say, Giacomo did not. The old man had a fanatical notion that his "young lord" could not have died so suddenly, and he grew so obstinate on the point that my wife declared he must be going crazy. Assunta, on the other hand, would talk volubly of my death and tell me with assured earnestness:

"It was to be expected, *eccellenza*–he was too good for us, and the saints took him. Of course our Lady wanted him–she always picks out the best among us. The poor Giacomo will not listen to me, he grows weak and childish, and he loved the master too well–better," and here her voice would deepen into reproachful solemnity, "yes, better actually than St. Joseph himself! And of course one is punished for such a thing. I always knew my master would die young–he was too gentle as a baby, and too kind-hearted as a man to stay here long."

And she would shake her gray head and feel for the beads of her rosary, and mutter many an Ave for the repose of my soul. Much as I wished it, I could never get her to talk about her mistress–it was the one subject on which she was invariably silent. On one occasion when I spoke with apparent enthusiasm of the beauty and accomplishments of the young countess, she glanced at me with sudden and earnest scrutiny–sighed–but said nothing. I was glad to see how thoroughly devoted she was to Stella, and the child returned her affection with interest–though as the November days came on, my little one looked far from strong. She paled and grew thin, her eyes looked preternaturally large and solemn, and she was very easily wearied. I called Assunta's attention to these signs of ill-health; she replied that she had spoken to the countess, but that "madam" had taken no notice of the child's weakly condition. Afterward I mentioned the matter myself to Nina, who merely smiled gratefully up in my face and answered:

"Really, my dear conte, you are too good! There is nothing the matter with Stella, her health is excellent; she eats too many bonbons, perhaps, and is growing rather fast, that is all. How kind you are to think of her! But, I assure you, she is quite well."

I did not feel so sure of this, yet I was obliged to conceal my anxiety, as overmuch concern about the child would not have been in keeping with my assumed character.

It was a little past the middle of November, when a circumstance occurred that gave impetus to my plans, and hurried them to full fruition. The days were growing chilly and sad even in Naples– yachting excursions were over, and I was beginning to organize a few dinners and balls for the approaching winter season, when one afternoon Ferrari entered my room unannounced and threw himself into the nearest chair with an impatient exclamation, and a vexed expression of countenance.

"What is the matter?" I asked, carelessly, as I caught a furtive glance of his eyes. "Anything financial? Pray draw upon me! I will be a most accommodating banker!"

He smiled uneasily though gratefully.

"Thanks, conte–but it is nothing of that sort–it is–gran Dio! what an unlucky wretch I am!"

"I hope," and here I put on an expression of the deepest anxiety, "I hope the pretty contessa has not played you false? she has refused to marry you?"

He laughed with a disdainful triumph in his laughter.

"Oh, as far as that goes there is no danger! She dares not play me false."

"DARES not! That is rather a strong expression, my friend!" And I stroked my beard and looked at him steadily. He himself seemed to think he had spoken too openly and hastily—for he reddened as he said with a little embarrassment:

"Well, I did not mean that exactly—of course she is perfectly free to do as she likes—but she cannot, I think, refuse me after showing me so much encouragement."

I waved my hand with an airy gesture of amicable agreement.

"Certainly not," I said, "unless she be an errant coquette and therefore a worthless woman, and you, who know so well her intrinsic goodness and purity, have no reason to fear. But, if not love or money, what is it that troubles you? It must be serious, to judge from your face."

He played absently with a ring I had given him, turning it round and round upon his finger many times before replying.

"Well, the fact is," he said at last, "I am compelled to go away—to leave Naples for a time."

My heart gave an expectant throb of satisfaction. Going away!— leaving Naples!—turning away from the field of battle and allowing me to gain the victory! Fortune surely favored me. But I answered with feigned concern:

"Going away! Surely you cannot mean it. Why?—what for? and where?"

"An uncle of mine is dying in Rome," he answered, crossly. "He has made me his heir, and I am bound for the sake of decency to attend his last moments. Rather protracted last moments they threaten to be too, but the lawyers say I had better be present, as the old man may take it into his head to disinherit me at the final gasp. I suppose I shall not be absent long–a fortnight at most–and in the meanwhile–"

Here he hesitated and looked at me anxiously.

"Continue, *caro mio*, continue!" I said with some impatience. "If I can do anything in your absence, you have only to command me."

He rose from his chair, and approaching the window where I sat in a half-reclining position, he drew a small chair opposite mine, and sitting down, laid one hand confidingly on my wrist.

"You can do much!" he replied, earnestly, "and I feel that I can thoroughly depend upon you. Watch over HER! She will have no other protector, and she is so beautiful and careless! You can guard her– your age, your rank and position, the fact of your being an old friend of the family–all these things warrant your censorship and vigilance over her, and you can prevent any other man from intruding himself upon her notice–"

"If he does," I exclaimed, starting up from my seat with a mock tragic air, "I will not rest till his body serves my sword as a sheath!"

And I laughed loudly, clapping him on the shoulder as I spoke. The words were the very same he had himself uttered when I had witnessed his interview with my wife in the avenue. He seemed to find something familiar in the phrase, for he looked confused and puzzled. Seeing this, I hastened to turn the current of his reflections. Stopping abruptly in my mirth, I assumed a serious gravity of demeanor, and said:

"Nay, nay! I see the subject is too sacred to be jested with– pardon my levity! I assure you, my good Ferrari, I will watch over the lady with the jealous scrutiny of a BROTHER–an elderly brother too, and therefore one more likely to be a model of propriety. Though I frankly admit it is a task I am not specially fitted for, and one that is rather distasteful to me, still, I would do much to please you, and enable you to leave Naples with an easy mind I promise you"–here I took his hand and shook it warmly–"that I will be worthy of your trust and true to it, with exactly the same fine loyalty and fidelity you yourself so nobly showed to your dead friend Fabio! History cannot furnish me with a better example!"

He started as if he had been stung, and every drop of blood receded from his face, leaving it almost livid. He turned his eyes in a kind of wondering doubt upon me, but I counterfeited an air of such good faith and frankness, that he checked some hasty utterance that rose to his lips, and mastering himself by a strong effort, said, briefly:

"I thank you! I know I can rely upon your honor."

"You can!" I answered, decisively–"as positively as you rely upon your own!" Again he winced, as though whipped smartly by an invisible lash. Releasing his hand, I asked, in a tone of affected regret

"And when must you leave us, carino?"

"Most unhappily, at once," he answered "I start by the early train to-morrow morning"

"Well, I am glad I knew of this in time," I said, glancing at my writing-table, which was strewn with unsent invitation cards, and estimates from decorators and ball furnishers. "I shall not think of starting any more gayeties till you return."

He looked gratefully at me "Really? It is very kind of you, but I should be sorry to interfere with any of your plans–"

"Say no more about it, amico" I interrupted him lightly "Everything can wait till you come back. Besides, I am sure you will prefer to think of *madame* as living in some sort of seclusion during your enforced absence–"

"I should not like her to be dull!" he eagerly exclaimed.

"Oh, no!" I said, with a slight smile at his folly, as if she– Nina–would permit herself to be dull! "I will take care of that. Little distractions, such as a drive now and then, or a very quiet, select musical evening! I understand–leave it all to me! But the dances, dinners, and other diversions shall wait till your return."

A delighted look flashed into his eyes. He was greatly flattered and pleased.

"You are uncommonly good to me, conte!" he said,

earnestly. "I can never thank you sufficiently."

"I shall demand a proof of your gratitude someday," I answered. "And now, had you not better be packing your portmanteau? To-morrow will soon be here. I will come and see you off in the morning."

Receiving this assurance as another testimony of my friendship, he left me. I saw him no more that day; it was easy to guess where he was! With my wife, of course!—no doubt binding her, by all the most sacred vows he could think of or invent, to be true to him—as true as she had been false to me. In fancy I could see him clasping her in his arms, and kissing her many times in his passionate fervor, imploring her to think of him faithfully, night and day, till he should again return to the joy of her caresses! I smiled coldly, as this glowing picture came before my imagination. Ay, Guido! kiss her and fondle her now to your heart's content—it is for the last time! Never again will that witching glance be turned to you in either fear or favor—never again will that fair body nestle in your jealous embrace—never again will your kisses burn on that curved sweet mouth; never, never again! Your day is done—the last brief moments of your sin's enjoyment have come—make the most of them!— no one shall interfere! Drink the last drop of sweet wine—MY hand shall not dash the cup from your lips on this, the final night of your amour! Traitor, liar, and hypocrite! make haste to be happy for the short time that yet remains to you—shut the door close, lest the pure pale stars behold your love ecstasies! but let the perfumed lamps shed their softest artificial luster on all that radiant beauty which tempted your sensual soul to ruin, and of which you are now permitted to take your last look! Let there be music too—the music of her voice, which murmurs in your ear such entrancing falsehoods! "She will be true," she says. You must believe her, Guido, as I did—and, believing her thus, part from her as lingeringly and tenderly as you will—part from her—FOREVER!

17

NEXT MORNING I kept my appointment and met Ferrari at the railway station. He looked pale and haggard, though he brightened a little on seeing me. He was curiously irritable and fussy with the porters concerning his luggage, and argued with them about some petty trifles as obstinately and pertinaciously as a deaf old woman. His nerves were evidently jarred and unstrung, and it was a relief when he at last got into his coupe. He carried a yellow paper-covered volume in his hand. I asked him if it contained any amusing reading.

"I really do not know," he answered, indifferently, "I have only just bought it. It is by Victor Hugo."

And he held up the title-page for me to see.

"*Le Dernier Jour d'un Condamne*," I read aloud with careful slowness. " Ah, indeed! You do well to read that. It is a very fine study!"

The train was on the point of starting, when he leaned out of the carriage window and beckoned me to approach more closely.

"Remember!" he whispered, "I trust you to take care of her!"

"Never fear!" I answered, "I will do my best to replace YOU!"

He smiled a pale uneasy smile, and pressed my hand. These were our last words, for with a warning shriek the train moved off, and in another minute had rushed out of sight. I was alone–alone with perfect freedom of action–I could do as I pleased with my wife now! I could even kill her if I chose–no one would interfere. I could visit her that evening and declare myself to her–could accuse her of her infidelity and stab her to the heart! Any Italian jury would find "extenuating circumstances" for me. But why? Why should I lay myself open to a charge of murder, even for a just cause? No! my original design was perfect, and I must keep to it and work it out with patience, though patience was difficult. While I thus meditated, walking from the station homeward, I was startled by the unexpected appearance of my valet, who came upon me quite suddenly. He was out of breath with running, and he carried a note for me marked "Immediate." It was from my wife, and ran briefly thus:

"Please come at once. Stella is very ill, and asks for you."

"Who brought this?" I demanded, quickening my pace, and signing to Vincenzo to keep beside me.

"The old man, *eccellenza*–Giacomo. He was weeping and in great trouble–he said the little *donzella* had the fever in her throat–it is the diphtheria he means, I think. She was taken ill in the middle of the night, but the nurse thought it was nothing serious. This morning she has been getting worse, and is in danger."

"A doctor has been sent for, of course?"

"Yes, *eccellenza*. So Giacomo said. But–"

"But WHAT?" I asked, quickly.

"Nothing, *eccellenza*! Only the old man said the doctor had come too late."

My heart sunk heavily, and a sob rose in my throat. I stopped in my rapid walk and bade Vincenzo call a carriage, one of the ordinary vehicles that are everywhere standing about for hire in the principal thoroughfares of Naples. I sprung into this and told the driver to take me as quickly as possible to the

Villa Romani, and adding to Vincenzo that I should not return to the hotel all day, I was soon rattling along the uphill road. On my arrival at the villa I found the gates open, as though in expectation of my visit, and as I approached the entrance door of the house, Giacomo himself met me.

"How is the child?" I asked him eagerly.

He made no reply, but shook his head gravely, and pointed to a kindly looking man who was at that moment descending the stairs–a man whom I instantly recognized as a celebrated English doctor resident in the neighborhood. To him I repeated my inquiry–he beckoned me into a side room and closed the door.

"The fact is," he said, simply, "it is a case of gross neglect. The child has evidently been in a weakly condition for some time past, and therefore is an easy prey to any disease that may be lurking about. She was naturally strong–I can see that–and had I been called in when the symptoms first developed themselves, I could have cured her. The nurse tells me she dared not enter the mother's room to disturb her after midnight, otherwise she would have called her to see the child– it is unfortunate, for now I can do nothing."

I listened like one in a dream. Not even old Assunta dared to enter her mistress's room after midnight–no! not though the child might be seriously ill and suffering. I knew the reason well–too well! And so while Ferrari had taken his fill of rapturous embraces and lingering farewells, my little one had been allowed to struggle in pain and fever without her mother's care or comfort. Not that such consolation would have been much at its best, but I was fool enough to wish there had been this one faint spark of womanhood left in her upon whom I had wasted all the first and only love of my life. The doctor watched me as I remained silent, and after a pause he spoke again.

"The child has earnestly asked to see you," he said, "and I persuaded the countess to send for you, though she was very reluctant to do so, as she said you might catch the disease. Of course there is always a risk—"

"I am no coward, monsieur," I interrupted him, "though many of us Italians prove but miserable panic-stricken wretches in time of plague—the more especially when compared with the intrepidity and pluck of Englishmen. Still there are exceptions—"

The doctor smiled courteously and bowed. "Then I have no more to say, except that it would be well for you to see my little patient at once. I am compelled to be absent for half an hour, but at the expiration of that time I will return."

"Stay!" I said, laying a detaining hand on his arm. "Is there any hope?"

He eyed me gravely. "I fear not."

"Can nothing be done?"

"Nothing—except to keep her as quiet and warm as possible. I have left some medicine with the nurse which will alleviate the pain. I shall be able to judge of her better when I return; the illness will have then reached its crisis." In a couple of minutes more he had left the house, and a young maid-servant showed me to the nursery.

"Where is the contessa?" I asked in a whisper, as I trod softly up the stairs.

"The contessa?" said the girl, opening her eyes in astonishment. "In her own bedroom, *eccellenza*—madame would not think of leaving it; because of the danger of infection." I smothered a rough oath that roses involuntarily to my lips. Another proof of the woman's utter heartlessness, I thought!

"Has she not seen her child?"

"Since the illness? Oh, no, *eccellenza!*"

Very gently and on tiptoe I entered the nursery. The blinds were partially drawn as the strong light worried the child, and by the little white bed sat Assunta, her brown face pale and almost rigid with anxiety. At my approach she raised her eyes to mine, muttering softly:

"It is always so. Our Lady will have the best of all, first the father, then the child; it is right and just—only the bad are left."

"Papa!" moaned a little voice feebly, and Stella sat up among her tumbled pillows, with wide-opened wild eyes, feverish cheeks, and parted lips through which the breath came in quick, uneasy gasps. Shocked at the marks of intense suffering in her face, I put my arms tenderly round her–she smiled faintly and tried to kiss me. I pressed the poor parched little mouth and murmured, soothingly:

"Stella must be patient and quiet–Stella must lie down, the pain will be better so; there! that is right!" as the child sunk back on her bed obediently, still keeping her gaze fixed upon me. I knelt at the bedside, and watched her yearningly–while Assunta moistened her lips, and did all she could to ease the pain endured so meekly by the poor little thing whose breathing grew quicker and fainter with every tick of the clock. "You are my papa, are you not?" she asked, a deeper flush crossing her forehead and cheeks. I made no answer–I only kissed the small hot hand I held. Assunta shook her head.

"Ah, *poverinetta*! The time is near–she sees her father. And why not? He loved her well–he would come to fetch her for certain if the saints would let him."

And she fell on her knees and began to tell over her rosary with great devotion. Meanwhile Stella threw one little arm round my neck–her eyes were half shut–she spoke and breathed with increasing difficulty.

"My throat aches so, papa!" she said, pitifully. "Can you not make it better?"

"I wish I could, my darling!" I murmured. "I would bear all the pain for you if it were possible!"

She was silent a minute. Then she said:

"What a long time you have been away! And now I am too ill to play with you!" Then a faint smile crossed her features. "See poor To- to!" she exclaimed, feebly, as her eyes fell on a battered old doll in the spangled dress of a carnival clown that lay at the foot of her bed. "Poor dear old To-to! He will think I do not love him anymore, because my throat hurts me. Give him to me, papa!"

And as I obeyed her request she encircled the doll with one arm, while she still clung to me with the other, and added:

"To-to remembers you, papa; you know you brought him from Rome, and he is fond of you, too—but not as fond as I am!" And her dark eyes glittered feverishly. Suddenly her glance fell on Assunta, whose gray head was buried in her hands as she knelt.

"Assunta!"

The old woman looked up.

"*Bambinetta!*" she answered, and her aged voice trembled.

"Why are you crying?" inquired Stella with an air of plaintive surprise. "Are you not glad to see papa?"

Her words were interrupted by a sharp spasm of pain which convulsed her whole body—she gasped for breath—she was nearly suffocated. Assunta and I raised her up gently and supported her against her pillows; the agony passed slowly, but left her little face white and rigid, while large drops of sweat gathered on her brow. I endeavored to soothe her.

"Darling, you must not talk," I whispered, imploringly; "try to be very still—then the poor throat will not ache so much."

She looked at me wistfully. After a minute or two she said, gently:

"Kiss me, then, and I will be quite good."

I kissed her fondly, and she closed her eyes. Ten, twenty, thirty minutes passed and she did not stir. At the end of that time the doctor entered. He glanced at her, gave me a warning look, and remained standing quietly at the foot of the bed. Suddenly the child woke, and smiled divinely on all three of us.

"Are you in pain, my dear?" I softly asked.

"No!" she answered in a tiny voice, so faint and far away that we held our breath to listen to it; "I am quite well now. Assunta must dress me in my white frock again now papa is here. I knew he would come back!"

And she turned her eyes upon me with a look of bright intelligence.

"Her brain wanders," said the doctor, in a low, pitying

voice; "it will soon be over."

Stella did not hear him; she turned and nestled in my arms, asking in a sort of babbling whisper:

"You did not go away because I was naughty, did you, papa?"

"No darling!" I answered, hiding my face in her curls.

"Why do you have those ugly black things on?" she asked, in the feeblest and most plaintive tone imaginable, so weak that I myself could scarcely hear it; "has somebody hurt your eyes? Let me see your eyes!" I hesitated. Dare I humor her in her fancy? I glanced up. The doctor's head again was turned away, Assunta was on her knees, her face buried in the bed-clothes, praying to her saints; quick as thought I slipped my spectacles slightly down, and looked over them full at my little one. She uttered a soft cry of delight– "Papa! papa!" and stretched out her arms, then a strong and terrible shudder shook her little frame. The doctor came closer–I replaced my glasses without my action being noticed, and we both bent anxiously over the suffering child. Her face paled and grew livid– she made another effort to speak–her beautiful eyes rolled upward and became fixed–she sighed–and sunk back on my shoulder– dying– dead! My poor little one! A hard sob stifled itself in my throat–I clasped the small lifeless body close in my embrace, and my tears fell hot and fast. There was a long silence in the room–a deep, an awe-struck, reverent silence, while the Angel of Death, noiselessly entering and departing, gathered my little white rose for his Immortal garden of flowers.

18

AFTER some little time the doctor's genial voice, slightly tremulous from kindly emotion, roused me from my grief-stricken attitude.

"Monsieur, permit me to persuade you to come away. Poor little child! she is free from pain now. Her fancy that you were her father was a fortunate delusion for her. It made her last moments happy. Pray come with me–I can see this has been a shock to your feelings."

Reverently I laid the fragile corpse back on the yet warm pillows. With a fond touch I stroked the flaxen head; I closed the dark, upturned, and glazing eyes–I kissed the waxen cheeks and lips, and folded the tiny hands in an attitude of prayer. There was a grave smile on the young dead face–a smile of superior wisdom and sweetness, majestic in its simplicity. Assunta rose from her knees and laid her crucifix on the little breast–the tears were running down her worn and withered countenance. As she strove to wipe them away with her apron, she said tremblingly:–

"It must be told to *madame*." A frown came on the doctor's face. He was evidently a true Britisher, decisive in his opinions, and frank enough to declare them openly. "Yes," he said, curtly, "*Madame*, as you call her, should have been here."

"The little angel did not once ask for her," murmured

Assunta.

"True!" he answered. And again there was silence. We stood round the small bed, looking at the empty casket that had held the lost jewel–the flawless pearl of innocent childhood that had gone, according to a graceful superstition, to ornament the festal robes of the Madonna as she walked in all her majesty through heaven. A profound grief was at my heart–mingled with a sense of mysterious and awful satisfaction. I felt, not as though I had lost my child, but had rather gained her to be more entirely mine than ever. She seemed nearer to me dead than she had been when living. Who could say what her future might have been? She would have grown to womanhood–what then? What is the usual fate that falls to even the best woman? Sorrow, pain, and petty worry, unsatisfied longings, incomplete aims, the disappointment of an imperfect and fettered life–for say what you will to the contrary, woman's inferiority to man, her physical weakness, her inability to accomplish any great thing for the welfare of the world in which she lives, will always make her more or less an object of pity. If good, she needs all the tenderness, support, and chivalrous guidance of her master, man–if bad, she merits what she receives, his pitiless disdain and measureless contempt. From all dangers and griefs of the kind my Stella had escaped–for her, sorrow no longer existed. I was glad of it, I thought, as I watched Assunta shutting the blinds close, as a signal to outsiders that death was in the house. At a sign from the doctor I followed him out of the room–on the stairs he turned round abruptly, and asked:

"Will YOU tell the countess?"

"I would rather be excused," I replied, decisively. "I am not at all in the humor for a SCENE."

"You think she will make a scene?" he said with an astonished uplifting of his eyebrows. "I dare say you are right though! She is an excellent actress."

By this time we had reached the foot of the stairs.

"She is very beautiful," I answered evasively.

"Oh, very! No doubt of that!" And here a strange frown contracted the doctor's brow. "For my own taste, I prefer an ugly woman to SUCH beauty."

And with these words he left me, disappearing down the passage which led to "*madama's*" boudoir. Left alone, I paced up and down the drawing-room, gazing abstractedly on its costly fittings, its many luxurious knickknacks and elegancies—most of which I had given to my wife during the first few months of our marriage. By and by I heard the sound of violent hysterical sobbing, accompanied by the noise of hurrying footsteps and the rapid whisking about of female garments. In a few moments the doctor entered with an expression of sardonic amusement on his face. "Yes!" he said in reply to my look of inquiry, "hysterics, lace handkerchiefs, eau-de-Cologne, and attempts at fainting. All very well done! I have assured the lady there is no fear of contagion, as under my orders everything will be thoroughly disinfected. I shall go now. Oh, by the way, the countess requests that you will wait here a few minutes—she has a message for you—she will not detain you long. I should recommend you to get back to your hotel as soon as you can, and take some good wine. *A rivederci!* Anything I can do for you pray command me!"

And with a cordial shake of the hand he left me, and I heard the street door close behind him. Again I paced wearily up and down, wrapped in sorrowful musings. I did not hear a stealthy tread on the carpet behind me, so that when I turned round abruptly, I was startled to find myself face to face with old Giacomo, who held out a note to me on a silver salver, and who meanwhile peered at me with his eager eyes in so inquisitive a manner that I felt almost uneasy.

"And so the little angel is dead!" he murmured in a thin, quavering voice. "Dead! Ay, that is a pity, a pity! But MY master is not dead—no, no! I am not such an old fool as to believe that."

I paid no heed to his rambling talk, but read the message Nina had sent to me through him.

"I am BROKEN-HEARTED!" so ran the delicately penciled lines. "Will you kindly telegraph my DREADFUL loss to Signor Ferrari? I shall be much obliged to you." I looked up from the perfumed missive and down at the old butler's wrinkled visage; he was a short man and much bent, and something in the downward glance I gave him evidently caught and riveted his attention, for Tie clasped his hands together and muttered something I could not hear.

"Tell your mistress," I said, speaking slowly and harshly, "that I will do as she wishes. That I am entirely at her service. Do you understand?"

"Yes, yes! I understand!" faltered Giacomo, nervously, "My master never thought me foolish–I could always understand him."

"Do you know, my friend," I observed, in a purposely cold and cutting tone, "that I have heard somewhat too much about your master? The subject is tiresome to me! Were your master alive, he would say you were in your dotage! Take my message to the countess at once."

The old man's face paled and his lips quivered–he made an attempt to draw up his shrunken figure with a sort of dignity as he answered *"Eccellenza*, my master would never speak to me so–never, never!" Then his countenance fell, and he muttered, softly–"Though it is just–I am a fool–I am mistaken–quite mistaken–there is no resemblance!" After a little pause he added, humbly, "I will take your message, *eccellenza.*" And stooping more than ever, he shambled out of the room. My heart smote me as he disappeared; I had spoken very harshly to the poor old fellow–but I instinctively felt that it was necessary to do so. His close and ceaseless examination of me–his timidity when he approached me–the strange tremors he experienced when I addressed him, were so many warnings to me to be on my guard with this devoted domestic. Were he, by some unforeseen chance, to recognize me, my plans would all be spoiled. I took my hat and left the house. As I crossed the upper terrace, I saw a small round object lying in the grass–it was Stella's ball that she used to throw for Wyvis to catch and bring to her. I picked up the poor plaything tenderly and put it in my pocket–and glancing up once more at the darkened nursery windows, I waved a kiss of farewell to my little one lying there in her last sleep. Then fiercely controlling all the weaker and softer emotions that threatened to overwhelm me, I hurried away. On my road to the hotel I stopped at the telegraph-office and dispatched the news of Stella's death to Guido Ferrari in Rome. He would be surprised, I thought, but certainly not grieved–the poor child had always been in his way. Would he come back to Naples to console the now childless widow? Not he!–he would know well that she stood in very small need of consolation–and that she took Stella's death as she had taken mine–as a blessing, and not a bereavement. On reaching my own rooms, I gave orders to Vincenzo that I was not at home to anyone who might call– and I passed the rest of the day in absolute solitude. I had much to think of. The last frail tie between my wife and myself had been snapped asunder–the child, the one innocent link in the long chain of falsehood and deception, no longer existed. Was I glad or sorry for this? I asked myself the question a hundred times, and I admitted the truth, though I trembled to realize it. I was GLAD–yes–GLAD! Glad that my own child was dead! You call this inhuman perhaps? Why? She was bound to have been miserable; she was now happy!

The tragedy of her parents' lives could be enacted without embittering and darkening her young days, she was out of it all, and I rejoiced to know it. For I was absolutely relentless; had my little Stella lived, not even for her sake would I have relaxed in one detail of my vengeance–nothing seemed to me so paramount as the necessity for restoring my own self-respect and damaged honor. In England I know these things are managed by the Divorce Court. Lawyers are paid exorbitant fees, and the names of the guilty and innocent are dragged through the revolting slums of the low London press. It may be an excellent method–but it does not tend to elevate a man in his own eyes, and it certainly does not do much to restore his lost dignity. It has one advantage–it enables the criminal parties to have their way without further interference–the wronged husband is set free–left out in the cold–and laughed at by those who wronged him. An admirable arrangement no doubt–but one that would not suit me. *Chacun a son gout!* It would be curious to know in matters of this kind whether divorced persons are really satisfied when they have got their divorce–whether the amount of red tape and parchment expended in their interest has done them good and really relieved their feelings. Whether, for instance, the betrayed husband is glad to have got rid of his unfaithful wife by throwing her (with the full authority and permission of the law) into his rival's arms? I almost doubt it! I heard of a strange case in England once. A man, moving in good society, having more than suspicions of his wife's fidelity, divorced her–the law pronounced her guilty. Some years afterward, he being free, met her again, fell in love with her for the second time and remarried her. She was (naturally!) delighted at his making such a fool of himself–for henceforth, whatever she chose to do, he could not reasonably complain without running the risk of being laughed at. So now the number and variety of her lovers is notorious in the particular social circle where she moves– while he, poor wretch, is perforce tongue-tied, and dare not consider himself wronged. There is no more pitiable object in the world than such a man–secretly derided and jeered at by his fellows, he occupies an almost worse position than that of a galley slave, while in his own esteem he has sunk so low that he dare not, even in secret, try to fathom the depth to which he has fallen. Some may assert that to be divorced is a social stigma. It used to be so perhaps, but society has grown very lenient nowadays. Divorced women hold their own in the best and most brilliant circles, and what is strange is that they are very generally petted and pitied.

"Poor thing!" says society, putting up its eyeglass to scan admiringly the beautiful heroine of the latest aristocratic scandal–"she had such a brute of a husband! No wonder she liked that DEAR Lord So-and-So! Very wrong of her, of course, but she is so young! She was married at sixteen–quite a child!–could not have known her own mind!"

The husband alluded to might have been the best and most chivalrous of men–anything but a "brute"–yet he always figures as such somehow, and gets no sympathy. And, by the way, it is rather a notable fact that all the beautiful, famous, or notorious women were "married at sixteen." How is this managed? I can account for it in southern climates, where girls are full-grown at sixteen and old at thirty–but I cannot understand its being the case in England, where a "miss" of sixteen is a most objectionable and awkward ingénue, without any of the "charms wherewith to charm," and whose conversation is always vapid and silly to the point of absolute exhaustion on the part of those who are forced to listen to it. These sixteen-year-old marriages are, however, the only explanation frisky English matrons can give for having such alarmingly prolific families of tall sons and daughters, and it is a happy and convenient excuse–one that provides a satisfactory reason for the excessive painting of their faces and dyeing of their hair. Being young (as they so nobly assert), they wish to look even younger. *A la bonne heure!* If men cannot see through the delicate fiction, they have only themselves to blame. As for me, I believe in the old, old, apparently foolish legend of Adam and Eve's sin and the curse which followed it–the curse on man is inevitably carried out to this day. God said:

"BECAUSE" (mark that BECAUSE!) "thou hast hearkened unto the voice of thy wife" (or thy WOMAN, whoever she be), "and hast eaten of the tree of which I commanded thee, saying, Thou shalt not eat of it" (the tree or fruit being the evil suggested FIRST to man by woman)," cursed is the ground for thy sake; in sorrow shalt thou eat of it all the days of thy life!"

True enough! The curse is upon all who trust woman too far–the sorrow upon all who are beguiled by her witching

flatteries. Of what avail her poor excuse in the ancient story—
"The serpent beguiled me and I did eat!" Had she never
listened she could not have been beguiled. The weakness, the
treachery, was in herself, and is there still. Through everything
the bitterness of it runs. The woman tempts—the man yields—
and the gate of Eden—the Eden of a clear conscience and an
untrammeled soul, is shut upon them. Forever and ever the
Divine denunciation re-echoes like muttering thunder through
the clouds of passing generations; forever and ever we
unconsciously carry it out in our own lives to its full extent till
the heart grows sick and the brain weary, and we long for the
end of it all, which is death—death, that mysterious silence and
darkness at which we sometimes shudder, wondering vaguely—
Can it be worse than life?

19

MORE THAN ten days had passed since Stella's death. Her mother had asked me to see to the arrangements for the child's funeral, declaring herself too ill to attend to anything. I was glad enough to accede to her request, for I was thus able to avoid the Romani vault as a place of interment. I could not bear to think of the little cherished body being laid to molder in that terrific place where I had endured such frantic horrors. Therefore, informing all whom it concerned that I acted under the countess's orders, I chose a pretty spot in the open ground of the cemetery, close to the tree where I had heard the nightingale singing in my hour of supreme misery and suffering. Here my little one was laid tenderly to rest in warm mother-earth, and I had sweet violets and primroses planted thickly all about the place, while on the simple white marble cross that marked the spot I had the words engraved— "Una Stella svanita," adding the names of her parents and the date of her birth and death. Since all this had been done I had visited my wife several times. She was always at home to me, though of course, for decency's sake, in consequence of the child's death, she denied herself to everybody else. She looked lovelier than ever; the air of delicate languor she assumed suited her as perfectly as its fragile whiteness suits a hot-house lily. She knew the power of her own beauty most thoroughly, and employed it in arduous efforts to fascinate me. But I had changed my tactics; I paid very little heed to her, and never went to see her unless she asked me very pressingly to do so. All compliments and attentions from me to her had ceased. SHE courted me, and I accepted her courtship in unresponsive silence. I played the part of a taciturn and reserved man, who preferred reading some ancient and abstruse treatise on metaphysics to even the charms of her society–and often, when she urgently desired my company, I would sit in her drawing-room, turning over the leaves of a book and feigning to be absorbed in it, while she, from her velvet fauteuil, would look at me with a pretty pensiveness made up half of respect, half of gentle admiration–a capitally acted facial expression, by the bye, and one that would do credit to Sarah Bernhardt. We had both heard from Guido Ferrari; his letter to my wife I of course did not see; she had, however, told me he was "much shocked and distressed to hear of Stella's death." The epistle he addressed to me had a different tale to tell. In it he wrote–

"YOU can understand, my dear conte, that I am not much grieved to hear of the death of Fabio's child. Had she lived, I confess her presence would have been a perpetual reminder to me of things I prefer to forget. She never liked me–she might have been a great source of trouble and inconvenience; so, on the whole, I am glad she is out of the way."

Further on in the letter he informed me:

"My uncle is at death's door, but although that door stands wide open for him, he cannot make up his mind to go in. His hesitation will not be allowed to last, so the doctors tell me–at any rate I fervently hope I shall not be kept waiting too long, otherwise I shall return to Naples and sacrifice my heritage, for I am restless and unhappy away from Nina, though I know she is safely guarded by your protecting care."

I read this particular paragraph to my wife, watching her closely as I slowly enunciated the words contained in it. She listened, and a vivid blush crimsoned her cheeks–a blush of indignation—and her brows contracted in the vexed frown I knew so well. Her lips parted in a half-sweet, half-chilly smile as she said, quietly:

"I owe you my thanks, conte, for showing me to what extent Signor Ferrari's impertinence may reach. I am surprised at his writing to you in such a manner! The fact is, my late husband's attachment for him was so extreme that he now presumes upon a supposed right that he has over me—he fancies I am really his sister, and that he can tyrannize, as brothers sometimes do! I really regret I have been so patient with him—I have allowed him too much liberty."

True enough! I thought and smiled bitterly. I was now in the heat of the game—the moves must be played quickly—there was no more time for hesitation or reflection.

"I think, madam," I said, deliberately, as I folded Guido's letter and replaced it in my pocket-book, "Signor Ferrari ardently aspires to be something more than a brother to you at no very distant date."

Oh, the splendid hypocrisy of women! No wonder they make such excellent puppets on the theatrical stage—acting is their natural existence, sham their breath of life! This creature showed no sign of embarrassment—she raised her eyes frankly to mine in apparent surprise—then she gave a little low laugh of disdain.

"Indeed!" she said. "Then I fear Signor Ferrari is doomed to have his aspirations disappointed! My dear conte," and here she rose and swept softly across the room toward me with that graceful gliding step that somehow always reminded me of the approach of a panther, "do you really mean to tell me that his audacity has reached such a height that—really it is TOO absurd!—that he hopes to marry me? "And sinking into a chair near mine she looked at me in calm inquiry. Lost in amazement at the duplicity of the Vroman, I answered, briefly:

"I believe so! He intimated as much to me." She smiled scornfully.

"I am too much honored! And did you, conte, think for a

moment that such an arrangement would meet with my approval?"

I was silent. My brain was confused—I found it difficult to meet with and confront such treachery as this. What! Had she no conscience? Were all the passionate embraces, the lingering kisses, the vows of fidelity, and words of caressing endearment as naught? Were they all blotted from her memory as the writing on a slate is wiped out by a sponge! Almost I pitied Guido! His fate, in her hands, was evidently to be the same as mine had been; yet after all, why should I be surprised? why should I pity? Had I not calculated it all? and was it not part of my vengeance?

"Tell me!" pursued my wife's dulcet voice, breaking in upon my reflections, "did you really imagine Signer Ferrari's suit might meet with favor at my hands?"

I must speak—the comedy had to be played out. So I answered, bluntly:

"Madam, I certainly did think so. It seemed a natural conclusion to draw from the course of events. He is young, undeniably handsome, and on his uncle's death will be fairly wealthy—what more could you desire? besides, he was your husband's friend—"

"And for that reason I would never marry him!" she interrupted me with a decided gesture. "Even if I liked him sufficiently, which I do not" (oh, miserable traitoress), "I would not run the risk of what the world would say of such a marriage."

"How, madam? Pardon me if I fail to comprehend you."

"Do you not see, conte?" she went on in a coaxing voice, as of one that begged to be believed, "if I were to marry one that was known to have been my husband's most intimate friend, society is so wicked—people would be sure to say that there had been something between us before my husband's death—I KNOW they would, and I could not endure such slander!"

"Murder will out" they say! Here was guilt partially

declaring itself. A perfectly innocent woman could not foresee so readily the condemnation of society. Not having the knowledge of evil she would be unable to calculate the consequences. The over-prudish woman betrays herself; the fine lady who virtuously shudders at the sight of a nude statue or picture, announces at once to all whom it may concern that there is something far coarser in the suggestions of her own mind than the work of art she condemns. Absolute purity has no fear of social slander; it knows its own value, and that it must conquer in the end. My wife—alas! that I should call her so—was innately vicious and false; yet how particular she was in her efforts to secure the blind world's good opinion! Poor old world! how exquisitely it is fooled, and how good-naturedly it accepts its fooling! But I had to answer the fair liar, whose net of graceful deceptions was now spread to entrap me, therefore I said with an effort of courtesy:

"No one would dare to slander you, contessa, in my presence." She bowed and smiled prettily. "But," I went on, "if it is true that you have no liking for Signer Ferrari—"

"It is true!" she exclaimed with sudden emphasis. "He is rough and ill-mannered; I have seen him the worse for wine, sometimes he is insufferable! I am afraid of him!"

I glanced at her quietly. Her face had paled, and her hands, which were busied with some silken embroidery, trembled a little.

"In that case," I continued, slowly, "though I am sorry for Ferrari, poor fellow! he will be immensely disappointed! I confess I am glad in other respects, because—"

"Because what?" she demanded, eagerly. "Why," I answered, feigning a little embarrassment, "because there will be more chance for other men who may seek to possess the hand of the accomplished and beautiful Contessa Romani."

She shook her fair head slightly. A transient expression of disappointment passed over her features.

"The 'other men' you speak of, conte, are not likely to indulge in such an ambition," she said, with a faint sigh; "more especially," and her eyes flashed indignantly, "since Signor Ferrari thinks it his duty to mount guard over me. I suppose he wishes to keep me for himself–a most impertinent and foolish notion! There is only one thing to do–I shall leave Naples before he returns."

"Why?" I asked.

She flushed deeply. "I wish to avoid him," she said, after a little pause; "I tell you frankly, he has lately given me much cause for annoyance. I will not be persecuted by his attentions; and as I before said to you, I am often afraid of him. Under YOUR protection I know I am quite safe, but I cannot always enjoy that."

The moment had come. I advanced a step or two.

"Why not?" I said. "It rests entirely with yourself."

She started and half rose from her chair–her work dropped from her hands.

"What do you mean, conte?" she faltered, half timidly, yet anxiously; "I do not understand!"

"I mean what I say," I continued in cool hard tones, and stooping, I picked up her work and restored it to her; "but pray do not excite yourself! You say you cannot always enjoy my protection; it seems to me that you can–by becoming my wife."

"Conte!" she stammered. I held up my hand as a sign to her to be silent.

"I am perfectly aware," I went on in business-like accents–"of the disparity in years that exists between us. I have neither youth, health, or good looks to recommend me to you. Trouble and bitter disappointment have made me what I am. But I have wealth which is almost inexhaustible–I have position and influence–and beside these things"–and here I looked at her steadily, "I have an ardent desire to do justice to your admirable qualities, and to give you all you deserve. If you think you could be happy with me, speak frankly–I cannot offer you the passionate adoration of a young man–my blood is cold and my pulse is slow–but what I CAN do, I will!"

Having spoken thus, I was silent–gazing at her intently. She paled and flushed alternately, and seemed for a moment lost in thought– then a sudden smile of triumph curved her mouth– she raised her large lovely eyes to mine, with a look of melting and wistful tenderness. She laid her needle-work gently down, and came close up to me–her fragrant breath fell warm on my cheek–her strange gaze fascinated me, and a sort of tremor shook my nerves.

"You mean," she said, with a tender pathos in her voice– "that you are willing to marry me, but that you do not really LOVE me?"

And almost appealingly she laid her white hand on my shoulder–her musical accents were low and thrilling–she sighed faintly. I was silent–battling violently with the foolish desire that had sprung up within me, the desire to draw this witching fragile thing to my heart, to cover her lips with kisses–to startle her with the passion of my embraces! But I forced the mad impulse down and stood mute. She watched me–slowly she lifted her hand from where it had rested, and passed it with a caressing touch through my hair.

"No–you do not really LOVE me," she whispered–"but I will tell you the truth–I LOVE YOU!"

And she drew herself up to her full height and smiled again as she uttered the lie. I knew it was a lie–but I seized the hand whose caresses stung me, and held it hard, as I answered:

"YOU love ME? No, no–I cannot believe it–it is impossible!"

She laughed softly. "It is true though," she said, emphatically, "the very first time I saw you I knew I should love you! I never even liked my husband, and though in some things you resemble him, you are quite different in others–and superior to him in every way. Believe it or not as you like, you are the only man in all the world I have ever loved!"

And she made the assertion unblushingly, with an air of conscious pride and virtue. Half stupefied at her manner, I asked:

"Then you will be my wife?"

"I will!" she answered—"and tell me—your name is Cesare, is it not?"

"Yes," I said, mechanically.

"Then, CESARE" she murmured, tenderly, "I will MAKE you love me very much!"

And with a quick lithe movement of her supple figure, she nestled softly against me, and turned up her radiant glowing face.

"Kiss me!" she said, and waited. As one in a whirling dream, I stooped and kissed those false sweet lips! I would have more readily placed my mouth upon that of a poisonous serpent! Yet that kiss roused a sort of fury in me. I slipped my arms round her half- reclining figure, drew her gently backward to the couch she had left, and sat down beside her, still embracing her. "You really love me?" I asked almost fiercely.

"Yes!"

"And I am the first man whom you have really cared for?

"You are!"

"You never liked Ferrari?"

"Never!"

"Did he ever kiss you as I have done?"

"Not once!"

God! how the lies poured forth! a very cascade of them! and they were all told with such an air of truth! I marveled at the ease and rapidity with which they glided off this fair woman's tongue, feeling somewhat the same sense of stupid astonishment a rustic exhibits when he sees for the first time a conjurer drawing yards and yards of many-colored ribbon out of his mouth. I took up the little hand on which the wedding-ring I had placed there was still worn, and quietly slipped upon the slim finger a circlet of magnificent rose-brilliants. I had long carried this trinket about with me in expectation of the moment that had now come. She started from my arms with an exclamation of delight.

"Oh, Cesare! how lovely! How good you are to me!"

And leaning toward me, she kissed me, then resting against

my shoulder, she held up her hand to admire the flash of the diamonds in the light. Suddenly she said, with some anxiety in her tone:

"You will not tell Guido? not yet?"

"No," I answered; "I certainly will not tell him till he returns. Otherwise he would leave Rome at once, and we do not want him back just immediately, do we?" And I toyed with her rippling gold tresses half mechanically, while I wondered within myself at the rapid success of my scheme. She, in the meantime grew pensive and abstracted, and for a few moments we were both silent. If she had known! I thought, if she could have imagined that she was encircled by the arm of HER OWN HUSBAND, the man whom she had duped and wronged, the poor fool she had mocked at and despised, whose life had been an obstruction in her path, whose death she had been glad of! Would she have smiled so sweetly? Would she have kissed me then?

* * *

She remained leaning against me in a reposeful attitude for some moments, ever and anon turning the ring I had given her round and round upon her finger. By and by she looked up.

"Will you do me one favor?" she asked, coaxingly; "such a little thing–a trifle! but it would give me such pleasure!"

"What is it?" I asked; "it is you to command and I to obey!"

"Well, to take off those dark glasses just for a minute! I want to see your eyes."

I rose from the sofa quickly, and answered her with some coldness.

"Ask anything you like but that, *mia bella*. The least light on my eyes gives me the most acute pain–pain that irritates my nerves for hours afterward. Be satisfied with me as I am for the present, though I promise you your wish shall be gratified–"

"When?" she interrupted me eagerly. I stooped and kissed

her hand.

"On the evening of our marriage day," I answered.

She blushed and turned away her head coquettishly.

"Ah! that is so long to wait!" she said, half pettishly.

"Not very long, I HOPE," I observed, with meaning emphasis. "We are now in November. May I ask you to make my suspense brief? to allow me to fix our wedding for the second month of the new year?"

"But my recent widowhood!—Stella's death!"—she objected faintly, pressing a perfumed handkerchief gently to her eyes.

"In February your husband will have been dead nearly six months," I said, decisively; "it is quite a sufficient period of mourning for one so young as yourself. And the loss of your child so increases the loneliness of your situation, that it is natural, even necessary, that you should secure a protector as soon as possible. Society will not censure you, you may be sure—besides, I shall know how to silence any gossip that savors of impertinence."

A smile of conscious triumph parted her lips.

"It shall be as you wish," she said, demurely; "if you, who are known in Naples as one who is perfectly indifferent to women like now to figure as an impatient lover. I shall not object!"

And she gave me a quick glance of mischievous amusement from under the languid lids of her dreamy dark eyes. I saw it, but answered, stiffly:

"YOU are aware, contessa, and I am also aware that I am not a 'lover' according to the accepted type, but that I am impatient I readily admit."

"And why?" she asked.

"Because," I replied, speaking slowly and emphatically; "I desire you to be mine and mine only, to have you absolutely in my possession, and to feel that no one can come between us, or interfere with my wishes concerning you."

She laughed gaily. "*A la bonne heure!* You ARE a lover without knowing it! Your dignity will not allow you to believe that you are actually in love with me, but in spite of yourself you ARE–you know you are!"

I stood before her in almost somber silence. At last I said: "If YOU say so, contessa, then it must be so. I have had no experience in affairs of the heart, as they are called, and I find it difficult to give a name to the feelings which possess me; I am only conscious of a very strong wish to become the absolute master of your destiny." And involuntarily I clinched my hand as I spoke. She did not observe the action, but she answered the words with a graceful bend of the head and a smile.

"I could not have a better fortune," she said, "for I am sure my destiny will be all brightness and beauty with YOU to control and guide it!"

"It will be what you desire," I half muttered; then with an abrupt change of manner I said: "I will wish you goodnight, contessa. It grows late, and my state of health compels me to retire to rest early."

She rose from her seat and gave me a compassionate look.

"You are really a great sufferer then?" she inquired tenderly. "I am sorry! But perhaps careful nursing will quite restore you. I shall be so proud if I can help you to secure better health."

"Rest and happiness will no doubt do much for me," I answered, "still I warn you, *cara mia*, that in accepting me as your husband you take a broken-down man, one whose whims are legion and whose chronic state of invalidism may in time prove to be a burden on your young life. Are you sure your decision is a wise one?"

"Quite sure!" she replied firmly. "Do I not LOVE you! And you will not always be ailing–you look so strong."

"I am strong to a certain extent," I said, unconsciously straightening myself as I stood. "I have plenty of muscle as far as that goes, but my nervous system is completely disorganized. I–why, what is the matter? Are you ill?"

For she had turned deathly pale, and her eyes look startled and terrified. Thinking she would faint, I extended my arms to save her from falling, but she put them aside with an alarmed yet appealing gesture.

"It is nothing," she murmured feebly, "a sudden giddiness–I thought–no matter what! Tell me, are you not related to the Romani family? When you drew yourself up just now you were so like–like FABIO! I fancied," and she shuddered, "that I saw his ghost!"

I supported her to a chair near the window, which I threw open for air, though the evening was cold.

"You are fatigued and overexcited," I said calmly, "your nature is too imaginative. No; I am not related to the Romanis, though possibly I may have some of their mannerisms. Many men are alike in these things. But you must not give way to such fancies. Rest perfectly quiet, you will soon recover."

And pouring out a glass of water I handed it to her. She sipped it slowly, leaning back in the fauteuil where I had placed her, and in silence we both looked out on the November night. There was a moon, but she was veiled by driving clouds, which ever and anon swept asunder to show her gleaming pallidly white, like the restless spirit of a deceived and murdered lady. A rising wind moaned dismally among the fading creepers and rustled the heavy branches of a giant cypress that stood on the lawn like a huge spectral mourner draped in black, apparently waiting for a forest funeral. Now and then a few big drops of rain fell-sudden tears wrung as though by force from the black heart of the sky. My wife shivered.

"Shut the window!" she said, glancing back at me where I stood behind her chair. "I am much better now. I was very silly. I do not know what came over me, but for the moment I felt afraid–horribly afraid!–of YOU!"

"That was not complimentary to your future husband," I remarked, quietly, as I closed and fastened the window in obedience to her request. "Should I not insist upon an apology?"

She laughed nervously, and played with her ring of rose-brilliants.

"It is not yet too late," I resumed, "if on second thoughts you would rather not marry me, you have only to say so. I shall accept my fate with equanimity, and shall not blame you."

At this she seemed quite alarmed, and rising, laid her hand pleadingly on my arm.

"Surely you are not offended?" she said. "I was not really afraid of you, you know–it was a stupid fancy–I cannot explain it. But I am quite well now, and I am only TOO happy. Why, I would not lose your love for all the world–you MUST believe me!"

And she touched my hand caressingly with her lips. I withdrew it gently, and stroked her hair with an almost parental tenderness; then I said quietly:

"If so, we are agreed, and all is well. Let me advise you to take a long night's rest: your nerves are weak and somewhat shaken. You wish me to keep our engagement secret?"

She thought for a moment, then answered musingly:

"For the present perhaps it would be best. Though," and she laughed, "it would be delightful to see all the other women jealous and envious of my good fortune! Still, if the news were told to any of our friends–who knows?–it might accidentally reach Guido, and–"

"I understand! You may rely upon my discretion. Good-night, contessa!"

"You may call me Nina," she murmured, softly.

"NINA, then," I said, with some effort, as I lightly kissed her. "Good-night!–may your dreams be of me!" She responded to this with a gratified smile, and as I left the room she waved her hand in a parting salute. My diamonds flashed on it like a small circlet of fire; the light shed through the rose-colored lamps that hung from the painted ceiling fell full on her exquisite loveliness, softening it into ethereal radiance and delicacy, and when I strode forth from the house into the night air heavy with the threatening gloom of coming tempest, the picture of that fair face and form flitted before me like a mirage–the glitter of her hair flashed on my vision like little snakes of fire–her lithe hands seemed to beckon me–her lips had left a scorching heat on mine. Distracted with the thoughts that tortured me, I walked on and on for hours. The storm broke at last; the rain poured in torrents, but heedless of wind and weather, I wandered on like a forsaken fugitive. I seemed to be the only human being left alive in a world of wrath and darkness. The rush and roar of the blast, the angry noise of waves breaking hurriedly on the shore, the swirling showers that fell on my defenseless head–all these things were unfelt, unheard by me. There are times in a man's life when mere physical feeling grows numb under the pressure of intense mental agony–when the indignant soul, smarting with the experience of some vile injustice, forgets for a little its narrow and poor house of clay. Some such mood was upon me then, I suppose, for in the very act of walking I was almost unconscious of movement. An awful solitude seemed to encompass me–a silence of my own creating. I fancied that even the angry elements avoided me as I passed; that there was nothing, nothing in all the wide universe but myself and a dark brooding horror called Vengeance. All suddenly, the mists of my mind cleared; I moved no longer in a deaf, blind stupor. A flash of lightning danced vividly before my eyes, followed by a crashing peal of thunder, I saw to what end of a wild journey I had come! Those heavy gates–that undefined stretch of land– those ghostly glimmers of motionless white like spectral mile-stones emerging from the gloom–I knew it all too well–it was the cemetery! I looked through the iron palisades with the feverish interest of one who watches the stage curtain rise on the last scene of a tragedy. The lightning sprung once more across the sky, and showed me for a brief second the distant marble outline of the Romani vault. There the drama began– where would it end? Slowly, slowly there flitted into my thoughts the face of my lost child–the young, serious face as it had looked when the calm, preternaturally wise smile of Death had rested upon it; and then a curious feeling of pity possessed me–pity that her little body should be lying stiffly out there, not in the vault, but under the wet sod, in such a relentless storm of rain. I wanted to take her up from that cold couch—to carry her to some home where there should be light and heat and laughter—to warm her to life again within my arms; and as my brain played with these foolish fancies, slow hot tears forced themselves into my eyes and scalded my cheeks as they fell. These tears relieved me—gradually the tightly strung tension of my nerves relaxed, and I recovered my usual composure by degrees. Turning deliberately away from the beckoning grave-stones, I walked back to the city through the thick of the storm, this time with an assured step and a knowledge of where I was going. I did not reach my hotel till past midnight, but this was not late for Naples, and the curiosity of the fat French hall-porter was not so much excited by the lateness of my arrival as by the disorder of my apparel.

"Ah, Heaven!" he cried; "that monsieur the distinguished should have been in such a storm all unprotected! Why did not monsieur send for his carriage?" I cut short his exclamations by dropping five francs into his ever-ready hand, assuring him that I had thoroughly enjoyed the novelty of a walk in bad weather, whereat he smiled and congratulated me as much as he had just commiserated me. On reaching my own rooms, my valet Vincenzo stared at my dripping and disheveled condition, but was discreetly mute. He quickly assisted me to change my wet clothes for a warm dressing-gown, and then brought a glass of mulled port wine, but performed these duties with such an air of unbroken gravity that I was inwardly amused while I admired the fellow's reticence. When I was about to retire for the night, I tossed him a napoleon. He eyed it musingly and inquiringly; then he asked:

"Your excellency desires to purchase something?"

"Your silence, my friend, that is all!" I replied, with a laugh. "Understand me, Vincenzo, you will serve yourself and me best by obeying implicitly, and asking no questions. Fortunate is the servant who, accustomed to see his master drunk every night, swears to all outsiders that he has never served so sober

and discreet a gentleman! That is your character, Vincenzo—
keep to it, and we shall not quarrel." He smiled gravely, and
pocketed my piece of gold without a word—like a true Tuscan
as he was. The sentimental servant, whose fine feelings will not
allow him to accept an extra "tip," is, you may be sure, a
humbug. I never believed in such a one. Labor can always
command its price, and what so laborious in this age as to be
honest? What so difficult as to keep silence on other people's
affairs? Such herculean tasks deserve payment! A valet who is
generously bribed, in addition to his wages, can be relied on; if
underpaid, all heaven and earth will not persuade him to hold
his tongue. Left alone at last in my sleeping chamber, I
remained for some time before actually going to bed. I took off
the black spectacles which served me so well, and looked at
myself in the mirror with some curiosity. I never permitted
Vincenzo to enter my bedroom at night, or before I was
dressed in the morning, lest he should surprise me without
these appendages which were my chief disguise, for in such a
case I fancy even his studied composure would have given way.
For, disburdened of my smoke-colored glasses, I appeared
what I was, young and vigorous in spite of my white beard and
hair. My face, which had been worn and haggard at first, had
filled up and was healthily colored; while my eyes, the
spokesmen of my thoughts, were bright with the clearness and
fire of constitutional strength and physical well-being. I
wondered, as I stared moodily at my own reflection, how it was
that I did not look ill. The mental suffering I continually
underwent, mingled though it was with a certain gloomy
satisfaction, should surely have left more indelible traces on my
countenance. Yet it has been proved that it is not always the
hollow-eyed, sallow and despairing-looking persons who are
really in sharp trouble—these are more often bilious or
dyspeptic, and know no more serious grief than the incapacity
to gratify their appetites for the high-flavored delicacies of the
table. A man may be endowed with superb physique, and a
constitution that is in perfect working order—his face and

outward appearance may denote the most harmonious action of the life principle within him—and yet his nerves may be so finely strung that he may be capable of suffering acuter agony in his mind than if his body were to be hacked slowly to pieces by jagged knives, and it will leave no mark on his features while YOUTH still has hold on his flesh and blood.

So it was with me; and I wondered what SHE—Nina—would say, could she behold me, unmasked as it were, in the solitude of my own room. This thought roused another in my mind—another at which I smiled grimly. I was an engaged man! Engaged to marry my own wife; betrothed for the second time to the same woman! What a difference between this and my first courtship of her! THEN, who so great a fool as I—who so adoring, passionate and devoted! NOW, who so darkly instructed, who so cold, so absolutely pitiless! The climax to my revenge was nearly reached. I looked through the coming days as one looks through a telescope out to sea, and I could watch the end approaching like a phantom ship—neither slow nor fast, but steadily and silently. I was able to calculate each event in its due order, and I knew there was no fear of failure in the final result. Nature itself—the sun, moon and stars, the sweeping circle of the seasons—all seem to aid in the cause of rightful justice. Man's duplicity may succeed in withholding a truth for a time, but in the end it must win its way. Once resolve, and then determine to carry out that resolve, and it is astonishing to note with what marvelous ease everything makes way for you, provided there be no innate weakness in yourself which causes you to hesitate. I had formerly been weak, I knew, very weak—else I had never been fooled by wife and friend; but now, now my strength was as the strength of a demon working within me. My hand had already closed with an iron grip on two false unworthy lives, and had I not sworn "never to relax, never to relent" till my vengeance was accomplished? I had! Heaven and earth had borne witness to my vow, and now held me to its stern fulfillment.

20

WINTER, or what the Neapolitans accept as winter, came on apace. For some time past the air had been full of that mild chill and vaporous murkiness, which, not cold enough to be bracing, sensibly lowered the system and depressed the spirits. The careless and jovial temperament of the people, however, was never much affected by the change of seasons— they drank more hot coffee than usual, and kept their feet warm by dancing from midnight up to the small hours of the morning. The cholera was a thing of the past—the cleansing of the city, the sanitary precautions, which had been so much talked about and recommended in order to prevent another outbreak in the coming year, were all forgotten and neglected, and the laughing populace tripped lightly over the graves of its dead hundreds as though they were odorous banks of flowers. "*Oggi! Oggi!*" is their cry—to-day, to-day! Never mind what happened yesterday, or what will happen to-morrow—leave that to *i signori Santi and la Signora Madonna*! And after all there is a grain of reason in their folly, for many of the bitterest miseries of man grow out of a fatal habit of looking back or looking forward, and of never living actually in the full-faced present. Then, too, Carnival was approaching; Carnival, which, though denuded of many of its best and brightest features, still reels through the streets of Naples with something of the picturesque madness that in old times used to accompany its prototype, the Feast of Bacchus. I was reminded of this coming festivity on the morning of the 21st of December, when I noted some unusual attempts on the part of Vincenzo to control his countenance, that often, in spite of his efforts, broadened into a sunny smile as though some humorous thought had flitted across his mind. He betrayed himself at last by asking me demurely whether I purposed taking any part in the carnival? I smiled and shook my head. Vincenzo looked dubious, but finally summoned up courage to say:

"Will the *eccellenza* permit—"

"You to make a fool of yourself?" I interrupted, "by all means! Take your own time, enjoy the fun as much as you please; I promise you I will ask no account of your actions."

He was much gratified, and attended to me with even more punctiliousness than usual. As he prepared my breakfast I asked him:

"By the way, when does the carnival begin?"

"On the 26th," he answered, with a slight air of surprise. "Surely the *eccellenza* knows."

"Yes, yes," I said, impatiently. "I know, but I had forgotten. I am not young enough to keep the dates of these follies in my memory. What letters have you there?"

He handed me a small tray full of different shaped missives, some from fair ladies who "desired the honor of my company," others from tradesmen, "praying the honor of my custom," all from male and female toadies as usual, I thought contemptuously, as I turned them over, when my glance was suddenly arrested by one special envelope, square in form and heavily bordered with black, on which the postmark "Roma" stood out distinctly. "At last!" I thought, and breathed heavily. I turned to my valet, who was giving the final polish to my breakfast cup and saucer:

"You may leave the room, Vincenzo," I said, briefly. He bowed, the door opened and shut noiselessly—he was gone.

Slowly I broke the seal of that fateful letter; a letter from Guido Ferrari, a warrant self-signed, for his own execution!

"My best friend," so it ran, "you will guess by the 'black flag' on my envelope the good news I have to give you. My uncle is dead AT LAST, thank God! and I am left his sole heir unconditionally. I am free, and shall of course return to Naples immediately, that is, as soon as some trifling law business has been got through with the executors. I believe I can arrange my return for the 23d or 24th instant, but will telegraph to you the exact day, and, if possible, the exact hour. Will you oblige me by NOT announcing this to the countess, as I wish to take her by surprise. Poor girl! she will have often felt lonely, I am sure, and I want to see the first beautiful look of rapture and astonishment in her eyes! You can understand this, can you not, amico, or does it seem to you a folly? At any rate, I should consider it very churlish were I to keep YOU in ignorance of my coming home, and I know you will humor me in my desire that the news should be withheld from Nina, How delighted she will be, and what a joyous carnival we will have this winter! I do not think I ever felt more light of heart; perhaps it is because I am so much heavier in pocket. I am glad of the money, as it places me on a more equal footing with HER, and though all her letters to me have been full of the utmost tenderness, still I feel she will think even better of me, now I am in a position somewhat nearer to her own. As for you, my good conte, on my return I shall make it my first duty to pay back with interest the rather large debt I owe to you—thus my honor will be satisfied, and you, I am sure, will have a better opinion of

"Yours to command,

"GUIDO FERRARI."

This was the letter, and I read it over and over again. Some of the words burned themselves into my memory as though they were living flame. "All her letters to me have been full of the utmost tenderness!" Oh, miserable-dupe! fooled, fooled to the acme of folly even as I had been! SHE, the arch-traitoress, to prevent his entertaining the slightest possible suspicion or jealousy of her actions during his absence, had written him, no doubt, epistles sweet as honey brimming over with endearing epithets and vows of constancy, even while she knew she had accepted me as her husband– me–good God! What a devil's dance of death it was!

"On my return I shall make it my first duty to pay back with interest the rather large debt I owe you" (rather large indeed, Guido, so large that you have no idea of its extent!), "thus my honor will be satisfied" (and so will mine in part), "and you, I am sure, will have a better opinion of yours to command." Perhaps I shall, Guido–mine to command as you are–perhaps when all my commands are fulfilled to the bitter end, I may think more kindly of you. But not till then! In the meantime–I thought earnestly for a few minutes, and then sitting down, I penned the following note.

"*Caro amico!* Delighted to hear of your good fortune, and still more enchanted to know you will soon enliven us all with your presence! I admire your little plan of surprising the countess, and will respect your wishes in the matter. But you, on your part, must do me a trifling favor: we have been very dull since you left, and I purpose to start the gayeties afresh by giving a dinner on the 24th (Christmas Eve), in honor of your return–an epicurean repast for gentlemen only. Therefore, I ask you to oblige me by fixing your return for that day, and on arrival at Naples, come straight to me at this hotel, that I may have the satisfaction of being the first to welcome you as you deserve. Telegraph your answer and the hour of your train; and my carriage shall meet you at the station. The dinner-hour can be fixed to suit your convenience of course; what say you to eight o'clock? After dinner you can betake yourself to the Villa Romani when you please–your enjoyment of the lady's surprise and rapture will be the more keen for having been slightly delayed. Trusting you will not refuse to gratify an old man's whim, I am,

"Yours for the time being,

"CESARE OLIVA."

This epistle finished and written in the crabbed disguised penmanship it was part of my business to effect, I folded, sealed and addressed it, and summoning Vincenzo, bade him post it immediately. As soon as he had gone on this errand, I sat down to my as yet untasted breakfast and made some effort to eat as usual. But my thoughts were too active for appetite–I counted on my fingers the days–there were four, only four, between me and–what? One thing was certain–I must see my wife, or rather I should say my BETROTHED–I must see her that very day. I then began to consider how my courtship had progressed since that evening when she had declared she loved me. I had seen her frequently, though not daily– her behavior had been by turns affectionate, adoring, timid, gracious and once or twice passionately loving, though the latter impulse in her I had always coldly checked. For though I could bear a great deal, any outburst of sham sentiment on her part sickened and filled me with such utter loathing that often when she was more than usually tender I dreaded lest my pent-up wrath should break loose and impel me to kill her swiftly and suddenly as one crushes the head of a poisonous adder–an all-too-merciful death for such as she. I preferred to woo her by gifts alone–and her hands were always ready to take whatever I or others chose to offer her. From a rare jewel to a common flower she never refused anything–her strongest passions were vanity and avarice. Sparkling gems from the pilfered store of Carmelo Neri-trinkets which I had especially designed for her–lace, rich embroideries, bouquets of hot-house blossoms, gilded boxes of costly sweets–nothing came amiss to her– she accepted all with a certain covetous glee which she was at no pains to hide from me–nay, she made it rather evident that she expected such things as her right.

And after all, what did it matter to me–I thought–of what value was anything I possessed save to assist me in carrying out the punishment I had destined for her? I studied her nature with critical coldness–I saw its inbred vice artfully concealed beneath the affectation of virtue–every day she sunk lower in my eyes, and I wondered vaguely how I could ever have loved so coarse and common a thing! Lovely she certainly was–lovely too are many of the wretched outcasts who sell themselves in the streets for gold, and who in spite of their criminal trade are less vile than such a woman as the one I had wedded. Mere beauty of face and form can be bought as easily as one buys a flower–but the loyal heart, the pure soul, the lofty intelligence which can make of woman an angel–these are unpurchasable wares, and seldom fall to the lot of man. For beauty, though so perishable, is a snare to us all–it maddens our blood in spite of ourselves–we men are made so. How was it that I–even I, who now loathed the creature I had once loved–could not look upon her physical loveliness without a foolish thrill of passion awaking within me–passion that had something of the murderous in it– admiration that was almost brutal–feelings which I could not control though I despised myself for them while they lasted! There is a weak point in the strongest of us, and wicked women know well where we are most vulnerable. One dainty pin-prick well-aimed–and all the barriers of caution and reserve are broken down–we are ready to fling away our souls for a smile or a kiss. Surely at the last day when we are judged–and may be condemned–we can make our last excuse to the Creator in the word? of the first misguided man:

"The woman whom thou pravest to be with me–she tempted me, and I did eat!"

I lost no time that day in going to the Villa Romani. I drove there in my carriage, taking with me the usual love-offering in the shape of a large gilded osier-basket full of white violets. Their delicious odor reminded me of that May morning when Stella was born–and then quickly there flashed into my mind the words spoken by Guido Ferrari at the time. How mysterious they had seemed to me then–how clear their meaning now! On arriving at the villa I found my fiancé in her own boudoir, attired in morning *deshabille*, if a trailing robe of white cashmere trimmed with Mechlin lace and swan's-down can be considered *deshabille*. Her rich hair hung loosely on her shoulders, and she was seated in a velvet easy-chair before a small sparkling wood fire, reading. Her attitude was one of luxurious ease and grace, but she sprung up as soon as her maid announced me, and came forward with her usual charming air of welcome, in which there was something imperial, as of a sovereign who receives a subject. I presented the flowers I had brought, with a few words of studied and formal compliment, uttered for the benefit of the servant who lingered in the room–then I added in a lower tone:

"I have news of importance–can I speak to you privately?"

She smiled assent, and motioning me by a graceful gesture of her hand to take a seat, she at once dismissed her maid. As soon as the door had closed behind the girl I spoke at once and to the point, scarcely waiting till my wife resumed her easy-chair before the fire.

"I have had a letter from Signor Ferrari."

She started slightly, but said nothing, she merely bowed her head and raised her delicately arched eyebrows with a look of inquiry as of one who should say, "Indeed! in what way does this concern me?" I watched her narrowly, and then continued, "He is coming back in two or three days–he says he is sure," and here I smiled, "that you will be delighted to see him."

This time she half rose from her seat, her lips moved as though she would speak, but she remained silent, and sinking back again among her violet velvet cushions, she grew very pale.

"If," I went on, "you have any reason to think that he may make himself disagreeable to you when he knows of your engagement to me, out of disappointed ambition, conceit, or self-interest (for of course YOU never encouraged him), I should advise you to go on a visit to some friends for a few days, till his irritation shall have somewhat passed. What say you to such a plan?"

She appeared to meditate for a few moments–then raising her lovely eyes with a wistful and submissive look, she replied:

"It shall be as you wish, Cesare! Signor Ferrari is certainly rash and hot-tempered, he might be presumptuous enough to— But you do not think of yourself in the matter! Surely YOU also are in danger of being insulted by him when he knows all?"

"I shall be on my guard!" I said, quietly. "Besides, I can easily pardon any outburst of temper on his part—it will be perfectly natural, I think! To lose all hope of ever winning such a love as yours must need be a sore trial to one of his hot blood and fiery impulses. Poor fellow!" and I sighed and shook my head with benevolent gentleness. "By the way, he tells me he has had letters from you?"

I put this question carelessly, but it took her by surprise. She caught her breath hard and looked at me sharply, with an alarmed expression. Seeing that my face was perfectly impassive, she recovered her composure instantly, and answered:

"Oh, yes! I have been compelled to write to him once or twice on matters of business connected with my late husband's affairs. Most unfortunately, Fabio made him one of the trustees of his fortune in case of his death—it is exceedingly awkward for me that he should occupy that position—it appears to give him some authority over my actions. In reality he has none. He has no doubt exaggerated the number of times I have written to him? it would be like his impertinence to do so."

Though this last remark was addressed to me almost as a question, I let it pass without response. I reverted to my original theme.

"What think you, then?" I said. "Will you remain here or will you absent yourself for a few days?"

She rose from her chair and approaching me, knelt down at my side, clasping her two little hands round my arm. "With your permission," she returned, softly, "I will go to the convent where I was educated. It is some eight or ten miles distant from here, and I think" (here she counterfeited the most wonderful expression of ingenuous sweetness and piety)—"I think I should

232

like to make a 'RETREAT'—that is, devote some time solely to the duties of religion before I enter upon a second marriage. The dear nuns would be so glad to see me—and I am sure you will not object? It will be a good preparation for my future."

I seized her caressing hands and held them hard, while I looked upon her kneeling there like the white-robed figure of a praying saint.

"It will indeed!" I said in a harsh voice. "The best of all possible preparations! We none of us know what may happen— we cannot tell whether life or death awaits us—it is wise to prepare for either by words of penitence and devotion! I admire this beautiful spirit in you, carina! Go to the convent by all means! I shall find you there and will visit you when the wrath and bitterness of our friend Ferrari have been smoothed into silence and resignation. Yes—go to the convent, among the good and pious nuns—and when you pray for yourself, pray for the peace of your dead husband's soul—and—for me! Such prayers, unselfish and earnest, uttered by pure lips like yours, fly swiftly to heaven! And as for young Guido—have no fear— I promise you he shall offend you no more!"

"Ah, you do not know him!" she murmured, lightly kissing my hands that still held hers; "I fear he will give you a great deal of trouble."

"I shall at any rate know how to silence him," I said, releasing her as I spoke, and watching her as she rose from her kneeling position and stood before me, supple and delicate as a white iris swaying in the wind. "You never gave him reason to hope—therefore he has no cause of complaint."

"True!" she replied, readily, with an untroubled smile. "But I am such a nervous creature! I am always imagining evils that never happen. And now, Cesare, when do you wish me to go to the convent?"

I shrugged my shoulders with an air of indifference.

"Your submission to my will, *mia bella*," I said, coldly, "is altogether charming, and flatters me much, but I am not your master—not yet! Pray choose your own time, and suit your departure to your own pleasure."

"Then," she replied, with an air of decision, "I will go today. The sooner the better—for some instinct tells me that Guido will play us a trick and return before we expect him. Yes—I will go to-day."

I rose to take my leave. "Then you will require leisure to make your preparations," I said, with ceremonious politeness. "I assure you I approve your resolve. If you inform the superioress of the convent that I am your betrothed husband, I suppose I shall be permitted to see you when I call?"

"Oh, certainly!" she replied. "The dear nuns will do anything for me. Their order is one of perpetual adoration, and their rules are very strict, but they do not apply them to their old pupils, and I am one of their great favorites."

"Naturally!" I observed. "And will you also join in the service of perpetual adoration?"

"Oh, yes!"

"It needs an untainted soul like yours," I said, with a satirical smile, which she did not see, "to pray before the unveiled Host without being conscience-smitten! I envy you your privilege. I could not do it—but YOU are probably nearer to the angels than we know. And so you will pray for me?"

She raised her eyes with devout gentleness. "I will indeed!"

"I thank you!"—and I choked back the bitter contempt and disgust I had for her hypocrisy as I spoke—"I thank you heartily—most heartily! Addio!"

She came or rather floated to my side, her white garments trailing about her and the gold of her hair glittering in the mingled glow of the firelight and the wintery sunbeams that shone through the window. She looked up—a witch-like languor lay in her eyes—her red lips pouted.

"Not one kiss before you go?" she said.

21

FOR A moment I lost my self-possession. I scarcely remember now what I did. I know I clasped her almost roughly in my arms–I know that I kissed her passionately on lips, throat and brow–and that in the fervor of my embraces, the thought of what manner of vile thing she was came swiftly upon me, causing me to release her with such suddenness that she caught at the back of a chair to save herself from falling. Her breath came and went in little quick gasps of excitement, her face was flushed–she looked astonished, yet certainly not displeased. No, SHE was not angry, but I was– thoroughly annoyed–bitterly vexed with myself, for being such a fool.

"Forgive me," I muttered. "I forgot–I–"

A little smile stole round the corners of her mouth.

"You are fully pardoned!" she said, in a low voice, "you need not apologize."

Her smile deepened; suddenly she broke into a rippling laugh, sweet and silvery as a bell–a laugh that went through me like a knife. Was it not the self-same laughter that had pierced my brain the night I witnessed her amorous interview with Guido in the avenue? Had not the cruel mockery of it nearly driven me mad? I could not endure it–I sprung to her side–she ceased laughing and looked at me in wide-eyed wonderment.

"Listen!" I said, in an impatient, almost fierce tone. "Do not laugh like that! It jars my nerves–it–hurts me! I will tell you why. Once–long ago–in my youth–I loved a woman. She was NOT like you– no–for she was false! False to the very heart's core–false in every word she uttered. You understand me? she resembled you in nothing–nothing! But she used to laugh at me–she trampled on my life and spoiled it–she broke my heart! It is all past now, I never think of her, only your laughter reminded me–there!" And I took her hands and kissed them. "I have told you the story of my early folly–forget it and forgive me! It is time you prepared for your journey, is it not? If I can be of service to you, command me–you know where to send for me. Good-bye! and the peace of a pure conscience be with you!"

And I laid my burning hand on her head weighted with its clustering curls of gold. SHE thought this gesture was one of blessing. I thought–God only knows what I thought–yet surely if curses can be so bestowed, my curse crowned her at that moment! I dared not trust myself longer in her presence, and without another word or look I left her and hurried from the house. I knew she was startled and at the same time gratified to think she could thus have moved me to any display of emotion–but I would not even turn my head to catch her parting glance. I could not–I was sick of myself and of her. I was literally torn asunder between love and hatred–love born basely of material feeling alone–hatred, the offspring of a deeply injured spirit for whose wrong there could scarce be found sufficient remedy. Once out of the influence of her bewildering beauty, my mind grew calmer–and the drive back to the hotel in my carriage through the sweet dullness of the December air quieted the feverish excitement of my blood and restored me to myself. It was a most lovely day–bright and fresh, with the savor of the sea in the wind. The waters of the bay were of a steel-like blue shading into deep olive-green, and a soft haze lingered about the shores of Amalfi like a veil of gray, shot through with silver and gold. Down the streets went women in picturesque garb carrying on their heads baskets full to the brim of purple violets that scented the air as they passed–children ragged and dirty ran along, pushing the luxuriant tangle of their dark locks away from their beautiful wild antelope eyes, and, holding up bunches of roses and narcissi with smiles as brilliant as the very sunshine, implored the passengers to buy "for the sake of the little Gesu who was soon coming!"

Bells clashed and clanged from the churches in honor of San Tommaso, whose festival it was, and the city had that aspect of gala gayety about it, which is in truth common enough to all continental towns, but which seems strange to the solemn Londoner who sees so much apparently reasonless merriment for the first time. He, accustomed to have his reluctant laughter pumped out of him by an occasional visit to the theater where he can witness the "original," English translation of a French farce, cannot understand WHY these foolish Neapolitans should laugh and sing and shout in the manner they do, merely because they are glad to be alive. And after much dubious consideration, he decides within himself that they are all rascals– the scum of the earth–and that he and he only is the true representative of man at his best–the model of civilized respectability. And a mournful spectacle he thus seems to the eyes of us "base" foreigners–in our hearts we are sorry for him and believe that if he could manage to shake off the fetters of his insular customs and prejudices, he might almost succeed in enjoying life as much as we do!

As I drove along I saw a small crowd at one of the street corners–a gesticulating, laughing crowd, listening to an *"improvisatore"* or wandering poet–a plump-looking fellow who had all the rhymes of Italy at his fingers' ends, and who could make a poem on any subject or an acrostic on any name, with perfect facility. I stopped my carriage to listen to his extemporized verses, many of which were really admirable, and tossed him three francs. He threw them up in the air, one after the other, and caught them, as they fell, in his mouth, appearing to have swallowed them all—then with an inimitable grimace, he pulled off his tattered cap and said:

"*Ancora affamato, excellenza!*" (I am still hungry!) amid the renewed laughter of his easily amused audience. A merry poet he was and without conceit—and his good humor merited the extra silver pieces I gave him, which caused him, to wish me—"*Buon appetito e un sorriso della Madonna!*"—(a good appetite to you and a smile of the Madonna!) Imagine the Lord Laureate of England standing at the corner of Regent Street swallowing half-pence for his rhymes! Yet some of the quaint conceits strung together by such a fellow as this *improvisatore* might furnish material for many of the so called "poets" whose names are mysteriously honored in Britain.

Further on I came upon a group of red-capped coral fishers assembled round a portable stove whereon roasting chestnuts cracked their glossy sides and emitted savory odors. The men were singing gaily to the thrumming of an old guitar, and the song they sung was familiar to me. Stay! where had I heard it?—let me listen!

"*Sciore limone Le voglio far mori de passione Zompa llari llira!*"

Ha! I remembered now. When I had crawled out of the vault through the brigand's hole of entrance—when my heart had bounded with glad anticipations never to be realized—when I had believed in the worth of love and friendship—when I had seen the morning sun glittering on the sea, and had thought—poor fool!—that his long beams were like so many golden flags of joy hung up in heaven to symbolize the happiness of my release from death and my restoration to liberty— then—then I had heard a sailor's voice in the distance singing that "ritornello," and I had fondly imagined its impassioned lines were all for me! Hateful music—most bitter sweetness! I could have put my hands up to my ears to shut out the sound of it now that I thought of the time when I had heard it last! For then I had possessed a heart—a throbbing, passionate, sensitive thing—alive to every emotion of tenderness and affection—now that heart was dead and cold as a stone. Only its corpse went with me everywhere, weighing me down with itself to the strange grave it occupied, a grave wherein were also buried so many dear delusions—such plaintive regrets, such pleading memories, that surely it was no wonder their small ghosts arose and haunted me, saying, "Wilt thou not weep for this lost sweetness?" "Wilt thou not relent before such a remembrance?" or "Hast thou no desire for that past delight?" But to all such inward temptations my soul was deaf and inexorable; justice—stern, immutable justice was what I sought and what I meant to have.

May be you find it hard to understand the possibility of Scheming and carrying out so prolonged a vengeance as mine? If you that read these pages are English, I know it will seem to you well-nigh incomprehensible. The temperate blood of the northerner, combined with his open, unsuspicious nature, has, I admit, the advantage over us in matters of personal injury. An Englishman, so I hear, is incapable of nourishing a long and deadly resentment, even against an unfaithful wife—he is too indifferent, he thinks it not worth his while. But we Neapolitans, we can carry a "vendetta" through a life-time—ay, through generation after generation! This is bad, you say— immoral, unchristian. No doubt! We are more than half pagans at heart; we are as our country and our traditions have made us. It will need another visitation of Christ before we shall learn how to forgive those that despitefully use us. Such a doctrine seems to us a mere play upon words—a weak maxim only fit for children and priests. Besides, did Christ himself forgive Judas? The gospel does not say so!

When I reached my own apartments at the hotel I felt worn out and fagged. I resolved to rest and receive no visitors that day. While giving my orders to Vincenzo a thought occurred to me. I went to a cabinet in the room and unlocked a secret drawer. In it lay a strong leather case. I lifted this, and bade Vincenzo unstrap and open it. He did so, nor showed the least sign of surprise when a pair of richly ornamented pistols was displayed to his view.

"Good weapons?" I remarked, in a casual manner.

My valet took each one out of the case, and examined them both critically.

"They need cleaning, *eccellenza.*"

"Good!" I said, briefly. "Then clean them and put them in good order. I may require to use them."

The imperturbable Vincenzo bowed, and taking the weapons, prepared to leave the room.

"Stay!"

He turned. I looked at him steadily.

"I believe you are a faithful fellow, Vincenzo," I said.

He met my glance frankly.

"The day may come," I went on, quietly, "when I shall perhaps put your fidelity to the proof."

The dark Tuscan eyes, keen and clear the moment before, flashed brightly and then grew humid.

"*Eccellenza,* you have only to command! I was a soldier once–I know what duty means. But there is a better service– gratitude. I am your poor servant, but you have won my heart. I would give my life for you should you desire it!"

He paused, half ashamed of the emotion that threatened to break through his mask of impassibility, bowed again and would have left me, but that I called him back and held out my hand.

"Shake hands, amico" I said, simply.

He caught it with an astonished yet pleased look–and stooping, kissed it before I could prevent him, and this time literally scrambled out of my presence with an entire oblivion of his usual dignity. Left alone, I considered this behavior of his with half- pained surprise. This poor fellow loved me it was evident–why, I knew not. I had done no more for him than any other master might have done for a good servant. I had often spoken to him with impatience, even harshness; and yet I had "won his heart"–so he said. Why should he care for me? why should my poor old butler Giacoma cherish me so devotedly in his memory; why should my very dog still love and obey me, when my nearest and dearest, my wife and my friend, had so gladly forsaken me, and were so eager to forget me! Perhaps fidelity was not the fashion now among educated persons? Perhaps it was a worn-out virtue, left to the *bas-peuple*–to the vulgar–and to animals? Progress might have attained this result–no doubt it had.

I sighed wearily, and threw myself clown in an arm-chair near the window, and watched the white-sailed boats skimming like flecks of silver across the blue-green water. The tinkling of a tambourine by and by attracted my wandering attention, and looking into the street just below my balcony I saw a young girl dancing. She was lovely to look at, and she danced with exquisite grace as well as modesty, but the beauty of her face was not so much caused by perfection of feature or outline as by a certain wistful expression that had in it something of nobility and pride. I watched her; at the conclusion of her dance she held up her tambourine with a bright but appealing smile. Silver and copper were freely flung to her, I contributing my quota to the amount; but all she received she at once emptied into a leather bag which was carried by a young and handsome man who accompanied her, and who, alas! was totally blind. I knew the couple well, and had often seen them; their history was pathetic enough. The girl had been betrothed to the young fellow when he had occupied a fairly good position as a worker in silver filigree jewelry. His eyesight, long painfully strained over his delicate labors, suddenly failed him– he lost his place, of course, and was utterly without resources. He offered to release his fiancé from her engagement, but she would not take her freedom–she insisted on marrying him at once. She had her way, and devoted herself to him soul and body– danced in the streets and sung to gain a living for herself and him; taught him to weave baskets so that he might not feel himself entirely dependent on her, and she sold these baskets for him so successfully that he was gradually making quite a little trade of them. Poor child! for she was not much more than a child–what a bright face she had!–glorified by the self-denial and courage of her everyday life. No wonder she had won the sympathy of the warmhearted and impulsive Neapolitans–they looked upon her as a heroine of romance; and as she passed through the streets, leading her blind husband tenderly by the hand, there was not a creature in the city, even among the most abandoned and vile characters, who would have dared to offer her the least insult, or who would have ventured to address her otherwise than respectfully. She was good, innocent, and true; how was it, I wondered dreamily, that I could not have won a woman's heart like hers? Were the poor alone to possess all the old world virtues–honor and faith, love and loyalty? Was there something in a life of luxury that sapped virtue at its root? Evidently early training had little to do with after results, for had not my wife been brought up among an order of nuns renowned for simplicity and sanctity; had not her own father declared her to be "as pure as a flower on the altar of the Madonna;" and yet the evil had been in her, and nothing had eradicated it; for even religion, with her, was a mere graceful sham, a kind of theatrical effect used to tone down her natural hypocrisy. My own thoughts began to harass and weary me. I took up a volume of philosophic essays and began to read, in an endeavor to distract my mind from dwelling on the one perpetual theme. The day wore on slowly enough; and I was glad when the evening closed in, and when Vincenzo, remarking that the night was chilly, kindled a pleasant wood-fire in my room, and lighted the lamps. A little while before my dinner was served he handed me a letter stating that it had just been brought by the Countess Romani's coachman. It bore my own seal and motto. I opened it; it was dated, "*La Santissima Annunziata*," and ran as follows:

"Beloved! I arrived here safely; the nuns are delighted to see me, and you will be made heartily welcome when you come. I think of you constantly–how happy I felt this morning! You seemed to love me so much; why are you not always so fond of your faithful

"NINA?"

I crumpled this note fiercely in my hand and flung it into the leaping flames of the newly lighted fire. There was a faint perfume about it that sickened me–a subtle odor like that of a civet cat when it moves stealthily after its prey through a tangle of tropical herbage. I always detested scented note-paper–I am not the only man who does so. One is led to fancy that the fingers of the woman who writes upon it must have some poisonous or offensive taint about them, which she endeavors to cover by the aid of a chemical concoction. I would not permit myself to think of this so "faithful Nina," as she styled herself. I resumed my reading, and continued it even at dinner, during which meal Vincenzo waited upon me with his usual silent gravity and decorum, though I could feel that he watched me with a certain solicitude. I suppose I looked weary–I certainly felt so, and retired to rest unusually early. The time seemed to me so long–would the end NEVER come? The next day dawned and trailed its tiresome hours after it, as a prisoner might trail his chain of iron fetters, until sunset, and then–then, when the gray of the wintry sky flashed for a brief space into glowing red– then, while the water looked like blood and the clouds like flame– then a few words sped along the telegraph wires that stilled my impatience, roused my soul, and braced every nerve and muscle in my body to instant action. They were plain, clear, and concise:

"From Guido Ferrari, Rome, to Il Conte Cesare Olfva, Naples.–Shall be with you on the 24th inst. Train arrives at 6:30 P.M. Will come to you as you desire without fail."

22

CHRISTMAS Eve! The day had been extra chilly, with frequent showers of stinging rain, but toward five o'clock in the afternoon the weather cleared. The clouds, which had been of a dull uniform gray, began to break asunder and disclose little shining rifts of pale blue and bright gold; the sea looked like a wide satin ribbon shaken out and shimmering with opaline tints. Flower girls trooped forth making the air musical with their mellow cries of "*Fiori! chi vuol fiori*" and holding up their tempting wares—not bunches of holly and mistletoe such as are known in England, but roses, lilies, jonquils, and sweet daffodils. The shops were brilliant with bouquets and baskets of fruits and flowers; a glittering show of *etrennes*, or gifts to suit all ages and conditions, were set forth in tempting array, from a box of bonbons costing one franc to a jeweled tiara worth a million, while in many of the windows were displayed models of the "Bethlehem," with babe Jesus lying in his manger, for the benefit of the round-eyed children—who, after staring fondly at His waxen image for some time, would run off hand in hand to the nearest church where the usual Christmas crèche was arranged, and there kneeling down, would begin to implore their "dear little Jesus," their "own little brother," not to forget them, with a simplicity of belief that was as touching as it was unaffected.

I am told that in England the principle sight on Christmas-eve are the shops of the butchers and poulterers hung with the dead carcasses of animals newly slaughtered, in whose mouths are thrust bunches of prickly holly, at which agreeable spectacle the passers-by gape with gluttonous approval. Surely there is nothing graceful about such a commemoration of the birth of Christ as this? nothing picturesque, nothing poetic?–nothing even orthodox, for Christ was born in the East, and the Orientals are very small eaters, and are particularly sparing in the use of meat. One wonders what such an unusual display of vulgar victuals has to do with the coming of the Savior, who arrived among us in such poor estate that even a decent roof was denied to Him. Perhaps, though, the English people read their gospels in a way of their own, and understood that the wise men of the East, who are supposed to have brought the Divine Child symbolic gifts of gold, frankincense, and myrrh, really brought joints of beef, turkeys, and "plum-pudding," that vile and indigestible mixture at which an Italian shrugs his shoulders in visible disgust. There is something barbaric, I suppose, in the British customs still–something that reminds one of their ancient condition when the Romans conquered them–when their supreme idea of enjoyment was to have an ox roasted whole before them while they drank "wassail" till they groveled under their own tables in a worse condition than overfed swine. Coarse and vulgar plenty is still the leading characteristic at the dinners of English or American parvenus; they have scarcely any idea of the refinements that can be imparted to the prosaic necessity of eating–of the many little graces of the table that are understood in part by the French, but that perhaps never reach such absolute perfection of taste and skill as at the banquets of a cultured and clever Italian noble. Some of these are veritable "feasts of the gods," and would do honor to the fabled Olympus, and such a one I had prepared for Guido Ferrari as a greeting to him on his return from Rome–a feast of welcome and– farewell!

All the resources of the hotel at which I stayed had been brought into requisition. The chef, a famous cordon bleu, had transferred the work of the usual *table d'hote* to his underlings, and had bent the powers of his culinary intelligence solely on the production of the magnificent dinner I had ordered. The landlord, in spite of himself, broke into exclamations of wonder and awe as he listened to and wrote down my commands for different wines of the rarest kinds and choicest vintages. The servants rushed hither and thither to obey my various behests, with looks of immense importance; the head waiter, a superb official who prided himself on his artistic taste, took the laying-out of the table under his entire superintendence, and nothing was talked of or thought of for the time but the grandeur of my proposed entertainment.

About six o'clock I sent my carriage down to the railway station to meet Ferrari as I had arranged; and then, at my landlord's invitation, I went to survey the stage that was prepared for one important scene of my drama—to see if the scenery, side-lights, and general effects were all in working order. To avoid disarranging my own apartments, I had chosen for my dinner-party a room on the ground-floor of the hotel, which was often let out for marriage- breakfasts and other purposes of the like kind; it was octagonal in shape, not too large, and I had had it most exquisitely decorated for the occasion. The walls were hung with draperies of gold-colored silk and crimson velvet, interspersed here and there with long mirrors, which were ornamented with crystal candelabra, in which twinkled hundreds of lights under rose-tinted glass shades. At the back of the room, a miniature conservatory was displayed to view, full of rare ferns and subtly perfumed exotics, in the center of which a fountain rose and fell with regular and melodious murmur. Here, later on, a band of stringed instruments and a choir of boys' voices were to be stationed, so that sweet music might be heard and felt without the performers being visible. One, and one only, of the long French windows of the room was left uncurtained, it was simply draped with velvet as one drapes a choice picture, and through it the eyes rested on a perfect view of the Bay of Naples, white with the wintery moonlight.

The dinner-table, laid for fifteen persons, glittered with sumptuous appointments of silver, Venetian glass, and the rarest flowers; the floor was carpeted with velvet pile, in which some grains of ambergris had been scattered, so that in walking the feet sunk, as it were, into a bed of moss rich with the odors of a thousand spring blossoms. The very chairs wherein my guests were to seat themselves were of a luxurious shape and softly stuffed, so that one could lean back in them or recline at ease–in short, everything was arranged with a lavish splendor almost befitting the banquet of an eastern monarch, and yet with such accurate taste that there was no detail one could have wished omitted.

I was thoroughly satisfied, but as I know what an unwise plan it is to praise servants too highly for doing well what they are expressly paid to do, I intimated my satisfaction to my landlord by a mere careless nod and smile of approval. He, who waited on my every gesture with abject humility, received this sign of condescension with as much delight as though it had come from the king himself, and I could easily see that the very fact of my showing no enthusiasm at the result of his labors, made him consider me a greater man than ever. I now went to my own apartments to don my evening attire; I found Vincenzo brushing every speck of dust from my dress coat with careful nicety–he had already arranged the other articles of costume neatly on my bed ready for wear. I unlocked a dressing-case and took from thence three studs, each one formed of a single brilliant of rare clearness and lusters and handed them to him to fix in my shirt-front. While he was polishing these admiringly on his coat-sleeve I watched him earnestly–then I suddenly addressed him.

"Vincenzo!" He started.

"*Eccellenza?*"

"To-night you will stand behind my chair and assist in

serving the wine."

"Yes, *eccellenza*."

"You will," I continued, "attend particularly to Sigor Ferrari, who will sit at my right hand. Take care that his glass is never empty."

"Yes, *eccellenza*."

"Whatever may be said or done," I went on, quietly, "you will show no sign of alarm or surprise. From the commencement of dinner till I tell you to move, remember your place is fixed by me."

The honest fellow looked a little puzzled, but replied as before:

"Yes, *eccellenza*."

I smiled, and advancing, laid my hand on his arm.

"How about the pistols, Vincenzo?"

"They are cleaned and ready for use, *eccellenza*," he replied. "I have placed them in your cabinet."

"That is well!" I said with a satisfied gesture. "You can leave me and arrange the salon for the reception of my friends."

He disappeared, and I busied myself with my toilet, about which I was for once unusually particular. The conventional dress-suit is not very becoming, yet there are a few men here and there who look well in it, and who, in spite of similarity in attire, will never be mistaken for waiters. Others there are who, passable in appearance when clad in their ordinary garments, reach the very acme of plebeianism when they clothe themselves in the unaccommodating evening-dress. Fortunately, I happened to be one of the former class—the sober black, the broad white display of starched shirt- front and neat tie became me, almost too well I thought. It would have been better for my purposes if I could have feigned an aspect of greater age and weightier gravity. I had scarcely finished my toilet when the rumbling of wheels in the court-yard outside made the hot blood rush to my face, and my heart beat with feverish excitement. I left my dressing-room, however, with a composed countenance and calm step, and entered my private salon just as its doors were flung open and "Signor Ferrari" was announced. He entered smiling–his face was alight with good humor and glad anticipation– he looked handsomer than usual.

"*Eccomi qua!*" he cried, seizing my hands enthusiastically in his own. "My dear conte, I am delighted to see you! What an excellent fellow you are! A kind of amiable Arabian Nights genius, who occupies himself in making mortals happy. And how are you? You look remarkably well!"

"I can return the compliment," I said, gaily. "You are more of an Antinous than ever."

He laughed, well pleased, and sat down, drawing off his gloves and loosening his traveling overcoat.

"Well, I suppose plenty of cash puts a man in good humor, and therefore in good condition," he replied. "But my dear fellow, you are dressed for dinner–*quel preux chevalier*! I am positively unfit to be in your company! You insisted that I should come to you directly, on my arrival, but I really must change my apparel. Your man took my valise; in it are my dress-clothes–I shall not be ten minutes putting them on."

"Take a glass of wine first," I said, pouring out some of his favorite Montepulciano. "There is plenty of time. It is barely seven, and we do not dine till eight. He took the wine from my hand and smiled. I returned the smile, adding, "It gives me great pleasure to receive you, Ferrari! I have been impatient for your return–almost as impatient as–" He paused in the act of drinking, and his eyes flashed delightedly.

"As SHE has? *Piccinina!* How I long to see her again! I swear to you, amico, I should have gone straight to the Villa Romani had I obeyed my own impulse–but I had promised you to come here, and, on the whole, the evening will do as well"– and he laughed with a covert meaning in his laughter–"perhaps better!"

My hands clinched, but I said with forced gayety:

"*Ma certamente!* The evening will be much better! Is it not

Byron who says that women, like stars, look best at night? You will find her the same as ever, perfectly well and perfectly charming. It must be her pure and candid soul that makes her face so fair! It may be a relief to your mind to know that I am the only man she has allowed to visit her during your absence!"

"Thank God for that!" cried Ferrari, devoutly, as he tossed off his wine. "And now tell me, my dear conte, what bacchanalians are coming to-night? Per Dio, after all I am more in the humor for dinner than love-making!"

I burst out laughing harshly. "Of course! Every sensible man prefers good eating even to good women! Who are my guests you ask? I believe you know them all. First, there is the Duca Filippo Marina."

"By Heaven!" interrupted Guido. "An absolute gentleman, who by his manner seems to challenge the universe to disprove his dignity! Can he unbend so far as to partake of food in public? My dear conte, you should have asked him that question!"

"Then," I went on, not heeding this interruption, "Signor Fraschetti and the Marchese Giuliano."

"Giuliano drinks deep'." laughed Ferrari, "and should he mix his wines, you will find him ready to stab all the waiters before the dinner is half over."

"In mixing wines," I returned, coolly, "he will but imitate your example, *caro mio.*"

"Ah, but I can stand it!" he said. "He cannot! Few Neapolitans are like me!"

I watched him narrowly, and went on with the list of my invited guests.

"After these, comes the Capitano Luigi Freccia."

"What! the raging fire-eater?" exclaimed Guido. "He who at every second word raps out a pagan or Christian oath, and cannot for his life tell any difference between the two!"

"And the illustrious gentleman Crispiano Dulci and Antonio Biscardi, artists like yourself," I continued.

He frowned slightly—then smiled.

"I wish them good appetites! Time was when I envied their skill–now I can afford to be generous. They are welcome to the whole field of art as far as I am concerned. I have said farewell to the brush and palette–I shall never paint again."

True enough! I thought, eying the shapely white hand with which he just then stroked his dark mustache; the same hand on which my family diamond ring glittered like a star. He looked up suddenly.

"Go on, conte I am all impatience. Who comes next?"

"More fire-eaters, I suppose you will call them," I answered, "and French fire-eaters, too. Monsieur le Marquis D'Avencourt, and le beau Capitaine Eugene de Hamal."

Ferrari looked astonished. "*Per Bacco!*" he exclaimed. "Two noted Paris duelists! Why–what need have you of such valorous associates? I confess your choice surprises me."

"I understood them to be YOUR friends," I said, composedly. "If you remember, YOU introduced me to them. I know nothing of the gentlemen beyond that they appear to be pleasant fellows and good talkers. As for their reputed skill I am inclined to set that down to a mere rumor, at any rate, my dinner-table will scarcely provide a field for the display of swordsmanship."

Guido laughed. "Well, no! but these fellows would like to make it one–why, they will pick a quarrel for the mere lifting of an eyebrow. And the rest of your company?"

"Are the inseparable brother sculptors Carlo and Francesco Respetti, Chevalier Mancini, scientist and man of letters, Luziano Salustri, poet and musician, and the fascinating Marchese Ippolito Gualdro, whose conversation, as you know, is more entrancing than the voice of Adelina Patti. I have only to add," and I smiled half mockingly, "the name of Signor Guido Ferrari, true friend and loyal lover–and the party is complete."

"Altro! Fifteen in all including yourself," said Ferrari, gaily, enumerating them on his fingers. "*Per la madre di Dio!* With such a goodly company and a host who entertains *en roi* we shall pass a merry time of it. And did you, amico, actually organize this banquet, merely to welcome back so unworthy a person as myself?"

"Solely and entirely for that reason," I replied.

He jumped up from his chair and clapped his two hands on my shoulders.

"*A la bonne heure!* But why, In the name of the saints or the devil, have you taken such a fancy to me?"

"Why have I taken such a fancy to you?" I repeated, slowly. "My dear Ferrari, I am surely not alone in my admiration for your high qualities! Does not Everyone like you? Are you not a universal favorite? Do you not tell me that your late friend the Count Romani held you as the dearest to him in the world after his wife? *Ebbene!* Why underrate yourself?"

He let his hands fall slowly from my shoulders and a look of pain contracted his features. After a little silence he said:

"Fabio again! How his name and memory haunt me! I told you he was a fool—it was part of his folly that he loved me too well—perhaps. Do you know I have thought of him very much lately?"

"Indeed?" and I feigned to be absorbed in fixing a star-like japonica in my button-hole. "How is that?"

A grave and meditative look softened the usually defiant brilliancy of his eyes.

"I saw my uncle die," he continued, speaking in a low tone. "He was an old man and had very little strength left,—yet his battle with death was horrible—horrible! I see him yet—his yellow convulsed face—his twisted limbs—his claw-like hands tearing at the empty air—then the ghastly grim and dropped jaw—the wide-open glazed eyes—pshaw! it sickened me!"

"Well, well!" I said in a soothing way, still busying myself with the arrangement of my button-hole, and secretly wondering what new emotion was at work in the volatile mind of my victim. "No doubt it was distressing to witness—but you could not have been very sorry— he was an old man, and, though it is a platitude not worth repeating—we must all die."

"Sorry!" exclaimed Ferrari, talking almost more to himself than to me. "I was glad! He was an old scoundrel, deeply dyed in every sort of social villainy. No–I was not sorry, only as I watched him in his frantic struggle, fighting furiously for each fresh gasp of breath–I thought–I know not why–of Fabio."

Profoundly astonished, but concealing my astonishment under an air of indifference, I began to laugh.

"Upon my word, Ferrari–pardon me for saying so, but the air of Rome seems to have somewhat obscured your mind! I confess I cannot follow your meaning."

He sighed uneasily. "I dare say not! I scarce can follow it myself. But if it was so hard for an old man to writhe himself out of life, what must it have been for Fabio! We were students together; we used to walk with our arms round each other's necks like school-girls, and he was young and full of vitality–physically stronger, too, than I am. He must have battled for life with every nerve and sinew stretched to almost breaking." He stopped and shuddered. "By Heaven! death should be made easier for us! It is a frightful thing!"

A contemptuous pity arose in me. Was he coward as well as traitor? I touched him lightly on the arm.

"Excuse me, my young friend, if I say frankly that your dismal conversation is slightly fatiguing. I cannot accept it as a suitable preparation for dinner! And permit me to remind you that you have still to dress."

The gentle satire of my tone made him look up and smile. His face cleared, and he passed his hand over his forehead, as though he swept it free of some unpleasant thought.

"I believe I am nervous," he said with a half laugh. "For the last few hours I have had all sorts of uncomfortable presentiments and forebodings."

"No wonder!" I returned carelessly, "with such a spectacle as you have described before the eyes of your memory. The Eternal City savors somewhat disagreeably of graves. Shake the dust of the Caesars from your feet, and enjoy your life, while it lasts!"

"Excellent advice!" he said, smiling, "and not difficult to follow. Now to attire for the festival. Have I your permission?"

I touched the bell which summoned Vincenzo, and bade him wait on Signer Ferrari's orders. Guido disappeared under his escort, giving me a laughing nod of salutation as he left the room. I watched his retiring figure with a strange pitifulness– the first emotion of the kind that had awakened in me for him since I learned his treachery. His allusion to that time when we had been students together–when we had walked with arms round each other's necks "like school- girls," as he said, had touched me more closely than I cared to realize. It was true, we had been happy then–two careless youths with all the world like an untrodden race-course before us. SHE had not then darkened the heaven of our confidence; she had not come with her false fair face to make of ME a blind, doting madman, and to transform him into a liar and hypocrite. It was all her fault, all the misery and horror; she was the blight on our lives; she merited the heaviest punishment, and she would receive it. Yet, would to God we had neither of us ever seen her! Her beauty, like a sword, had severed the bonds of friendship that after all, when it DOES exist between two men, is better and braver than the love of woman. However, all regrets were unavailing now; the evil was done, and there was no undoing it. I had little time left me for reflection; each moment that passed brought me nearer to the end I had planned and foreseen.

23

AT ABOUT a quarter to eight my guests began to arrive, and one by one they all came in save two–the brothers Respetti. While we were awaiting them, Ferrari entered in evening-dress, with the conscious air of a handsome man who knows he is looking his best. I readily admitted his charm of manner; had I not myself been subjugated and fascinated by it in the old happy, foolish days? He was enthusiastically greeted and welcomed back to Naples by all the gentlemen assembled, many of whom were his own particular friends. They embraced him in the impressionable style common to Italians, with the exception of the stately Duca di Marina, who merely bowed courteously, and inquired if certain families of distinction whom he named had yet arrived in Rome for the winter season. Ferrari was engaged in replying to these questions with his usual grace and ease and fluency, when a note was brought to me marked "Immediate." It contained a profuse and elegantly worded apology from Carlo Respetti, who regretted deeply that an unforeseen matter of business would prevent himself and his brother from having the inestimable honor and delight of dining with me that evening. I thereupon rang my bell as a sign that the dinner need no longer be delayed; and, turning to those assembled, I announced to them the unavoidable absence of two of the party.

"A pity Francesco could not have come," said Captain Freccia, twirling the ends of his long mustachios. "He loves good wine, and, better still, good company."

"*Caro Capitano!*" broke in the musical voice of the Marchese Gualdro, "you know that our Francesco goes nowhere without his beloved Carlo. Carlo CANNOT come–altro! Francesco WILL NOT. Would that all men were such brothers!"

"If they were," laughed Luziano Salustri, rising from the piano where he had been playing softly to himself, "half the world would be thrown out of employment. You, for instance," turning to the Marquis D'Avencourt, "would scarce know what to do with your time."

The marquis smiled and waved his hand with a deprecatory gesture– that hand, by the by, was remarkably small and delicately formed–it looked almost fragile. Yet the strength and suppleness of D'Avencourt's wrist was reputed to be prodigious by those who had seen him handle the sword, whether in play or grim earnest.

"It is an impossible dream," he said, in reply to the remarks of Gualdro and Salustri, "that idea of all men fraternizing together in one common pig-sty of equality. Look at the differences of caste! Birth, breeding and education make of man that high-mettled, sensitive animal known as gentleman, and not all the socialistic theories in the world can force him down on the same level with the rough boor, whose flat nose and coarse features announce him as plebeian even before one hears the tone of his voice. We cannot help these things. I do not think we WOULD help them even if we could."

"You are quite right," said Ferrari. "You cannot put race-horses to draw the plow. I have always imagined that the first quarrel–the Cain and Abel affair–must have occurred through some difference of caste as well as jealousy–for instance, perhaps Abel was a negro and Cain a white man, or vice versa; which would account for the antipathy existing between the races to this day."

The Duke di Marina coughed a stately cough, and shrugged his shoulders.

"That first quarrel," he said, "as related in the Bible, was exceedingly vulgar. It must have been a kind of prize-fight. *Ce n'etait pas fin.*"

Gualdro laughed delightedly.

"So like you, Marina!" he exclaimed, "to say that! I sympathize with your sentiments! Fancy the butcher Abel piling up his reeking carcasses and setting them on fire, while on the other side stood Cain the green-grocer frizzling his cabbages, turnips, carrots, and other vegetable matter! What a spectacle! The gods of Olympus would have sickened at it! However, the Jewish Deity, or rather, the well- fed priest who represented him, showed his good taste in the matter; I myself prefer the smell of roast meat to the rather disagreeable odor of scorching vegetables!"

We laughed–and at that moment the door was thrown open, and the head-waiter announced in solemn tones befitting his dignity–

"*Le diner de Monsieur le Conte est servi!*"

I at once led the way to the banqueting-room–my guests followed gaily, talking and jesting among themselves. They were all in high good humor, none of them had as yet noticed the fatal blank caused by the absence of the brothers Respetti. I had–for the number of my guests was now thirteen instead of fifteen. Thirteen at table! I wondered if any of the company were superstitious? Ferrari was not, I knew–unless his nerves had been latterly shaken by witnessing the death of his uncle. At any rate, I resolved to say nothing that could attract the attention of my guests to the ill-omened circumstance; if anyone should notice it, it would be easy to make light of it and of all similar superstitions. I myself was the one most affected by it–it had for me a curious and fatal significance. I was so occupied with the consideration of it that I scarcely attended to the words addressed to me by the Duke di Marina, who, walking beside me, seemed disposed to converse with more familiarity than was his usual custom. We reached the door of the dining-room; which at our approach was thrown wide open, and delicious strains of music met our ears as we entered. Low murmurs of astonishment and admiration broke from all the gentlemen as they viewed the sumptuous scene before them. I pretended not to hear their eulogies, as I took my seat at the head of the table, with Guido Ferrari on my right and the Duke di Manna on my left. The music sounded louder and more triumphant, and while all the company were seating themselves in the places assigned to them, a choir of young fresh voices broke forth into a Neapolitan "*madrigale*"– which as far as I can translate it ran as follows:

"Welcome the festal hour! Pour the red wine into cups of gold! Health to the men who are strong and bold! Welcome the festal hour! Waken the echoes with riotous mirth– Cease to remember the sorrows of earth In the joys of the festal hour! Wine is the monarch of laughter and light, Death himself shall be merry to-night! Hail to the festal hour!"

An enthusiastic clapping of hands rewarded this effort on the part of the unseen vocalists, and the music having ceased, conversation became general.

"By heaven!" exclaimed Ferrari, "if this Olympian carouse is meant as a welcome to me, amico, all I can say is that I do not deserve it. Why, it is more fit for the welcome of one king to his neighbor sovereign!"

"*Ebbene!*" I said. "Are there any better kings than honest men? Let us hope we are thus far worthy of each other's esteem."

He flashed a bright look of gratitude upon me and was silent, listening to the choice and complimentary phrases uttered by the Duke di Manna concerning the exquisite taste displayed in the arrangement of the table.

"You have no doubt traveled much in the East, conte," said this nobleman. "Your banquet reminds me of an Oriental romance I once read, called 'Vathek.'"

"Exactly" exclaimed Guido. "I think Oliva must be Vathek

himself?"

"Scarcely!" I said, smiling coldly. "I lay no claim to supernatural experiences. The realities of life are sufficiently wonderful for me."

Antonio Biscardi the painter, a refined, gentle-featured man, looked toward us and said modestly:

"I think you are right, conte. The beauties of nature and of humanity are so varied and profound that were it not for the inextinguishable longing after immortality which has been placed in Every one of us, I think we should be perfectly satisfied with this world as it is."

"You speak like an artist and a man of even temperament," broke in the Marchese Gualdro, who had finished his soup quickly in order to be able to talk—talking being his chief delight. "For me, I am never contented. I never have enough of anything! That is my nature. When I see lovely flowers, I wish more of them—when I behold a fine sunset, I desire many more such sunsets—when I look upon a lovely woman—"

"You would have lovely women ad infinitum!" laughed the French Capitaine de Hamal. "*En verite*, Gualdro, you should have been a Turk!"

"And why not?" demanded Gualdro. "The Turks are very sensible people—they know how to make coffee better than we do. And what more fascinating than a harem? It must be like a fragrant hot-house, where one is free to wander every day, sometimes gathering a gorgeous lily, sometimes a simple violet—sometimes—" "A thorn?" suggested Salustri.

"Well, perhaps!" laughed the Marchese. "Yet one would run the risk of that for the sake of a perfect rose."

Chevalier Mancini, who wore in his button-hole the decoration of the Legion d'Honneur, looked up—he was a thin man with keen eyes and a shrewd face which, though at a first glance appeared stern, could at the least provocation break up into a thousand little wrinkles of laughter.

"There is undoubtedly something *entrainant* about the idea," he observed, in his methodical way. "I have always fancied that marriage as we arrange it is a great mistake."

"And that is why you have never tried it?" queried Ferrari, looking amused.

"*Certissimamente!*" and the chevalier's grim countenance began to work with satirical humor. "I have resolved that I will never be bound over by the law to kiss only one woman. As matters stand, I can kiss them all if I like."

A shout of merriment and cries of "Oh! oh!" greeted this remark, which Ferrari, however, did not seem inclined to take in good part.

"All?" he said, with a dubious air. "You mean all except the married ones?"

The chevalier put on his spectacles, and surveyed him with a sort of comic severity.

"When I said ALL, I meant all," he returned–"the married ones in particular. They, poor things, need such attentions–and often invite them–why not? Their husbands have most likely ceased to be amorous after the first months of marriage."

I burst out laughing. "You are right, Mancini," I said; "and even if the husbands are fools enough to continue their gallantries they deserve to be duped–and they generally are! Come, amico."" I added, turning to Ferrari, "those are your own sentiments–you have often declared them to me."

He smiled uncomfortably, and his brows contracted. I could easily perceive that he was annoyed. To change the tone of the conversation I gave a signal for the music to recommence, and instantly the melody of a slow, voluptuous Hungarian waltz-measure floated through the room. The dinner was now fairly on its way; the appetites of my guests were stimulated and tempted by the choicest and most savory viands, prepared with all the taste and intelligence a first rate chef can bestow on his work, and good wine flowed freely.

Vincenzo obediently following my instructions, stood behind my chair, and seldom moved except to refill Ferrari's glass, and occasionally to proffer some fresh vintage to the Duke di Marina. He, however, was an abstemious and careful man, and followed the good example shown by the wisest Italians, who never mix their wines. He remained faithful to the first beverage he had selected—a specially fine Chianti, of which he partook freely without its causing the slightest flush to appear on his pale aristocratic features. Its warm and mellow flavor did but brighten his eyes and loosen his tongue, inasmuch that he became almost as elegant a talker as the Marchese Gualdro. This latter, who scarce had a *scudo* to call his own, and who dined sumptuously every day at other people's expense for the sake of the pleasure his company afforded, was by this time entertaining Everyone near him by the most sparkling stories and witty pleasantries.

The merriment increased as the various courses were served; shouts of laughter frequently interrupted the loud buzz of conversation, mingling with the clinking of glasses and clattering of porcelain. Every now and then might be heard the smooth voice of Captain Freccia rolling out his favorite oaths with the sonority and expression of a *primo tenore*; sometimes the elegant French of the Marquis D'Avencourt, with his high, sing-song Parisian accent, rang out above the voices of the others; and again, the choice Tuscan of the poet Luziano Salustri rolled forth in melodious cadence as though he were chanting lines from Dante or Ariosto, instead of talking lightly on indifferent matters. I accepted my share in the universal hilarity, though I principally divided my conversation between Ferrari and the duke, paying to both, but specially to Ferrari, that absolute attention which is the greatest compliment a host can bestow on those whom he undertakes to entertain.

We had reached that stage of the banquet when the game was about to be served—the invisible choir of boys' voices had just completed an enchanting *stornello* with an accompaniment of mandolins—when a stillness, strange and unaccountable, fell upon the company—a pause—an ominous hush, as though some person supreme in authority had suddenly entered the room and commanded "Silence!" No one seemed disposed to speak or to move, the very footsteps of the waiters were muffled in the velvet pile of the carpets–no sound was heard but the measured plash of the fountain that played among the ferns and flowers. The moon, shining frostily white through the one uncurtained window, cast a long pale green ray, like the extended arm of an appealing ghost, against one side of the velvet hangings– a spectral effect which was heightened by the contrast of the garish glitter of the waxen tapers. Each man looked at the other with a sort of uncomfortable embarrassment, and somehow, though I moved my lips in an endeavor to speak and thus break the spell, I was at a loss, and could find no language suitable to the moment. Ferrari toyed with his wine-glass mechanically–the duke appeared absorbed in arranging the crumbs beside his plate into little methodical patterns; the stillness seemed to last so long that it was like a suffocating heaviness in the air. Suddenly Vincenzo, in his office of chief butler, drew the cork of a champagne-bottle with a loud- sounding pop! We all started as though a pistol had been fired in our ears, and the Marchese Gualdro burst out laughing.

"*Corpo di Baceo!*" he cried. "At last you have awakened from sleep! Were you all struck dumb, amici, that you stared at the table-cloth so persistently and with such admirable gravity? May Saint Anthony and his pig preserve me, but for the time I fancied I was attending a banquet on the wrong side of the Styx, and that you, my present companions, were all dead men!"

"And that idea made YOU also hold your tongue, which is quite an unaccountable miracle in its way," laughed Luziano Salustri. "Have you never heard the pretty legend that attaches to such an occurrence as a sudden silence in the midst of high festivity? An angel enters, bestowing his benediction as he passes through."

"That story is more ancient than the church," said Chevalier Mancini. "It is an exploded theory–for we have ceased to believe in angels–we call them women instead."

"*Bravo, mon vieux gaillard!*" cried Captain de Hamal. "Your

264

sentiments are the same as mine, with a very trifling difference. You believe women to be angels–I know them to be devils–*mas il n'y agu'un pas entre es deux*? We will not quarrel over a word–*a votre sante, mon cher*!"

And he drained his glass, nodding to Mancini, who followed his example.

"Perhaps," said the smooth, slow voice of Captain Freccia, "our silence was caused by the instinctive consciousness of something wrong with our party–a little inequality–which I dare say our noble host has not thought it worthwhile to mention."

Every head was turned in his direction. "What do you mean?" "What inequality?" "Explain yourself!" chorused several voices.

"Really it is a mere nothing," answered Freccia, lazily, as he surveyed with the admiring air of a gourmet the dainty portion of pheasant just placed before him. "I assure you, only the uneducated would care two scudi about such a circumstance. The excellent brothers Respetti are to blame–their absence to-night has caused– but why should I disturb your equanimity? I am not superstitious– ma, chi sa?–some of you may be."

"I see what you mean!" interrupted Salustri, quickly. "We are thirteen at table!"

24

AT THIS announcement my guests looked furtively at each other, and I could see they were counting up the fatal number for themselves. They were undeniably clever, cultivated men of the world, but the superstitious element was in their blood, and all, with the exception perhaps of Freccia and the ever-cool Marquis D'Avencourt, were evidently rendered uneasy by the fact now discovered. On Ferrari it had a curious effect–he started violently and his face flushed. "*Diabolo!*" he muttered, under his breath, and seizing his never-empty glass, he swallowed its contents thirstily and quickly at one gulp as though attacked by fever, and pushed away his plate with a hand that trembled nervously. I, meanwhile, raised my voice and addressed my guests cheerfully!

"Our distinguished friend Salustri is perfectly right, gentlemen. I myself noticed the discrepancy in our number some time ago–but I knew that you were all advanced thinkers, who had long since liberated yourselves from the trammels of superstitious observances, which are the result of priest craft, and are now left solely to the vulgar. Therefore I said nothing. The silly notion of any misfortune attending the number thirteen arose, as you are aware, out of the story of the Last Supper, and children and women may possibly still give credence to the fancy that one out of thirteen at table must be a traitor and doomed to die. But we men know better. None of us here to-night have reason to put ourselves in the position of a Christ or a Judas—we are all good friends and boon companions, and I cannot suppose for a moment that this little cloud can possibly affect you seriously. Remember also that this is Christmas-eve, and that according to the world's greatest poet, Shakespeare,

"'Then no planet strikes, No fairy tales, nor witch hath power to charm, So hallowed and so gracious is the time.'"

A murmur of applause and a hearty clapping of hands rewarded this little speech, and the Marchese Gualdro sprung to his feet—

"By Heaven!" he exclaimed, "we are not a party of terrified old women to shiver on the edge of a worn-out omen! Fill your glasses, signori! More wine, garcon! *Per bacco!* if Judas Iscariot himself had such a feast as ours before he hanged himself, he was not much to be pitied! *Hola amici!* To the health of our noble host, Conte Cesare Oliva!"

He waved his glass in the air three times—Everyone followed his example and drank the toast with enthusiasm. I bowed my thanks and acknowledgments—and the superstitious dread which at first bad undoubtedly seized the company passed away quickly—the talking, the merriment, and laughter were resumed, and soon it seemed as though the untoward circumstance were entirely forgotten. Only Guido Ferrari seemed still somewhat disturbed in his mind—but even his uneasiness dissipated itself by degrees, and heated by the quantity of wine he had taken, he began to talk with boastful braggartism of his many successful gallantries, and related his most questionable anecdotes in such a manner as to cause some haughty astonishment in the mind of the Duke di Marina, who eyed him from time to time with ill-disguised impatience that bordered on contempt. I, on the contrary, listened to everything he said with urbane courtesy—I humored him and drew him out as much as possible—I smiled complacently at his poor jokes and vulgar witticisms–and when he said something that was more than usually outrageous, I contented myself with a benevolent shake of my head, and the mild remark:

"Ah! young blood! young blood!" uttered in a bland sotto-voce.

The dessert was now served, and with it came the costly wines which I had ordered to be kept back till then. Priceless "Chateau Yquem," "Clos Vougeot," of the rarest vintages, choice "Valpulcello" and an exceedingly superb "Lacrima Cristi"–one after the other, these were tasted, criticised, and heartily appreciated. There was also a very unique brand of champagne costing nearly forty francs a bottle, which was sparkling and mellow to the palate, but fiery in quality. This particular beverage was so seductive in flavor that Everyone partook of it freely, with the result that the most discreet among the party now became the most uproarious. Antonio Biscardi, the quiet and unobtrusive painter, together with his fellow-student, Crispiano Dulci, usually the shyest of young men, suddenly grew excited, and uttered blatant nothings concerning their art. Captain Freccia argued the niceties of sword-play with the Marquis D'Avencourt, both speakers illustrating their various points by thrusting their dessert-knives skillfully into the pulpy bodies of the peaches they had on their plates. Luziano Salustri lay back at ease in his chair, his classic head reclining on the velvet cushions, and recited in low and measured tones one of his own poems, caring little or nothing whether his neighbors attended to him or not. The glib tongue of the Marchese Gualdro ran on smoothly and incessantly, though he frequently lost the thread of his anecdotes and became involved in a maze of contradictory assertions. The rather large nose of the Chevalier Mancini reddened visibly as he laughed joyously to himself at nothing in particular–in short, the table had become a glittering whirlpool of excitement and feverish folly, which at a mere touch, or word out of season, might rise to a raging storm of frothy dissension. The Duke di

Marina and myself alone of all the company were composed as usual–he had resisted the champagne, and as for me, I had let all the splendid wines go past me, and had not taken more than two glasses of a mild Chianti.

I glanced keenly round the riotous board–I noted the flushed faces and rapid gesticulations of my guests, and listened to the Babel of conflicting tongues. I drew a long breath as I looked–I calculated that in two or three minutes at the very least I might throw down the trump card I had held so patiently in my hand all the evening.

I took a close observation of Ferrari. He had edged his chair a little away from mine, and was talking confidentially to his neighbor, Captain de Hamal–his utterance was low and thick, but yet I distinctly heard him enumerating in somewhat coarse language the exterior charms of a woman–what woman I did not stop to consider– the burning idea struck me that he was describing the physical perfections of my wife to this De Hamal, a mere *spadaccino*, for whom there was nothing sacred in heaven or earth. My blood rapidly heated itself to boiling point–to this day I remember how it throbbed in my temples, leaving my hands and feet icy cold. I rose in my seat, and tapped on the table to call for silence and attention–but for some time the noise of argument and the clatter of tongues were so great that I could not make myself heard. The duke endeavored to second my efforts, but in vain. At last Ferrari's notice was attracted–he turned round, and seizing a dessert knife beat with it on the table and on his own plate so noisily and persistently that the loud laughter and conversation ceased suddenly. The moment had come–I raised my head, fixed my spectacles more firmly over my eyes, and spoke in distinct and steady tones, first of all stealing a covert glance toward Ferrari. He had sunk back again lazily in his chair and was lighting a cigarette.

"My friends," I said, meeting with a smile the inquiring looks that were directed toward me, "I have presumed to interrupt your mirth for a moment, not to restrain it, but rather to give it a fresh impetus. I asked you all here tonight, as you know, to honor me by your presence and to give a welcome to our mutual friend, Signor Guido Ferrari." Here I was interrupted by a loud clapping of hands and ejaculations of approval, while Ferrari himself murmured affably between two puffs of his cigarette. "*Tropp' onore, amico, tropp' onore!*" I resumed, "This young and accomplished gentleman, who is, I believe, a favorite with you all, has been compelled through domestic affairs to absent himself from our circle for the past few weeks, and I think he must himself be aware how much we have missed his pleasant company. It will, however, be agreeable to you, as it has been for me, to know that he has returned to Naples a richer man than when he left it–that fortune has done him justice, and that with the possession of abundant wealth he is at last called upon to enjoy the reward due to his merits!"

Here there was more clapping of hands and exclamations of pleasure, while those who were seated near Ferrari raised their glasses and drank to his health with congratulations, all of which courtesies he acknowledged by a nonchalant, self-satisfied bow. I glanced at him again–how tranquil he looked!–reclining among the crimson cushions of his chair, a brimming glass of champagne beside him, the cigarette between his lips, and his handsome face slightly upturned, though his eyes rested half drowsily on the uncurtained window through which the Bay of Naples was seen glittering in the moonlight.

I continued: "It was, gentlemen, that you might welcome and congratulate Signor Ferrari as you have done, that I assembled you here to-night–or rather, let me say it was PARTLY the object of our present festivity–but there is yet another reason which I shall now have the pleasure of explaining to you–a reason which, as it concerns myself and my immediate happiness, will, I feel confident, secure your sympathy and good wishes."

This time Everyone was silent, intently following my words.

"What I am about to say," I went on, calmly, "may very possibly surprise you. I have been known to you as a man of few words, and, I fear, of abrupt and brusque manners"–cries of "No, no!" mingled with various complimentary assurances reached my ears from all sides of the table. I bowed with a gratified air, and when silence was restored–"At any rate you would not think me precisely the sort of man to take a lady's fancy." A look of wonder and curiosity was now exchanged among my guests. Ferrari took his cigarette out of his mouth and stared at me in blank astonishment.

"No," I went on, meditatively, "old as I am, and a half-blind invalid besides, it seems incredible that any woman should care to look at me more than twice en passant. But I have met–let me say with the Chevalier Mancini–an angel–who has found me not displeasing to her, and–in short–I am going to marry!"

There was a pause. Ferrari raised himself slightly from his reclining position and seemed about to speak, but apparently changing his mind he remained silent–his face had somewhat paled. The momentary hesitation among my guests passed quickly. All present, except Guido, broke out into a chorus of congratulations, mingled with good-humored jesting and laughter.

"Say farewell to jollity, conte!" cried Chevalier Mancini; "once drawn along by the rustling music of a woman's gown, no more such feasts as we have had to-night!"

And he shook his head with tipsy melancholy.

"By all the gods!" exclaimed Gualdro, "your news has surprised me! I should have thought you were the last man to give up liberty for the sake of a woman. ONE woman, too! Why, man, freedom could give you twenty!"

"Ah!" murmured Salustri, softly and sentimentally, "but the one perfect pearl–the one flawless diamond–"

"Bah! Salustri, *caro mio*, you are half asleep!" returned Gualdro. "'Tis the wine talks, not you. Thou art conquered by the bottle, amico. You, the darling of all the women in Naples, to talk of one*! Buona notte, bambino!*"

I still maintained my standing position, leaning my two hands on the table before me.

"What our worthy Gualdro says," I went on, "is perfectly true. I have been noted for my antipathy to the fair sex. I know it. But when one of the loveliest among women comes out of her way to tempt me—when she herself displays the matchless store of her countless fascinations for my attraction—when she honors me by special favors and makes me plainly aware that I am not too presumptuous in venturing to aspire to her hand in marriage—what can I do but accept with a good grace the fortune thrown to me by Providence? I should be the most ungrateful of men were I to refuse so precious a gift from Heaven, and I confess I feel no inclination to reject what I consider to be the certainty of happiness. I therefore ask you all to fill your glasses, and do me the favor to drink to the health and happiness of my future bride."

Gualdro sprung erect, his glass held high in the air; every man followed his example, Ferrari rose to his feet with some unsteadiness, while the hand that held his full champagne glass trembled.

The Duke di Marina, with a courteous gesture, addressed me: "You will, of course, honor us by disclosing the name of the fair lady whom we are prepared to toast with all befitting reverence?"

"I was about to ask the same question," said Ferrari, in hoarse accents—his lips were dry, and he appeared to have some difficulty in speaking. "Possibly we are not acquainted with her?"

"On the contrary," I returned, eying him steadily with a cool smile. "You all know her name well! *Illustrissimi Signori!*" and my voice rang out clearly—"to the health of my betrothed wife, the Contessa Romani!"

"Liar!" shouted Ferrari—and with all a madman's fury he dashed his brimming glass of champagne full in my face! In a second the wildest scene of confusion ensued. Every man left his place at table and surrounded us. I stood erect and perfectly calm—wiping with my handkerchief the little runlets of wine that dripped from my clothing—the glass had fallen at my feet, striking the table as it fell and splitting itself to atoms.

"Are you drunk or mad, Ferrari?" cried Captain de Hamal, seizing him by the arm—"do you know what you have done?"

Ferrari glared about him like a tiger at bay—his face was flushed and swollen like that of a man in apoplexy—the veins in his forehead stood out like knotted cords—his breath came and went hard as though he had been running. He turned his rolling eyes upon me. "Damn you!" he muttered through his clinched teeth—then suddenly raising his voice to a positive shriek, he cried, "I will have your blood if I have to tear your heart for it!"—and he made an effort to spring upon me. The Marquis D'Avencourt quietly caught his other arm and held it as in a vise.

"Not so fast, not so fast, *mon cher*" he said, coolly. "We are not murderers, we! What devil possesses you, that you offer such unwarrantable insult to our host?"

"Ask HIM!" replied Ferrari, fiercely, struggling to release himself from the grasp of the two Frenchmen—"he knows well enough! Ask HIM!"

All eyes were turned inquiringly upon me. I was silent.

"The noble conte is really not bound to give any explanation," remarked Captain Freccia—"even admitting he were able to do so."

"I assure you, my friends," I said, "I am ignorant of the cause of this fracas, except that this young gentleman had pretensions himself to the hand of the lady whose name affects him so seriously!"

For a moment I thought Ferrari would have choked.

"Pretensions—pretensions!" he gasped. "Gran Dio! Hear him!—hear the miserable scoundrel!"

"*Ah, basta!*" exclaimed Chevalier Mancini, scornfully—"Is that all? A mere *bagatelle*! Ferrari, you were wont to be more sensible! What! quarrel with an excellent friend for the sake of a woman who happens to prefer him to you! *Ma che!* Women are plentiful–friends are few."

"If," I resumed, still methodically wiping the stains of wine from my coat and vest–"if Signor Ferrari's extraordinary display of temper is a mere outcome of natural disappointment, I am willing to excuse it. He is young and hot blooded–let him apologize, and I shall freely pardon him."

"By my faith!" said the Duke di Marina with indignation, "such generosity is unheard of, conte! Permit me to remark that it is altogether exceptional, after such ungentlemanly conduct."

Ferrari looked from one to the other in silent fury. His face had grown pale as death. He wrenched himself from the grasp of D'Avencourt and De Hamal.

"Fools! let me go!" he said, savagely. "None of you are on my side– I see that!" He stepped to the table, poured out a glass of water and drank it off. He then turned and faced me– his head thrown back, his eyes blazing with wrath and pain.

"Liar!" he cried again, "double-faced accursed liar! You have stolen HER–you have fooled ME–but, by God, you shall pay for it with your life!"

"Willingly!" I said, with a mocking smile, restraining by a gesture the hasty exclamations of those around me who resented this fresh attack–"most willingly, *caro signor*! But excuse me if I fail to see wherein you consider yourself wronged. The lady who is now my fiancée has not the slightest affection for you–she told me so herself. Had she entertained any such feelings I might have withdrawn my proposals–but as matters stand, what harm have I done you?"

A chorus of indignant voices interrupted me. "Shame on you, Ferrari!" cried Gualdro. "The count speaks like a gentleman and a man of honor. Were I in his place you should have had no word of explanation whatever. I would not have condescended to parley with you–by Heaven I would not!"

"Nor I!" said the duke, stiffly.

"Nor I!" said Mancini.

"Surely," said Luziana Salustri, "Ferrari will make the *amende* honorable."

There was a pause. Each man looked at Ferrari with some anxiety. The suddenness of the quarrel had sobered the whole party more effectually than a cold douche. Ferrari's face grew more and more livid till his very lips turned a ghastly blue–he laughed aloud in bitter scorn. Then, walking steadily up to me, with his eyes full of baffled vindictiveness, he said, in a low clear tone:

"You say that–you say she never cared for me–YOU! and I am to apologize to you! Thief, coward, traitor–take that for my apology!" And he struck me across the mouth with his bare hand so fiercely that the diamond ring he wore (my diamond ring) cut my flesh and slightly drew blood. A shout of anger broke from all present! I turned to the Marquis D'Avencourt.

"There can be but one answer to this," I said, with indifferent coldness. "Signor Ferrari has brought it on himself. Marquis, will you do me the honor to arrange the affair?"

The marquis bowed, "I shall be most happy!"

Ferrari glared about him for a moment and then said, "Freccia, you will second me?"

Captain Freccia shrugged his shoulders. "You must positively excuse me," he said. "My conscience will not permit me to take up such a remarkably wrong cause as yours, *cara mio*! I shall be pleased to act with D'Avencourt for the count, if he will permit me." The marquis received him with cordiality, and the two engaged in earnest conversation. Ferrari next proffered his request to his quondam friend De Hamal, who also declined to second him, as did Everyone among the company. He bit his lips in mortification and wounded vanity, and seemed hesitating what to do next, when the marquis approached him with frigid courtesy and appeared to offer him some suggestions in a low tone of voice–for after a few minutes' converse, Ferrari suddenly turned on his heel and abruptly left the room without another word or look. At the same instant I touched Vincenzo, who, obedient to his orders, had remained an impassive but evidently astonished spectator of all that had passed, and whispered—"Follow that man and do not let him see you." He obeyed so instantly that the door had scarcely closed upon Ferrari when Vincenzo had also disappeared. The Marquis D'Avencourt now came up to me.

"Your opponent has gone to find two seconds," he said. "As you perceived, no one here would or could support him. It is a most unfortunate affair."

"Most unfortunate," chorused De Hamal, who, though not in it, appeared thoroughly to enjoy it.

"For my part," said the Duke di Marina, "I wonder how our noble friend could be so lenient with such a young puppy. His conceit is insufferable!"

Others around me made similar remarks, and were evidently anxious to show how entirely they were on my side. I however remained silent, lest they should see how gratified I was at the success of my scheme. The marquis addressed me again:

"While awaiting the other seconds, who are to find us here," he said, with a glance at his watch, "Freccia and I have arranged a few preliminaries. It is now nearly midnight. We propose that the affair should come off in the morning at six precisely. Will that suit you?"

I bowed.

"As the insulted party you have the choice of weapons. Shall we say—"

"Pistols," I replied briefly.

"*A la bonne heure!* Then, suppose we fix upon the plot of open ground just behind the hill to the left of the Casa Ghirlande–between that and the Villa Romani–it is quiet and secluded, and there will be no fear of interruption."

I bowed again.

"Thus it stands," continued the marquis, affably–"the hour of six– the weapons pistols–the paces to be decided hereafter when the other seconds arrive."

I professed myself entirely satisfied with these

arrangements, and shook hands with my amiable coadjutor. I then looked round at the rest of the assembled company with a smile at their troubled faces.

"Gentlemen," I said, "our feast has broken up in a rather disagreeable manner–and I am sorry for it, the more especially as it compels me to part from you. Receive my thanks for your company, and for the friendship you have displayed toward me! I do not believe that this is the last time I shall have the honor of entertaining you–but if it should be so, I shall at any rate carry a pleasant remembrance of you into the next world! If on the contrary I should survive the combat of the morning, I hope to see you all again on my marriage-day, when nothing shall occur to mar our merriment. In the meantime–good-night!"

They closed round me, pressing my hands warmly and assuring me of their entire sympathy with me in the quarrel that had occurred. The duke was especially cordial, giving me to understand that had the others failed in their services, he himself, in spite of his dignity and peace-loving disposition, would have volunteered as my second. I escaped from them all at last and reached the quiet of my own apartments. There I sat alone for more than an hour, waiting for the return of Vincenzo, whom I had sent to track Ferrari. I heard the departing footsteps of my guests as they left the hotel by twos and threes–I heard the equable voices of the marquis and Captain Freccia ordering hot coffee to be served to them in a private room where they were to await the other seconds–now and then I caught a few words of the excited language of the waiters who were volubly discussing the affair as they cleared away the remains of the superb feast at which, though none knew it save myself, death had been seated. Thirteen at table! One was a traitor and one must die. I knew which one. No presentiment lurked in my mind as to the doubtful result of the coming combat. It was not my lot to fall–my time had not come yet–I felt certain of that! No! All the fateful forces of the universe would help me to keep alive till my vengeance was fulfilled. Oh, what bitter shafts of agony Ferrari carried in his heart at that moment, I thought. HOW he had looked when I said she never cared for him! Poor wretch! I pitied him even while I rejoiced at his torture. He suffered now as I had suffered–he was duped as I had been duped–and each quiver of his convulsed face and tormented frame had been fraught with satisfaction to me! Each moment of his life was now a pang to him. Well! it would soon be over–thus far at least I was merciful. I drew out pens and paper and commenced to write a few last instructions, in case the result of the fight should be fatal to me. I made them very concise and brief–I knew, while writing, that they would not be needed. Still–for the sake of form I wrote–and sealing the document, I directed it to the Duke di Marina. I looked at my watch–it was past one o'clock and Vincenzo had not yet returned. I went to the window, and drawing back the curtains, surveyed the exquisitely peaceful scene that lay before me. The moon was still high and bright– and her reflection made the waters of the bay appear like a warrior's coat of mail woven from a thousand glittering links of polished steel. Here and there, from the masts of anchored brigs and fishing-boats gleamed a few red and green lights burning dimly like fallen and expiring stars. There was a heavy unnatural silence everywhere–it oppressed me, and I threw the window wide open for air. Then came the sound of bells chiming softly. People passed to and fro with quiet footsteps– some paused to exchange friendly greetings. I remembered the day with a sort of pang at my heart. The night was over, though as yet there was no sign of dawn–and–it was Christmas morning!

25

THE OPENING of the room door aroused me from my meditations. I turned–to find Vincenzo standing near me, hat in hand–he had just entered.

"Ebbene!" I said, with a cheerful air–"what news?"

"*Eccellenza*, you have been obeyed. The young Signor Ferrari is now at his studio."

"You left him there?"

"Yes, *eccellenza*"–and Vincenzo proceeded to give me a graphic account of his adventures. On leaving the banqueting-room, Ferrari had taken a carriage and driven straight to the Villa Romani– Vincenzo, unperceived, had swung himself on to the back of the vehicle and had gone also.

"Arriving there," continued my valet, "he dismissed the *fiacre*–and rang the gate-bell furiously six or seven times. No one answered. I hid myself among the trees and watched. There were no lights in the villa windows–all was darkness. He rang it again–he even shook the gate as though he would break it open. At last the poor Giacomo came, half undressed and holding a lantern in his hand–he seemed terrified, and trembled so much that the lantern jogged up and down like a corpse-candle on a tomb.

"'I must see the contessa,' said the young signor, Giacomo

blinked like an owl, and coughed as though the devil scratched in his throat.

"'The contessa!' he said. 'She is gone!'

"The signor then threw himself upon Giacomo and shook him to and fro as though he were a bag of loose wheat.

"'Gone!' and he screamed like a madman! 'WHERE? Tell me WHERE, dolt! idiot! driveler! before I twist your neck for you!'

"Truly, *eccellenza*, I would have gone to the rescue of the poor Giacomo, but respect for your commands kept me silent. 'A thousand pardons, signor!' he whispered, out of breath with his shaking.' I will tell you instantly–most instantly. She is at the Convento dell' Annunziata–ten miles from here–the saints know I speak the truth–she left two days since.'

"The Signor Ferrari then flung away the unfortunate Giacomo with so much force that he fell in a heap on the pavement and broke his lantern to pieces. The old man set up a most pitiful groaning, but the signor cared nothing for that. He was mad, I think. 'Get to bed!' he cried, 'and sleep–sleep till you die! Tell your mistress when you see her that I came to kill her! My curse upon this house and all who dwell in it!' And with that he ran so quickly through the garden into the high-road that I had some trouble to follow him. There after walking unsteadily for a few paces, he suddenly fell down, senseless."

Vincenzo paused. "Well," I said, "what happened next?"

"*Eccellenza*, I could not leave him there without aid. I drew my cloak well up to my mouth and pulled my hat down over my eyes so that he could not recognize me. Then I took water from the fountain close by and dashed it on his face. He soon came to himself, and, taking me for a stranger, thanked me for my assistance, saying that he had a sudden shock. He then drank greedily from the fountain and went on his way."

"You followed?"

"Yes, *eccellenza*–at a little distance. He next visited a common tavern in one of the back streets of the city and came out with two men. They were well dressed–they had the air of gentlemen spoiled by bad fortune. The signor talked with them for some time–he seemed much excited. I could not hear what they said except at the end, when these two strangers consented to appear as seconds for Signor Ferrari, and they at once left him, to come straight to this hotel. And they are arrived, for I saw them through a half-opened door as I came in, talking with the Marquis D'Avencourt."

"Well!" I said, "and what of Signor Ferrari when he was left alone by his two friends?"

"There is not much more to tell, *eccellenza*. He went up the little hill to his own studio, and I noticed that he walked like a very old man with his head bent. Once he stopped and shook his fist in the air as though threatening someone. He let himself in at his door with a private key–and I saw him no more. I felt that he would not come out again for some time. And as I moved away to return here, I heard a sound as of terrible weeping."

"And that is all, Vincenzo?"

"That is all, *eccellenza*."

I was silent. There was something in the simple narration that touched me, though I remained as determinately relentless as ever. After a few moments I said:

"You have done well, Vincenzo. You are aware how grossly this young man has insulted me–and that his injurious treatment can only be wiped out in one way. That way is already arranged. You can set out those pistols you cleaned."

Vincenzo obeyed–but as he lifted the heavy case of weapons and set them on the table, he ventured to remark, timidly:

"The *eccellenza* knows it is now Christmas-day?"

"I am quite aware of the fact," I said somewhat frigidly.

In nowise daunted he went on, "Coming back just now I saw the big Nicolo–the *eccellenza* has doubtless seen him often?–he is a vine- grower, and they say he is the largest man in Naples–three months since he nearly killed his brother–

ebbene! To-night that same big Nicolo is drinking Chianti with that same brother, and both shouted after me as I passed, '*Hola*! Vincenzo Flamma! all is well between us because it is the blessed Christ's birthday.'" Vincenzo stopped and regarded me wistfully.

"Well!" I said, calmly, "what has the big Nicolo or his brother to do with me?"

My valet hesitated–looked up–then down–finally he said, simply, "May the saints preserve the *eccellenza* from all harm!"

I smiled gravely. "Thank you, my friend! I understand what you mean. Have no fear for me. I am now going to lie down and rest till five o'clock or thereabouts–and I advise you to do the same. At that time you can bring me some coffee."

And I nodded kindly to him as I left him and entered my sleeping apartment, where I threw myself on the bed, dressed as I was. I had no intention of sleeping–my mind was too deeply engrossed by all I had gone through. I could enter into Guido's feelings–had I not suffered as he was now suffering?– nay! more than he–for HE, at any rate, would not be buried alive! I should take care of that! HE would not have to endure the agony of breaking loose from the cold grasp of the grave to come back to life and find his name slandered, and his vacant place filled up by a usurper. Do what I would, I could not torture him as much as I myself had been tortured. That was a pity–death, sudden and almost painless, seemed too good for him. I held up my hand in the half light and watched it closely to see if it trembled ever so slightly. No! it was steady as a rock–I felt I was sure of my aim. I would not fire at his heart, I thought but just above it–for I had to remember one thing–he must live long enough to recognize me before he died. THAT was the sting I reserved for his last moments! The sick dreams that had bewildered my brain when I was taken ill at the *auberge* recurred to me. I remembered the lithe figure, so like Guido, that had glided in the Indian canoe toward me and had plunged a dagger three times in my heart? Had it not been realized? Had not Guido stabbed me thrice?– in his theft of my wife's affections–in his contempt for my little dead child–in his slanders on my name? Then why such foolish notions of pity– of forgiveness, that were beginning to steal into my mind? It was too late now for forgiveness–the very idea of it only rose out of a silly sentimentalism awakened by Ferrari's allusion to our young days–days for which, after all, he really cared nothing. Meditating on all these things, I suppose I must have fallen by imperceptible degrees into a doze which gradually deepened till it became a profound and refreshing sleep. From this I was awakened by a knocking at the door. I arose and admitted Vincenzo, who entered bearing a tray of steaming coffee.

"Is it already so late?" I asked him.

"It wants a quarter to five," replied Vincenzo–then looking at me in some surprise, he added, "Will not the *eccellenza* change his evening-dress?"

I nodded in the affirmative–and while I drank my coffee my valet set out a suit of rough tweed, such as I was accustomed to wear every day. He then left me, and I quickly changed my attire, and while I did so I considered carefully the position of affairs. Neither the Marquis D'Avencourt nor Captain Freccia had ever known me personally when I was Fabio Romani–nor was it at all probable that the two tavern companions of Ferrari had ever seen me. A surgeon would be on the field–most probably a stranger. Thinking over these points, I resolved on a bold stroke–it was this–that when I turned to face Ferrari in the combat, I would do so with uncovered eyes–I would abjure my spectacles altogether for the occasion. Vaguely I wondered what the effect would be upon him. I was very much changed even without these disguising glasses–my white beard and hair had seemingly altered my aspect–yet I knew there was something familiar in the expression of my eyes that could not fail to startle one who had known me well. My seconds would consider it very natural that I should remove the smoke-colored spectacles in order to see my aim unencumbered–the only person likely to be disconcerted by my action was Ferrari himself. The more I thought of it the more determined I was to do it. I had scarcely finished dressing when Vincenzo entered with my overcoat, and informed me that the marquis waited for me, and that a close carriage was in attendance at the private door of the hotel.

"Permit me to accompany you, *eccellenza!*" pleaded the faithful fellow, with anxiety in the tone of his voice.

"Come then, amico!" I said, cheerily. "If the marquis makes no objection I shall not. But you must promise not to interrupt any of the proceedings by so much as an exclamation."

He promised readily, and when I joined the marquis he followed, carrying my case of pistols.

"He can be trusted, I suppose?" asked D'Avencourt, glancing keenly at him while shaking hands cordially with me.

"To the death!" I replied, laughingly. "He will break his heart if he is not allowed to bind up my wounds!"

"I see you are in good spirits, conte," remarked Captain Freccia, as we took our seats in the carriage. "It is always the way with the man who is in the right. Ferrari, I fear, is not quite so comfortable."

And he proffered me a cigar, which I accepted. Just as we were about to start, the fat landlord of the hotel rushed toward us, and laying hold of the carriage door–"*Eccellenza,*" he observed in a confidential whisper, "of course this is only a matter of coffee and glorias? They will be ready for you all on your return. I know–I understand!" And he smiled and nodded a great many times, and laid his finger knowingly on the side of his nose. We laughed heartily, assuring him that his perspicuity was wonderful, and he stood on the broad steps in high good humor, watching us as our vehicle rumbled heavily away.

"Evidently," I remarked, "he does not consider a duel as a serious affair."

"Not he!" replied Freccia. "He has known of too many sham fights to be able to understand a real one. D'Avencourt knows something about that too, though he always kills his man. But very often it is sufficient to scratch one another with the sword-point so as to draw a quarter of a drop of blood, and honor is satisfied! Then the coffee and glorias are brought, as suggested by our friend the landlord."

"It is a ridiculous age," said the marquis, taking his cigar from his mouth, and complacently surveying his small, supple white hand, "thoroughly ridiculous, but I determined it should never make a fool of ME. You see, my dear conte, nowadays a duel is very frequently decided with swords rather than pistols, and why? Because cowards fancy it is much more difficult to kill with the sword. But not at all. Long ago I made up my mind that no man should continue to live who dared to insult me. I therefore studied swordplay as an art. And I assure you it is a simple matter to kill with the sword– remarkably simple. My opponents are astonished at the ease with which I dispatch them!"

Freccia laughed. "De Hamal is a pupil of yours, marquis, is he not?"

"I regret to say yes! He is marvelously clumsy. I have often earnestly requested him to eat his sword rather than handle it so boorishly. Yet he kills his men, too, but in a butcher-like manner– totally without grace or refinement. I should say he was about on a par with our two associates, Ferrari's seconds."

I roused myself from a reverie into which I had fallen.

"What men are they?" I inquired.

"One calls himself the Capitano Ciabatti, the other Cavaliere Dursi, at your service," answered Freccia, indifferently. "Good swearers both and hard drinkers–filled with stock phrases, such as 'our distinguished dear friend, Ferrari, 'wrongs which can only be wiped out by blood'–all bombast and *braggadocio*! These fellows would as soon be on one side as the other."

He resumed his smoking, and we all three lapsed into silence. The drive seemed very long, though in reality the distance was not great. At last we passed the Casa Ghirlande, a superb chateau belonging to a distinguished nobleman who in former days had been a friendly neighbor to me, and then our vehicle jolted down a gentle declivity which sloped into a small valley, where there was a good- sized piece of smooth flat greensward. From this spot could be faintly discerned the castellated turrets of my own house, the Villa Romani. Here we came to a standstill. Vincenzo jumped briskly down from his seat beside the coachman, and assisted us to alight. The carriage then drove off to a retired corner behind some trees. We surveyed the ground, and saw that as yet only one person beside ourselves had arrived. This was the surgeon, a dapper good-humored little German who spoke bad French and worse Italian, and who shook hands cordially with us all. On learning who I was he bowed low and smiled very amiably. "The best wish I can offer to you, signor," he said, "is that you may have no occasion for my services. You have reposed yourself? That is well–sleep steadies the nerves. Ach! you shiver! True it is, the morning is cold."

I did indeed experience a passing shudder, but not because the air was chilly. It was because I felt certain–so terribly certain, of killing the man I had once loved well. Almost I wished I could also feel that there was the slightest possibility of his killing me; but no!–all my instincts told me there was no chance of this. I had a sort of sick pain at my heart, and as I thought of HER, the jewel- eyed snake who had wrought all the evil, my wrath against her increased tenfold. I wondered scornfully what she was doing away in the quiet convent where the sacred Host, unveiled, glittered on the altar like a star of the morning. No doubt she slept; it was yet too early for her to practice her sham sanctity. She slept, in all probability most peacefully, while her husband and her lover called upon death to come and decide between them. The slow clear strokes of a bell chiming from the city tolled six, and as its last echo trembled mournfully on the wind there was a slight stir among my companions. I looked and saw Ferrari approaching with his two associates. He walked slowly, and was muffled in a thick cloak; his hat was pulled over his brows, and I could not see the expression of his face, as he did not turn his head once in my direction, but stood apart leaning against the trunk of a leafless tree. The seconds on both sides now commenced measuring the ground.

"We are agreed as to the distance, gentlemen," said the marquis. "Twenty paces, I think?"

"Twenty paces," stiffly returned one of Ferrari's friends—a battered-looking middle-aged rogue with ferocious mustachios, whom I presumed was Captain Ciabatti.

They went on measuring carefully and in silence. During the pause I turned my back on the whole party, slipped off my spectacles and put them in my pocket. Then I lowered the brim of my hat slightly so that the change might not be observed too suddenly—and resuming my first position, I waited. It was daylight though not full morning— the sun had not yet risen, but there was an opaline luster in the sky, and one pale pink streak in the east like the floating pennon from the lance of a hero, which heralded his approach. There was a gentle twittering of awakening birds—the grass sparkled with a million tiny drops of frosty dew. A curious calmness possessed me. I felt for the time as though I were a mechanical automaton moved by some other will than my own. I had no passion left.

The weapons were now loaded—and the marquis, looking about him with a cheerful business-like air, remarked:

"I think we may now place our men?"

This suggestion agreed to, Ferrari left his place near the tree against which he had in part inclined as though fatigued, and advanced to the spot his seconds pointed out to him. He threw off his hat and overcoat, thereby showing that he was still in his evening-dress. His face was haggard and of a sickly paleness—his eyes had dark rings of pain round them, and were full of a keen and bitter anguish. He eagerly grasped the pistol they handed to him, and examined it closely with vengeful interest. I meanwhile also threw off my hat and coat—the marquis glanced at me with careless approval.

"You look a much younger man without your spectacles,

conte," he remarked as he handed me my weapon. I smiled indifferently, and took up my position at the distance indicated, exactly opposite Ferrari. He was still occupied in the examination of his pistol, and did not at once look up.

"Are we ready, gentlemen?" demanded Freccia, with courteous coldness.

"Quite ready," was the response. The Marquis D'Avencourt took out his handkerchief. Then Ferrari raised his head and faced me fully for the first time. Great Heaven! shall I ever forget the awful change that came over his pallid countenance–the confused mad look of his eyes–the startled horror of his expression! His lips moved as though he were about to utter an exclamation–he staggered.

"One!" cried D'Avencourt.

We raised our weapons.

"Two!"

The scared and bewildered expression of Ferrari's face deepened visibly as he eyed me steadily in taking aim. I smiled proudly–I gave him back glance for glance–I saw him waver–his hand shook.

"Three!" and the white handkerchief fluttered to the ground. Instantly, and together, we fired. Ferrari's bullet whizzed past me, merely tearing my coat and grazing my shoulder. The smoke cleared– Ferrari still stood erect, opposite to me, staring straight forward with the same frantic far-off look–the pistol had dropped from his hand. Suddenly he threw up his arms–shuddered–and with a smothered groan fell, face forward, prone on the sward. The surgeon hurried to his side and turned him so that he lay on his back. He was unconscious–though his dark eyes were wide open, and turned blindly upward to the sky. The front of his shirt was already soaked with blood. We all gathered round him.

"A good shot?" inquired the marquis, with the indifference of a practiced duelist.

"Ach! a good shot indeed!" replied the little German doctor, shaking his head as he rose from his examination of the wound. "Excellent! He will be dead in ten minutes. The bullet has passed through the lungs close to the heart. Honor is satisfied certainly!"

At that moment a deep anguished sigh parted the lips of the dying man. Sense and speculation returned to those glaring eyes so awfully upturned. He looked upon us all doubtfully one after the other–till finally his gaze rested upon me. Then he grew strangely excited–his lips moved–he eagerly tried to speak. The doctor, watchful of his movements, poured brandy between his teeth. The cordial gave him momentary strength–he raised himself by a supreme effort.

"Let me speak," he gasped faintly, "to HIM!" And he pointed to me– then he continued to mutter like a man in a dream–"to him–alone– alone!–to him alone!"

The others, slightly awed by his manner, drew aside out of ear-shot, and I advanced and knelt beside him, stooping my face between his and the morning sky. His wild eyes met mine with a piteous beseeching terror.

"In God's name," he whispered, thickly, "WHO ARE YOU?"

"You know me, Guido!" I answered, steadily. "I am Fabio Romani, whom you once called friend! I am he whose wife you stole!–whose name you slandered!–whose honor you despised! Ah! look at me well! your own heart tells you who I am!"

He uttered a low moan and raised his hand with a feeble gesture.

"Fabio? Fabio?" he gasped. "He died–I saw him in his coffin!"

I leaned more closely over him. "I was BURIED ALIVE," I said with thrilling distinctness. "Understand me, Guido– buried alive! I escaped–no matter how. I came home–to learn your treachery and my own dishonor! Shall I tell you more?"

A terrible shudder shook his frame–his head moved restlessly to and fro, the sweat stood in large drops upon his forehead. With my own handkerchief I wiped his lips and brow tenderly–my nerves were strung up to an almost brittle tension–I smiled as a woman smiles when on the verge of hysterical weeping.

"You know the avenue," I said, "the dear old avenue, where the nightingales sing? I saw you there, Guido–with HER!–on the very night of my return from death–SHE was in your arms–you kissed her–you spoke of me–you toyed with the necklace on her white breast!"

He writhed under my gaze with a strong convulsive movement.

"Tell me–quick!" he gasped. "Does–SHE–know you?"

"Not yet!" I answered, slowly. "But soon she will–when I have married her!"

A look of bitter anguish filled his straining eyes. "Oh, God, God!" he exclaimed with a groan like that of a wild beast in pain. "This is horrible, too horrible! Spare me–spare–" A rush of blood choked his utterance. His breathing grew fainter and fainter; the livid hue of approaching dissolution spread itself gradually over his countenance. Staring wildly at me, he groped with his hands as though he searched for some lost thing. I took one of those feebly wandering hands within my own, and held it closely clasped.

"You know the rest," I said gently; "you understand my vengeance! But it is all over, Guido–all over, now! She has played us both false. May God forgive you as I do!"

He smiled–a soft look brightened his fast-glazing eyes–the old boyish look that had won my love in former days.

"All over!" he repeated in a sort of plaintive babble. "All over now! God–Fabio–forgive!–" A terrible convulsion wrenched and contorted his limbs and features, his throat rattled, and stretching himself out with a long shivering sigh–he died! The first beams of the rising sun, piercing through the dark, moss-covered branches of the pine-trees, fell on his clustering hair, and lent a mocking brilliancy to his wide-open sightless eyes: there was a smile on the closed lips! A burning, suffocating sensation rose in my throat, as of rebellious tears trying to force a passage. I still held the hand of my friend and enemy–it had grown cold in my clasp. Upon it sparkled my family diamond–the ring SHE had given him. I drew the jewel off: then I kissed that poor passive hand as I laid it gently down–kissed it tenderly, reverently. Hearing footsteps approaching, I rose from my kneeling posture and stood erect with folded arms, looking tearlessly down on the stiffening clay before me. The rest of the party came up; no one spoke for a minute, all surveyed the dead body in silence. At last Captain Freccia said, softly in half- inquiring accents:

"He is gone, I suppose?"

I bowed. I could not trust myself to speak.

"He made you his apology?" asked the marquis.

I bowed again. There was another pause of heavy silence. The rigid smiling face of the corpse seemed to mock all speech. The doctor stooped and skillfully closed those glazed appealing eyes–and then it seemed to me as though Guido merely slept and that a touch would waken him. The Marquis D'Avencourt took me by the arm and whispered, "Get back to the city, amico, and take some wine–you look positively ill! Your evident regret does you credit, considering the circumstances– but what would you?–it was a fair fight. Consider the provocation you had! I should advise you to leave Naples for a couple of weeks–by that time the affair will be forgotten. I know how these things are managed–leave it all to me."

I thanked him and shook his hand cordially and turned to depart. Vincenzo was in waiting with the carriage. Once I looked back, as with slow steps I left the field; a golden radiance illumined the sky just above the stark figure stretched so straightly on the sward; while almost from the very side of that pulseless heart a little bird rose from its nest among the grasses and soared into the heavens, singing rapturously as it flew into the warmth and glory of the living, breathing day.

26

ENTERING the fiacre, I drove in it a very little way toward the city. I bade the driver stop at the corner of the winding road that led to the Villa Romani, and there I alighted. I ordered Vincenzo to go on to the hotel and send from thence my own carriage and horses up to the villa gates, where I would wait for it. I also bade him pack my portmanteau in readiness for my departure that evening, as I proposed going to Avellino, among the mountains, for a few days. He heard my commands in silence and evident embarrassment. Finally he said:

"Do I also travel with the *eccellenza?*"

"Why, no!" I answered with a forced sad smile. "Do you not see, amico, that I am heavy-hearted, and melancholy men are best left to themselves. Besides–remember the carnival–I told you that you were free to indulge in its merriment, and shall I not deprive you of your pleasure? No, Vincenzo; stay and enjoy yourself, and take no concern for me."

Vincenzo saluted me with his usual respectful bow, but his features wore an expression of obstinacy.

"The *eccellenza* must pardon me," he said, "but I have just looked at death, and my taste is spoiled for carnival. Again–the *eccellenza* is sad–it is necessary that I should accompany him to Avellino."

I saw that his mind was made up, and I was in no humor for argument.

"As you will," I answered, wearily, "only believe me, you make a foolish decision. But do what you like; only arrange all so that we leave to-night. And now get back quickly–give no explanation at the hotel of what has occurred, and lose no time in sending on my carriage. I will wait alone at the Villa Romani till it comes."

The vehicle rumbled off, bearing Vincenzo seated on the box beside the driver. I watched it disappear, and then turned into the road that led me to my own dishonored home. The place looked silent and deserted–not a soul was stirring. The silken blinds of the reception-rooms were all closely drawn, showing that the mistress of the house was absent; it was as if someone lay dead within. A vague wonderment arose in my mind. WHO was dead? Surely it must be I–I the master of the household, who lay stiff and cold in one of those curtained rooms! This terrible white-haired man who roamed feverishly up and down outside the walls was not me–it was some angry demon risen from the grave to wreak punishment on the guilty. I was dead–I could never have killed the man who had once been my friend. And he also was dead–the same murderess had slain us both–and SHE lived! Ha! that was wrong–she must now die–but in such torture that her very soul shall shrink and shrivel under it into a devil's flame for the furnace of hell!

With my brain full of hot whirling thoughts like these I looked through the carved heraldic work of the villa gates. Here had Guido stood, poor wretch, last night, shaking these twisted wreaths of iron in impotent fury. There on the mosaic pavement he had flung the trembling old servant who had told him of the absence of his traitoress. On this very spot he had launched his curse, which, though he knew it not, was the curse of a dying man. I was glad he had uttered it–such maledictions cling! There was nothing but compassion for him in my heart now that he was dead. He had been duped and wronged even as I; and I felt that his spirit, released from its grosser clay, would work with mine and aid in her punishment.

I paced round the silent house till I came to the private wicket that led into the avenue; I opened it and entered the familiar path. I had not been there since the fatal night on which I had learned my own betrayal. How intensely still were those solemn pines–how gaunt and dark and grim! Not a branch quivered–not a leaf stirred. A cold dew that was scarcely a frost glittered on the moss at my feet, No bird's voice broke the impressive hush of the wood-lands morning dream. No bright-hued flower unbuttoned its fairy cloak to the breeze; yet there was a subtle perfume everywhere–the fragrance of unseen violets whose purple eyes were still closed in slumber.

I gazed on the scene as a man may behold in a vision the spot where he once was happy. I walked a few paces, then paused with a strange beating at my heart. A shadow fell across my path–it flitted before me, it stopped–it lay still. I saw it resolve itself into the figure of a man stretched out in rigid silence, with the light beating full on its smiling, dead face, and also on a deep wound just above his heart, from which the blood oozed redly, staining the grass on which he lay. Mastering the sick horror which seized me at this sight, I sprung forward–the shadow vanished instantly–it was a mere optical delusion, the result of my overwrought and excited condition. I shuddered involuntarily at the image my own heated fancy had conjured up; should I always see Guido thus, I thought, even in my dreams?

Suddenly a ringing, swaying rush of sound burst joyously on the silence–the slumbering trees awoke, their leaves moved, their dark branches quivered, and the grasses lifted up their green Lilliputian sword-blades. Bells!–and SUCH bells!– tongues of melody that stormed the air with sweetest eloquence–round, rainbow bubbles of music that burst upon the wind, and dispersed in delicate broken echoes.

"Peace on earth, good will to men! Peace–on–earth–good–will–to–men!" they seemed to say over and over again, till my ears ached with the repetition. Peace! What had I to do with peace or good- will? The Christ Mass could teach me nothing. I was as one apart from human life-an alien from its customs and affections–for me no love, no brotherhood remained. The swinging song of the chimes jarred my nerves. Why, I thought, should the wild erring world, with all its wicked men and women, presume to rejoice at the birth of the Savior?–they, who were not worthy to be saved! I turned swiftly away; I strode fiercely past the kingly pines that, now thoroughly awakened, seemed to note me with a stern disdain as though they said among themselves: "What manner of small creature is this that torments himself with passions unknown to US in our calm converse with the stars?"

I was glad when I stood again on the high-road, and infinitely relieved when I heard the rapid trot of horses rumbling of wheels, and saw my closed brougham, drawn by its prancing black Arabians, approaching. I walked to meet it; the coachman seeing me drew up instantly, I bade him take me to the Convento dell'Annunziata, and entering the carriage, I was driven rapidly away.

The convent was situated, I knew, somewhere between Naples and Sorrento. I guessed it to be near Castellamare, but it was fully three miles beyond that, and was a somewhat long drive of more than two hours. It lay a good distance out of the direct route, and was only attained by a by-road, which from its rough and broken condition was evidently not much frequented. The building stood apart from all other habitations in a large open piece of ground, fenced in by a high stone wall spiked at the top. Roses climbed thickly among the spikes, and almost hid their sharp points from view, and from a perfect nest of green foliage, the slender spire of the convent chapel rose into the sky like a white finger pointing to heaven. My coachman drew up before the heavily barred gates. I alighted, and bade him take the carriage to the principal hostelry at Castellamare, and wait for me there. As soon as he had driven off, I rang the convent bell. A little wicket fixed in the gate opened immediately, and the wrinkled visage of a very old and ugly nun looked out. She demanded in low tones what I sought. I handed her my card, and stated my desire to see the Countess Romani, if agreeable to the superioress. While I spoke she looked at me curiously–my spectacles, I suppose, excited her wonder–for I had replaced these disguising glasses immediately on leaving the scene of the duel–I needed them yet a little while longer. After peering at me a minute or two with her bleared and aged eyes, she shut the wicket in my face with a smart click and disappeared. While I awaited her return I heard the sound of children's laughter and light footsteps running trippingly on the stone passage within.

"*Fi donc*, Rosie!" said the girl's voice in French; "*la bonne Mere Marguerite sera tres tres fachee avec toi.*"

"*Tais-toi, petite sainte!*" cried another voice more piercing and silvery in tone. "*Je veux voir qui est la! C'est un homme je sais bien–parceque la vieille Mere Laura a rougi!*" and both young voices broke into a chorus of renewed laughter.

Then came the shuffling noise of the old nun's footsteps returning; she evidently caught the two truants, whoever they were, for I heard her expostulating, scolding and praying to the saints all in a breath, as she bade them go inside the house and ask the good little Jesus to forgive their naughtiness. A silence ensued, then the bolts and bars of the huge gate were undone slowly–it opened, and I was admitted. I raised my hat as I entered, and walked bareheaded through a long, cold corridor, guided by the venerable nun, who looked at me no more, but told her beads as she walked, and never spoke till she had led me into the building, through a lofty hall glorious with sacred paintings and statues, and from thence into a large, elegantly furnished room, whose windows commanded a fine view of the grounds. Here she motioned me to take a seat, and without lifting her eyelids, said:

"Mother Marguerite will wait upon you instantly, signor."

I bowed, and she glided from the room so noiselessly that I did not even hear the door close behind her. Left alone in what

I rightly concluded was the reception-room for visitors, I looked about me with some faint interest and curiosity. I had never before seen the interior of what is known as an educational convent. There were many photographs on the walls and mantelpiece—portraits of girls, some plain of face and form, others beautiful—no doubt they had all been sent to the nuns as souvenirs of former pupils. Rising from my chair I examined a few of them carelessly, and was about to inspect a fine copy of Murillo's Virgin, when my attention was caught by an upright velvet frame surmounted with my own crest and coronet. In it was the portrait of my wife, taken in her bridal dress, as she looked when she married me. I took it to the light and stared at the features dubiously. This was she—this slim, fairy-like creature clad in gossamer white, with the marriage veil thrown back from her clustering hair and child-like face—this was the THING for which two men's lives had been sacrificed! With a movement of disgust I replaced the frame in its former position; I had scarcely done so when the door opened quietly and a tall woman, clad in trailing robes of pale blue with a nun's band and veil of fine white cashmere, stood before me. I saluted her with a deep reverence; she responded by the slightest possible bend of her head. Her outward manner was so very still and composed that when she spoke her colorless lips scarcely moved, her very breathing never stirred the silver crucifix that lay like a glittering sign-manual on her quiet breast. Her voice, though low, was singularly clear and penetrating.

"I address the Count Oliva?" she inquired.

I bowed in the affirmative. She looked at me keenly: she had dark, brilliant eyes, in which the smoldering fires of many a conquered passion still gleamed.

"You would see the Countess Romani, who is in retreat here?"

"If not inconvenient or out of rule—" I began.

The shadow of a smile flitted across the nun's pale, intellectual face; it was gone almost as soon as it appeared.

"Not at all," she replied, in the same even monotone. "The

Countess Nina is, by her own desire, following a strict regime, but to-day being a universal feast-day all rules are somewhat relaxed. The reverend mother desires me to inform you that it is now the hour for mass—she has herself already entered the chapel. If you will share in our devotions, the countess shall afterward be informed of your presence here."

I could do no less than accede to this proposition, though in truth it was unwelcome to me. I was in no humor for either prayers or praise; I thought moodily how startled even this impassive nun might have been, could she have known what manner of man it was that she thus invited to kneel in the sanctuary. However, I said no word of objection, and she bade me follow her. As we left the room I asked:

"Is the countess well?"

"She seems so," returned Mere Marguerite; "she follows her religious duties with exactitude, and makes no complaint of fatigue."

We were now crossing the hall. I ventured on another inquiry.

"She was a favorite pupil of yours, I believe?"

The nun turned her passionless face toward me with an air of mild surprise and reproof.

"I have no favorites," she answered, coldly. "All the children educated here share my attention and regard equally."

I murmured an apology, and added with a forced smile:

"You must pardon my apparent inquisitiveness, but as the future husband of the lady who was brought up under your care, I am naturally interested in all that concerns her."

Again the searching eyes of the religieuse surveyed me; she sighed slightly.

"I am aware of the connection between you," she said, in rather a pained tone. "Nina Romani belongs to the world, and follows the ways of the world. Of course, marriage is the natural fulfillment of most young girls' destinies; there are comparatively few who are called out of the ranks to serve Christ. Therefore, when Nina married the estimable Count

Romani, of whom report spoke ever favorably, we rejoiced greatly, feeling that her future was safe in the hands of a gentle and wise protector. May his soul rest in peace! But a second marriage for her is what I did not expect, and what I cannot in my conscience approve. You see I speak frankly."

"I am honored that you do so, *madame*!" I said, earnestly, feeling a certain respect for this sternly composed yet patient-featured woman; "yet, though in general you may find many reasonable objections to it, a second marriage is I think, in the Countess Romani's case almost necessary. She is utterly without a protector– she is very young and how beautiful!"

The nun's eyes grew solemn and almost mournful.

"Such beauty is a curse," she answered, with emphasis; "a fatal–a fearful curse! As a child it made her wayward. As a woman it keeps her wayward still. Enough of this, signor!" and she bowed her head; "excuse my plain speaking. Rest assured that I wish you both happiness."

We had by this time reached the door of the chapel, through which the sound of the pealing organ poured forth in triumphal surges of melody. Mere Marguerite dipped her fingers in the holy water, and signing herself with the cross, pointed out a bench at the back of the church as one that strangers were allowed to occupy. I seated myself, and looked with a certain soothed admiration at the picturesque scene before me. There was the sparkle of twinkling lights–the bloom and fragrance of flowers. There were silent rows of nuns blue-robed and white-veiled, kneeling and absorbed in prayer. Behind these a little cluster of youthful figures in black, whose drooped heads were entirely hidden in veils of flowing white muslin. Behind these again, one woman's slight form arrayed in heavy mourning garments; her veil was black, yet not so thick but that I could perceive the sheeny glitter of golden hair–that was my wife, I knew. Pious angel! how devout she looked! I smiled in dreary scorn as I watched her; I cursed her afresh in the name of the man I had killed. And above all, surrounded with the luster of golden rays and incrusted jewels, the uncovered Host shone serenely like the gleam of the morning star. The stately service went on–the organ music swept through and through the church as though it were a strong wind striving to set itself free–but amid it all I sat as one in a dark dream, scarcely seeing, scarcely hearing–inflexible and cold as marble. The rich plaintive voice of one of the nuns in the choir, singing the Agnus Dei, moved me to a chill sort of wonder. "*Qui tollis peccata mundi*–Who takest away the sin of the world." No, no! there are some sins that cannot be taken away–the sins of faithless women, the "LITTLE" sins as they are called nowadays–for we have grown very lenient in some things, and very severe in others. We will imprison the miserable wretch who steals five francs from our pockets, but the cunning feminine thief who robs us of our prestige, our name and honorable standing among our fellow-men, escapes almost scot-free; she cannot be put in prison, or sentenced to hard labor–not she! A pity it is that Christ did not leave us some injunction as to what was to be done with such women– not the penitent Magdalenes, but the creatures whose mouths are full of lies even when they pretend to pray–they who would be capable of trying to tempt the priest who comes to receive their last confessions– they who would even act out a sham repentance on their deathbeds in order to look well. What can be done with devils such as these? Much has been said latterly of the wrongs perpetrated on women by men; will no one take up the other side of the question? We, the stronger sex, are weak in this–we are too chivalrous. When a woman flings herself on our mercy we spare her and are silent. Tortures will not wring her secrets out of us; something holds us back from betraying her. I know not what it can be–perhaps it is the memory of our mothers. Whatever it is, it is certain that many a man allows himself to be disgraced rather than he will disgrace a woman. But a time is at hand when this foolish chivalry of ours will die out. *On changera tout cela!* When once our heavy masculine brains shall have grasped the novel idea that woman has by her own wish and choice resigned all claim on our respect or forbearance, we shall have our revenge. We are slow to change the traditions of our forefathers, but no doubt we shall soon manage to quench the last spark of knightly reverence left in us for the female sex, as this is evidently the point the women desire to bring us to. We shall meet them on that low platform of the "equality" they seek for, and we shall treat them with the unhesitating and regardless familiarity they so earnestly invite!

Absorbed in thought, I knew not when the service ended. A hand touched me, and looking up I saw Mere Marguerite, who whispered:

"Follow me, if you please."

I rose and obeyed her mechanically. Outside the chapel door she said:

"Pray excuse me for hurrying you, but strangers are not permitted to see the nuns and boarders passing out."

I bowed, and walked on beside her. Feeling forced to say something, I asked:

"Have you many boarders at this holiday season?"

"Only fourteen," she replied, "and they are children whose parents live far away. Poor little ones!" and the set lines of the nun's stern face softened into tenderness as she spoke. "We do our best to make them happy, but naturally they feel lonely. We have generally fifty or sixty young girls here, besides the day scholars."

"A great responsibility," I remarked.

"Very great indeed!" and she sighed; "almost terrible. So much of a woman's after life depends on the early training she receives. We do all we can, and yet in some cases our utmost efforts are in vain; evil creeps in, we know not how—some unsuspected fault spoils a character that we judged to be admirable, and we are often disappointed in our most promising pupils. Alas! there is nothing entirely without blemish in this world."

Thus talking, she showed me into a small, comfortable-looking room, lined with books and softly carpeted.

"This is one of our libraries," she explained. "The countess will receive you here, as other visitors might disturb you in the drawing-room. Pardon me," and her steady gaze had something of compassion in it, "but you do not look well. Can I send you some wine?"

I declined this offer with many expressions of gratitude, and assured her I was perfectly well. She hesitated, and at last said, anxiously:

"I trust you were not offended at my remark concerning Nina Romani's marriage with you? I fear I was too hasty?"

"Not so, *madame*," I answered, with all the earnestness I felt. "Nothing is more pleasant to me than a frank opinion frankly spoken. I have been so accustomed to deception—" Here I broke off and added hastily, "Pray do not think me capable of judging you wrongly."

She seemed relieved, and smiling that shadowy, flitting smile of hers, she said:

"No doubt you are impatient, signor; Nina shall come to you directly," and with a slight salutation she left me.

Surely she was a good woman, I thought, and vaguely wondered about her past history—that past which she had buried forever under a mountain of prayers. What had she been like when young—before she had shut herself within the convent walls—before she had set the crucifix like a seal on her heart? Had she ever trapped a man's soul and strangled it with lies? I fancied not—her look was too pure and candid; yet who could tell? Were not Nina's eyes trained to appear as though they held the very soul of truth? A few minutes passed. I heard the fresh voices of children singing in the next room:

"*D'ou vient le petit Gesu? Ce joli bouton de rose Qui fleurit, enfant cheri Sur le coeur de notre mere Marie.*"

Then came a soft rustle of silken garments, the door opened, and my wife entered.

27

S HE APPROACHED with her usual panther-like grace and supple movement, her red lips parted in a charming smile.

"So good of you to come!" she began, holding out her two hands as though she invited an embrace; "and on Christmas morning too!" She paused, and seeing that I did not move or speak, she regarded me with some alarm. "What is the matter?" she asked, in fainter tones; "has anything happened?"

I looked at her. I saw that she was full of sudden fear, I made no attempt to soothe her, I merely placed a chair.

"Sit down," I said, gravely. "I am the bearer of bad news."

She sunk into the chair as though unnerved, and gazed at me with terrified eyes. She trembled. Watching her keenly, I observed all these outward signs of trepidation with deep satisfaction. I saw plainly what was passing in her mind. A great dread had seized her– the dread that I had found out her treachery. So indeed I had, but the time had not yet come for her to know it. Meanwhile she suffered–suffered acutely with that gnawing terror and suspense eating into her soul. I said nothing, I waited for her to speak. After a pause, during which her cheeks had lost their delicate bloom, she said, forcing a smile as she spoke–

"Bad news? You surprise me! What can it be? Some unpleasantness with Guido? Have you seen him?"

"I have seen him," I answered in the same formal and serious tone; "I have just left him. He sends you THIS," and I held out my diamond ring that I had drawn off the dead man's finger.

If she had been pale before, she grew paler now. All the brilliancy of her complexion faded for the moment into an awful haggardness. She took the ring with fingers that shook visibly and were icy cold. There was no attempt at smiling now. She drew a sharp quick breath; she thought I knew all. I was again silent. She looked at the diamond signet with a bewildered air.

"I do not understand," she murmured, petulantly. "I gave him this as a remembrance of his friend, my husband, why does he return it?"

Self-tortured criminal! I studied her with a dark amusement, but answered nothing. Suddenly she looked up at me and her eyes filled with tears.

"Why are you so cold and strange, Cesare?" she pleaded, in a sort of plaintive whimper. "Do not stand there like a gloomy sentinel; kiss me and tell me at once what has happened."

Kiss her! So soon after kissing the dead hand of her lover! No, I could not and would not. I remained standing where I was, inflexibly silent. She glanced at me again, very timidly, and whimpered afresh.

"Ah, you do not love me!" she murmured. "You could not be so stern and silent if you loved me! If there is indeed any bad news, you ought to break it to me gently and kindly. I thought you would always make everything easy for me–"

"Such has been my endeavor, *madame*," I said interrupting her complaint. "From your own statement, I judged that your adopted brother Guido Ferrari had rendered himself obnoxious to you. I promised that I would silence him–you remember! I have kept my word. He IS silenced–forever!"

She started.

"Silenced? How? You mean—"

I moved away from my place behind her chair, and stood so that I faced her as I spoke.

"I mean that he is dead."

She uttered a slight cry, not of sorrow but of wonderment.

"DEAD!" she exclaimed. "Not possible! Dead! You have killed him?"

I bent my head gravely. "I killed him—yes! But in open combat, openly witnessed. Last night he insulted me grossly; we fought this morning. We forgave each other before he died."

She listened attentively. A little color came back into her cheeks.

"In what way did he insult you?" she asked, in a low voice.

I told her all, briefly. She still looked anxious.

"Did he mention my name?" she said.

I glanced at her troubled features in profound contempt. She feared the dying man might have made some confession to me! I answered:

"No; not after our quarrel. But I hear he went to your house to kill you! Not finding you there, he only cursed you."

She heaved a sigh of relief. She was safe now, she thought! Her red lips widened into a cruel smile.

"What bad taste!" she said, coldly. "Why he should curse me I cannot imagine! I have always been kind to him—TOO kind."

Too kind indeed! kind enough to be glad when the object of all her kindness was dead! For she WAS glad! I could see that in the murderous glitter of her eyes.

"You are not sorry?" I inquired, with an air of pretended surprise.

"Sorry? Not at all! Why should I be? He was a very agreeable friend while my husband was alive to keep him in order, but after my poor Fabio's death, his treatment of me was quite unbearable."

Take care, beautiful hypocrite! take care! Take care lest your "poor Fabio's" fingers should suddenly nip your slim throat with a convulsive twitch that means death! Heaven only knows how I managed to keep my hands off her at that moment! Why, any groveling beast of the field had more feeling than this wretch whom I had made my wife! Even for Guido's sake—such are the strange inconsistencies of the human heart—I could have slain her then. But I restrained my fury; I steadied my voice and said calmly: "Then I was mistaken? I thought you would be deeply grieved, that my news would shock and annoy you greatly, hence my gravity and apparent coldness. But it seems I have done well?"

She sprung up from her chair like a pleased child and flung her arms round my neck.

"You are brave, you are brave!" she exclaimed, in a sort of exultation. "You could not have done otherwise! He insulted you and you killed him. That was right! I love you all the more for being such a man of honor!"

I looked down upon her in loathing and disgust. Honor! Its very name was libeled coming from HER lips. She did not notice the expression of my face—she was absorbed, excellent actress as she was, in the part she had chosen to play.

"And so you were dull and sad because you feared to grieve me! Poor Cesare!" she said, in child-like caressing accents, such as she could assume when she chose. "But now that you see I am not unhappy, you will be cheerful again? Yes? Think how much I love you, and how happy we will be! And see, you have given me such lovely jewels, so many of them too, that I scarcely dare offer you such a trifle as this; but as it really belonged to Fabio, and to Fabio's father, whom you knew, I think you ought to have it. Will you take it and wear it to please me?" and she slipped on my finger the diamond signet—my own ring!

I could have laughed aloud! but I bent my head gravely as I accepted it.

"Only as a proof of your affection, cara mia," I said, "though it has a terrible association for me. I took it from

Ferrari's hand when—"

"Oh, yes, I know!" she interrupted me with a little shiver; "it must have been trying for you to have seen him dead. I think dead people look so horrid—the sight upsets the nerves! I remember when I was at school here, they WOULD take me to see a nun who died; it sickened me and made me ill for days. I can quite understand your feelings. But you must try and forget the matter. Duels are very common occurrences, after all!"

"Very common," I answered, mechanically, still regarding the fair upturned face, the lustrous eyes, the rippling hair; "but they do not often end so fatally. The result of this one compels me to leave Naples for some days. I go to Avellino to-night."

"To Avellino?" she exclaimed, with interest. "Oh, I know it very well. I went there once with Fabio when I was first married."

"And were you happy there?" I inquired, coldly.

I remembered the time she spoke of—a time of such unreasoning, foolish joy!

"Happy? Oh, yes; everything was so new to me then. It was delightful to be my own mistress, and I was so glad to be out of the convent."

"I thought you liked the nuns?" I said.

"Some of them—yes. The reverend mother is a dear old thing. But Mere Marguerite, the Vicaire as she is called—the one that received you—oh, I do detest her!"

"Indeed! and why?"

The red lips curled mutinously.

"Because she is so sly and silent. Some of the children here adore her; but they MUST have something to love, you know," and she laughed merrily.

"Must they?"

I asked the question automatically, merely for the sake of saying something.

"Of course they must," she answered, gaily. "You foolish Cesare! The girls often play at being one another's lovers, only they are careful not to let the nuns know their game. It is very amusing. Since I have been here they have what is called a 'CRAZE' for me. They give me flowers, run after me in the garden, and sometimes kiss my dress, and call me by all manner of loving names. I let them do it because it vexes Madame la Vicaire; but of course it is very foolish."

I was silent. I thought what a curse it was–this necessity of loving. Even the poison of it must find its way into the hearts of children–young things shut within the walls of a secluded convent, and guarded by the conscientious care of holy women.

"And the nuns?" I said, uttering half my thoughts aloud. "How do they manage without love or romance?"

A wicked little smile, brilliant and disdainful, glittered in her eyes.

"DO they always manage without love or romance?" she asked, half indolently. "What of Abelard and Heloise, or Fra Lippi?"

Roused by something in her tone, I caught her round the waist, and held her firmly while I said, with some sternness:

"And you–is it possible that YOU have sympathy with, or find amusement in, the contemplation of illicit and dishonorable passion–tell me?"

She recollected herself in time; her white eyelids drooped demurely.

"Not I!" she answered, with a grave and virtuous air; "how can you think so? There is nothing to my mind so horrible as deceit; no good ever comes of it."

I loosened her from my embrace.

"You are right," I said, calmly; "I am glad your instincts are so correct! I have always hated lies."

"So have I!" she declared, earnestly, with a frank and open look; "I have often wondered why people tell them. They are so sure to be found out!"

I bit my lips hard to shut in the burning accusations that my tongue longed to utter. Why should I damn the actress or the play before the curtain was ready to fall on both? I changed the subject of converse.

"How long do you propose remaining here in retreat?" I asked. "There is nothing now to prevent your returning to Naples."

She pondered for some minutes before replying, then she said:

"I told the superioress I came here for a week. I had better stay till that time is expired. Not longer, because as Guido is really dead, my presence is actually necessary in the city."

"Indeed! May I ask why?"

She laughed a little consciously.

"Simply to prove his last will and testament," she replied. "Before he left for Rome, he gave it into my keeping."

A light flashed on my mind.

"And its contents?" I inquired.

"Its contents make ME the owner of everything he died possessed of!" she said, with an air of quiet yet malicious triumph.

Unhappy Guido! What trust he had reposed in this vile, self- interested, heartless woman! He had loved her, even as I had loved her–she who was unworthy of any love! I controlled my rising emotion, and merely said with gravity:

"I congratulate you! May I be permitted to see this document?"

"Certainly; I can show it to you now. I have it here," and she drew a Russia-leather letter-case from her pocket, and opening it, handed me a sealed envelope. "Break the seal!" she added, with childish eagerness. "He closed it up like that after I had read it."

With reluctant hand, and a pained piteousness at my heart, I opened the packet. It was as she had said, a will drawn up in perfectly legal form, signed and witnessed, leaving everything UNCONDITIONALLY to "Nina, Countess Romani, of the Villa Romani, Naples." I read it through and returned it to her.

"He must have loved you!" I said.

She laughed.

"Of course," she said, airily. "But many people love me–
that is nothing new; I am accustomed to be loved. But you
see," she went on, reverting to the will again, "it specifies,
'EVERYTHING HE DIES POSSESSED OF;' that means all
the money left to him by his uncle in Rome, does it not?"

I bowed. I could not trust myself to speak.

"I thought so," she murmured, gleefully, more to herself
than to me; "and I have a right to all his papers and letters."
There she paused abruptly and checked herself.

I understood her. She wanted to get back her own letters to
the dead man, lest her intimacy with him should leak out in
some chance way for which she was unprepared. Cunning
devil! I was almost glad she showed me to what a depth of
vulgar vice she had fallen. There was no question of pity or
forbearance in HER case. If all the tortures invented by
savages or stern inquisitors could be heaped upon her at once,
such punishment would be light in comparison with her
crimes– crimes for which, mark you, the law gives you no
remedy but divorce. Tired of the wretched comedy, I looked at
my watch.

"It is time for me to take my leave of you," I said, in the
stiff, courtly manner I affected. "Moments fly fast in your
enchanting company! But I have still to walk to Castellamare,
there to rejoin my carriage, and I have many things to attend to
before my departure this evening. On my return from Avellino
shall I be welcome?"

"You know it," she returned, nestling her head against my
shoulder, while for mere form's sake I was forced to hold her
in a partial embrace. "I only wish you were not going at all.
Dearest, do not stay long away–I shall be so unhappy till you
come back!"

"Absence strengthens love, they say," I observed, with a
forced smile. "May it do so in our case. Farewell, *cara mia*! Pray
for me; I suppose you DO pray a great deal here?"

"Oh, yes," she replied, naively; "there is nothing else to

do."

I held her hands closely in my grasp. The engagement ring on her finger, and the diamond signet on my own, flashed in the light like the crossing of swords.

"Pray then," I said, "storm the gates of heaven with sweet-voiced pleadings for the repose of poor Ferrari's soul! Remember he loved you, though YOU never loved him. For YOUR sake he quarreled with me, his best friend—for YOUR sake he died! Pray for him—who knows," and I spoke in thrilling tones of earnestness—"who knows but that his too-hastily departed spirit may not be near us now—hearing our voices, watching our looks?"

She shivered slightly, and her hands in mine grew cold.

"Yes, yes," I continued, more calmly; "you must not forget to pray for him—he was young and not prepared to die."

My words had some of the desired effect upon her—for once her ready speech failed—she seemed as though she sought for some reply and found none. I still held her hands.

"Promise me!" I continued; "and at the same time pray for your dead husband! He and poor Ferrari were close friends, you know; it will be pious and kind of you to join their names in one petition addressed to Him 'from whom no secrets are hid,' and who reads with unerring eyes the purity of your intentions. Will you do it?"

She smiled, a forced, faint smile.

"I certainly will," she replied, in a low voice; "I promise you."

I released her hands—I was satisfied. If she dared to pray thus I felt—I KNEW that she would draw down upon her soul the redoubled wrath of Heaven; for I looked beyond the grave! The mere death of her body would be but a slight satisfaction to me; it was the utter destruction of her wicked soul that I sought. She should never repent, I swore; she should never have the chance of casting off her vileness as a serpent casts its skin, and, reclothing herself in innocence, presume to ask admittance into that Eternal Gloryland whither my little child had gone–never, never! No church should save her, no priest should absolve her–not while I lived!

She watched me as I fastened my coat and began to draw on my gloves.

"Are you going now?" she asked, somewhat timidly.

"Yes, I am going now, *cara mia*," I said. "Why! what makes you look so pale?"

For she had suddenly turned very white.

"Let me see your hand again," she demanded, with feverish eagerness, "the hand on which I placed the ring!"

Smilingly and with readiness I took off the glove I had just put on.

"What odd fancy possesses you now, little one?" I asked, with an air of playfulness.

She made no answer, but took my hand and examined it closely and curiously. Then she looked up, her lips twitched nervously, and she laughed a little hard mirthless laugh.

"Your hand," she murmured, incoherently, "with–that–signet–on it–is exactly like–like Fabio's!"

And before I had time to say a word she went off into a violent fit of hysterics–sobs, little cries, and laughter all intermingled in that wild and reasonless distraction that generally unnerves the strongest man who is not accustomed to it. I rang the bell to summon assistance; a lay-sister answered it, and seeing Nina's condition, rushed for a glass of water and summoned Madame la Vicaire. This latter, entering with her quiet step and inflexible demeanor, took in the situation at a glance, dismissed the lay-sister, and possessing herself of the tumbler of water, sprinkled the forehead of the interesting patient, and forced some drops between her clinched teeth. Then turning to me she inquired, with some stateliness of manner, what had caused the attack?

"I really cannot tell you, *madame*," I said, with an air of affected concern and vexation. "I certainly told the countess of the unexpected death of a friend, but she bore the news with exemplary resignation. The circumstance that appears to have so greatly distressed her is that she finds, or says she finds, a resemblance between my hand and the hand of her deceased husband. This seems to me absurd, but there is no accounting for ladies' caprices."

And I shrugged my shoulders as though I were annoyed and impatient.

Over the pale, serious face of the nun there flitted a smile in which there was certainly the ghost of sarcasm.

"All sensitiveness and tenderness of heart, you see!" she said, in her chill, passionless tones, which, icy as they were, somehow conveyed to my ear another meaning than that implied by the words she uttered. "We cannot perhaps understand the extreme delicacy of her feelings, and we fail to do justice to them."

Here Nina opened her eyes, and looked at us with piteous plaintiveness, while her bosom heaved with those long, deep sighs which are the finishing chords of the Sonata Hysteria.

"You are better, I trust?" continued the nun, without any sympathy in her monotonous accents, and addressing her with some reserve. "You have greatly alarmed the Count Oliva."

"I am sorry—" began Nina, feebly.

I hastened to her side.

"Pray do not speak of it!" I urged, forcing something like a lover's ardor into my voice. "I regret beyond measure that it is my misfortune to have hands like those of your late husband! I assure you I am quite miserable about it. Can you forgive me?"

She was recovering quickly, and she was evidently conscious that she had behaved somewhat foolishly. She smiled a weak pale smile; but she looked very scared, worn and ill. She rose from her chair slowly and languidly.

"I think I will go to my room," she said, not regarding Mere Marguerite, who had withdrawn to a little distance, and who stood rigidly erect, immovably featured, with her silver crucifix glittering coldly on her still breast.

"Good-bye, Cesare! Please forget my stupidity, and write to me from Avellino."

I took her outstretched hand, and bowing over it, touched it gently with my lips. She turned toward the door, when suddenly a mischievous idea seemed to enter her mind. She looked at Madame la Vicaire and then came back to me.

"*Addio, amor mio!*" she said, with a sort of rapturous emphasis, and throwing her arms round my neck she kissed me almost passionately.

Then she glanced maliciously at the nun, who had lowered her eyes till they appeared fast shut, and breaking into a low peal of indolently amused laughter, waved her hand to me, and left the room.

I was somewhat confused. The suddenness and warmth of her caress had been, I knew, a mere monkish trick, designed to vex the religious scruples of Mere Marguerite. I knew not what to say to the stately woman who remained confronting me with downcast eyes and lips that moved dumbly as though in prayer. As the door closed after my wife's retreating figure, the nun looked up; there was a slight flush on her pallid cheeks, and to my astonishment, tears glittered on her dark lashes.

"Madame," I began, earnestly, "I assure you–"

"Say nothing, signor," she interrupted me with a slight deprecatory gesture; "it is quite unnecessary. To mock a *religieuse* is a common amusement with young girls and women of the world. I am accustomed to it, though I feel its cruelty more than I ought to do. Ladies like the Countess Romani think that we–we, the sepulchers of womanhood–sepulchers that we have emptied and cleansed to the best of our ability, so that they may more fittingly hold the body of the crucified Christ; these *grandes dames*, I say, fancy that WE are ignorant of all they know–that we cannot understand love, tenderness or passion. They never reflect–how should they?–that we also have had our histories–histories, perhaps, that would make angels weep for pity! I, even I–" and she struck her breast fiercely, then suddenly recollecting herself, she continued coldly: "The rule of our convent, signer, permits no visitor to remain longer than one hour–that hour has expired. I will summon a sister to show you the way out."

"Wait one instant, *madame*," I said, feeling that to enact my part thoroughly I ought to attempt to make some defense of Nina's conduct; "permit me to say a word! My fiancée is very young and thoughtless. I really cannot think that her very innocent parting caress to me had anything in it that was meant to purposely annoy you."

The nun glanced at me—her eyes flashed disdainfully.

"You think it was all affection for you, no doubt, signor? very natural supposition, and—I should be sorry to undeceive you."

She paused a moment and then resumed:

"You seem an earnest man—may be you are destined to be the means of saving Nina; I could say much—yet it is wise to be silent. If you love her do not flatter her; her overweening vanity is her ruin. A firm, wise, ruling master-hand may perhaps—who knows?" She hesitated and sighed, then added, gently, "Farewell, signor! Benedicite!" and making the sign of the cross as I respectfully bent my head to receive her blessing, she passed noiselessly from the room.

One moment later, and a lame and aged lay-sister came to escort me to the gate. As I passed down the stone corridor a side door opened a very little way, and two fair young faces peeped out at me. For an instant I saw four laughing bright eyes; I heard a smothered voice say, "Oh! *c'est un vieux papa!*" and then my guide, who though lame was not blind, perceived the opened door and shut it with an angry bang, which, however, did not drown the ringing merriment that echoed from within. On reaching the outer gates I turned to my venerable companion, and laying four twenty-franc pieces in her shriveled palm, I said:

"Take these to the reverend mother for me, and ask that mass may be said in the chapel to-morrow for the repose of the soul of him whose name is written here."

And I gave her Guido Ferrari's visiting-card, adding in lower and more solemn tones:

"He met with a sudden and unprepared death. Of your charity, pray also for the man who killed him!"
The old woman looked startled, and crossed herself devoutly; but she promised that my wishes should be fulfilled, and I bade her farewell and passed out, the convent gates closing with a dull clang behind me. I walked on a few yards, and then paused, looking back. What a peaceful home it seemed; how calm and sure a retreat, with the white Noisette roses crowning its ancient gray walls! Yet what embodied curses were pent up in there in the shape of girls growing to be women; women for whom all the care, stern training and anxious solicitude of the nuns would be unavailing; women who would come forth from even that abode of sanctity with vile natures and animal impulses, and who would hereafter, while leading a life of vice and hypocrisy, hold up this very strictness of their early education as proof of their unimpeachable innocence and virtue! To such, what lesson is learned by the daily example of the nuns who mortify their flesh, fast, pray and weep? No lesson at all–nothing save mockery and contempt. To a girl in the heyday of youth and beauty the life of a *religieuse* seems ridiculous. "The poor nuns!" she says, with a laugh; "they are so ignorant. Their time is over–mine has not yet begun." Few, very few, among the thousands of young women who leave the scene of their quiet schooldays for the social whirligig of the world, ever learn to take life in earnest, love in earnest, sorrow in earnest. To most of them life is a large dressmaking and millinery establishment; love a question of money and diamonds; sorrow a solemn calculation as to how much or how little mourning is considered becoming or fashionable. And for creatures such as these we men work–work till our hairs are gray and our backs bent with toil–work till all the joy and zest of living has gone from us, and our reward is–what? Happiness?–seldom. Infidelity?–often. Ridicule? Truly we ought to be glad if we are only ridiculed and thrust back to occupy the second place in our own houses; our lady-wives call that "kind treatment." Is there a married woman living who

does not now and then throw a small stone of insolent satire at her husband when his back is turned? What, *madame*? You, who read these words–you say with indignation: "Certainly there is, and I am that woman!" Ah, truly? I salute you profoundly!–you are, no doubt, the one exception!

28

AVELLINO is one of those dreamy, quiet and picturesque towns which have not as yet been desecrated by the Vandal tourist. Persons holding "through tickets" from Messrs. Cook or Gaze do not stop there–there are no "sights" save the old sanctuary called Monte Virgine standing aloft on its rugged hill, with all the memories of its ancient days clinging to it like a wizard's cloak, and wrapping it in a sort of mysterious meditative silence. It can look back through a vista of eventful years to the eleventh century, when it was erected, so the people say, on the ruins of a temple of Cybele. But what do the sheep and geese that are whipped abroad in herds by the drovers Cook and Gaze know of Monte Virgine or Cybele? Nothing– and they care less; and quiet Avellino escapes from their depredations, thankful that it is not marked on the business map of the drovers' "RUNS." Shut in by the lofty Apennines, built on the slope of the hill that winds gently down into a green and fruitful valley through which the river Sabato rushes and gleams white against cleft rocks that look like war-worn and deserted castles, a drowsy peace encircles it, and a sort of stateliness, which, compared with the riotous fun and folly of Naples only thirty miles away, is as though the statue of a nude Egeria were placed in rivalry with the painted waxen image of a half-dressed ballet- dancer. Few lovelier sights are to be seen in nature than a sunset from one of the smaller hills round Avellino–when the peaks of the Apennines seem to catch fire from the flaming clouds, and below them, the valleys are full of those tender purple and gray shadows that one sees on the canvases of Salvator Rosa, while the town itself looks like a bronzed carving on an old shield, outlined clearly against the dazzling luster of the sky. To this retired spot I came–glad to rest for a time from my work of vengeance–glad to lay down my burden of bitterness for a brief space, and become, as it were, human again, in the sight of the near mountains. For within their close proximity, things common, things mean seem to slip from the soul–a sort of largeness pervades the thoughts, the cramping prosiness of daily life has no room to assert its sway–a grand hush falls on the stormy waters of passion, and like a chidden babe the strong man stands, dwarfed to an infinite littleness in his own sight, before those majestic monarchs of the landscape whose large brows are crowned with the blue circlet of heaven.

I took up my abode in a quiet, almost humble lodging, living simply, and attended only by Vincenzo. I was tired of the ostentation I had been forced to practice in Naples in order to attain my ends–and it was a relief to me to be for a time as though I were a poor man. The house in which I found rooms that suited me was a ramblingly built, picturesque little place, situated on the outskirts of the town, and the woman who owned it, was, in her way, a character. She was a Roman, she told me, with pride flashing in her black eyes–I could guess that at once by her strongly marked features, her magnificently molded figure, and her free, firm tread–that step which is swift without being hasty, which is the manner born of Rome. She told me her history in a few words, with such eloquent gestures that she seemed to live through it again as she spoke: her husband had been a worker in a marble quarry–one of his fellows had let a huge piece of the rock fall on him, and he was crushed to death.

"And well do I know," she said, "that he killed my Toni purposely, for he would have loved me had he dared. But I am a common woman, see you—and it seems to me one cannot lie. And when my love's poor body was scarce covered in the earth, that miserable one—the murderer—came to me—he offered marriage. I accused him of his crime—he denied it—he said the rock slipped from his hands, he knew not how. I struck him on the mouth, and bade him leave my sight and take my curse with him! He is dead now—and surely if the saints have heard me, his soul is not in heaven!"

Thus she spoke with flashing eyes and purposeful energy, while with her strong brown arms she threw open the wide casement of the sitting-room I had taken, and bade me view her orchard. It was a fresh green strip of verdure and foliage—about eight acres of good land, planted entirely with apple-trees.

"Yes, truly!" she said, showing her white teeth in a pleased smile as I made the admiring remark she expected. "Avellino has long had a name for its apples—but, thanks to the Holy Mother, I think in the season there is no fruit in all the neighborhood finer than mine. The produce of it brings me almost enough to live upon—that and the house, when I can find signori willing to dwell with me. But few strangers come hither; sometimes an artist, sometimes a poet—such as these are soon tired of gayety, and are glad to rest. To common persons I would not open my door—not for pride, ah, no! but when one has a girl, one cannot be too careful."

"You have a daughter, then?"

Her fierce eyes softened.

"One—my Lilla. I call her my blessing, and too good for me. Often I fancy that it is because she tends them that the trees bear so well, and the apples are so sound and sweet! And when she drives the load of fruit to market, and sits so smilingly behind the team, it seems to me that her very face brings luck to the sale."

I smiled at the mother's enthusiasm, and sighed. I had no

fair faiths left–I could not even believe in Lilla. My landlady, Signora Monti as she was called, saw that I looked fatigued, and left me to myself–and during my stay I saw very little of her, Vincenzo constituting himself my majordomo, or rather becoming for my sake a sort of amiable slave, always looking to the smallest details of my comfort, and studying my wishes with an anxious solicitude that touched while it gratified me. I had been fully three days in my retreat before he ventured to enter upon any conversation with me, for he had observed that I always sought to be alone, that I took long, solitary rambles through the woods and, across the hills–and, not daring to break through my taciturnity, he had contented himself by merely attending to my material comforts in silence. One afternoon, however, after clearing away the remains of my light luncheon, he lingered in the room.

"The *eccellenza* has not yet seen Lilla Monti?" he asked, hesitatingly.

I looked at him in some surprise. There was a blush on his olive- tinted cheeks and an unusual sparkle in his eyes. For the first time I realized that this valet of mine was a handsome young fellow.

"Seen Lilla Monti!" I repeated, half absently; "oh, you mean the child of the landlady? No, I have not seen her. Why do you ask?"

Vincenzo smiled. "Pardon, *eccellenza*! but she is beautiful, and there is a saying in my province: Be the heart heavy as stone, the sight of a fair face will lighten it!"

I gave an impatient gesture. "All folly, Vincenzo! Beauty is the curse of the world. Read history, and you shall find the greatest conquerors and sages ruined and disgraced by its snares."

He nodded gravely. He probably thought of the announcement I had made at the banquet of my own approaching marriage, and strove to reconcile it with the apparent inconsistency of my present observation. But he was too discreet to utter his mind aloud–he merely said:

"No doubt you are right, *eccellenza*. Still one is glad to see the roses bloom, and the stars shine, and the foam-bells sparkle on the waves–so one is glad to see Lilla Monti."

I turned round in my chair to observe him more closely– the flush deepened on his cheek as I regarded him. I laughed with a bitter sadness.

"In love, amico, art thou? So soon!–three days–and thou hast fallen a prey to the smile of Lilla! I am sorry for thee!"

He interrupted me eagerly.

"The *eccellenza* is in error! I would not dare–she is too innocent– she knows nothing! She is like a little bird in the nest, so soft and tender–a word of love would frighten her; I should be a coward to utter it."

Well, well! I thought, what was the use of sneering at the poor fellow! Why, because my own love had turned to ashes in my grasp, should I mock at those who fancied they had found the golden fruit of the Hesperides? Vincenzo, once a soldier, now half courier, half valet, was something of a poet at heart; he had the grave meditative turn of mind common to Tuscans, together with that amorous fire that ever burns under their lightly worn mask of seeming reserve.

I roused myself to appear interested.

"I see, Vincenzo," I said, with a kindly air of banter, "that the sight of Lilla Monti more than compensates you for that portion of the Neapolitan carnival which you lose by being here. But why you should wish me to behold this paragon of maidens I know not, unless you would have me regret my own lost youth."

A curious and perplexed expression flitted over his face, At last he said firmly, as though his mind were made up:

"The *eccellenza* must pardon me for seeing what perhaps I ought not to have seen, but–"

"But what?" I asked.

"*Eccellenza*, you have not lost your youth."

I turned my head toward him again–he was looking at me in some alarm–he feared some outburst of anger.

"Well!" I said, calmly. "That is your idea, is it? and why?"

"*Eccellenza*, I saw you without your spectacles that day when you fought with the unfortunate Signor Ferrari. I watched you when you fired. Your eyes are beautiful and terrible–the eyes of a young man, though your hair is white."

Quietly I took off my glasses and laid them on the table beside me.

"As you have seen me once without them, you can see me again," I observed, gently. "I wear them for a special purpose. Here in Avellino the purpose does not hold. Thus far I confide in you. But beware how you betray my confidence."

"*Eccellenza!*" cried Vincenzo, in truly pained accents, and with a grieved look.

I rose and laid my hand on his arm.

"There! I was wrong–forgive me. You are honest; you have served your country well enough to know the value of fidelity and duty. But when you say I have not lost my youth, you are wrong, Vincenzo! I HAVE lost it–it has been killed within me by a great sorrow. The strength, the suppleness of limb, the brightness of eye these are mere outward things: but in the heart and soul are the chill and drear bitterness of deserted age. Nay, do not smile; I am in truth very old–so old that I tire of my length of days; yet again, not too old to appreciate your affection, amico, and"–here I forced a faint smile–"when I see the maiden Lilla, I will tell you frankly what I think of her."

Vincenzo stooped his head, caught my hand within his own, and kissed it, then left the room abruptly, to hide the tears that my words had brought to his eyes. He was sorry for me, I could see, and I judged him rightly when I thought that the very mystery surrounding me increased his attachment. On the whole, I was glad he had seen me undisguised, as it was a relief to me to be without my smoked glasses for a time, and during all the rest of my stay at Avellino I never wore them once.

One day I saw Lilla. I had strolled up to a quaint church situated on a rugged hill and surrounded by fine old chestnut-trees, where there was a picture of the Scourging of Christ, said to have been the work of Fra Angelico. The little sanctuary was quite deserted when I entered it, and I paused on the threshold, touched by the simplicity of the place and soothed by the intense silence. I walked on my tiptoe up to the corner where hung the picture I had come to see, and as I did so a girl passed me with a light step, carrying a basket of fragrant winter narcissi and maiden-hair fern. Something in her graceful, noiseless movements caused me to look after her; but she had turned her back to me and was kneeling at the shrine consecrated to the Virgin, having placed her flowers on the lowest step of the altar. She was dressed in peasant costume—a simple, short blue skirt and scarlet bodice, relieved by the white kerchief that was knotted about her shoulders; and round her small well- shaped head the rich chestnut hair was coiled in thick shining braids.

I felt that I must see her face, and for that reason went back to the church door and waited till she should pass out. Very soon she came toward me, with the same light timid step that I had often before noticed, and her fair young features were turned fully upon me. What was there in those clear candid eyes that made me involuntarily bow my head in a reverential salutation as she passed? I know not. It was not beauty—for though the child was lovely I had seen lovelier; it was something inexplicable and rare—something of a maidenly composure and sweet dignity that I had never beheld on any woman's face before. Her cheeks flushed softly as she modestly returned my salute, and when she was once outside the church door she paused, her small white fingers still clasping the carven brown beads of her rosary. She hesitated a moment, and then spoke shyly yet brightly:

"If the *eccellenza* will walk yet a little further up the hill he will see a finer view of the mountains."

Something familiar in her look—a sort of reflection of her mother's likeness—made me sure of her identity. I smiled.

"Ah! you are Lilla Monti?"

She blushed again.

"Si, signor. I am Lilla."

I let my eyes dwell on her searchingly and almost sadly. Vincenzo was right: the girl was beautiful, not with the forced hot-house beauty of the social world and its artificial constraint, but with the loveliness and fresh radiance which nature gives to those of her cherished ones who dwell with her in peace. I had seen many exquisite women–women of Juno-like form and face–women whose eyes were basilisks to draw and compel the souls of men–but I had never seen any so spiritually fair as this little peasant maiden, who stood fearlessly yet modestly regarding me with the innocent inquiry of a child who suddenly sees something new, to which it is unaccustomed. She was a little fluttered by my earnest gaze, and with a pretty courtesy turned to descend the hill. I said gently:

"You are going home, *fanciulla mia?*"

The kind protecting tone in which I spoke reassured her. She answered readily:

"Si signor. My mother waits for me to help her with the *eccellenza's* dinner."

I advanced and took the little hand that held the rosary.

"What!" I exclaimed, playfully, "do you still work hard, little Lilla, even when the apple season is over?"

She laughed musically.

"Oh! I love work. It is good for the temper. People are so cross when their hands are idle. And many are ill for the same reason. Yes, truly!" and she nodded her head with grave importance, "it is often so. Old Pietro, the cobbler, took to his bed when he had no shoes to mend–yes; he sent for the priest and said he would die, not for want of money–oh no! he has plenty, he is quite rich–but because he had nothing to do. So my mother and I found some shoes with holes, and took them to him; he sat up in bed to mend them, and now he is as well as ever! And we are careful to give him something always."

She laughed again, and again looked grave.

"Yes, yes!" she said, with a wise shake of her little glossy head, "one cannot live without work. My mother says that good women are never tired, it is only wicked persons who are lazy. And that reminds me I must make haste to return and prepare the *eccellenza's* coffee."

"Do you make my coffee, little one?" I asked, "and does not Vincenzo help you?"

The faintest suspicion of a blush tinged her pretty cheeks.

"Oh, he is very good, Vincenzo," she said, demurely, with downcast eyes; "he is what we call *buon' amico*, yes, indeed! But he is often glad when I make coffee for him also; he likes it so much! He says I do it so well! But perhaps the *eccellenza* will prefer Vincenzo?"

I laughed. She was so naive, so absorbed in her little duties–such a child altogether.

"Nay, Lilla, I am proud to think you make anything for me. I shall enjoy it more now that I know what kind hands have been at work. But you must not spoil Vincenzo–you will turn his head if you make his coffee too often."

She looked surprised. She did not understand. Evidently to her mind Vincenzo was nothing but a good-natured young fellow, whose palate could be pleased by her culinary skill; she treated him, I dare say, exactly as she would have treated one of her own sex. She seemed to think over my words, as one who considers a conundrum, then she apparently gave it up as hopeless, and shook her head lightly as though dismissing the subject.

"Will the *eccellenza* visit the Punto d'Angelo?" she said brightly, as she turned to go.

I had never heard of this place, and asked her to what she alluded.

"It is not far from here," she explained, "it is the view I spoke of before. Just a little further up the hill you will see a flat gray rock, covered with blue gentians. No one knows how they grow–they are always there, blooming in summer and winter. But it said that one of God's own great angels comes once in every month at midnight to bless the Monte Vergine, and that he stands on that rock. And of course wherever the angels tread there are flowers, and no storm can destroy them— not even an avalanche. That is why the people call it the Punto d'Angelo. It will please you to see it, *eccellenza*—it is but a walk of a little ten minutes."

And with a smile, and a courtesy as pretty and as light as a flower might make to the wind, she left me, half running, half dancing down the hill, and singing aloud for sheer happiness and innocence of heart. Her pure lark-like notes floated upward toward me where I stood, wistfully watching her as she disappeared. The warm afternoon sunshine caught lovingly at her chestnut hair, turning it to a golden bronze, and touched up the whiteness of her throat and arms, and brightened the scarlet of her bodice, as she descended the grassy slope, and was at last lost to my view amid the foliage of the surrounding trees.

29

I SIGHED heavily as I resumed my walk. I realized all that I had lost. This lovely child with her simple fresh nature, why had I not met such a one and wedded HER instead of the vile creature who had been my soul's undoing? The answer came swiftly. Even if I HAD seen her when I was free, I doubt if I should have known her value. We men of the world who have social positions to support, we see little or nothing in the peasant type of womanhood; we must marry "ladies," so-called–educated girls who are as well versed in the world's ways as ourselves, if not more so. And so we get the Cleopatras, the Du Barrys, the Pompadours, while unspoiled maidens such as Lilla too often become the household drudges of common mechanics or day- laborers, living and dying in the one routine of hard work, and often knowing and caring for nothing better than the mountain-hut, the farm-kitchen, or the covered stall in the market-place. Surely it is an ill-balanced world–so many mistakes are made; Fate plays us so many apparently unnecessary tricks, and we are all of us such blind madmen, knowing not whither we are going from one day to another! I am told that it is no longer fashionable to believe in a devil–but I care nothing for fashion! A devil there is I am sure, who for some inscrutable reason has a share in the ruling of this planet–a devil who delights in mocking us from the cradle to the grave. And perhaps we are never so hopelessly, utterly fooled as in our marriages!

Occupied in various thoughts, I scarcely saw where I wandered, till a flashing glimmer of blue blossoms recalled me to the object of my walk. I had reached the Punto d'Angelo. It was, as Lilla had said, a flat rock bare in every place save at the summit, where it was thickly covered with the lovely gentians, flowers that are rare in this part of Italy. Here then the fabled angel paused in his flight to bless the venerable sanctuary of Monte Vergine. I stopped and looked around me. The view was indeed superb—from the leafy bosom of the valley, the green hills like smooth, undulating billows rolled upward, till their emerald verdure was lost in the dense purple shadows and tall peaks of the Apennines; the town of Avellino lay at my feet, small yet clearly defined as a miniature painting on porcelain; and a little further beyond and above me rose the gray tower of the Monte Vergine itself, the one sad and solitary-looking object in all the luxuriant riante landscape.

I sat down to rest, not as an intruder on the angel's flower-embroidered throne, but on a grassy knoll close by. And then I bethought me of a packet I had received from Naples that morning—a packet that I desired yet hesitated to open. It had been sent by the Marquis D'Avencourt, accompanied by a courteous letter, which informed me that Ferrari's body had been privately buried with all the last religious rites in the cemetery, "close to the funeral vault of the Romani family," wrote D'Avencourt, "as, from all we can hear or discover, such seems to have been his own desire. He was, it appears, a sort of adopted brother of the lately deceased count, and on being informed of this circumstance, we buried him in accordance with the sentiments he would no doubt have expressed had he considered the possible nearness of his own end at the time of the combat."

With regard to the packet enclosed, D'Avencourt continued—"The accompanying letters were found in Ferrari's breast-pocket, and on opening the first one, in the expectation of finding some clue as to his last wishes, we came to the conclusion that you, as the future husband of the lady whose signature and handwriting you will here recognize, should be made aware of the contents, not only for your own sake, but in justice to the deceased. If all the letters are of the same tone as the one I unknowingly opened, I have no doubt Ferrari considered himself a sufficiently injured man. But of that you will judge for yourself, though, if I might venture so far in the way of friendship, I should recommend you to give careful consideration to the enclosed correspondence before tying the matrimonial knot to which you alluded the other evening. It is not wise to walk on the edge of a precipice with one's eyes shut! Captain Ciabatti was the first to inform me of what I now know for a fact–namely, that Ferrari left a will in which everything he possessed is made over unconditionally to the Countess Romani. You will of course draw your own conclusions, and pardon me if I am guilty of *trop de zele* in your service. I have now only to tell you that all the unpleasantness of this affair is passing over very smoothly and without scandal–I have taken care of that. You need not prolong your absence further than you feel inclined, and I, for one, shall be charmed to welcome you back to Naples. With every sentiment of the highest consideration and regard, I am, my dear conte, "Your very true friend and servitor, "PHILIPPE D'AVENCOURT."

I folded this letter carefully and put it aside. The little package he had sent me lay in my hand–a bundle of neatly folded letters tied together with a narrow ribbon, and strongly perfumed with the faint sickly perfume I knew and abhorred. I turned them over and over; the edges of the note-paper were stained with blood–Guido's blood–as though in its last sluggish flowing it had endeavored to obliterate all traces of the daintily penned lines that now awaited my perusal. Slowly I untied the ribbon. With methodical deliberation I read one letter after the other. They were all from Nina–all written to Guido while he was in Rome, some of them bearing the dates of the very days when she had feigned to love ME–me, her newly accepted husband. One very amorous epistle had been written on the self-same evening she had plighted her troth to me! Letters burning and tender, full of the most passionate protestations of fidelity, overflowing with the sweetest terms of endearment; with such a ring of truth and love throughout them that surely it was no wonder that Guido's suspicions were all unawakened, and that he had reason to believe himself safe in his fool's paradise. One passage in this poetical and romantic correspondence fixed my attention: it ran thus:

"Why do you write so much of marriage to me, Guido mio? it seems to my mind that all the joy of loving will be taken from us when once the hard world knows of our passion. If you become my husband you will assuredly cease to be my lover, and that would break my heart. Ah, my best beloved! I desire you to be my lover always, as you were when Fabio lived–why bring commonplace matrimony into the heaven of such a passion as ours?"

I studied these words attentively. Of course I understood their drift. She had tried to feel her way with the dead man. She had wanted to marry me, and yet retain Guido for her lonely hours, as "her lover always!" Such a pretty, ingenious plan it was! No thief, no murderer ever laid more cunning schemes than she, but the law looks after thieves and murderers. For such a woman as this, law says, "Divorce her–that is your best remedy." Divorce her! Let the criminal go scot-free! Others may do it that choose–I have different ideas of justice!

Tying up the packet of letters again, with their sickening perfume and their blood-stained edges, I drew out the last graciously worded missive I had received from Nina. Of course I heard from her every day–she was a most faithful correspondent! The same affectionate expressions characterized her letters to me as those that had deluded her dead lover–with this difference, that whereas she inveighed much against the prosiness of marriage to Guido, to me she drew the much touching pictures of her desolate condition:

how lonely she had felt since her "dear husband's" death, how rejoiced she was to think that she was soon again to be a happy wife–the wife of one so noble, so true, so devoted as I was! She had left the convent and was now at home–when should she have the happiness of welcoming me, her best beloved Cesare, back to Naples? She certainly deserved some credit for artistic lying; I could not understand how she managed it so well. Almost I admired her skill, as one sometimes admires a cool-headed burglar, who has more skill, cunning, and pluck than his comrades. I thought with triumph that though the wording of Ferrari's will enabled her to secure all other letters she might have written to him, this one little packet of documentary evidence was more than sufficient for MY purposes. And I resolved to retain it in my own keeping till the time came for me to use it against her.

And how about D'Avencourt's friendly advice concerning the matrimonial knot? "A man should not walk on the edge of a precipice with his eyes shut." Very true. But if his eyes are open, and he has his enemy by the throat, the edge of a precipice is a convenient position for hurling that enemy down to death in a quiet way, that the world need know nothing of! So for the present I preferred the precipice to walking on level ground.

I rose from my seat near the Punto d'Angelo. It was growing late in the afternoon. From the little church below me soft bells rang out the Angelus, and with them chimed in a solemn and harsher sound from the turret of the Monte Vergine. I lifted my hat with the customary reverence, and stood listening, with my feet deep in the grass and scented thyme, and more than once glanced up at the height whereon the venerable sanctuary held its post, like some lonely old god of memory brooding over vanished years. There, according to tradition, was once celebrated the worship of the many-breasted Cybele; down that very slope of grass dotted with violets had rushed the howling, naked priests beating their discordant drums and shrinking their laments for the loss of

Atys, the beautiful youth, their goddess's paramour. Infidelity again!–even in this ancient legend, what did Cybele care for old Saturn, whose wife she was? Nothing, less than nothing!–and her adorers worshiped not her chastity, but her faithlessness; it is the way of the world to this day!

The bells ceased ringing; I descended the hill and returned homeward through a shady valley, full of the odor of pines and bog-myrtle. On reaching the gate of the Signora Monti's humble yet picturesque dwelling, I heard the sound of laughter and clapping of hands, and looking in the direction of the orchard, I saw Vincenzo hard at work, his shirt-sleeves rolled up to the shoulder, splitting some goodly logs of wood, while Lilla stood beside him, merrily applauding and encouraging his efforts. He seemed quite in his element, and wielded his ax with a regularity and vigor I should scarcely have expected from a man whom I was accustomed to see performing the somewhat effeminate duties of a *valet-de-chambre*. I watched him and the fair girl beside him for a few moments, myself unperceived.

If this little budding romance were left alone it would ripen into a flower, and Vincenzo would be a happier man than his master. He was a true Tuscan, from the very way he handled his wood-ax; I could see that he loved the life of the hills and fields–the life of a simple farmer and fruit-grower, full of innocent enjoyments, as sweet as the ripe apples in his orchard. I could foresee his future with Lilla beside him. He would have days of unwearying contentment, rendered beautiful by the free fresh air and the fragrance of flowers–his evenings would slip softly by to the tinkle of the mandolin, and the sound of his wife and children's singing.

What fairer fate could a man desire?–what life more certain to keep health in the body and peace in the mind? Could I not help him to his happiness, I wondered? I, who had grown stern with long brooding upon my vengeance–could I not aid in bringing joy to others! If I could, my mind would be somewhat lightened of its burden–a burden grown heavier since Guide's death, for from his blood had sprung forth a new group of Furies, that lashed me on to my task with scorpion whips of redoubled wrath and passionate ferocity. Yet if I could do one good action now–would it not be as a star shining in the midst of my soul's storm and darkness? Just then Lilla laughed– how sweetly!–the laugh of a very young child. What amused her now? I looked, and saw that she had taken the ax from Vincenzo, and lifting it in her little hands, was endeavoring bravely to imitate his strong and telling stroke; he meanwhile stood aside with an air of smiling superiority, mingled with a good deal of admiration for the slight active figure arrayed in the blue kirtle and scarlet bodice, on which the warm rays of the late sun fell with so much amorous tenderness. Poor little Lilla! A penknife would have made as much impression as her valorous blows produced on the inflexible, gnarled, knotty old stump she essayed to split in twain. Flushed and breathless with her efforts, she looked prettier than ever, and at last, baffled, she resigned her ax to Vincenzo, laughing gaily at her incapacity for wood-cutting, and daintily shaking her apron free from the chips and dust, till a call from her mother caused her to run swiftly into the house, leaving Vincenzo working away as arduously as ever. I went up to him; he saw me approaching, and paused in his labors with an air of slight embarrassment.

"You like this sort of work, amico?" I said, gently.

"An old habit, *eccellenza*–nothing more. It reminds me of the days of my youth, when I worked for my mother. Ah! a pleasant place it was–the old home just above Fiesole." His eyes grew pensive and sad. "It is all gone now–finished. That was before I became a soldier. But one thinks of it sometimes."

"I understand. And no doubt you would be glad to return to the life of your boyhood?"

He looked a little startled.

"Not to leave YOU, *eccellenza*!"

I smiled rather sadly. "Not to leave ME? Not if you wedded Lilla Monti?"

His olive cheek flushed, but he shook his head.

"Impossible! She would not listen to me. She is a child."

"She will soon be a woman, believe me! A little more of your company will make her so. But there is plenty of time. She is beautiful, as you said: and something better than that, she is innocent–think of that, Vincenzo! Do you know how rare a thing innocence is–in a woman? Respect it as you respect God; let her young life be sacred to you."

He glanced upward reverently.

"*Eccellenza*, I would as soon tear the Madonna from her altars as vex or frighten Lilla!"

I smiled and said no more, but turned into the house. From that moment I resolved to let this little love-idye have a fair chance of success. Therefore I remained at Avellino much longer than I had at first intended, not for my own sake, but for Vincenzo's. He served me faithfully; he should have his reward. I took a pleasure in noticing that my efforts to promote his cause were not altogether wasted. I spoke with Lilla often on indifferent matters that interested her, and watched her constantly when she was all unaware of my observant gaze. With me she was as frank and fearless as a tame robin; but after some days I found that she grew shy of mentioning the name of Vincenzo, that she blushed when he approached her, that she was timid of asking him to do anything for her; and from all these little signs I knew her mind, as one knows by the rosy streaks in the sky that the sunrise is near.

One afternoon I called the Signora Monti to my room. She came, surprised, and a little anxious. Was anything wrong with the service? I reassured her housewifely scruples, and came to the point at once.

"I would speak to you of your child, the little Lilla," I said, kindly. "Have you ever thought that she may marry?"

Her dark bold eyes filled with tears and her lips quivered.

"Truly I have," she replied with a wistful sadness; "but I have prayed, perhaps foolishly, that she would not leave me yet. I love her so well; she is always a babe to me, so small and sweet! I put the thought of her marriage from me as a sorrowful thing."

"I understand your feeling," I said. "Still, suppose your daughter wedded a man who would be to you as a son, and who would not part her from you?–for instance, let us say Vincenzo?"

Signora Monti smiled through her tears.

"Vincenzo! He is a good lad, a very good lad, and I love him; but he does not think of Lilla–he is devoted to the *eccellenza.*"

"I am aware of his devotion," I answered. "Still I believe you will find out soon that he loves your Lilla. At present he says nothing– he fears to offend you and alarm her; but his eyes speak–so do hers. You are a good woman, a good mother; watch them both, you will soon tell whether love is between them or no. And see," here I handed her a sealed envelope, "in this you will find notes to the amount of four thousand francs." She uttered a little cry of amazement. "It is Lilla's dowry, whoever she marries, though I think she will marry Vincenzo. Nay–no thanks, money is of no value to me; and this is the one pleasure I have had for many weary months. Think well of Vincenzo–he is an excellent fellow. And all I ask of you is, that you keep this little dowry a secret till the day of your fair child's espousals."

Before I could prevent her the enthusiastic woman had seized my hand and kissed it. Then she lifted her head with the proud free-born dignity of a Roman matron; her broad bosom heaved, and her strong voice quivered with suppressed emotion.

"I thank you, signor," she said, simply, "for Lilla's sake! Not that my little one needs more than her mother's hands have toiled for, thanks be to the blessed saints who have had us both in their keeping! But this is a special blessing of God sent through your hands, and I should be unworthy of all prosperity were I not grateful. *Eccellenza*, pardon me, but my eyes are quick to see that you have suffered sorrow. Good actions lighten grief! We will pray for your happiness, Lilla and I, till the last breath leaves our lips. Believe it–the name of our benefactor shall be lifted to the saints night and morning, and who knows but good may come of it!"

I smiled faintly.

"Good will come of it, my excellent signora, though I am all unworthy of your prayers. Rather pray," and I sighed heavily, "for the dead, 'that they may be loosed from their sins.'"

The good woman looked at me with a sort of kindly pity mingled with awe, then murmuring once more her thanks and blessing, she left the room. A few minutes afterward Vincenzo entered. I addressed him cheerfully.

"Absence is the best test of love, Vincenzo; prepare all for our departure! We shall leave Avellino the day after to-morrow."

And so we did. Lilla looked slightly downcast, but Vincenzo seemed satisfied, and I augured from their faces, and from the mysterious smile of Signor Monti, that all was going well. I left the beautiful mountain town with regret, knowing I should see it no more. I touched Lilla's fair cheek lightly at parting, and took what I knew was my last look into the sweet candid young face. Yet the consciousness that I had done some little good gave my tired heart a sense of satisfaction and repose–a feeling I had not experienced since I died and rose again from the dead.

On the last day of January I returned to Naples, after an absence of more than a month, and was welcomed back by all my numerous acquaintance with enthusiasm. The Marquis D'Avencourt had informed me rightly–the affair of the duel was a thing of the past–an almost forgotten circumstance. The carnival was in full riot, the streets were scenes of fantastic mirth and revelry; there was music and song, dancing and masquerading, and feasting. But I withdrew from the tumult of merriment, and absorbed myself in the necessary preparations for–my marriage.

30

LOOKING back on the incidents of those strange feverish weeks that preceded my wedding-day, they seemed to me like the dreams of a dying man. Shifting colors, confused images, moments of clear light, hours of long darkness—all things gross, refined, material, and spiritual were shaken up in my life like the fragments in a kaleidoscope, ever changing into new forms and bewildering patterns. My brain was clear; yet I often questioned myself whether I was not going mad—whether all the careful methodical plans I formed were but the hazy fancies of a hopelessly disordered mind? Yet no; each detail of my scheme was too complete, too consistent, too business- like for that. A madman may have a method of action to a certain extent, but there is always some slight slip, some omission, some mistake which helps to discover his condition. Now, I forgot nothing—I had the composed exactitude of a careful banker who balances his accounts with the most elaborate regularity. I can laugh to think of it all now; but THEN—then I moved, spoke, and acted like a human machine impelled by stronger forces than my own— in all things precise, in all things inflexible.

Within the week of my return from Avellino my coming marriage with the Countess Romani was announced. Two days after it had been made public, while sauntering across the

Largo del Castello, I met the Marquis D'Avencourt. I had not seen him since the morning of the duel, and his presence gave me a sort of nervous shock. He was exceedingly cordial, though I fancied he was also slightly embarrassed After a few commonplace remarks he said, abruptly:

"So your marriage will positively take place?"

I forced a laugh.

"*Ma! certamente!* Do you doubt it?"

His handsome face clouded and his manner grew still more constrained.

"No; but I thought–I had hoped–"

"*Mon cher*," I said, airily, "I perfectly understand to what you allude. But we men of the world are not fastidious–we know better than to pay any heed to the foolish love-fancies of a woman before her marriage, so long as she does not trick us afterward. The letters you sent me were trifles, mere trifles! In wedding the Contessa Romani I assure you I believe I secure the most virtuous as well as the most lovely woman in Europe!" And I laughed again heartily.

D'Avencourt looked puzzled; but he was a punctilious man, and knew how to steer clear of a delicate subject. He smiled.

"*A la bonne heure*," he said–"I wish you joy with all my heart! You are the best judge of your own happiness; as for me–*vive la liberte!*"

And with a gay parting salute he left me. No one else in the city appeared to share his foreboding scruples, if he had any, about my forthcoming marriage. It was everywhere talked of with as much interest and expectation as though it were some new amusement invented to heighten the merriment of carnival. Among other things, I earned the reputation of being a most impatient lover, for now I would consent to no delays. I hurried all the preparations on with feverish precipitation. I had very little difficulty in persuading Nina that the sooner our wedding took place the better; she was to the full as eager as myself, as ready to rush on her own destruction as Guido had been. Her chief passion was avarice, and the repeated rumors of my supposed fabulous wealth had aroused her greed from the very moment she had first met me in my assumed character of the Count Oliva. As soon as her engagement to me became known in Naples, she was an object of envy to all those of her own sex who, during the previous autumn, had laid out their store of fascinations to entrap me in vain—and this made her perfectly happy. Perhaps the supreme satisfaction a woman of this sort can attain to is the fact of making her less fortunate sisters discontented and miserable! I loaded her, of course, with the costliest gifts, and she, being the sole mistress of the fortune left her by her "late husband," as well as of the unfortunate Guido's money, set no limits to her extravagance. She ordered the most expensive and elaborate costumes; she was engaged morning after morning with dressmakers, tailors, and milliners, and she was surrounded by a certain favored "set" of female friends, for whose benefit she displayed the incoming treasures of her wardrobe till they were ready to cry for spite and vexation, though they had to smile and hold in their wrath and outraged vanity beneath the social mask of complacent composure. And Nina loved nothing better than to torture the poor women who were stinted of pocket-money with the sight of shimmering satins, soft radiating plushes, rich velvets, embroidery studded with real gems, pieces of costly old lace, priceless scents, and articles of bijouterie; she loved also to dazzle the eyes and bewilder the brains of young girls, whose finest toilet was a garb of simplest white stuff unadorned save by a cluster of natural blossoms, and to send them away sick at heart, pining for they knew not what, dissatisfied with everything, and grumbling at fate for not permitting them to deck themselves in such marvelous "arrangements" of costume as those possessed by the happy, the fortunate future Countess Oliva.

Poor maidens! had they but known all they would not have envied her! Women are too fond of measuring happiness by the amount of fine clothes they obtain, and I truly believe dress is the one thing that never fails to console them. How often a fit of hysterics can be cut short by the opportune arrival of a new gown!

My wife, in consideration of her approaching second nuptial, had thrown off her widow's crape, and now appeared clad in those soft subdued half-tints of color that suited her fragile, fairy-like beauty to perfection. All her old witcheries and her graceful tricks of manner and speech were put forth again for my benefit. I knew them all so well! I understood the value of her light caresses and languishing looks so thoroughly! She was very anxious to attain the full dignity of her position as the wife of so rich a nobleman as I was reputed to be, therefore she raised no objection when I fixed the day of our marriage for Giovedi Grasso. Then the fooling and mumming, the dancing, shrieking, and screaming would be at its height; it pleased my whim to have this other piece of excellent masquerading take place at the same time.

The wedding was to be as private as possible, owing to my wife's "recent sad bereavements," as she herself said with a pretty sigh and tearful, pleading glance. It would take place in the chapel of San Gennaro, adjoining the cathedral. We were married there before! During the time that intervened, Nina's manner was somewhat singular. To me she was often timid, and sometimes half conciliatory. Now and then I caught her large dark eyes fixed on me with a startled, anxious look, but this expression soon passed away. She was subject, too, to wild fits of merriment, and anon to moods of absorbed and gloomy silence. I could plainly see that she was strung up to an extreme pitch of nervous excitement and irritability, but I asked her no questions. If–I thought–if she tortured herself with memories, all the better–if she saw, or fancied she saw, the resemblance between me and her "dear dead Fabio," it suited me that she should be so racked and bewildered.

I came and went to and fro from the villa as I pleased. I wore my dark glasses as usual, and not even Giacomo could follow me with his peering, inquisitive gaze; for since the night he had been hurled so fiercely to the ground by Guido's reckless and impatient hand, the poor old man had been paralyzed, and had spoken no word. He lay in an upper chamber, tended by Assunta, and my wife had already written to his relatives in Lombardy, asking them to send for him home.

"Of what use to keep him?" she had asked me.

True! Of what use to give even roof-shelter to a poor old human creature, maimed, broken, and useless for evermore? After long years of faithful service, turn him out, cast him forth! If he die of neglect, starvation, and ill-usage, what matter?–he is a worn-out tool, his day is done–let him perish. I would not plead for him– why should I? I had made my own plans for his comfort–plans shortly to be carried out; and in the meantime Assunta nursed him tenderly as he lay speechless, with no more strength than a year-old baby, and only a bewildered pain in his upturned, lack-luster eyes. One incident occurred during these last days of my vengeance that struck a sharp pain to my heart, together with a sense of the bitterest anger. I had gone up to the villa somewhat early in the morning, and on crossing the lawn I saw a dark form stretched motionless on one of the paths that led directly up to the house. I went to examine it, and started back in horror–it was my dog Wyvis shot dead. His silky black head and forepaws were dabbled in blood–his honest brown eyes were glazed with the film of his dying agonies. Sickened and infuriated at the sight, I called to a gardener who was trimming the shrubbery.

"Who has done this?" I demanded.

The man looked pityingly at the poor bleeding remains, and said, in a low voice:

"It was *madame's* order, signor. The dog bit her yesterday; we shot him at daybreak."

I stooped to caress the faithful animal's body, and as I stroked the silky coat my eyes were dim with tears.

"How did it happen?" I asked in smothered accents. "Was your lady hurt?"

The gardener shrugged his shoulders and sighed.

"Ma!—no! But he tore the lace on her dress with his teeth and grazed her hand. It was little, but enough. He will bite no more— *povera bestia!*"

I gave the fellow five francs.

"I liked the dog," I said briefly, "he was a faithful creature. Bury him decently under that tree," and I pointed to the giant cypress on the lawn, "and take this money for your trouble."

He looked surprised but grateful, and promised to do my bidding. Once more sorrowfully caressing the fallen head of perhaps the truest friend I ever possessed, I strode hastily into the house, and met Nina coming out of her morning-room, clad in one of her graceful trailing garments, in which soft lavender hues were blended like the shaded colors of late and early violets.

"So Wyvis has been shot?" I said, abruptly.

She gave a slight shudder.

"Oh, yes; is it not sad? But I was compelled to have it done. Yesterday I went past his kennel within reach of his chain, and he sprung furiously at me for no reason at all. See!" And holding up her small hand she showed me three trifling marks in the delicate flesh. "I felt that you would be so unhappy if you thought I kept a dog that was at all dangerous, so I determined to get rid of him. It is always painful to have a favorite animal killed; but really Wyvis belonged to my poor husband, and I think he has never been quite safe since his master's death, and now Giacomo is ill—"

"I see!" I said, curtly, cutting her explanations short.

Within myself I thought how much more sweet and valuable was the dog's life than hers. Brave Wyvis—good Wyvis! He had done his best—he had tried to tear her dainty flesh; his honest instincts had led him to attempt rough vengeance on the woman he had felt was his master's foe. And he had met his fate, and died in the performance of duty. But I said no more on the subject. The dog's death was not alluded to again by either Nina or myself. He lay in his mossy grave under the cypress boughs–his memory untainted by any lie, and his fidelity enshrined in my heart as a thing good and gracious, far exceeding the self-interested friendship of so-called Christian humanity.

The days passed slowly on. To the revelers who chased the flying steps of carnival with shouting and laughter, no doubt the hours were brief, being so brimful of merriment; but to me, who heard nothing save the measured ticking of my own timepiece of revenge, and who saw naught save its hands, that every second drew nearer to the last and fatal figure on the dial, the very moments seemed long and laden with weariness. I roamed the streets of the city aimlessly, feeling more like a deserted stranger than a well-known envied nobleman, whose wealth made him the cynosure of all eyes. The riotous glee, the music, the color that whirled and reeled through the great street of Toledo at this season bewildered and pained me. Though I knew and was accustomed to the wild vagaries of carnival, yet this year they seemed to be out of place, distracting, senseless, and all unfamiliar.

Sometimes I escaped from the city tumult and wandered out to the cemetery. There I would stand, dreamily looking at the freshly turned sods above Guido Ferrari's grave. No stone marked the spot as yet, but it was close to the Romani vault– not more than a couple of yards away from the iron grating that barred the entrance to that dim and fatal charnel-house. I had a drear fascination for the place, and more than once I went to the opening of that secret passage made by the brigands to ascertain if all was safe and undisturbed. Everything was as I had left it, save that the tangle of brush-wood had become thicker, and weeds and brambles had sprung up, making it less visible than before, and probably rendering it more impassable. By a fortunate accident I had secured the key of the vault. I knew that for family burial-places of this kind there are always two keys–one left in charge of the keeper of the cemetery, the other possessed by the person or persons to whom the mausoleum belongs, and this other I managed to obtain.

On one occasion, being left for some time alone in my own library at the villa, I remembered that in an upper drawer of an old oaken escritoire that stood there, had always been a few keys belonging to the doors of cellars and rooms in the house. I looked, and found them lying there as usual; they all had labels attached to them, signifying their use, and I turned them over impatiently, not finding what I sought. I was about to give up the search, when I perceived a large rusty iron key that had slipped to the back of the drawer; I pulled it out, and to my satisfaction it was labeled "Mausoleum." I immediately took possession of it, glad to have obtained so useful and necessary an implement; I knew that I should soon need it. The cemetery was quite deserted at this festive season—no one visited it to lay wreaths of flowers or sacred mementoes on the last resting-places of their friends. In the joys of the carnival who thinks of the dead? In my frequent walks there I was always alone; I might have opened my own vault and gone down into it without being observed, but I did not; I contented myself with occasionally trying the key in the lock, and assuring myself that it worked without difficulty.

Returning from one of these excursions late on a mild afternoon toward the end of the week preceding my marriage, I bent my steps toward the Molo, where I saw a picturesque group of sailors and girls dancing one of those fantastic, graceful dances of the country, in which impassioned movement and expressive gesticulation are everything. Their steps were guided and accompanied by the sonorous twanging of a full-toned guitar and the tinkling beat of a tambourine. Their handsome, animated faces, their flashing eyes and laughing lips, their gay, many-colored costumes, the glitter of beads on the brown necks of the maidens, the red caps jauntily perched on the thick black curls of the fishermen—all made up a picture full of light and life thrown up into strong relief against the pale gray and amber tints of the February sky and sea; while shadowing overhead frowned the stern dark walls of the Castel Nuovo.

It was such a scene as the English painter Luke Fildes might love to depict on his canvas–the one man of to-day who, though born of the land of opaque mists and rain-burdened clouds, has, notwithstanding these disadvantages, managed to partly endow his brush with the exhaustless wealth and glow of the radiant Italian color. I watched the dance with a faint sense of pleasure–it was full of so much harmony and delicacy of rhythm. The lad who thrummed the guitar broke out now and then into song–a song in dialect that fitted into the music of the dance as accurately as a rosebud into its calyx. I could not distinguish all the words he sung, but the refrain was always the same, and he gave it in every possible inflection and variety of tone, from grave to gay, from pleading to pathetic.

"*Che bella cosa e de morire acciso, Nnanze a la porta de la nnamorata!*" –meaning literally–"How beautiful a thing to die, suddenly slain at the door of one's beloved!"

There was no sense in the thing, I thought half angrily–it was a stupid sentiment altogether. Yet I could not help smiling at the ragged, barefooted rascal who sung it: he seemed to feel such a gratification in repeating it, and he rolled his black eyes with lovelorn intensity, and breathed forth sighs that sounded through his music with quite a touching earnestness. Of course he was only following the manner of all Neapolitans, namely, acting his song; they all do it, and cannot help themselves. But this boy had a peculiarly roguish way of pausing and crying forth a plaintive "Ah!" before he added "*Che bella cosa,*" etc., which gave point and piquancy to his absurd ditty. He was evidently brimful of mischief– his expression betokened it; no doubt he was one of the most thorough little scamps that ever played at "*morra,*" but there was a charm about his handsome dirty face and unkempt hair, and I watched him amusedly, glad to be distracted for a few minutes from the tired inner workings of my own unhappy thoughts. In time to come, so I mused, this very boy might learn to set his song about the "beloved" to a sterner key, and might find it meet, not to be slain himself, but to slay HER! Such a thing–in Naples–was more than probable. By and by the dance ceased, and I recognized in one of the breathless, laughing sailors my old acquaintance Andrea Luziani, with whom I had sailed to Palermo. The sight of him relieved me from a difficulty which had puzzled me for some days, and as soon as the little groups of men and women had partially dispersed, I walked up to him and touched him on the shoulder. He started, looked round surprised, and did not appear to recognize me. I remembered that when he had seen me I had not grown a beard, neither had I worn dark spectacles. I recalled my name to him; his face cleared and he smiled.

"*Ah! buon giorno, eccellenza!*" he cried. "A thousand pardons that I did not at first know you! Often have I thought of you! often have I heard your name–ah! what a name! Rich, great, generous!–ah! what a glad life! And on the point of marrying–ah, Dio! love makes all the troubles go–so!" and taking his cigar from his mouth, he puffed a ring of pale smoke into the air and laughed gaily. Then suddenly lifting his cap from his clustering black hair, he added, "All joy be with you, *eccellenza!*"

I smiled and thanked him. I noticed he looked at me curiously.

"You think I have changed in appearance?" I said.

The Sicilian looked embarrassed.

"Ebbene! we must all change," he answered, lightly, evading my glance. "The days pass on–each day takes a little bit of youth away with it. One grows old without knowing it!"

I laughed.

"I see," I observed. "You think I have aged somewhat since you saw me?"

"A little, *eccellenza,*" he frankly confessed.

"I have suffered severe illness," I said, quietly, "and my eyes are still weak, as you perceive," and I touched my glasses. "But I shall get stronger in time. Can you come with me for a few moments? I want your help in a matter of importance."

He nodded a ready assent and followed me.

31

W E LEFT the Molo, and paused at a retired street corner leading from the Chiaja.

"You remember Carmelo Neri?" I asked.

Andrea shrugged his shoulders with an air of infinite commiseration.

"Ah! *povero diavolo!* Well do I remember him! A bold fellow and brave, with a heart in him, too, if one did but know where to find it. And now he drags the chain! Well, well, no doubt it is what he deserves; but I say, and always will maintain, there are many worse men than Carmelo."

I briefly related how I had seen the captured brigand in the square at Palermo and had spoken with him. "I mentioned you," I added, "and he bade me tell you Teresa had killed herself."

"Ah! that I well know," said the little captain, who had listened to me intently, and over whose mobile face flitted a shadow of tender pity, as he sighed. "*Poverinetta!* So fragile and small! To think she had the force to plunge the knife in her breast! As well imagine a little bird flying down to pierce itself on an uplifted bayonet. Ay, ay! women will do strange things— and it is certain she loved Carmelo."

"You would help him to escape again if you could, no doubt?" I inquired with a half-smile.

The ready wit of the Sicilian instantly asserted itself.

"Not I, *eccellenza*," he replied, with an air of dignity and most virtuous honesty. "No, no, not now. The law is the law, and I, Andrea Luziani, am not one to break it. No, Carmelo must take his punishment; it is for life they say–and hard as it seems, it is but just. When the little Teresa was in the question, look you, what could I do? but now–let the saints that choose help Carmelo, for I will not."

I laughed as I met the audacious flash of his eyes; I knew, despite his protestations, that if Carmelo Neri ever did get clear of the galleys, it would be an excellent thing for him if Luziani's vessel chanced to be within reach.

"You have your brig the 'Laura' still?" I asked him.

"Yes, *eccellenza*, the Madonna be praised! And she has been newly rigged and painted, and she is as trig and trim a craft as you can meet with in all the wide blue waters of the Mediterranean."

"Now you see," I sad, impressively, "I have a friend, a relative, who is in trouble: he wishes to get away from Naples quietly and in secret. Will you help him? You shall be paid whatever you think proper to demand."

The Sicilian looked puzzled. He puffed meditatively at his cigar and remained silent.

"He is not pursued by the law," I continued, noting his hesitation. "He is simply involved in a cruel difficulty brought upon him by his own family–he seeks to escape from unjust persecution."

Andrea's brow cleared.

"Oh, if that is the case, *eccellenza*, I am at your service. But where does your friend desire to go?"

I paused for a moment and considered.

"To Civita Vecchia," I said at last, "from that port he can obtain a ship to take him to his further destination."

The captain's expressive face fell–he looked very dubious.

"To Civita Vecchia is a long way, a very long way," he said, regretfully; "and it is the bad season, and there are cross currents and contrary winds. With all the wish in the world to please you, *eccellenza*, I dare not run the 'Laura' so far; but there is another means."

And interrupting himself he considered awhile in silence. I waited patiently for him to speak.

"Whether it would suit your friend I know not," he said at last, laying his hand confidentially on my arm, "but there is a stout brig leaving here for Civita Vecchia on Friday morning next—"

"The day after Giovedi Grasso?" I queried, with a smile he did not understand. He nodded.

"Exactly so. She carries a cargo of Lacrima Cristi, and she is a swift sailer. I know her captain—he is a good soul; but," and Andrea laughed lightly, "he is like the rest of us—he loves money. You do not count the francs—no, they are nothing to you—but we look to the *soldi*. Now, if it please you I will make him a certain offer of passage money, as large as you shall choose, also I will tell him when to expect his one passenger, and I can almost promise you that he will not say no!"

This proposal fitted in so excellently with my plans that I accepted it, and at once named an exceptionally munificent sum for the passage required. Andrea's eyes glistened as he heard.

"It is a little fortune!" he cried, enthusiastically. "Would that I could earn as much in twenty voyages! But one should not be churlish—such luck cannot fall in all men's way."

I smiled.

"And do you think, amico, I will suffer you to go unrewarded?" I said. And placing two twenty-franc pieces in his brown palm I added, "As you rightly said, francs are nothing to me. Arrange this little matter without difficulty, and you shall not be forgotten. You can call at my hotel to-morrow or the next day, when you have settled everything—here is the address," and I penciled it on my card and gave it to him; "but remember, this is a secret matter, and I rely upon you to explain it as such to your friend who commands the brig going to Civita Vecchia. He must ask no questions of his passenger—the more silence the more discretion—and when once he has landed him at his destination he will do well to straightway forget all about him. You understand?"

Andrea nodded briskly.

"*Sì, sì, signer.* He has a bad memory as it is—it shall grow worse at your command! Believe it!"

I laughed, shook hands, and parted with the friendly little fellow, he returning to the Molo, and I slowly walking homeward by way of the Villa Reale. An open carriage coming swiftly toward me attracted my attention; as it drew nearer I recognized the prancing steeds and the familiar liveries. A fair woman clad in olive velvets and Russian sables looked out smiling, and waved her hand.

It was my wife—my betrothed bride, and beside her sat the Duchess di Marina, the most irreproachable of matrons, famous for her piety not only in Naples but throughout Italy. So immaculate was she that it was difficult to imagine her husband daring to caress that upright, well-dressed form, or venturing to kiss those prim lips, colder than the carven beads of her jeweled rosary. Yet there was a story about her too—an old story that came from Padua—of how a young and handsome nobleman had been found dead at her palace doors, stabbed to the heart. Perhaps—who knows—he also might have thought—

"*Che bella cosa e de morire accisa, Nnanze a la porta de la nnamorata!*"

Some said the duke had killed him; but nothing could be proved, nothing was certain. The duke was silent, so was is duchess; and Scandal herself sat meekly with closed lips in the presence of this stately and august couple, whose bearing toward each other in society was a lesson of complete etiquette to the world. What went on behind the scenes no one could tell. I raised my hat with the profoundest deference as the carriage containing the two ladies dashed by; I knew not which was the cleverest hypocrite of the two, therefore I did equal honor to both. I was in a meditative and retrospective mood, and when I reached the Toledo the distracting noises, the cries of the flower-girls, and venders of chestnuts and confetti, the nasal singing of the street-rhymers, the yells of *punchinello*, and the answering laughter of the populace, were all beyond my endurance. To gratify a sudden whim that seized me, I made my way into the lowest and dirtiest quarters of the city, and roamed through wretched courts and crowded alleys, trying to discover that one miserable street which until now I had always avoided even the thought of, where I had purchased the coral-fisher's clothes on the day of my return from the grave. I went in many wrong directions, but at last I found it, and saw at a glance that the old rag- dealer's shop was still there, in its former condition of heterogeneous filth and disorder. A man sat at the door smoking, but not the crabbed and bent figure I had before seen—this was a younger and stouter individual, with a Jewish cast of countenance, and dark, ferocious eyes. I approached him, and seeing by my dress and manner that I was some person of consequence, he rose, drew his pipe from his mouth, and raised his greasy cap with a respectful yet suspicious air.

"Are you the owner of this place?" I asked.

"*Si, signor!*"

"What has become of the old man who used to live here?"

He laughed, shrugged his shoulders, and drew his pipe-stem across his throat with a significant gesture.

"So, signor!—with a sharp knife! He had a good deal of blood, too, for so withered a body. To kill himself in that fashion was stupid: he spoiled an Indian shawl that was on his bed, worth more than a thousand francs. One would not have thought he had so much blood."

And the fellow put back his pipe in his mouth and smoked complacently. I heard in sickened silence.

"He was mad, I suppose?" I said at last.

The long pipe was again withdrawn.

"Mad? Well, the people say so. I for one think he was very

reasonable–all except that matter of the shawl–he should have taken that off his bed first. But he was wise enough to know that he was of no use to anybody–he did the best he could! Did you know him, signor?"

"I gave him money once," I replied, evasively; then taking out a few francs I handed them to this evil-eyed, furtive-looking son of Israel, who received the gift with effusive gratitude.

"Thank you for your information," I said coldly. "Good-day."

"Good-day to you, signor," he replied, resuming his seat and watching me curiously as I turned away.

I passed out of the wretched street feeling faint and giddy. The end of the miserable rag-dealer been told to me briefly and brutally enough–yet somehow I was moved to a sense of regret and pity. Abjectly poor, half crazy, and utterly friendless, he had been a brother of mine in the same bitterness and irrevocable sorrow. I wondered with a half shudder–would my end be like his? When my vengeance was completed should I grow shrunken, and old, and mad, and one lurid day draw a sharp knife across my throat as a finish to my life's history? I walked more rapidly to shake off the morbid fancies that thus insidiously crept in on my brain; and as before, the noise and glitter of the Toledo had been unbearable, so now I found it a relief and a distraction. Two maskers bedizened in violet and gold whizzed past me like a flash, one of them yelling a stale jest concerning *la namorata*–a jest I scarcely heard, and certainly had no heart or wit to reply to. A fair woman I knew leaned out of a gaily draped balcony and dropped a bunch of roses at my feet; out of courtesy I stooped to pick them up, and then raising my hat I saluted the dark-eyed donor, but a few paces on I gave them away to a ragged child. Of all flowers that bloom, they were, and still are, the most insupportable to me. What is it the English poet Swinburne says–

"I shall never be friends again with roses!"

My wife wore them always: even on that night when I had

seen her clasped in Guido's arms, a red rose on her breast had been crushed in that embrace–a rose whose withered leaves I still possess. In the forest solitude where I now dwell there are no roses–and I am glad! The trees are too high, the tangle of bramble and coarse brushwood too dense–nothing grows here but a few herbs and field flowers–weeds unfit for wearing by fine ladies, yet to my taste infinitely sweeter than all the tenderly tinted cups of fragrance, whose colors and odors are spoiled to me forever. I am unjust, say you? the roses are innocent of evil? True enough, but their perfume awakens memory, and–I strive always to forget!

I reached my hotel that evening to find that I was an hour late for dinner, an unusual circumstance, which had caused Vincenzo some disquietude, as was evident from the relieved expression of his face when I entered. For some days the honest fellow had watched me with anxiety; my abstracted moods, the long solitary walks I was in the habit of taking, the evenings I passed in my room writing, with the doors locked– all this behavior on my part exercised his patience, I have no doubt, to the utmost limit, and I could see he had much ado to observe his usual discretion and tact, and refrain from asking questions. On this particular occasion I dined very hastily, for I had promised to join my wife and two of her lady friends at the theater that night.

When I arrived there, she was already seated in her box, looking radiantly beautiful. She was attired in some soft, sheeny, clinging primrose stuff, and the brigand's jewels I had given her through Guido's hands, flashed brilliantly on her uncovered neck and arms. She greeted me with her usual child-like enthusiasm as I entered, bearing the customary offering–a costly bouquet, set in a holder of mother-of-pearl studded with turquois, for her acceptance. I bowed to her lady friends, both of whom I knew, and then stood beside her watching the stage. The *comedietta* played there was the airiest trifle–it turned on the old worn-out story–a young wife, an aged, doting husband, and a lover whose principles were, of course, of the "noblest" type.

The husband was fooled (naturally), and the chief amusement of the piece appeared to consist in his being shut out of his own house in dressing-gown and slippers during a pelting storm of rain, while his spouse (who was particularly specified as "pure") enjoyed a luxurious supper with her highly moral and virtuous admirer. My wife laughed delightedly at the poor jokes and the stale epigrams, and specially applauded the actress who successfully supported the chief role. This actress, by the way, was a saucy, brazen-faced jade, who had a trick of flashing her black eyes, tossing her head, and heaving her ample bosom tumultuously whenever she hissed out the words *Vecchiaccio maladetto*, or accursed, villainous old monster, at her discomfited husband, which had an immense effect on the audience–an audience which entirely sympathized with her, though she was indubitably in the wrong. I watched Nina in some derision as she nodded her fair head and beat time to the music with her painted fan. I bent over her.

"The play pleases you?" I asked, in a low tone.

"Yes, indeed!" she answered, with a laughing light in her eyes. "The husband is so droll! It is all very amusing."

"The husband is always droll!" I remarked, smiling coldly. "It is not a temptation to marry when one knows that as a husband one must always look ridiculous."

She glanced up at me.

"Cesare! You surely are not vexed? Of course it is only in plays that it happens so!"

"Plays, *cara mia*, are often nothing but the reflex of real life," I said. "But let us hope there are exceptions, and that all husbands are not fools."

She smiled expressively and sweetly, toyed with the flowers I had given her, and turned her eyes again to the stage. I said no more, and was a somewhat moody companion for the rest of the evening. As we all left the theater one of the ladies who had accompanied Nina said lightly:

"You seem dull and out of spirits, conte?"

I forced a smile.

"Not I, signora! Surely you do not find me guilty of such ungallantry? Were I dull in YOUR company I should prove myself the most ungrateful of my sex."

She sighed somewhat impatiently. She was very young and very lovely, and, as far as I knew, innocent, and of a more thoughtful and poetical temperament than most women.

"That is the mere language of compliment," she said, looking straightly at me with her clear, candid eyes. "You are a true courtier! Yet often I think your courtesy is reluctant."

I looked at her in some surprise.

"Reluctant? Signora, pardon me if I do not understand!"

"I mean," she continued, still regarding me steadily, though a faint blush warmed the clear pallor of her delicate complexion, "that you do not really like us women; you say pretty things to us, and you try to be amiable in our company, but you are in truth averse to our ways–you are skeptical–you think we are all hypocrites."

I laughed a little coldly.

"Really, signora, your words place me in a very awkward position. Were I to tell you my real sentiments–"

She interrupted me with a touch of her fan on my arm, and smiled gravely.

"You would say, 'Yes, you are right, signora. I never see one of your sex without suspecting treachery.' Ah, Signor Conte, we women are indeed full of faults, but nothing can blind our instinct!" She paused, and her brilliant eyes softened as she added gently, "I pray your marriage may be a very happy one."

I was silent. I was not even courteous enough to thank her for the wish. I was half angered that this girl should have been able to probe my thoughts so quickly and unerringly. Was I so bad an actor after all? I glanced down at her as she leaned lightly on my arm,

"Marriage is a mere *comedietta*," I said, abruptly and harshly. "We have seen it acted to-night. In a few days I shall play the part of the chief buffoon–in other words, the husband."

And I laughed. My young companion looked startled, almost frightened, and over her fair face there flitted an expression of something like aversion. I did not care—why should I?—and there was no time for more words between us, for we had reached the outer vestibule of the theater.

My wife's carriage was drawn up at the entrance—my wife herself was stepping into it. I assisted her, and also her two friends, and then stood with uncovered head at the door wishing them all the "*felicissima notte.*" Nina put her tiny jeweled hand through the carriage window—I stooped and kissed it lightly. Drawing it back quickly, she selected a white gardenia from her bouquet and gave it to me with a bewitching smile.

Then the glittering equipage dashed away with a whirl and clatter of prancing hoofs and rapid wheels, and I stood alone under the wide portico of the theater—alone, amid the pressing throngs of the people who were still coming out of the house—holding the strongly scented gardenia in my hand as vaguely as a fevered man who finds a strange flower in one of his sick dreams.

After a minute or two I suddenly recollected myself, and throwing the blossom on the ground, I crushed it savagely beneath my heel— the penetrating odor rose from its slain petals as though a vessel of incense had been emptied at my feet. There was a nauseating influence in it; where had I inhaled that subtle perfume last? I remembered—Guido Ferrari had worn one of those flowers in his coat at my banquet—it had been still in his buttonhole when I killed him!

I strode onward and homeward; the streets were full of mirth and music, but I heeded none of it. I felt, rather than saw, the quiet sky bending above me dotted with its countless millions of luminous worlds; I was faintly conscious of the soft plash of murmuring waves mingling with the dulcet chords of deftly played mandolins echoing from somewhere down by the shore; but my soul was, as it were, benumbed—my mind, always on the alert, was for once utterly tired out—my very limbs ached, and when I at last flung myself on my bed, exhausted, my eyes closed instantly, and I slept the heavy, motionless sleep of a man weary unto death.

32

"*TOUT le monde vient a celui qui sait attendre.*" So wrote the great Napoleon. The virtue of the aphorism consists in the little words '*qui sait*'. All the world comes to him who KNOWS HOW to wait, I knew this, and I had waited, and my world–a world of vengeance– came to me at last.

The slow-revolving wheel of Time brought me to the day before my strange wedding–the eve of my remarriage with my own wife! All the preparations were made–nothing was left undone that could add to the splendor of the occasion. For though the nuptial ceremony was to be somewhat quiet and private in character, and the marriage breakfast was to include only a few of our more intimate acquaintances, the proceedings were by no means to terminate tamely. The romance of these remarkable espousals was not to find its conclusion in bathos. No; the bloom and aroma of the interesting event were to be enjoyed in the evening, when a grand supper and ball, given by me, the happy and much-to-be-envied bridegroom, was to take place in the hotel which I had made my residence for so long. No expense was spared for this, the last entertainment offered by me in my brilliant career as a successful Count Cesare Oliva. After it, the dark curtain would fall on the played-out drama, never to rise again.

Everything that art, taste, and royal luxury could suggest was included in the arrangements for this brilliant ball, to which a hundred and fifty guests had been invited, not one of whom had refused to attend.

And now—now, in the afternoon of this, the last of my self-imposed probation—I sat alone with my fair wife in the drawing-room of the Villa Romani, conversing lightly on various subjects connected with the festivities of the coming morrow. The long windows were open— the warm spring sunlight lay like a filmy veil of woven gold on the tender green of the young grass, birds sung for joy and flitted from branch to branch, now poising hoveringly above their nests, now soaring with all the luxury of perfect liberty into the high heaven of cloudless blue—the great creamy buds of the magnolia looked ready to burst into wide and splendid flower between their large, darkly shining leaves, the odor of violets and primroses floated on every delicious breath of air, and round the wide veranda the climbing white china roses had already unfurled their little crumpled rosette-like blossoms to the balmy wind. It was spring in Southern Italy—spring in the land where, above all other lands, spring is lovely—sudden and brilliant in its beauty as might be the smile of a happy angel. Gran Dio!—talk of angels! Had I not a veritable angel for my companion at that moment? What fair being, even in Mohammed's Paradise of Houris, could outshine such charms as those which it was my proud privilege to gaze upon without rebuke— dark eyes, rippling golden hair, a dazzling and perfect face, a form to tempt the virtue of a Galahad, and lips that an emperor might long to touch—in vain? Well, no!—not altogether in vain: if his imperial majesty could offer a bribe large enough—let us say a diamond the size of a pigeon's egg—he might possibly purchase one, nay!—perhaps two kisses from that seductive red mouth, sweeter than the ripest strawberry. I glanced at her furtively from time to time when she was not aware of my gaze; and glad was I of the sheltering protection of the dark glasses I wore, for I knew and felt that there was a terrible look in my eyes–the look of a half-famished tiger ready to spring on some long-desired piece of prey. She herself was exceptionally bright and cheerful; with her riante features and agile movements, she reminded me of some tropical bird of gorgeous plumage swaying to and fro on a branch of equally gorgeous blossom.

"You are like a prince in a fairy tale, Cesare," she said, with a little delighted laugh; "everything you do is superbly done! How pleasant it is to be so rich–there is nothing better in all the world."

"Except love!" I returned, with a grim attempt to be sentimental.

Her large eyes softened like the pleading eyes of a tame fawn.

"Ay, yes!" and she smiled with expressive tenderness, "except love. But when one has both love and wealth, what a paradise life can be!"

"So great a paradise," I assented, "that it is hardly worth while trying to get into heaven at all! Will you make earth a heaven for me, Nina mia, or will you only love me as much–or as little–as you loved your late husband?"

She shrugged her shoulders and pouted like a spoilt child.

"Why are you so fond of talking about my late husband, Cesare?" she asked, peevishly; "I am so tired of his name! Besides, one does not always care to be reminded of dead people–and he died so horribly too! I have often told you that I did not love him at all. I liked him a little, and I was quite ill when that dreadful monk, who looked like a ghost himself, came and told me he was dead. Fancy hearing such a piece of news suddenly, while I was actually at luncheon with Gui– Signore Ferrari! We were both shocked, of course, but I did not break my heart over it. Now I really DO love YOU–"

I drew nearer to her on the couch where she sat, and put one arm round her.

"You really DO?" I asked, in a half-incredulous tone; "you are quite sure?"

She laughed and nestled her head on my shoulder.

"I am quite sure! How many times have you asked me that absurd question? What can I say, what can I do–to make you believe me?"

"Nothing," I answered, and answered truly, for certainly nothing she could say or do would make me believe her for a moment. "But HOW do you love me–for myself or for my wealth?"

She raised her head with a proud, graceful gesture.

"For yourself, of course! Do you think mere wealth could ever win MY affection? No, Cesare! I love you for your own sake–your own merits have made you dear to me."

I smiled bitterly. She did not see the smile. I slowly caressed her silky hair.

"For that sweet answer, *carissima mia*, you shall have your reward. You called me a fairy prince just now–perhaps I merit that title more than you know. You remember the jewels I sent you before we ever met?"

"Remember them!" she exclaimed. "They are my choicest ornaments. Such a *parure* is fit for an empress."

"And an empress of beauty wears them!" I said, lightly. "But they are mere trifles compared to other gems which I possess, and which I intend to offer for your acceptance."

Her eyes glistened with avarice and expectancy.

"Oh, let me see them!" she cried. "If they are lovelier than those I already have, they must be indeed magnificent! And are they all for me?"

"All for you!" I replied, drawing her closer, and playing with the small white hand on which the engagement-ring I had placed there sparkled so bravely. "All for my bride. A little hoard of bright treasures; red rubies, ay–as red as blood-diamonds as brilliant as the glittering of crossed daggers–sapphires as blue as the lightning–pearls as pure as the little folded hands of a dead child–opals as dazzlingly changeful as woman's love! Why do you start?" for she had moved restlessly in my embrace. "Do I use bad similes? Ah, *cara mia*, I am no poet! I can but speak of things as they seem to my poor judgment. Yes, these precious things are for you, *bellissima*; you have nothing to do but to take them, and may they bring you much joy!"

A momentary pallor had stolen over her face while I was speaking– speaking in my customary hard, harsh voice, which I strove to render even harder and harsher than usual–but she soon recovered from whatever passing emotion she may have felt, and gave herself up to the joys of vanity and greed, the paramount passions of her nature.

"I shall have the finest jewels in all Naples!" she laughed, delightedly. "How the women will envy me! But where are these treasures? May I see them now–immediately?"

"No, not quite immediately," I replied, with a gentle derision that escaped her observation. "To-morrow night–our marriage night–you shall have them. And I must also fulfill a promise I made to you. You wish to see me for once without these," and I touched my dark glasses–"is it not so?"

She raised her eyes, conveying into their lustrous depths an expression of melting tenderness.

"Yes," she murmured; "I want to see you as you ARE!"

"I fear you will be disappointed," I said, with some irony, "for my eyes are not pleasant to look at."

"Never mind," she returned, gaily. "I shall be satisfied if I see them just once, and we need not have much light in the room, as the light gives you pain. I would not be the cause of suffering to you– no, not for all the world!"

"You are very amiable," I answered, "more so than I deserve. I hope I may prove worthy of your tenderness! But to return to the subject of the jewels. I wish you to see them for yourself and choose the best among them. Will you come with me to-morrow night? and I will show you where they are."

She laughed sweetly.

"Are you a miser, Cesare?–and have you some secret hiding-place full of treasure like Aladdin?"

I smiled.

"Perhaps I have," I said. "There are exceptional cases in which one fears to trust even to a bank. Gems such as those I have to offer you are almost priceless, and it would be unwise, almost cruel to place such tempting toys within the reach of even an honest man. At any rate, if I have been something of a miser, it is for your sake, for your sake I have personally guarded the treasure that is to be your bridal gift. You cannot blame me for this?"

In answer she threw her fair arms round my neck and kissed me. Strive against it as I would, I always shuddered at the touch of her lips–a mingled sensation of loathing and longing possessed me that sickened while it stung my soul.

"Amor mio!" she murmured. "As if I could blame you! You have no faults in my estimation of you. You are good, brave and generous– the best of men; there is only one thing I wish sometimes–" Here she paused, and her brow knitted itself frowningly, while a puzzled, pained expression came into her eyes.

"And that one thing is?" I inquired.

"That you did not remind me so often of Fabio," she said, abruptly and half angrily. "Not when you speak of him, I do not mean that. What I mean is, that you have ways like his. Of course I know there is no actual resemblance, and yet–" She paused again, and again looked troubled.

"Really, *carina mia*," I remarked, lightly and jestingly, "you embarrass me profoundly! This fancy of yours is a most awkward one for me. At the convent where I visited you, you became quite ill at the contemplation of my hand, which you declared was like the hand of your deceased husband; and now–this same foolish idea is returning, when I hoped it had gone, with other morbid notions of an oversensitive brain, forever. Perhaps you think I am your late husband?"

And I laughed aloud! She trembled a little, but soon laughed also.

"I know I am very absurd," she said, "perhaps I am a little nervous and unstrung: I have had too much excitement lately.

Tell me more about the jewels. When will you take me to see them?"

"To-morrow night," I answered, "while the ball is going on, you and I will slip away together—we shall return again before any of our friends can miss us. You will come with me?"

"Of course I will," she replied, readily, "only we must not be long absent, because my maid will have to pack my wedding-dress, and then there will be the jewels also to put in my strong box. Let me see! We stay the night at the hotel, and leave for Rome and Paris the first thing in the morning, do we not?"

"That is the arrangement, certainly," I said, with a cold smile.

"The little place where you have hidden your jewels, you droll Cesare, is quite near then?" she asked.

"Quite near," I assented, watching her closely.

She laughed and clapped her hands.

"Oh, I must have them," she exclaimed. "It would be ridiculous to go to Paris without them. But why will you not get them yourself, Cesare, and bring them here to me?"

"There are so many," I returned, quietly, "and I do not know which you would prefer. Some are more valuable than others. And it will give me a special satisfaction—one that I have long waited for—to see you making your own choice."

She smiled half shyly, half cunningly.

"Perhaps I will make no choice," she whispered, "perhaps I will take them ALL, Cesare. What will you say then?"

"That you are perfectly welcome to them," I replied.

She looked slightly surprised.

"You are really too good to me, *caro mio*," she said; "you spoil me."

"CAN you be spoiled?" I asked, half jestingly. "Good women are like fine brilliants—the more richly they are set the more they shine."

She stroked my hand caressingly.

"No one ever made such pretty speeches to me as you do!" she murmured.

"Not even Guido Ferrari?" I suggested, ironically.

She drew herself up with an inimitably well-acted gesture of lofty disdain.

"Guido Ferrari!" she exclaimed. "He dared not address me save with the greatest respect! I was as a queen to him! It was only lately that he began to presume on the trust left him by my husband, and then he became too familiar–a mistake on his part, for which YOU punished him–as he deserved!"

I rose from my seat beside her. I could not answer for my own composure while sitting so close to the actual murderess of MY friend and HER lover. Had she forgotten her own "familiar" treatment of the dead man–the thousand nameless wiles and witcheries and tricks of her trade, by which she had beguiled his soul and ruined his honor?

"I am glad you are satisfied with my action in that affair," I said, coldly and steadily. "I myself regret the death of the unfortunate young man, and shall continue to do so. My nature, unhappily, is an oversensitive one, and is apt to be affected by trifles. But now, *mia bella*, farewell until to-morrow–happy to-morrow!–when I shall call you mine indeed!"

A warm flush tinted her cheeks; she came to me where I stood, and leaned against me.

"Shall I not see you again till we meet in the church?" she inquired, with a becoming bashfulness.

"No. I will leave you this last day of your brief widowhood alone. It is not well that I should obtrude myself upon your thoughts or prayers. Stay!" and I caught her hand which toyed with the flower in my buttonhole. "I see you still wear your former wedding-ring. May I take it off?"

"Certainly." And she smiled while I deftly drew off the plain gold circlet I had placed there nearly four years since.

"Will you let me keep it?"

"If you like. I would rather not see it again."

"You shall not," I answered, as I slipped it into my pocket.

"It will be replaced by a new one to-morrow—one that I hope may be the symbol of more joy to you than this has been."

And as her eyes turned to my face in all their melting, perfidious languor, I conquered my hatred of her by a strong effort, and stooped and kissed her. Had I yielded to my real impulses, I would have crushed her cruelly in my arms, and bruised her delicate flesh with the brutal ferocity of caresses born of bitterest loathing, not love. But no sign of my aversion escaped me—all she saw was her elderly looking admirer, with his calmly courteous demeanor, chill smile, and almost parental tenderness; and she judged him merely as an influential gentleman of good position and unlimited income, who was about to make her one of the most envied women in all Italy.

The fugitive resemblance she traced in me to her "dead" husband was certainly attributed by her to a purely accidental likeness common to many persons in this world, where every man, they say, has his double, and for that matter every woman also. Who does not remember the touching surprise of Heinrich Heine when, on visiting the picture-gallery of the Palazzo Durazzo in Genoa, he was brought face to face with the portrait, as he thought, of a dead woman he had loved—"*Maria la morte.*" It mattered not to him that the picture was very old, that it had been painted by Giorgio Barbarelli centuries before his "Maria" could have lived; he simply declares: "*Il est vraiment d une ressemblance admirable, ressemblant jusqu'au silence de la mort!*"

Such likenesses are common enough, and my wife, though my resemblance to myself (!) troubled her a little, was very far from imagining the real truth of the matter, as indeed how should she? What woman, believing and knowing, as far as anything can be known, her husband to be dead and fast buried, is likely to accept even the idea of his possible escape from the tomb! Not one!—else the disconsolate widows would indeed have reason to be more inconsolable than they appear!

When I left her that morning I found Andrea Luziani waiting for me at my hotel. He was seated in the outer entrance hall; I bade him follow me into my private salon. He did so. Abashed at the magnificence of the apartment, he paused at the doorway, and stood, red cap in hand, hesitating, though with an amiable smile on his sunburned merry countenance.

"Come in, amico," I said, with an inviting gesture, "and sit down. All this tawdry show of velvet and gilding must seem common to your eyes, that have rested so long on the sparkling pomp of the foaming waves, the glorious blue curtain of the sky, and the sheeny white of the sails of the 'Laura' gleaming in the gold of the sun. Would I could live such a life as yours, Andrea!–there is nothing better under the width of heaven."

The poetical temperament of the Sicilian was caught and fired by my words. He at once forgot the splendid appurtenances of wealth and the costly luxuries that surrounded him; he advanced without embarrassment, and seated himself on a velvet and gold chair with as much ease as though it were a coil of rough rope on board the "Laura."

"You say truly, *eccellenza*," he said, with a gleam of his white teeth through his jet-black mustache, while his warm southern eyes flashed fire, "there is nothing sweeter than the life of the *marinaro*. And truly there are many who say to me, 'Ah, ah! Andrea! *buon amico*, the time comes when you will wed, and the home where the wife and children sit will seem a better thing to you than the caprice of the wind and waves.' But I–see you!–I know otherwise. The woman I wed must love the sea; she must have the fearless eyes that can look God's storms in the face–her tender words must ring out all the more clearly for the sound of the bubbling waves leaping against the 'Laura' when the wind is high! And as for our children," he paused and laughed, "per la Santissima Madonna! if the salt and iron of the ocean be not in their blood, they will be no children of mine!"

I smiled at his enthusiasm, and pouring out some choice Montepulciano, bade him taste it. He did so with a keen appreciation of its flavor, such as many a so-called connoisseur of wines does not possess.

"To your health, *eccellenza!*" he said, "and may you long

enjoy your life!"

I thanked him; but in my heart I was far from echoing the kindly wish.

"And are you going to fulfill the prophecy of your friends, Andrea?" I asked. "Are you about to marry?"

He set down his glass only partly emptied, and smiled with an air of mystery.

"*Ebbene! chi sa!*" he replied, with a gay little shrug of his shoulders, yet with a sudden tenderness in his keen eyes that did not escape me. "There is a maiden–my mother loves her well–she is little and fair as Carmelo Neri's Teresa–so high," and he laid his brown hand lightly on his breast, "her head touches just here," and he laughed. "She looks as frail as a lily, but she is hardy as a sea-gull, and no one loves the wild waves more than she. Perhaps, in the month of the Madonna, when the white lilies bloom–perhaps!–one can never tell–the old song may be sung for us–

"*Chi sa fervente amar Solo e felice!*"

And humming the tune of the well-known love-ditty under his breath, he raised his glass of wine to his lips and drained it off with a relish, while his honest face beamed with gayety and pleasure. Always the same story, I thought, moodily. Love, the tempter–Love, the destroyer–Love, the curse! Was there NO escape possible from this bewildering snare that thus caught and slew the souls of men?

33

HE SOON roused himself from his pleasant reverie, and drawing his chair closer to mine, assumed an air of mystery.

"And for your friend who is in trouble," he said, in a confidential tone, then paused and looked at me as though waiting permission to proceed.

I nodded.

"Go on, amico. What have you arranged?"

"Everything!" he announced, with an air of triumph. "All is smooth sailing. At six o'clock on Friday morning the 'Rondinella,' that is the brig I told you of, *eccellenza*, will weigh anchor for Civita Vecchia. Her captain, old Antonio Bardi, will wait ten minutes or even a quarter of an hour if necessary for the—the—"

"Passenger," I supplemented. "Very amiable of him, but he will not need to delay his departure for a single instant beyond the appointed hour. Is he satisfied with the passage money?"

"Satisfied!" and Andrea swore a good-natured oath and laughed aloud. "By San Pietro! if he were not, he would deserve to drown like a dog on the voyage! Though truly, it is always difficult to please him, he being old and cross and crusty. Yes; he is one of those men who have seen so much of life that they are tired of it. Believe it! even the stormiest sea is a tame fish-pond to old Bardi. But he is satisfied this time, *eccellenza*, and his tongue and eyes are so tied up that I should not wonder if your friend found him to be both dumb and blind when he steps on board."

"That is well," I said, smiling. "I owe you many thanks, Andrea. And yet there is one more favor I would ask of you."

He saluted me with a light yet graceful gesture.

"*Eccellenza*, anything I can do–command me."

"It is a mere trifle," I returned. "It is merely to take a small valise belonging to my friend, and to place it on board the 'Rondmella' under the care of the captain. Will you do this?"

"Most willingly. I will take it now if it so please you."

"That is what I desire. Wait here and I will bring it to you."

And leaving him for a minute or two, I went into my bedroom and took from a cupboard I always kept locked a common rough leather bag, which I had secretly packed myself, unknown to Vincenzo, with such things as I judged to be useful and necessary. Chief among them was a bulky roll of bank-notes. These amounted to nearly the whole of the remainder of the money I had placed in the bank at Palermo. I had withdrawn it by gradual degrees, leaving behind only a couple of thousand francs, for which I had no special need. I locked and strapped the valise; there was no name on it and it was scarcely any weight to carry. I took it to Andrea, who swung it easily in his right hand and said, smilingly:

"Your friend is not wealthy, *eccellenza*, if this is all his luggage!"

"You are right," I answered, with a slight sigh; "he is truly very poor–beggared of everything that should be his through the treachery of those whom he has benefited." I paused; Andrea was listening sympathetically. "That is why I have paid his passage- money, and have done my best to aid him."

"Ah! you have the good heart, *eccellenza*," murmured the Sicilian, thoughtfully. "Would there were more like you! Often when fortune gives a kick to a man, nothing will suit but that all who see him must kick him also. And thus the *povero diavolo* dies of so many kicks, often! This friend of yours is young, *senza dubbio?*"

"Yes, quite young, not yet thirty."

"It is as if you were a father to him!" exclaimed Andrea, enthusiastically. "I hope he may be truly grateful to you, *eccellenza.*"

"I hope so too," I said, unable to resist a smile. "And now, amico, take this," and I pressed a small sealed packet into his hand. "It is for yourself. Do not open it till you are at home with the mother you love so well, and the little maiden you spoke of by your side. If its contents please you, as I believe they will, think that I am also rendered happier by your happiness."

His dark eyes sparkled with gratitude as I spoke, and setting the valise he held down on the ground, he stretched out his hand half timidly, half frankly. I shook it warmly and bade him farewell.

"*Per Bacco!*" he said, with a sort of shamefaced eagerness, "the very devil must have caught my tongue in his fingers! There is something I ought to say to you, *eccellenza*, but for my life I cannot find the right words. I must thank you better when I see you next."

"Yes," I answered, dreamily and somewhat wearily, "when you see me next, Andrea, you shall thank me if you will; but believe me, I need no thanks."

And thus we parted, never to meet again–he to the strong glad life that is born of the wind and sea, and I to–. But let me not anticipate. Step by step through the labyrinths of memory let me go over the old ground watered with blood and tears, not missing one sharp stone of detail on the drear pathway leading to the bitter end.

That same evening I had an interview with Vincenzo. He was melancholy and taciturn–a mood which was the result of an announcement I had previously made to him–namely, that his services would not be required during my wedding-trip. He had hoped to accompany me and to occupy the position of courier, valet, major- domo, and generally confidential attendant–a hope which had partially soothed the vexation he had evidently felt at the notion of my marrying at all.

His plans were now frustrated, and if ever the good-natured fellow could be ill-tempered, he was assuredly so on this occasion. He stood before me with his usual respectful air, but he avoided my glance, and kept his eyes studiously fixed on the pattern of the carpet. I addressed him with an air of gayety.

"*Ebbene*, Vincenzo! Joy comes at last, you see, even to me! To-morrow I shall wed the Countess Romani–the loveliest and perhaps the richest woman in Naples!"

"I know it, *eccellenza*."

This with the same obstinately fixed countenance and downward look.

"You are not very pleased, I think, at the prospect of my happiness?" I asked, banteringly.

He glanced up for an instant, then as quickly down again.

"If one could be sure that the *illustrissimo eccellenza* was indeed happy, that would be a good thing," he answered, dubiously.

"And are you not sure?"

He paused, then replied firmly:

"No; the *eccellenza* does not look happy. No, no, *davvero*! He has the air of being sorrowful and ill, both together."

I shrugged my shoulders indifferently.

"You mistake me, Vincenzo. I am well–very well–and happy! *Gran Dio!* who could be happier? But what of my health or happiness?–they are nothing to me, and should be less to you. Listen; I have something I wish you to do for me."

He gave me a sidelong and half-expectant glance. I went on:

"To-morrow evening I want you to go to Avellino."

He was utterly astonished.

"To Avellino!" he murmured under his breath, "to Avellino!"

"Yes, to Avellino," I repeated, somewhat impatiently. "Is

there anything so surprising in that? You will take a letter from me to the Signora Monti. Look you, Vincenzo, you have been faithful and obedient so far, I expect implicit fidelity and obedience still. You will not be needed here to-morrow after the marriage ball has once begun; you can take the nine o'clock train to Avellino, and– understand me–you will remain there till you receive further news from me. You will not have to wait long, and in the meantime," here I smiled, "you can make love to Lilla."

Vincenzo did not return the smile.

"But–but," he stammered, sorely perplexed–"if I go to Avellino I cannot wait upon the *eccellenza*. There is the portmanteau to pack– and who will see to the luggage when you leave on Friday morning for Rome? And–and–I had thought to see you to the station–" He stopped, his vexation was too great to allow him to proceed.

I laughed gently.

"How many more trifles can you think of, my friend, in opposition to my wishes? As for the portmanteau, you can pack it this very day if you so please–then it will be in readiness. The rest of your duties can for once be performed by others. It is not only important, but imperative that you should go to Avellino on my errand. I want you to take this with you," and I tapped a small square iron box, heavily made and strongly padlocked, which stood on the table near me.

He glanced at the box, but still hesitated, and the gloom on his countenance deepened. I grew a little annoyed.

"What is the matter with you?" I said at last with some sternness. "You have something on your mind–speak out!"

The fear of my wrath startled him. He looked up with a bewildered pain in his eyes, and spoke, his mellow Tuscan voice vibrating with his own eloquent entreaty.

"*Eccellenza!*" he exclaimed, eagerly, "you must forgive me– yes, forgive your poor servant who seems too bold, and who yet is true to you–yes, indeed, so true!–and who would go with you to death if there were need! I am not blind, I can see your sufferings, for you do suffer, *'lustrissimo*, though you hide it well. Often have I watched you when you have not known it. I feel that you have what we call a wound in the heart, bleeding, bleeding always. Such a thing means death often, as much as a straight shot in battle. Let me watch over you, *eccellenza*; let me stay with you! I have learned to love you! *Ah, mio signor*," and he drew nearer and caught my hand timidly, "you do not know–how should you?–the look that is in your face sometimes, the look of one who is stunned by a hard blow. I have said to myself 'That look will kill me if I see it often.' And your love for this great lady, whom you will wed to-morrow, has not lightened your soul as love should lighten it. No! you are even sadder than before, and the look I speak of comes ever again and again. Yes, I have watched you, and lately I have seen you writing, writing far into the night, when you should have slept. Ah, signor! you are angry, and I know I should not have spoken; but tell me, how can I look at Lilla and be happy when I feel that you are alone and sad?"

I stopped the flood of his eloquence by a mute gesture and withdrew my hand from his clasp.

"I am not angry," I said, with quiet steadiness, and yet with something of coldness, though my whole nature, always highly sensitive, was deeply stirred by the rapid, unstudied expressions of affection that melted so warmly from his lips in the liquid music of the mellow Tuscan tongue. "No, I am not angry, but I am sorry to have been the object of so much solicitude on your part. Your pity is misplaced, Vincenzo, it is indeed! Pity an emperor clad in purples and seated on a throne of pure gold, but do not pity ME! I tell you that, to-morrow, yes, to-morrow, I shall obtain all that I have ever sought–my greatest desire will be fulfilled. Believe it. No man has ever been so thoroughly satiated with–satisfaction–as I shall be!"

Then seeing him look still sad and incredulous, I clapped my hand on his shoulder and smiled.

"Come, come, amico, wear a merrier face for my bridal day, or you will not deserve to wed Lilla. I thank you from my heart," and I spoke more gravely, "for your well-meant care and kindness, but I assure you there is nothing wrong with me. I am well—perfectly well—and happy. It is understood that you go to Avellino to-morrow evening?"

Vincenzo sighed, but was passive.

"It must be as the *eccellenza* pleases," he murmured, resignedly.

"That is well," I answered, good-humoredly; "and as you know my pleasure, take care that nothing interferes with your departure. And—one word more—you must cease to watch me. Plainly speaking, I do not choose to be under your surveillance. Nay—I am not offended, far from it, fidelity and devotion are excellent virtues, but in the present case I prefer obedience—strict, implicit obedience. Whatever I may do, whether I sleep or wake, walk or sit still— attend to YOUR duties and pay no heed to MY actions. So will you best serve me—you understand?"

"Si, signor!" and the poor fellow sighed again, and reddened with his own inward confusion. "You will pardon me, *eccellenza*, for my freedom of speech? I feel I have done wrong—"

"I pardon you for what in this world is never pardoned—excess of love," I answered, gently. "Knowing you love me, I ask you to obey me in my present wishes, and thus we shall always be friends."

His face brightened at these last words, and his thoughts turned in. a new direction. He glanced at the iron box I had before pointed out to him.

"That is to go to Avellino, *eccellenza?*" he asked, with more alacrity than he had yet shown.

"Yes," I answered. "You will place it in the hands of the good Signora Monti, for whom I have a great respect. She will take care of it till—I return."

"Your commands shall be obeyed, signor," he said, rapidly, as though eager to atone for his past hesitation. "After all," and he smiled, "it will be pleasant to see Lilla; she will be interested, too, to hear the account of the *eccellenza's* marriage."

And somewhat consoled by the prospect of the entertainment his unlooked-for visit would give to the charming little maiden of his choice, he left me, and shortly afterward I heard him humming a popular love-song softly under his breath, while he busied himself in packing my portmanteau for the honeymoon trip—a portmanteau destined never to be used or opened by its owner.

That night, contrary to my usual habit, I lingered long over my dinner; at its close I poured out a full glass of fine Lacrima Cristi, and secretly mixing with it a dose of a tasteless but powerful opiate, I called my valet and bade him drink it and wish me joy. He did so readily, draining the contents to the last drop. It was a tempestuous night; there was a high wind, broken through by heavy sweeping gusts of rain. Vincenzo cleared the dinner-table, yawning visibly as he did so, then taking my out-door *paletot* on his arm, he went to his bedroom, a small one adjoining mine, for the purpose of brushing it, according to his customary method. I opened a book, and pretending to be absorbed in its contents, I waited patiently for about half an hour.

At the expiration of that time I stole softly to his door and looked in. It was as I had expected; overcome by the sudden and heavy action of the opiate, he had thrown himself on his bed, and was slumbering profoundly, the unbrushed overcoat by his side. Poor fellow! I smiled as I watched him; the faithful dog was chained, and could not follow my steps for that night at least.

I left him thus, and wrapping myself in a thick Almaviva that muffled me almost to the eyes, I hurried out, fortunately meeting no one on my way—out into the storm and darkness, toward the Campo Santo, the abode of the all-wise though speechless dead. I had work to do there—work that must be done. I knew that if I had not taken the precaution of drugging my too devoted servitor, he might, despite his protestations, have been tempted to track me whither I went. As it was, I felt myself safe, for four hours must pass, I knew, before Vincenzo could awake from his lethargy. And I was absent for some time.

Though I performed my task as quickly as might be, it took me longer than I thought, and filled me with more loathing and reluctance than I had deemed possible. It was a gruesome, ghastly piece of work–a work of preparation–and when I had finished it entirely to my satisfaction, I felt as though the bony fingers of death itself had been plunged into my very marrow. I shivered with cold, my limbs would scarce bear me upright, and my teeth chattered as though I were seized by strong ague. But the fixity of my purpose strengthened me till all was done– till the stage was set for the last scene of the tragedy. Or comedy? What you will! I know that in the world nowadays you make a husband's dishonor more of a whispered jest than anything else–you and your heavy machinery of the law. But to me–I am so strangely constituted–dishonor is a bitterer evil than death. If all those who are deceived and betrayed felt thus, then justice would need to become more just. It is fortunate– for the lawyers–that we are not all honorable men!

When I returned from my dreary walk in the driving storm I found Vincenzo still fast asleep. I was glad of this, for had he seen me in the plight I was, he would have had good reason to be alarmed concerning both my physical and mental condition. Perceiving myself in the glass, I recoiled as from an image of horror. I saw a man with haunted, hungry eyes gleaming out from under a mass of disordered white hair, his pale, haggard face set and stern as the face of a merciless inquisitor of old Spain, his dark cloak dripping with glittering raindrops, his hands and nails stained as though he had dug them into the black earth, his boots heavy with mire and clay, his whole aspect that of one who had been engaged in some abhorrent deed, too repulsive to be named. I stared at my own reflection thus and shuddered; then I laughed softly with a sort of fierce enjoyment. Quickly I threw off all my soiled habiliments, and locked them out of sight, and arraying myself in dressing-gown and slippers, I glanced at the time. It was half-past one—already the morning of my bridal. I had been absent three hours and a half. I went into my salon and remained there writing. A few minutes after two o'clock had struck the door opened noiselessly, and Vincenzo, looking still very sleepy, appeared with an expression of inquiring anxiety. He smiled drowsily, and seemed relieved to see me sitting quietly in my accustomed place at the writing-table. I surveyed him with an air of affected surprise.

"*Ebbene*, Vincenzo! What has become of you all this while?"

"*Eccellenza*," he stammered, "it was the Lacrima; I am not used to wine! I have been asleep."

I laughed, pretended to stifle a yawn on my own account, and rose from my easy-chair.

"*Veramente*," I said, lightly, "so have I, very nearly! And if I would appear as a gay bridegroom, it is time I went to bed. *Buona notte.*"

"*Buona notte, signor.*"

And we severally retired to rest, he satisfied that I had been in my own room all the evening, and I, thinking with a savage joy at my heart of what I had prepared out there in the darkness, with no witnesses of my work save the whirling wind and rain.

34

MY MARRIAGE morning dawned bright and clear, though the high wind of the past night still prevailed and sent the white clouds scudding rapidly, like ships running a race, across the blue fairness of the sky. The air was strong, fresh, and exhilarating, and the crowds that swarmed into the Piazza del Popolo, and the Toledo, eager to begin the riot and fun of Giovedi Grasso, were one and all in the highest good humor. As the hours advanced, many little knots of people hurried toward the cathedral, anxious, if possible, to secure places in or near the Chapel of San Gennaro, in order to see to advantage the brilliant costumes of the few distinguished persons who had been invited to witness my wedding. The ceremony was fixed to take place at eleven, and at a little before half past ten I entered my carriage, in company with the Duke di Marina as best man, and drove to the scene of action. Clad in garments of admirable cut and fit, with well-brushed hair and beard, and wearing a demeanor of skillfully mingled gravity and gayety, I bore but little resemblance to the haggard, ferocious creature who had faced me in the mirror a few hours previously.

A strange and secret mirth too possessed me, a sort of half-frenzied merriment that threatened every now and then to break through the mask of dignified composure it was necessary for me to wear. There were moments when I could have laughed, shrieked, and sung with the fury of a drunken madman. As it was, I talked incessantly; my conversation was flavored with bitter wit and pungent sarcasm, and once or twice my friend the duke surveyed me with an air of wondering inquiry, as though he thought my manner forced or unnatural. My coachman was compelled to drive rather slowly, owing to the pressing throngs that swarmed at every corner and through every thoroughfare, while the yells of the masqueraders, the gambols of street clowns, the firing of toy guns, and the sharp explosion of colored bladders, that were swung to and fro and tossed in the air by the merry populace, startled my spirited horses frequently, and caused them to leap and prance to a somewhat dangerous extent, thus attracting more than the customary attention to my equipage. As it drew up at last at the door of the chapel, I was surprised to see what a number of spectators had collected there. There was a positive crowd of loungers, beggars, children, and middle-class persons of all sorts, who beheld my arrival with the utmost interest and excitement.

In accordance with my instructions a rich crimson carpet had been laid down from the very edge of the pavement right into the church as far as the altar; a silken awning had also been erected, under which bloomed a miniature avenue of palms and tropical flowers. All eyes were turned upon me curiously as I stepped from my carriage and entered the chapel, side by side with the duke, and murmurs of my vast wealth and generosity were audibly whispered as I passed along. One old crone, hideously ugly, but with large, dark piercing eyes, the fading lamps of a lost beauty, chuckled and mumbled as she craned her skinny throat forward to observe me more closely. "Ay, ay! The saints know he need be rich and generous—*pover'uomo* to fill HER mouth. A little red cruel mouth always open, that swallows money like macaroni, and laughs at the suffering poor! Ah! that is bad, bad! He need be rich to satisfy HER!"

The Duke di Marina caught these words and glanced

quickly at me, but I affected not to have heard. Inside the chapel there were a great number of people, but my own invited guests, not numbering more than twenty or thirty, were seated in the space apportioned to them near the altar, which was divided from the mere sight-seers by means of a silken rope that crossed the aisle. I exchanged greetings with most of these persons, and in return received their congratulations; then I walked with a firm deliberate step up to the high altar and there waited. The magnificent paintings on the wall round me seemed endowed with mysterious life–the grand heads of saints and martyrs were turned upon me as though they demanded–"MUST thou do this thing? Hast thou no forgiveness?"

And ever my stern answer, "Nay; if hereafter I am tortured in eternal flame for all ages, yet now–now while I live, I will be avenged!"

A bleeding Christ suspended on His cross gazed at me reproachfully with long-enduring eyes of dreadful anguish–eyes that seemed to say, "Oh, erring man, that tormentest thyself with passing passions, shall not thine own end approach speedily?–and what comfort wilt thou have in thy last hour?"

And inwardly I answered, "None! No shred of consolation can ever again be mine–no joy, save fulfilled revenge! And this I will possess though the heavens should crack and the earth split asunder! For once a woman's treachery shall meet with punishment–for once such strange uncommon justice shall be done!"

And my spirit wrapped itself again in somber meditative silence. The sunlight fell gloriously through the stained windows–blue, gold, crimson, and violet shafts of dazzling radiance glittered in lustrous flickering patterns on the snowy whiteness of the marble altar, and slowly, softly, majestically, as though an angel stepped forward, the sound of music stole on the incense-laden air. The unseen organist played a sublime voluntary of Palestrina's, and the round harmonious notes came falling gently on one another like drops from a fountain trickling on flowers.

I thought of my last wedding-day, when I had stood in this very place, full of hope, intoxicated with love and joy, when Guido Ferrari had been by my side, and had drunk in for the first time the poisoned draught of temptation from the loveliness of my wife's face and form; when I, poor fool! would us soon have thought that God could lie, as that either of these whom I adored could play me false. I drew the wedding-ring from my pocket and looked at it–it was sparklingly bright and appeared new. Yet it was old–it was the very same ring I had drawn off my wife's finger the day before; it had only been burnished afresh by a skilled jeweler, and showed no more marks of wear than if it had been bought that morning.

The great bell of the cathedral boomed out eleven, and as the last stroke swung from the tower, the chapel doors were flung more widely open: then came the gentle rustle of trailing robes, and turning, I beheld my wife. She approached, leaning lightly on the arm of the old Chevalier Mancini, who, true to his creeds of gallantry, had accepted with alacrity the post of paternal protector to the bride on this occasion; and I could not well wonder at the universal admiration that broke in suppressed murmurs from all assembled, as this most fair masterpiece of the devil's creation paced slowly and gracefully up the aisle. She wore a dress of clinging white velvet made with the greatest simplicity–a lace veil, priceless in value and fine as gossamer, draped her from head to foot–the jewels I had given her flashed about her like scintillating points of light, in her hair, at her waist, on her breast and uncovered arms.

Being as she deemed herself, a widow, she had no bride-maids; her train was held up by a handsome boy clad in the purple and gold costume of a sixteenth century page–he was the youngest son of the Duke di Marina. Two tiny girls of five and six years of age went before, strewing white roses and lilies, and stepping daintily backward as though in attendance on a queen; they looked like two fairies who had slipped out of a midnight dream, in their little loose gowns of gold-colored plush, with wreaths of meadow daffodils on their tumbled curly hair. They had been well trained by Nina herself, for on arrival at the altar they stood demurely, one on each side of her, the pretty page occupying his place behind, and still holding up the end of the velvet train with a charming air of hauteur and self-complacency.

The whole cortege was a picture in its way, as Nina had meant it to be: she was fond of artistic effects. She smiled languishingly upon me as she reached the altar, and sunk on her knees beside me in prayer. The music swelled forth with redoubled grandeur, the priests and acolytes appeared, the marriage service commenced. As I placed the ring on the book I glanced furtively at the bride; her fair head was bent demurely–she seemed absorbed in holy meditations. The priest having performed the ceremony of sprinkling it with holy water, I took it back, and set it for the second time on my wife's soft white little hand–set it in accordance with the Catholic ritual, first on the thumb, then on the second finger, then on the third, and lastly on the fourth, where I left it in its old place, wondering as I did so, and murmured, *"In Nomine Patris et Filii et Spiritus Sancti, Amen!"* whether she recognized it as the one she had worn so long! But it was evident she did not; her calm was unbroken by even so much as a start or tremor; she had the self-possession of a perfectly satisfied, beautiful, vain, and utterly heartless woman.

The actual ceremony of marriage was soon over; then followed the Mass, in which we, the newly-wedded pair, were compelled, in submission to the rule of the Church, to receive the Sacrament. I shuddered as the venerable priest gave me the Sacred Host. What had I to do with the inward purity and peace this memento of Christ is supposed to leave in our souls? Methought the Crucified Image in the chapel regarded me afresh with those pained eyes, and said, "Even so dost thou seal thine own damnation!" Yet SHE, the true murderess, the arch liar, received the Sacrament with the face of a rapt angel– the very priest himself seemed touched by those upraised, candid, glorious eyes, the sweet lips so reverently parted, the absolute, reliable peace that rested on that white brow, like an aureole round the head of a saint!

"If I am damned, then is SHE thrice damned!" I said to myself, recklessly. "I dare say hell is wide enough for us to live apart when we get there."

Thus I consoled my conscience, and turned resolutely away from the painted appealing faces on the wall—the faces that in their various expressions of sorrow, resignation, pain, and death seemed now to be all pervaded by another look, that of astonishment—astonishment, so I fancied, that such a man as I, and such a woman as she, should be found in the width of the whole world, and should be permitted to kneel at God's altar without being struck dead for their blasphemy!

Ah, good saints, well may you be astonished! Had you lived in our day you must have endured worse martyrdoms than the boiling oil or the wrenching rack! What you suffered was the mere physical pain of torn muscles and scorching flesh, pain that at its utmost could not last long; but your souls were clothed with majesty and power, and were glorious in the light of love, faith, hope, and charity with all men. WE have reversed the position YOU occupied! We have partly learned, and are still learning, how to take care of our dearly beloved bodies, how to nourish and clothe them and guard them from cold and disease; but our souls, good saints, the souls that with you were everything—THESE we smirch, burn, and rack, torture and destroy—these we stamp upon till we crush out God's image therefrom—these we spit and jeer at, crucify and drown! THERE is the difference between you, the strong and wise of a fruitful olden time, and we, the miserable, puny weaklings of a sterile modern age.

Had you, sweet St. Dorothy, or fair child-saint Agnes, lived in this day, you would have felt something sharper than the executioner's sword; for being pure, you would have been dubbed the worst of women—being prayerful, you would have been called hypocrites—being faithful, you would have been suspected of all vileness–being loving, you would have been mocked at more bitterly than the soldiers of Pontius Pilate mocked Christ; but you would have been FREE–free to indulge your own opinions, for ours is the age of liberty. Yet how much better for you to have died than have lived till now!

Absorbed in strange, half-morose, half-speculative fancies, I scarcely heard the close of the solemn service. I was roused by a delicate touch from my wife, and I woke, as it were, with a start, to hear the sonorous, crashing chords of the wedding-march in "Lohengrin" thundering through the air. All was over: my wife was MINE indeed–mine most thoroughly–mine by the exceptionally close- tied knot of a double marriage–mine to do as I would with "TILL DEATH SHOULD US PART." How long, I gravely mused, how long before death could come to do us this great service? And straightway I began counting, counting certain spaces of time that must elapse before–I was still absorbed in this mental arithmetic, even while I mechanically offered my arm to my wife as we entered the vestry to sign our names in the marriage register. So occupied was I in my calculations that I nearly caught myself murmuring certain numbers aloud. I checked this, and recalling my thoughts by a strong effort, I strove to appear interested and delighted, as I walked down the aisle with my beautiful bride, through the ranks of admiring and eager spectators.

On reaching the outer doors of the chapel several flower-girls emptied their full and fragrant baskets at our feet; and in return, I bade one of my servants distribute a bag of coins I had brought for the purpose, knowing from former experience that it would be needed. To tread across such a heap of flowers required some care, many of the blossoms clinging to Nina's velvet train–we therefore moved forward slowly.

Just as we had almost reached the carriage, a young girl, with large laughing eyes set like flashing jewels in her soft oval face, threw down in my path a cluster of red roses. A sudden fury of impotent passion possessed me, and I crushed my heel instantly and savagely upon the crimson blossoms, stamping upon them again and again so violently that my wife raised her delicate eyebrows in amazement, and the pressing people who stood round us, shrugged their shoulders, and gazed at one another with looks of utter bewilderment–while the girl who had thrown them shrunk back in terror, her face paling as she murmured, "Santissima Madonna! mi fa paura!" I bit my lip with vexation, inwardly cursing the weakness of my own behavior. I laughed lightly in answer to Nina's unspoken, half-alarmed inquiry.

"It is nothing–a mere fancy of mine. I hate red roses! They look to me like human blood in flower!"

She shuddered slightly.

"What a horrible idea! How can you think of such a thing?"

I made no response, but assisted her into the carriage with elaborate care and courtesy; then entering it myself, we drove together back to the hotel, where the wedding breakfast awaited us.

This is always a feast of general uneasiness and embarrassment everywhere, even in the sunny, pleasure-loving south; Everyone is glad when it is over, and when the flowery, unmeaning speeches and exaggerated compliments are brought to a fitting and happy conclusion. Among my assembled guests, all of whom belonged to the best and most distinguished families in Naples, there was a pervading atmosphere of undoubted chilliness: the women were dull, being rendered jealous of the bride's beauty and the richness of her white velvets and jewels; the men were constrained, and could scarcely force themselves into even the appearance of cordiality– they evidently thought that, with such wealth as mine, I would have done much better to remain a bachelor. In truth, Italians, and especially Neapolitans, are by no means enthusiastic concerning the supposititious joys of marriage. They are apt to shake their heads, and to look upon it as a misfortune rather than a blessing. "L'altare e la tomba dell' amore," is a very common saying with us, and very commonly believed.

It was a relief to us all when we rose from the splendidly appointed table, and separated for a few hours. We were to meet again at the ball, which was fixed to commence at nine o'clock in the evening. The cream of the event was to be tasted THEN–the final toasting of the bride was to take place THEN–THEN there would be music, mirth and dancing, and all the splendor of almost royal revelry. I escorted my wife with formal courtesy to a splendid apartment which had been prepared for her, for she had, as she told me, many things to do–as, for instance, to take off her bridal robes, to study every detail of her wondrous ball costume for the night, and to superintend her maid in the packing of her trunks for the next day's journey. THE NEXT DAY! I smiled grimly–I wondered how she would enjoy her trip! Then I kissed her hand with the most profound respect and left her to repose–to refresh and prepare herself for the brilliant festivity of the evening.

Our marriage customs are not as coarse as those of some countries; a bridegroom in Italy thinks it scarcely decent to persecute his bride with either his presence or his caresses as soon as the Church has made her his. On the contrary, if ardent, he restrains his ardor–he forbears to intrude, he strives to keep up the illusion, the rose- colored light, or rather mist, of love as long as possible, and he has a wise, instinctive dread of becoming overfamiliar; well knowing that nothing kills romance so swiftly and surely as the bare blunt prose of close and constant proximity. And I, like other gentlemen of my rank and class, gave my twice-wedded wife her liberty–the last hours of liberty she would ever know. I left her to busy herself with the trifles she best loved–trifles of dress and personal adornment, for which many women barter away their soul's peace and honor, and divest themselves of the last shred of right and honest principle merely to outshine others of their own sex, and sow broadcast heart-burnings, petty envies, mean hatreds and contemptible spites, where, if they did but choose, there might be a widely different harvest.

It is easy to understand the feelings of Marie Stuart when

she arrayed herself in her best garments for her execution: it was simply the heroism of supreme vanity, the desire to fascinate if possible the very headsman. One can understand any beautiful woman being as brave as she. Harder than death itself would it have seemed to her had she been compelled to appear on the scaffold looking hideous. She was resolved to make the most of her charms so long as life lasted. I thought of that sweet-lipped, luscious-smiling queen as I parted from my wife for a few brief hours: royal and deeply injured lady though she was, she merited her fate, for she was treacherous—there can be no doubt of that. Yet most people reading her her story pity her—I know not why. It is strange that so much of the world's sympathy is wasted on false women!

I strolled into one of the broad *loggie* of the hotel, from whence I could see a portion of the Piazza del Popolo, and lighting a cigar, I leisurely watched the frolics of the crowd. The customary fooling proper to the day was going on, and no detail of it seemed to pall on the good-natured, easily amused folks who must have seen it all so often before. Much laughter was being excited by the remarks of a vender of quack medicines, who was talking with extreme volubility to a number of gaily dressed girls and fishermen. I could not distinguish his words, but I judged he was selling the "elixir of love," from his absurd amatory gestures—an elixir compounded, no doubt, of a little harmless *eau sucre*.

Flags tossed on the breeze, trumpets brayed, drums beat; *improvisatores* twanged their guitars and mandolins loudly to attract attention, and failing in their efforts, swore at each other with the utmost joviality and heartiness; flower-girls and lemonade- sellers made the air ring with their conflicting cries: now and then a shower of chalky confetti flew out from adjacent windows, dusting with white powder the coats of the passers-by; clusters of flowers tied with favors of gay-colored ribbon were lavishly flung at the feet of bright-eyed peasant girls, who rejected or accepted them at pleasure, with light words of badinage or playful repartee; clowns danced and tumbled, dogs barked, church bells clanged, and through all the waving width of color and movement crept the miserable, shrinking forms of diseased and loathly beggars whining for a *soldo*, and clad in rags that barely covered their halting, withered limbs.

It was a scene to bewilder the brain and dazzle the eyes, and I was just turning away from it out of sheer fatigue, when a sudden cessation of movement in the swaying, whirling crowd, and a slight hush, caused me to look out once more. I perceived the cause of the momentary stillness–a funeral cortege appeared, moving at a slow and solemn pace; as it passed across the square, heads were uncovered, and women crossed themselves devoutly. Like a black shadowy snake it coiled through the mass of shifting color and brilliance– another moment, and it was gone. The depressing effect of its appearance was soon effaced–the merry crowds resumed their thousand and one freaks of folly, their shrieking, laughing and dancing, and all was as before. Why not?

The dead are soon forgotten; none knew that better than I! Leaning my arms lazily on the edge of the balcony, I finished smoking my cigar. That glimpse of death in the midst of life had filled me with a certain satisfaction. Strangely enough, my thoughts began to busy themselves with the old modes of torture that used to be legal, and that, after all, were not so unjust when practiced upon persons professedly vile. For instance, the iron coffin of Lissa–that ingeniously contrived box in which the criminal was bound fast hand and foot, and then was forced to watch the huge lid descending slowly, slowly, slowly, half an inch at a time, till at last its ponderous weight crushed into a flat and mangled mass the writhing wretch within, who had for long agonized hours watched death steadily approaching. Suppose that I had such a coffin now! I stopped my train of reflection with a slight shudder. No, no; she whom I sought to punish was so lovely, such a softly colored, witching, gracious body, though tenanted by a wicked soul–she should keep her beauty! I would not destroy that–I would be satisfied with my plan as already devised.

I threw away the end of my smoked-out cigar and entered my own rooms. Calling Vincenzo, who was now resigned and even eager to go to Avellino, I gave him his final instructions, and placed in his charge the iron cash-box, which, unknown to him, contained 12,000 francs in notes and gold. This was the last good action I could do: it was a sufficient sum to set him up as a well-to-do farmer and fruit-grower in Avellino with Lilla and her little dowry combined. He also carried a sealed letter to Signora Monti, which I told him she was not to open till a week had elapsed; this letter explained the contents of the box and my wishes concerning it; it also asked the good woman to send to the Villa Romani for Assunta and her helpless charge, poor old paralyzed Giacomo, and to tend the latter as well as she could till his death, which I knew could not be far off.

I had thought of everything as far as possible, and I could already foresee what a happy, peaceful home there would be in the little mountain town guarded by the Monte Vergine. Lilla and Vincenzo would wed, I knew; Signora Monti and Assunta would console each other with their past memories and in the tending of Lilla's children; for some little time, perhaps, they would talk of me and wonder sorrowfully where I had gone; then gradually they would forget me, even as I desired to be forgotten.

Yes; I had done all I could for those who had never wronged me. I had acquitted myself of my debt to Vincenzo for his affection and fidelity; the rest of my way was clear. I had no more to do save the ONE THING, the one deed which had clamored so long for accomplishment. Revenge, like a beckoning ghost, had led me on step by step for many weary days and months, which to me had seemed cycles of suffering; but now it paused–it faced me–and turning its blood-red eyes upon my soul said, "Strike!"

35

THE BALL opened brilliantly. The rooms were magnificently decorated, and the soft luster of a thousand lamps shone on a scene of splendor almost befitting the court of a king. Some of the stateliest nobles in all Italy were present, their breasts glittering with jeweled orders and ribbons of honor; some of the loveliest women to be seen anywhere in the world flitted across the polished floors, like poets' dreams of the gliding sylphs that haunt rivers and fountains by moonlight.

But fairest where all were fair, peerless in the exuberance of her triumphant vanity, and in the absolute faultlessness of her delicate charms, was my wife–the bride of the day, the heroine of the night. Never had she looked so surpassingly beautiful, and I, even I, felt my pulse beat quicker, and the blood course more hotly through my veins, as I beheld her, radiant, victorious, and smiling–a veritable queen of the fairies, as dainty as a drop of dew, as piercing to the eye as a flash of light. Her dress was some wonderful mingling of misty lace, with the sheen of satin and glimmering showers of pearl; diamonds glittered on her bodice like sunlight on white foam; the brigand's jewels flashed gloriously on her round white throat and in her tiny shell-like ears, while the masses of her gold hair were coiled to the top of her small head and there caught by a priceless circlet of rose-brilliants–brilliants that I remembered well–they had belonged to my mother. Yet more lustrous than the light of the gems she wore was the deep, ardent glory of her eyes, dark as night and luminous as stars; more delicate than the filmy robes that draped her was the pure, pearl- like whiteness of her neck, which was just sufficiently displayed to be graceful without suggesting immodesty.

For Italian women do not uncover their bosoms for the casual inspection of strangers, as is the custom of their English and German sisters; they know well enough that any lady venturing to wear a *decollete* dress would find it impossible to obtain admittance to a court ball at the Palazzo Quirinale. She would be looked upon as one of a questionable class, and no matter how high her rank and station, would run the risk of ejection from the doors, as on one occasion did unfortunately happen to an English peeress, who, ignorant of Italian customs, went to an evening reception in Rome arrayed in a very low bodice with straps instead of sleeves. Her remonstrances were vain; she was politely but firmly refused admittance, though told she might gain her point by changing her costume, which I believe she wisely did.

Some of the *grandes dames* present at the ball that night wore dresses the like of which are seldom or never seen out of Italy– robes sown with jewels, and thick with wondrous embroidery, such as have been handed down from generation to generation through hundreds of years. As an example of this, the Duchess of Marina's cloth of gold train, stitched with small rubies and seed-pearls, had formerly belonged to the family of Lorenzo de Medici. Such garments as these, when they are part of the property of a great house, are worn only on particular occasions, perhaps once in a year; and then they are laid carefully by and sedulously protected from dust and moths and damp, receiving as much attention as the priceless pictures and books of a famous historical mansion. Nothing ever designed by any great modern tailor or milliner can hope to compete with the magnificent workmanship and durable material of the *festa* dresses that are locked preciously away in the old oaken coffers of the greatest Italian families–dresses that are beyond valuation, because of the romances and tragedies attached to them, and which, when worn, make all the costliest fripperies of to-day look flimsy and paltry beside them, like the attempts of a servant to dress as tastefully as her mistress.

Such glitter of gold and silver, such scintillations from the burning eyes of jewels, such cloud-like wreaths of floating laces, such subtle odors of rare and exquisite perfume, all things that most keenly prick and stimulate the senses were round me in fullest force this night–this one dazzling, supreme and terrible night, that was destined to burn into my brain like a seal of scorching fire. Yes; till I die, that night will remain with me as though it were a breathing, sentient thing; and after death, who knows whether it may not uplift itself in some tangible, awful shape, and confront me with its flashing mock-luster, and the black heart of its true meaning in its menacing eyes, to take its drear place by the side of my abandoned soul through all eternity! I remember now how I shivered and started out of the bitter reverie into which I had fallen at the sound of my wife's low, laughing voice.

"You must dance, Cesare," she said, with a mischievous smile. "You are forgetting your duties. You should open the ball with me!"

I rose at once mechanically.

"What dance is it?" I asked, forcing a smile. "I fear you will find me but a clumsy partner."

She pouted.

"Oh, surely not! You are not going to disgrace me–you really must try and dance properly just this once. It will look so stupid if you make any mistake. The band was going to play a quadrille; I would not have it, and told them to strike up the Hungarian waltz instead. But I assure you I shall never forgive you if you waltz badly– nothing looks so awkward and absurd."

I made no answer, but placed my arm round her waist and

stood ready to begin. I avoided looking at her as much as possible, for it was growing more and more difficult with each moment that passed to hold the mastery over myself. I was consumed between hate and love. Yes, love!—of an evil kind, I own, and in which there was no shred of reverence—filled me with a sort of foolish fury, which mingled itself with another and manlier craving, namely, to proclaim her vileness then and there before all her titled and admiring friends, and to leave her shamed in the dust of scorn, despised and abandoned. Yet I knew well that were I to speak out—to declare my history and hers before that brilliant crowd—I should be accounted mad, and that for a woman such as she there existed no shame.

The swinging measure of the slow Hungarian waltz, that most witching of dances, danced perfectly only by those of the warm-blooded southern temperament, now commenced. It was played pianissimo, and stole through the room like the fluttering breath of a soft sea wind. I had always been an excellent waltzer, and my step had fitted in with that of Nina as harmoniously as the two notes of a perfect chord. She found it so on this occasion, and glanced up with a look of gratified surprise as I bore her lightly with languorous, dreamlike ease of movement through the glittering ranks of our guests, who watched us admiringly as we circled the room two or three times.

Then—all present followed our lead, and in a couple of minutes the ball-room was like a moving flower-garden in full bloom, rich with swaying colors and rainbow-like radiance; while the music, growing stronger, and swelling out in marked and even time, echoed forth like the sound of clear-toned bells broken through by the singing of birds. My heart beat furiously, my brain reeled, my senses swam as I felt my wife's warm breath on my cheek; I clasped her waist more closely, I held her little gloved hand more firmly. She felt the double pressure, and, lifting her white eyelids fringed with those long dark lashes that gave such a sleepy witchery to her eyes, her lips parted in a little smile.

"At last you love me!" she whispered.

"At last, at last," I muttered, scarce knowing what I said. "Had I not loved you at first, *bellissima*, I should not have been to you what I am to-night."

A low ripple of laughter was her response.

"I knew it," she murmured again, half breathlessly, as I drew her with swifter and more voluptuous motion into the vortex of the dancers. "You tried to be cold, but I knew I could make you love me–yes, love me passionately–and I was right." Then with an outburst of triumphant vanity she added, "I believe you would die for me!"

I bent over her more closely. My hot quick breath moved the feathery gold of her hair.

"I HAVE died for you," I said; "I have killed my old self for your sake."

Dancing still, encircled by my arms, and gliding along like a sea- nymph on moonlighted foam, she sighed restlessly.

"Tell me what you mean, *amor mio*," she asked, in the tenderest tone in the world.

Ah, God! that tender seductive cadence of her voice, how well I knew it!–how often had it lured away my strength, as the fabled siren's song had been wont to wreck the listening mariner.

"I mean that you have changed me, sweetest!" I whispered, in fierce, hurried accents. "I have seemed old–for you to-night I will be young again–for you my chilled slow blood shall again be hot and quick as lava–for you my long-buried past shall rise in all its pristine vigor; for you I will be a lover, such as perhaps no woman ever had or ever will have again!"

She heard, and nestled closer to me in the dance. My words pleased her. Next to her worship of wealth her delight was to arouse the passions of men. She was very panther-like in her nature–her first tendency was to devour, her next to gambol with any animal she met, though her sleek, swift playfulness might mean death. She was by no means exceptional in this; there are many women like her.

As the music of the waltz grew slower and slower, dropping down to a sweet and persuasive conclusion, I led my wife to her fauteuil, and resigned her to the care of a distinguished Roman prince who was her next partner. Then, unobserved, I slipped out to make inquiries concerning Vincenzo. He had gone; one of the waiters at the hotel, a friend of his, had accompanied him and seen him into the train for Avellino. He had looked in at the ball-room before leaving, and had watched me stand up to dance with my wife, then "with tears in his eyes"–so said the vivacious little waiter who had just returned from the station–he had started without daring to wish me good-bye.

I heard this information of course with an apparent kindly indifference, but in my heart I felt a sudden vacancy, a drear, strange loneliness. With my faithful servant near me I had felt conscious of the presence of a friend, for friend he was in his own humble, unobtrusive fashion; but now I was alone–alone in a loneliness beyond all conceivable comparison–alone to do my work, without prevention or detection. I felt, as it were, isolated from humanity, set apart with my victim on some dim point of time, from which the rest of the world receded, where the searching eye of the Creator alone could behold me. Only she and I and God–these three were all that existed for me in the universe; between these three must justice be fulfilled.

Musingly, with downcast eyes, I returned to the ball-room. At the door a young girl faced me–she was the only daughter of a great Neapolitan house. Dressed in pure white, as all such maidens are, with a crown of snow-drops on her dusky hair, and her dimpled face lighted with laughter, she looked the very embodiment of early spring. She addressed me somewhat timidly, yet with all a child's frankness.

"Is not this delightful? I feel as if I were in fairy-land! Do you know this is my first ball?"

I smiled wearily.

"Ay, truly? And you are happy?"

"Oh, happiness is not the word–it is ecstasy! How I wish it

could last forever! And–is it not strange?–I did not know I was beautiful till to-night."

She said this with perfect simplicity, and a pleased smile radiated her fair features. I glanced at her with cold scrutiny.

"Ah! and someone has told you so."

She blushed and laughed a little consciously.

"Yes; the great Prince de Majano. And he is too noble to say what is not true, so I MUST be '*la piu bella donzella,*' as he said, must I not?"

I touched the snow-drops that she wore in a white cluster at her breast.

"Look at your flowers, child," I said, earnestly. "See how they begin to droop in this heated air. The poor things! How glad they would feel could they again grow in the cool wet moss of the woodlands, waving their little bells to the wholesome, fresh wind! Would they revive now, think you, for your great Prince de Majano if he told them they were fair? So with your life and heart, little one–pass them through the scorching fire of flattery, and their purity must wither even as these fragile blossoms. And as for beauty–are you more beautiful than SHE?"

And I pointed slightly to my wife, who was at that moment courtesying to her partner in the stately formality of the first quadrille.

My young companion looked, and her clear eyes darkened enviously.

"Ah, no, no! But if I wore such lace and satin and pearls, and had such jewels, I might perhaps be more like her!"

I sighed bitterly. The poison had already entered this child's soul. I spoke brusquely.

"Pray that you may never be like her," I said, with somber sternness, and not heeding her look of astonishment. "You are young–you cannot yet have thrown off religion. Well, when you go home to- night, and kneel beside your little bed, made holy by the cross above it and your mother's blessing–pray– pray with all your strength that you may never resemble in the smallest degree that exquisite woman yonder! So may you be spared her fate."

I paused, for the girl's eyes were dilated in extreme wonder and fear. I looked at her, and laughed abruptly and harshly.

"I forgot," I said; "the lady is my wife–I should have thought of that! I was speaking of–another whom you do not know. Pardon me! when I am fatigued my memory wanders. Pay no attention to my foolish remarks. Enjoy yourself, my child, but do not believe all the pretty speeches of the Prince de Majano. *A rivederci!*"

And smiling a forced smile I left her, and mingled with the crowd of my guests, greeting one here, another there, jesting lightly, paying unmeaning compliments to the women who expected them, and striving to distract my thoughts with the senseless laughter and foolish chatter of the glittering cluster of society butterflies, all the while desperately counting the tedious minutes, and wondering whether my patience, so long on the rack, would last out its destined time. As I made my way through the brilliant assemblage, Luziano Salustri, the poet, greeted me with a grave smile.

"I have had little time to congratulate you, conte," he said, in those mellifluous accents of his which were like his own improvised music, "but I assure you I do so with all my heart. Even in my most fantastic dreams I have never pictured a fairer heroine of a life's romance than the lady who is now the Countess Oliva."

I silently bowed my thanks.

"I am of a strange temperament, I suppose," he resumed. "To-night this ravishing scene of beauty and splendor makes me sad at heart, I know not why. It seems too brilliant, too dazzling. I would as soon go home and compose a dirge as anything."

I laughed satirically.

"Why not do it?" I said. "You are not the first person who, being present at a marriage, has, with perverse incongruity, meditated on a funeral!"

A wistful look came into his brilliant poetic eyes.

"I have thought once or twice," he remarked in a low tone, "of that misguided young man Ferrari. A pity, was it not, that the quarrel occurred between you?"

"A pity indeed!" I replied, brusquely. Then taking him by the arm I turned him round so that he faced my wife, who was standing not far off. "But look at the–the–ANGEL I have married! Is she not a fair cause for a dispute even unto death? Fy on thee, Luziano!–why think of Ferrari? He is not the first man who has been killed for the sake of a woman, nor will he be the last!"

Salustri shrugged his shoulders, and was silent for a minute or two. Then he added with his own bright smile:

"Still, amico, it would have been much better if it had ended in coffee and cognac. Myself, I would rather shoot a man with an epigram than a leaden bullet! By the do you remember our talking of Cain and Abel that night?"

"Perfectly."

"I have wondered since," he continued half merrily, half seriously, "whether the real cause of their quarrel has ever been rightly told. I should not be at all surprised if one of these days some savant does not discover a papyrus containing a missing page of Holy Writ, which will ascribe the reason of the first bloodshed to a love affair. Perhaps there were wood nymphs in those days, as we are assured there were giants, and some dainty Dryad might have driven the first pair of human brothers to desperation by her charms! What say you?"

"It is more than probable," I answered, lightly. "Make a poem of it, Salustri; people will say you have improved on the Bible!"

And I left him with a gay gesture to join other groups, and to take my part in the various dances which were now following quickly on one another. The supper was fixed to take place at midnight. At the first opportunity I had, I looked at the time. Quarter to eleven!– my heart beat quickly, the blood rushed to my temples and surged noisily in my ears. The hour I had waited for so long and so eagerly had come! At last! at last!

* * *

Slowly and with a hesitating step I approached my wife. She was resting after her exertions in the dance, and reclined languidly in a low velvet chair, chatting gaily with that very Prince de Majano whose honeyed compliments had partly spoiled the budding sweet nature of the youngest girl in the room. Apologizing for interrupting the conversation, I lowered my voice to a persuasive tenderness as I addressed her.

"*Cara, sposina mia!* permit me to remind you of your promise."

What a radiant look she gave me!

"I am all impatience to fulfill it! Tell me when—and how?"

"Almost immediately. You know the private passage through which we entered the hotel this morning on our return from church?"

"Perfectly."

"Well, meet me there in twenty minutes. We must avoid being observed as we pass out. But," and I touched her delicate dress, "you will wear something warmer than this?"

"I have a long sable cloak that will do," she replied, brightly. "We are not going far?"

"No, not far."

"We shall return in time for supper, of course?"

I bent my head.

"Naturally!"

Her eyes danced mirthfully.

"How romantic it seems! A moonlight stroll with you will be charming! Who shall say you are not a sentimental bridegroom? Is there a bright moon?"

"I believe so."

"*Cosa bellissima!*" and she laughed sweetly. "I look forward to the trip! In twenty minutes then I shall be with you at the place you name, Cesare; in the meanwhile the Marchese

Gualdro claims me for this mazurka."

And she turned with her bewitching grace of manner to the *marchese*, who at that moment advanced with his courteous bow and fascinating smile, and I watched them as they glided forward together in the first figure of the elegant Polish dance, in which all lovely women look their loveliest.

Then, checking the curse that rose to my lips, I hurried away. Up to my own room I rushed with feverish haste, full of impatience to be rid of the disguise I had worn so long.

Within a few minutes I stood before my mirror, transformed into my old self as nearly as it was possible to be. I could not alter the snowy whiteness of my hair, but a few deft quick strokes of the razor soon divested me of the beard that had given me so elderly an aspect, and nothing remained but the mustache curling slightly up at the corners of the lip, as I had worn it in past days. I threw aside the dark glasses, and my eyes, densely brilliant, and fringed with the long lashes that had always been their distinguishing feature, shone with all the luster of strong and vigorous youth. I straightened myself up to my full height, I doubled my fist and felt it hard as iron; I laughed aloud in the triumphant power of my strong manhood. I thought of the old rag-dealing Jew—"You could kill anything easily." Ay, so I could!—even without the aid of the straight swift steel of the Milanese dagger which I now drew from its sheath and regarded steadfastly, while I carefully felt the edge of the blade from hilt to point. Should I take it with me? I hesitated. Yes! it might be needed. I slipped it safely and secretly into my vest.

And now the proofs—the proofs! I had them all ready to my hand, and gathered them quickly together; first the things that had been buried with me—the gold chain on which hung the locket containing the portraits of my wife and child, the purse and card-case which Nina herself had given me, the crucifix the monk had laid on my breast in the coffin. The thought of that coffin moved me to a stern smile—that splintered, damp, and moldering wood must speak for itself by and by. Lastly I look the letters sent me by the Marquis D'Avencourt–the beautiful, passionate love epistles she had written to Guido Ferrari in Rome.

Now, was that all? I thoroughly searched both my rooms, ransacking every corner. I had destroyed everything that could give the smallest clew to my actions; I left nothing save furniture and small valuables, a respectable present enough in their way, to the landlord of the hotel.

I glanced again at myself in the mirror. Yes; I was once more Fabio Romani, in spite of my white hair; no one that had ever known me intimately could doubt my identity. I had changed my evening dress for a rough, every-day suit, and now over this I threw my long Almaviva cloak, which draped me from head to foot. I kept its folds well up about my mouth and chin, and pulled on a soft slouched hat, with the brim far down over my eyes. There was nothing unusual in such a costume; it was common enough to many Neapolitans who have learned to dread the chill night winds that blow down from the lofty Apennines in early spring. Thus attired, too, I knew my features would be almost invisible to HER more especially as the place of our rendezvous was a long dim entresol lighted only by a single oil- lamp, a passage that led into the garden, one that was only used for private purposes, having nothing to do with the ordinary modes of exit and entrance to and from the hotel.

Into this hall I now hurried with an eager step; it was deserted; she was not there. Impatiently I waited–the minutes seemed hours! Sounds of music floated toward me from the distant ball-room–the dreamy, swinging measure of a Viennese waltz. I could almost hear the flying feet of the dancers. I was safe from all observation where I stood–the servants were busy preparing the grand marriage supper, and all the inhabitants of the hotel were absorbed in watching the progress of the brilliant and exceptional festivities of the night.

Would she never come? Suppose, after all, she should escape me! I trembled at the idea, then put it from me with a smile at my own folly. No, her punishment was just, and in her case the Fates were inflexible. So I thought and felt. I paced up and down feverishly; I could count the thick, heavy throbs of my own heart. How long the moments seemed! Would she never come? Ah! at last! I caught the sound of a rustling robe and a light step–a breath of delicate fragrance was wafted on the air like the odor of falling orange- blossoms. I turned, and saw her approaching. With swift grace she ran up to me as eagerly as a child, her heavy cloak of rich Russian sable falling back from her shoulders and displaying her glittering dress, the dark fur of the hood heightening by contrast the fairness of her lovely flushed face, so that it looked like the face of one of Correggio's angels framed in ebony and velvet. She laughed, and her eyes flashed saucily.

"Did I keep you waiting, *caro mio*?" she whispered; and standing on tiptoe she kissed the hand with which I held my cloak muffled about me. "How tall you look in that Almaviva! I am so sorry I am a little late, but that last waltz was so exquisite I could not resist it; only I wish YOU had danced it with me."

"You honor me by the wish," I said, keeping one arm about her waist and drawing her toward the door that opened into the garden. "Tell me, how did you manage to leave the ball-room?"

"Oh, easily. I slipped away from my partner at the end of the waltz, and told him I should return immediately. Then I ran upstairs to my room, got my cloak–and here I am."

And she laughed again. She was evidently in the highest spirits.

"You are very good to come with me at all, *mia bella*," I murmured as gently as I could; "it is kind of you to thus humor my fancy. Did you see your maid? does she know where you are going?"

"She? Oh, no, she was not in my room at all. She is a great coquette, you know; I dare say she is amusing herself with the waiters in the kitchen. Poor thing! I hope she enjoys it."

I breathed freely; we were so far undiscovered. No one had

as yet noticed our departure—no one had the least clew to my intentions, I opened the door of the passage noiselessly, and we passed out. Wrapping my wife's cloak more closely about her with much apparent tenderness, I led her quickly across the garden. There was no one in sight—we were entirely unobserved. On reaching the exterior gate of the enclosure I left her for a moment, while I summoned a carriage, a common fiacre. She expressed some surprise on seeing the vehicle.

"I thought we were not going far?" she said.

I reassured her on this point, telling her that I only desired to spare her all possible fatigue. Satisfied with this explanation, she suffered me to assist her into the carriage. I followed her, and calling to the driver, "A la Villa Guarda," we rattled away over the rough uneven stones of the back streets of the city.

"La Villa Guarda!" exclaimed Nina. "Where is that?"

"It is an old house," I replied, "situated near the place I spoke to you of, where the jewels are."

"Oh!"

And apparently contented, she nestled back in the carriage, permitting her head to rest lightly on my shoulder. I drew her closer to me, my heart beating with a fierce, terrible joy.

"Mine—mine at last!" I whispered in her ear. "Mine forever!"

She turned her face upward and smiled victoriously; her cool fragrant lips met my burning, eager ones in a close, passionate kiss. Yes, I kissed her now—why should I not? She was as much mine as any purchased slave, and merited less respect than a sultan's occasional female toy. And as she chose to caress me, I let her do so: I allowed her to think me utterly vanquished by the battery of her charms. Yet whenever I caught an occasional glimpse of her face as we drove along in the semi-darkness, I could not help wondering at the supreme vanity of the woman! Her self-satisfaction was so complete, and, considering her approaching fate, so tragically absurd!

She was entirely delighted with herself, her dress, and her conquest—as she thought—of me. Who could measure the height of the dazzling visions she indulged in; who could fathom the depths of her utter selfishness!

Seeing one like her, beautiful, wealthy, and above all—society knows I speak the truth—WELL DRESSED, for by the latter virtue alone is a woman allowed any precedence nowadays—would not all the less fortunate and lovely of her sex feel somewhat envious? Ah, yes; they would and they do; but believe me, the selfish feminine thing, whose only sincere worship is offered at the shrines of Fashion and Folly, is of all creatures the one whose life is to be despised and never desired, and whose death makes no blank even in the circles of her so-called best friends.

I knew well enough that there was not a soul in Naples who was really attached to my wife—not one who would miss her, no, not even a servant—though she, in her superb self-conceit, imagined herself to be the adored beauty of the city. Those who had indeed loved her she had despised, neglected, and betrayed. Musingly I looked down upon her as she rested back in the carriage, encircled by my arm, while now and then a little sigh of absolute delight in herself broke from her lips—but we spoke scarcely at all. Hate has almost as little to say as love!

The night was persistently stormy, though no rain fell—the gale had increased in strength, and the white moon only occasionally glared out from the masses of white and gray cloud that rushed like flying armies across the sky, and her fitful light shone dimly, as though she were a spectral torch glimmering through a forest of shadow. Now and again bursts of music, or the blare of discordant trumpets, reached our ears from the more distant thoroughfares where the people were still celebrating the feast of Giovedi Grasso, or the tinkle of passing mandolins chimed in with the rolling wheels of our carriage; but in a few moments we were out of reach of even such sounds as these.

We passed the outer suburbs of the city and were soon on the open road. The man I had hired drove fast; he knew nothing of us, he was probably anxious to get back quickly to the crowded squares and illuminated quarters where the principal merriment of the evening was going on, and no doubt thought I showed but a poor taste in requiring to be driven away, even for a short distance, out of Naples on such a night of feasting and folly. He stopped at last; the castellated turrets of the villa I had named were faintly visible among the trees; he jumped down from his box and came to us.

"Shall I drive up to the house?" he asked, looking as though he would rather be spared this trouble.

"No," I answered, indifferently, "you need not. The distance is short, we will walk."

And I stepped out into the road and paid him his money.

"You seem anxious to get back to the city, my friend," I said, half jocosely.

"Si, davvero!" he replied, with decision, "I hope to get many a good fare from the Count Oliva's marriage-ball to-night."

"Ah! he is a rich fellow, that count," I said, as I assisted my wife to alight, keeping her cloak well muffled round her so that this common fellow should not perceive the glitter of her costly costume; "I wish I were he!"

The man grinned and nodded emphatically. He had no suspicion of my identity. He took me, in all probability, for one of those "gay gallants" so common in Naples, who, on finding at some public entertainment a "*dama*" to their taste, hurry her off, carefully cloaked and hooded, to a mysterious nook known only to themselves, where they can complete the romance of the evening entirely to their own satisfaction. Bidding me a lively *buona notte*, he sprung on his box again, jerked his horse's head violently round with a volley of oaths, and drove away at a rattling pace. Nina, standing on the road beside me, looked after him with a bewildered air.

"Could he not have waited to take us back?" she asked.

"No," I answered, brusquely; "we shall return by a different route. Come."

And passing my arm round her, I led her onward. She

shivered slightly, and there was a sound of querulous complaint in her voice as she said:

"Have we to go much further, Cesare?"

"Three minutes, walk will bring us to our destination," I replied, briefly, adding in a softer tone, "Are you cold?"

"A little," and she gathered her sables more closely about her and pressed nearer to my side. The capricious moon here suddenly leaped forth like the pale ghost of a frenzied dancer, standing tiptoe on the edge of a precipitous chasm of black clouds. Her rays, pallidly green and cold, fell full on the dreary stretch of land before us, touching up with luminous distinctness those white mysterious milestones of the Campo Santo which mark where the journeys of men, women, and children began and where they left off, but never explain in what new direction they are now traveling. My wife saw and stopped, trembling violently.

"What place is this?" she asked, nervously.

In all her life she had never visited a cemetery—she had too great a horror of death.

"It is where I keep all my treasures," I answered, and my voice sounded strange and harsh in my own ears, while I tightened my grasp of her full, warm waist. "Come with me, my beloved!" and in spite of my efforts, my tone was one of bitter mockery. "With me you need have no fear! Come."

And I led her on, too powerless to resist my force, too startled to speak—on, on, on, over the rank dewy grass and unmarked ancient graves—on, till the low frowning gate of the house of my dead ancestors faced me—on, on, on, with the strength of ten devils in my arm as I held her—on, on, on, to her just doom!

36

THE MOON had retreated behind a dense wall of cloud, and the landscape was enveloped in semi-darkness. Reaching the door of the vault, I unlocked it; it opened instantly, and fell back with a sudden clang. She whom I held fast with my iron grip shrunk back, and strove to release herself from my grasp.

"Where are you going?" she demanded, in a faint tone. "I–I am afraid!"

"Of what?"–I asked, endeavoring to control the passionate vibrations of my voice and to speak unconcernedly. "Because it is dark? We shall have a light directly–you will see–you–you," and to my own surprise I broke into a loud and violent laugh. "You have no cause to be frightened! Come!"

And I lifted her swiftly and easily over the stone step of the entrance and set her safely inside. INSIDE at last, thank Heaven! I shut the great gate upon us both and locked it! Again that strange undesired laugh broke from my lips involuntarily, and the echoes of the charnel house responded to it with unearthly and ghastly distinctness. Nina clung to me in the dense gloom.

"Why do you laugh like that?" she cried, loudly and impatiently. "It sounds horrible."

I checked myself by a strong effort.

"Does it? I am sorry–very sorry! I laugh because–because, *cara mia*, our moonlight ramble is so pleasant–and amusing–is it not?"

And I caught her to my heart and kissed her roughly. "Now," I whispered, "I will carry you–the steps are too rough for your little feet–dear, dainty, white little feet! I will carry you, you armful of sweetness!–yes, carry you safely down into the fairy grotto where the jewels are–SUCH jewels, and all for you–my love, my wife!"

And I raised her from the ground as though she were a young, frail child. Whether she tried to resist me or not I cannot now remember. I bore her down the moldering stairway, setting my foot on each crooked step with the firmness of one long familiar with the place. But my brain reeled–rings of red fire circled in the darkness before my eyes; every artery in my body seemed strained to bursting; the pent-up agony and fury of my soul were such that I thought I should go mad or drop down dead ere I gained the end of my long desire. As I descended I felt her clinging to me; her hands were cold and clammy on my neck, as though she were chilled to the blood with terror. At last I reached the lowest step–I touched the floor of the vault. I set my precious burden down. Releasing my clasp of her, I remained for a moment inactive, breathing heavily. She caught my arm–she spoke in a hoarse whisper.

"What place is this? Where is the light you spoke of?"

I made no answer. I moved from her side, and taking matches from my pocket, I lighted up six large candles which I had fixed in various corners of the vault the night previously. Dazzled by the glare after the intense darkness, she did not at once perceive the nature of the place in which she stood. I watched her, myself still wrapped in the heavy cloak and hat that so effectually disguised my features. What a sight she was in that abode of corruption! Lovely, delicate, and full of life, with the shine of her diamonds gleaming from under the folds of rich fur that shrouded her, and the dark hood falling back as though to display the sparkling wonder of her gold hair.

Suddenly, and with a violent shock, she realized the gloom of her surroundings–the yellow flare of the waxen torches showed her the stone niches, the tattered palls, the decaying trophies of armor, the drear shapes of worm-eaten coffins, and with a shriek of horror she rushed to me where I stood, as immovable as a statue clad in coat of mail, and throwing her arms about me clung to me in a frenzy of fear.

"Take me away, take me away!" she moaned, hiding her face against my breast. "'Tis a vault–oh, Santissima Madonna!– a place for the dead! Quick–quick! take me out to the air–let us go home–home–"

She broke off abruptly, her alarm increasing at my utter silence. She gazed up at me with wild wet eyes.

"Cesare! Cesare! speak! What ails you? Why have you brought me here? Touch me–kiss me! say something– anything–only speak!"

And her bosom heaved convulsively; she sobbed with terror.

I put her from me with a firm hand. I spoke in measured accents, tinged with some contempt.

"Hush, I pray you! This is no place for an hysterical *scena*. Consider where you are! You have guessed aright–this is a vault– your own mausoleum, fair lady!–if I mistake not–the burial-place of the Romani family."

At these words her sobs ceased, as though they had been frozen in her throat; she stared at me in speechless fear and wonder.

"Here," I went on with methodical deliberation, "here lie all the great ancestors of your husband's family, heroes and martyrs in their day. Here will your own fair flesh molder. Here," and my voice grew deeper and more resolute, "here, six months ago, your husband himself, Fabio Romani, was buried."

She uttered no sound, but gazed at me like some beautiful pagan goddess turned to stone by the Furies. Having spoken thus far I was silent, watching the effect of what I had said, for I sought to torture the very nerves of her base soul. At last her dry lips parted–her voice was hoarse and indistinct.

"You must be mad!" she said, with smothered anger and horror in her tone.

Then seeing me still immovable, she advanced and caught my hand half commandingly, half coaxingly. I did not resist her.

"Come," she implored, "come away at once!" and she glanced about her with a shudder. "Let us leave this horrible place; as for the jewels, if you keep them here, they may stay here; I would not wear them for the world! Come."

I interrupted her, holding her hand in a fierce grasp; I turned her abruptly toward a dark object lying on the ground near us–my own coffin broken asunder. I drew her close to it.

"Look!" I said in a thrilling whisper, "what is this? Examine it well: it is a coffin of flimsiest wood, a cholera coffin! What says this painted inscription? Nay, do not start! It bears your husband's name; he was buried in it. Then how comes it to be open? WHERE IS HE?"

I felt her sway under me; a new and overwhelming terror had taken instant possession of her, her limbs refused to support her, she sunk on her knees. Mechanically and feebly she repeated the words after me–

"WHERE IS HE? WHERE IS HE?"

"Ay!" and my voice rang out through the hollow vault, its passion restrained no more. "WHERE IS HE?–the poor fool, the miserable, credulous dupe, whose treacherous wife played the courtesan under his very roof, while he loved and blindly trusted her? WHERE IS HE? Here, here!" and I seized her hands and forced her up from her kneeling posture. "I promised you should see me as I am! I swore to grow young to-night for your sake!–Now I keep my word! Look at me, Nina!–look at me, my twice-wedded wife!–Look at me!–do you not know your HUSBAND?"

And throwing my dark habiliments from me, I stood

before her undisguised! As though some defacing disease had swept over her at my words and look, so her beauty suddenly vanished. Her face became drawn and pinched and almost old– her lips turned blue, her eyes grew glazed, and strained themselves from their sockets to stare at me; her very hands looked thin and ghost-like as she raised them upward with a frantic appealing gesture; there was a sort of gasping rattle in her throat as she drew herself away from me with a convulsive gesture of aversion, and crouched on the floor as though she sought to sink through it and thus avoid my gaze.

"Oh, no, no, no!" she moaned, wildly, "not Fabio!–no, it cannot be-Fabio is dead–dead! And you!–you are mad!–this is some cruel jest of yours–some trick to frighten me!"

She broke off breathlessly, and her large, terrified eyes wandered to mine again with a reluctant and awful wonder. She attempted to arise from her crouching position; I approached, and assisted her to do so with ceremonious politeness. She trembled violently at my touch, and slowly staggering to her feet, she pushed back her hair from her forehead and regarded me fixedly with a searching, anguished look, first of doubt, then of dread, and lastly of convinced and hopeless certainty, for she suddenly covered her eyes with her hands as though to shut out some repulsive object. and broke into a low wailing sound like that of one in bitter physical pain. I laughed scornfully.

"Well, do you know me at last?" I cried. "'Tis true I have somewhat altered. This hair of mine was black, if you remember–it is white enough now, blanched by the horrors of a living death such as you cannot imagine, but which," and I spoke more slowly and impressively, "you may possibly experience ere long. Yet in spite of this change I think you know me! That is well. I am glad your memory serves you thus far!"

A low sound that was half a sob and half a cry broke from her.

"Oh, no, no!" she muttered, again, incoherently–"it cannot

be! It must be false–it is some vile plot–it cannot be true! True! Oh, Heaven! it would be too cruel, too horrible!"

I strode up to her. I drew her hands away from her eyes and grasped them tightly in my own.

"Hear me!" I said, in clear, decisive tones. "I have kept silence, God knows, with a long patience, but now–now I can speak. Yes! you thought me dead–you had every reason to think so, you had every proof to believe so. How happy my supposed death made you! What a relief it was to you!–what an obstruction removed from your path! But–I was buried alive!" She uttered a faint shriek of terror, and looking wildly about her, strove to wrench her hands from my clasp. I held them more closely. "Ay, think of it, wife of mine!–you to whom luxury has been second nature, think of this poor body straightened in a helpless swoon, packed and pressed into yonder coffin and nailed up fast, shut out from the blessed light and air, as one would have thought, forever! Who could have dreamed that life still lingered in me–life still strong enough to split asunder the boards that enclosed me, and leave them shattered, as you see them now!"

She shuddered and glanced with aversion toward the broken coffin, and again tried to loosen her hands from mine. She looked at me with a burning anger in her face.

"Let me go!" she panted. "Madman! liar!–let me go!"

I released her instantly and stood erect, regarding her fixedly.

"I am no madman," I said, composedly; "and you know as well as I do that I speak the truth. When I escaped from that coffin I found myself a prisoner in this very vault–this house of my perished ancestry, where, if old legends could be believed, the very bones that are stored up here would start and recoil from YOUR presence as pollution to the dead, whose creed was HONOR."

The sound of her sobbing breath ceased suddenly; she fixed her eyes on mine; they glittered defiantly.

"For one long awful night," I resumed, "I suffered here. I

might have starved–or perished of thirst. I thought no agony could surpass what I endured! But I was mistaken: there was a sharper torment in store for me. I discovered a way of escape; with grateful tears I thanked God for my rescue, for liberty, for life! Oh, what a fool was I! How could I dream that my death was so desired!–how could I know that I had better far have died than have returned to SUCH a home!"

Her lips moved, but she uttered no word; she shivered as though with intense cold. I drew nearer to her.

"Perhaps you doubt my story?"

She made no answer. A rapid impulse of fury possessed me.

"Speak!" I cried, fiercely, "or by the God above us I will MAKE you! Speak!" and I drew the dagger I carried from my vest. "Speak the truth for once–'twill be difficult to you who love lies–but this time I must be answered! Tell me, do you know me? DO you or do you NOT believe that I am indeed your husband–your living husband, Fabio Romani?"

She gasped for breath. The sight of my infuriated figure–the glitter of the naked steel before her eyes–the suddenness of my action, the horror of her position, all terrified her into speech. She flung herself down before me in an attitude of abject entreaty. She found her voice at last.

"Mercy! mercy!" she cried. "Oh, God! you will not kill me? Anything–anything but death; I am too young to die! Yes, yes; I know you are Fabio–Fabio, my husband, Fabio, whom I thought dead–Fabio–oh!" and she sobbed convulsively. "You said you loved me to-day–when you married me! Why did you marry me? I was your wife already–why–why? Oh, horrible, horrible! I see–I understand it all now! But do not, do not kill me, Fabio–I am afraid to die!"

And she hid her face at my feet and groveled there. As quickly calmed as I had been suddenly furious, I put back the dagger. I smoothed my voice and spoke with mocking courtesy.

"Pray do not alarm yourself," I said, coolly. "I have not the slightest intention of killing you! I am no vulgar murderer, yielding to mere brute instincts. You forget: a Neapolitan has hot passions, but he also has finesse, especially in matters of vengeance. I brought you here to tell you of my existence, and to confront you with the proofs of it. Rise, I beg of you, we have plenty of time to talk; with a little patience I shall make things clear to you–rise!"

She obeyed me, lifting herself up reluctantly with a long, shuddering sigh. As she stood upright I laughed contemptuously.

"What! no love words for me?" I cried, "not one kiss, not one smile, not one word of welcome? You say you know me– well!–are you not glad to see your husband?–you, who were such an inconsolable widow?"

A strange quiver passed over her face–she wrung her hands together hard, but she said no word.

"Listen!" I said, "there is more to tell. When I broke loose from the grasp of death, when I came HOME–I found my vacant post already occupied. I arrived in time to witness a very pretty pastoral play. The scene was the ilex avenue–the actors, you, my wife, and Guido, my friend!"

She raised her head and uttered a low exclamation of fear. I advanced a step or two and spoke more rapidly.

"You hear? There was moonlight, and the song of nightingales–yes; the stage effects were perfect! I watched the progress of the comedy–with what emotions you may imagine. I learned much that was news to me. I became aware that for a lady of your large heart and sensitive feelings ONE husband was not sufficient"–here I laid my hand on her shoulder and gazed into her face, while her eyes, dilated with terror, stared hopelessly up to mine–"and that within three little months of your marriage to me you provided yourself with another. Nay, no denial can serve you! Guido Ferrari was husband to you in all things but the name. I mastered the situation–I rose to the emergency. Trick for trick, comedy for comedy! You know the rest. As the Count Oliva you cannot deny that I acted well! For the second time I courted you, but not half so eagerly as YOU courted ME! For the second time I have married you! Who shall deny that you are most thoroughly mine–mine, body and soul, till death do us part!"

And I loosened my grasp of her: she writhed from me like some glittering wounded serpent. The tears had dried on her cheeks, her features were rigid and wax-like as the features of a corpse; only her dark eyes shone, and these seemed preternaturally large, and gleamed with an evil luster. I moved a little away, and turning my own coffin on its side, I sat down upon it as indifferently as though it were an easy-chair in a drawing-room. Glancing at her then, I saw a wavering light upon her face. Some idea had entered into her mind. She moved gradually from the wall where she leaned, watching me fearfully as she did so. I made no attempt to stir from the seat I occupied.

Slowly, slowly, still keeping her eyes on me, she glided step by step onward and passed me–then with a sudden rush she reached the stairway and bounded up it with the startled haste of a hunted deer. I smiled to myself. I heard her shaking the iron gateway to and fro with all her feeble strength; she called aloud for help several times. Only the sullen echoes of the vault answered her, and the wild whistle of the wind as it surged through the trees of the cemetery. At last she screamed furiously, as a savage cat might scream–the rustle of her silken robes came swiftly sweeping down the steps, and with a spring like that of a young tigress she confronted me, the blood now burning wrathfully in her face, and transforming it back to something of its old beauty.

"Unlock that door!" she cried, with a furious stamp of her foot. "Assassin! traitor! I hate you! I always hated you! Unlock the door, I tell you! You dare not disobey me; you have no right to murder me!"

I looked at her coldly; the torrent of her words was suddenly checked, something in my expression daunted her; she trembled and shrunk back.

"No right!" I said, mockingly. "I differ from you! A man ONCE married has SOME right over his wife, but a man TWICE married to the same woman has surely gained a double authority! And as for 'DARE NOT!' there is nothing I 'dare not' do to-night."

And with that I rose and approached her. A torrent of passionate indignation boiled in my veins; I seized her two white arms and held her fast.

"You talk of murder!" I muttered, fiercely. "YOU—you who have remorselessly murdered two men! Their blood be on your head! For though I live, I am but the moving corpse of the man I was—hope, faith, happiness, peace—all things good and great in me have been slain by YOU. And as for Guido—"

She interrupted me with a wild sobbing cry.

"He loved me! Guido loved me!"

"Ay, he loved you, oh, devil in the shape of a woman! he loved you! Come here, here!" and in a fury I could not restrain I dragged her, almost lifted her along to one corner of the vault, where the light of the torches scarcely illumined the darkness, and there I pointed upward. "Above our very heads— to the left of where we stand—the brave strong body of your lover lies, festering slowly in the wet mould, thanks to you!—the fair, gallant beauty of it all marred by the red-mouthed worms— the thick curls of hair combed through by the crawling feet of vile insects—the poor frail heart pierced by a gaping wound—"

"You killed him; you—you are to blame," she moaned, restlessly, striving to turn her face away from me.

"I killed him? No, no, not I, but YOU! He died when he learned your treachery—when he knew you were false to him for the sake of wedding a supposed wealthy stranger—my pistol-shot but put him out of torment. You! you were glad of his death—as glad as when you thought of mine! YOU talk of murder! Oh, vilest among women! if I could murder you twenty times over, what then? Your sins outweigh all punishment!"

And I flung her from me with a gesture of contempt and

loathing. This time my words had struck home. She cowered before me in horror—her sables were loosened and scarcely protected her, the richness of her ball costume was fully displayed, and the diamonds on her bosom heaved restlessly up and down as she panted with excitement, rage and fear.

"I do not see," she muttered, sullenly, "why you should blame ME! I am no worse than other women!"

"No worse! no worse!" I cried. "Shame, shame upon you that thus outrage your sex! Learn for once what MEN think of unfaithful wives—for maybe you are ignorant. The novels you have read in your luxurious, idle hours have perhaps told you that infidelity is no sin—merely a little social error easily condoned, or set right by the divorce court. Yes! modern books and modern plays teach you so: in them the world swerves upside down, and vice looks like virtue. But I will tell you what may seem to you a strange and wonderful thing! There is no mean animal, no loathsome object, no horrible deformity of nature so utterly repulsive to a true man as a faithless wife! The cowardly murderer who lies in wait for his victim behind some dark door, and stabs him in the back as he passes by unarmed—he, I say, is more to be pardoned than the woman who takes a husband's name, honor, position, and reputation among his fellows, and sheltering herself with these, passes her beauty promiscuously about like some coarse article of commerce, that goes to the highest bidder! Ay, let your French novels and books of their type say what they will—infidelity is a crime, a low, brutal crime, as bad if not worse than murder, and deserves as stern a sentence!"

A sudden spirit of defiant insolence possessed her. She drew herself erect, and her level brows knitted in a dark frown.

"Sentence!" she exclaimed, imperiously. "How dare you judge me! What harm have I done? If I am beautiful, is that my fault? If men are fools, can I help it? You loved me—Guido loved me—could I prevent it? I cared nothing for him, and less for you!"

"I know it," I said, bitterly. "Love was never part of YOUR

nature! Our lives were but cups of wine for your false lips to drain; once the flavor pleased you, but now—now, think you not the dregs taste somewhat cold?"

She shrunk at my glance—her head drooped, and drawing near a projecting stone in the wall, she sat down upon it, pressing one hand to her heart.

"No heart, no conscience, no memory!" I cried. "Great Heaven! that such a thing should live and call itself woman! The lowest beast of the field has more compassion for its kind! Listen: before Guido died he knew me, even as my child, neglected by you, in her last agony knew her father. She being innocent, passed in peace; but he!—imagine if you can, the wrenching torture in which he perished, knowing all! How his parted spirit must curse you!"

She raised her hands to her head and pushed away the light curls from her brow. There was a starving, hunted, almost furious look in her eyes, but she fixed them steadily on me.

"See," I went on—"here are more proofs of the truth of my story. These things were buried with me," and I threw into her lap as she sat before me the locket and chain, the card-case and purse she herself had given me. "You will no doubt recognize them. This—"and I showed her the monk's crucifix—"this was laid on my breast in the coffin. It may be useful to you—you can pray to it presently!"

She interrupted me with a gesture of her hand; she spoke as though in a dream.

"You escaped from this vault?" she said, in a low tone, looking from right to left with searching eagerness. "Tell me how—and—where?"

I laughed scornfully, guessing her thoughts.

"It matters little," I replied. "The passage I discovered is now closed and fast cemented. I have seen to that myself! No other living creature left here can escape as I did. Escape is impossible."

A stifled cry broke from her; she threw herself at my feet, letting the things I had given her as proofs of my existence fall heedlessly on the floor.

"Fabio! Fabio!" she cried, "save me, pity me! Take me out to the light–the air–let me live! Drag me through Naples–let all the crowd see me dishonored, brand me with the worst of names, make of me a common outcast–only let me feel the warm life throbbing in my veins! I will do anything, say anything, be anything–only let me live! I loathe the cold and darkness–the horrible–horrible ways of death!" She shuddered violently and clung to me afresh. "I am so young! and after all, am I so vile? There are women who count their lovers by the score, and yet they are not blamed; why should I suffer more than they?"

"Why, why?" I echoed, fiercely. "Because for once a husband takes the law into his own hands–for once a wronged man insists on justice–for once he dares to punish the treachery that blackens his honor! Were there more like me there would be fewer like you! A score of lovers! 'Tis not your fault that you had but one! I have something else to say which concerns you. Not content with fooling two men, you tried the same amusement on a supposed third. Ay, you wince at that! While you thought me to be the Count Oliva–while you were betrothed to me in that character, you wrote to Guido Ferrari in Rome. Very charming letters! here they are," and I flung them down to her. "I have no further use for them–I have read them all!"

She let them lie where they fell; she still crouched at my feet, and her restless movements loosened her cloak so far that it hung back from her shoulders, showing the jewels that flashed on her white neck and arms like points of living light. I touched the circlet of diamonds in her hair–I snatched it from her.

"These are mine!" I cried, "as much as this signet I wear, which was your love-gift to Guido Ferrari, and which you afterward returned to me, its rightful owner. These are my mother's gems–how dared you wear them? The stones I gave you are your only fitting ornaments– they are stolen goods, filched by the blood-stained hands of the blackest brigand in Sicily! I promised you more like them; behold them!"–and I threw open the coffin-shaped chest containing the remainder of Carmelo Neri's spoils. It occupied a conspicuous position near where I stood, and I had myself arranged its interior so that the gold ornaments and precious stones should be the first things to meet her eyes. "You see now," I went on, "where the wealth of the supposed Count Oliva came from. I found this treasure hidden here on the night of my burial–little did I think then what dire need I should have for its usage! It has served me well; it is not yet exhausted; the remainder is at your service!"

37

AT THESE words she rose from her knees and stood upright. Making an effort to fasten her cloak with her trembling hands, she moved hesitatingly toward the brigand's coffin and leaned over it, looking in with a faint light of hope as well as curiosity in her haggard face. I watched her in vague wonderment–she had grown old so suddenly. The peach-like bloom and delicacy of her flesh had altogether disappeared–her skin appeared drawn and dry as though parched in tropical heat. Her hair was disordered, and fell about her in clustering showers of gold– that, and her eyes, were the only signs of youth about her. A sudden wave of compassion swept over my soul.

"Oh wife!" I exclaimed–"wife that I so ardently loved–wife that I would have died for indeed, had you bade me!–why did you betray me? I thought you truth itself–ay! and if you had but waited for one day after you thought me dead, and THEN chosen Guido for your lover, I tell you, so large was my tenderness, I would have pardoned you! Though risen from the grave, I would have gone away and made no sign–yes if you had waited–if you had wept for me ever so little! But when your own lips confessed your crime–when I knew that within three months of our marriage-day you had fooled me–when I learned that my love, my name, my position, my honor, were used as mere screens to shelter your intrigue with the man I called friend!–God! what creature of mortal flesh and blood could forgive such treachery? I am no more than others–but I loved you–and in proportion to my love, so is the greatness of my wrongs!"

She listened–she advanced a little toward me–a faint smile dawned on her pallid lips–she whispered:

"Fabio! Fabio!"

I looked at her–unconsciously my voice dropped into a cadence of intense melancholy softened by tenderness.

"Ay–Fabio! What wouldst thou with a ghost of him? Does it not seem strange to thee–that hated name?–thou, Nina, whom I loved as few men love women–thou who gavest me no love at all–thou, who hast broken my heart and made me what I am!"

A hard, heavy sob rose in my throat and choked my utterance. I was young; and the cruel waste and destruction of my life seemed at that moment more than I could bear. She heard me, and the smile brightened more warmly on her countenance. She came close to me– half timidly yet coaxingly she threw one arm about my neck–her bosom heaved quickly.

"Fabio," she murmured–"Fabio, forgive me! I spoke in haste–I do not hate thee! Come! I will make amends for all thy suffering–I will love thee–I will be true to thee, I will be all thine! See! thou knowest I have not lost my beauty!"

And she clung to me with passion, raising her lips to mine, while with her large inquiring eyes she searched my face for the reply to her words. I gazed down upon her with sorrowful sternness.

"Beauty? Mere food for worms–I care not for it! Of what avail is a fair body tenanted by a fiendish soul? Forgiveness?– you ask too late! A wrong like mine can never be forgiven."

There ensued a silence. She still embraced me, but her eyes roved over me as though she searched for some lost thing. The wind tore furiously among the branches of the cypresses outside, and screamed through the small holes and crannies of the stone-work, rattling the iron gate at the summit of the stairway with a clanking sound, as though the famous brigand chief had escaped with all his chains upon him, and were clamoring for admittance to recover his buried property. Suddenly her face lightened with an expression of cunning intensity–and before I could perceive her intent–with swift agility she snatched from my vest the dagger I carried!

"Too late!" she cried, with a wild laugh. "No; not too late! Die– wretch!"

For one second the bright steel flashed in the wavering light as she poised it in act to strike–the next, I had caught her murderous hand and forced it down, and was struggling with her for the mastery of the weapon. She held it with a desperate grip–she fought with me breathlessly, clinging to me with all her force–she reminded me of that ravenous unclean bird with which I had had so fierce a combat on the night of my living burial. For some brief moments she was possessed of supernatural strength–she sprung and tore at my clothes, keeping the poniard fast in her clutch. At last I thrust her down, panting and exhausted, with fury flashing in her eyes–I wrenched the steel from her hand and brandished it above her.

"Who talks of murder NOW?" I cried, in bitter derision. "Oh, what a joy you have lost! What triumph for you, could you have stabbed me to the heart and left me here dead indeed! What a new career of lies would have been yours! How sweetly you would have said your prayers with the stain of my blood upon your soul! Ay! you would have fooled the world to the end, and died in the odor of sanctity. And you dared to ask my forgiveness–"

I stopped short–a strange, bewildered expression suddenly passed over her face–she looked about her in a dazed, vague way–then her gaze became suddenly fixed, and she pointed toward a dark corner and shuddered.

"Hush–hush!" she said, in a low, terrified whisper. "Look! how still he stands! how pale he seems! Do not speak–do not move–hush! he must not hear your voice–I will go to him and tell him all–all–" She rose and stretched out her arms with a gesture of entreaty:

"Guido! Guido!"

With a sudden chilled awe at my heart I looked toward the spot that thus riveted her attention–all was shrouded in deep gloom. She caught my arm.

"Kill him!" she whispered, fiercely–"kill him, and then I will love you! Ah!" and with an exclamation of fear she began to retire swiftly backward as though confronted by some threatening figure. "He is coming–nearer! No, no, Guido! You shall not touch me–you dare not–Fabio is dead and I am free– free!" She paused–her wild eyes gazed upward–did she see some horror there? She put up both hands as though to shield herself from some impending blow, and uttering a loud cry she fell prone on the stone floor insensible. Or dead? I balanced this question indifferently, as I looked down upon her inanimate form. The flavor of vengeance was hot in my mouth, and filled me with delirious satisfaction. True, I had been glad, when my bullet whizzing sharply through the air had carried death to Guido, but my gladness had been mingled with ruthfulness and regret. NOW, not one throb of pity stirred me–not the faintest emotion of tenderness, Ferrari's sin was great, but SHE tempted him–her crime outweighed his. And now–there she lay white and silent–in a swoon that was like death–that might be death for aught I knew–or cared! Had her lover's ghost indeed appeared before the eyes of her guilty conscience? I did not doubt it–I should scarcely have been startled had I seen the poor pale shadow of him by my side, as I musingly gazed upon the fair fallen body of the traitoress who had wantonly wrecked both our lives.

"Ay, Guido," I muttered, half aloud–"dost see the work? Thou art avenged, frail spirit–avenged as well as I–part thou in peace from earth and its inhabitants!–haply thou shalt cleanse in pure fire the sins of thy lower nature, and win a final pardon; but for her– is hell itself black enough to match HER soul?"

And I slowly moved toward the stairway; it was time, I

thought, with a grim resolve–TO LEAVE HER! Possibly she was dead–if not–why then she soon would be! I paused irresolute–the wild wind battered ceaselessly at the iron gateway, and wailed as though with a hundred voices of aerial creatures, lamenting. The torches were burning low, the darkness of the vault deepened. Its gloom concerned me little– I had grown familiar with its unsightly things, its crawling spiders, its strange uncouth beetles, the clusters of blue fungi on its damp walls. The scurrying noises made by bats and owls, who, scared by the lighted candles, were hiding themselves in holes and corners of refuge, startled me not at all–I was well accustomed to such sounds. In my then state of mind, an emperor's palace were less fair to me than this brave charnel house–this stone-mouthed witness of my struggle back to life and all life's misery. The deep-toned bell outside the cemetery struck ONE! We had been absent nearly two hours from the brilliant assemblage left at the hotel. No doubt we were being searched for everywhere–it mattered not! they would not come to seek us HERE. I went on resolutely toward the stair–as I placed my foot on the firm step of the ascent, my wife stirred from her recumbent position–her swoon had passed. She did not perceive me where I stood, ready to depart–she murmured something to herself in a low voice, and taking in her hand the falling tresses of her own hair she seemed to admire its color and texture, for she stroked it and restroked it and finally broke into a gay laugh–a laugh so out of all keeping with her surroundings, that it startled me more than her attempt to murder me.

She presently stood up with all her own lily-like grace and fairy majesty; and smiling as though she were a pleased child, she began to arrange her disordered dress with elaborate care. I paused wonderingly and watched her. She went on to the brigand's chest of treasure and proceeded to examine its contents–laces, silver and gold embroideries, antique ornaments, she took carefully in her hands, seeming mentally to calculate their cost and value. Jewels that were set as necklaces, bracelets and other trinkets of feminine wear she put on, one after the other, till her neck and arms were loaded—and literally blazed with the myriad scintillations of different-colored gems. I marveled at her strange conduct, but did not as yet guess its meaning. I moved away from the staircase and drew imperceptibly nearer to her—Hark! what was that? A strange, low rumbling like a distant earthquake, followed by a sharp cracking sound; I stopped to listen attentively. A furious gust of wind rushed round the mausoleum shrieking wildly like some devil in anger, and the strong draught flying through the gateway extinguished two of the flaring candles. My wife, entirely absorbed in counting over Carmelo Neri's treasures, apparently saw and heard nothing. Suddenly she broke into another laugh—a chuckling, mirthless laugh such as might come from the lips of the aged and senile. The sound curdled the blood in my veins—it was the laugh of a mad-woman! With an earnest, distinct voice I called to her:

"Nina! Nina!"

She turned toward me still smiling—her eyes were bright, her face had regained its habitual color, and as she stood in the dim light, with her rich tresses falling about her, and the clustering gems massed together in a glittering fire against her white skin, she looked unnaturally, wildly beautiful. She nodded to me, half graciously, half haughtily, but gave me no answer. Moved with quick pity I called again:

"Nina!"

She laughed again—the same terrible laugh.

"*Si, si! Son' bella, son' bellissima!*" she murmured. "*E tu, Guido mio? Tu m'ami?*"

Then raising one hand as though commanding attention she cried:

"*Ascolta!*" and began to sing clearly though feebly:

"*Ti saluto, Rosignuolo! Nel tuo duolo—ti saluto! Sei l'amante della rosa Che morendo si fa sposa!*"

As the old familiar melody echoed through the dreary vault, my bitter wrath against her partially lessened; with the swiftness of my southern temperament a certain compassion stirred my soul. She was no longer quite the same woman who had wronged and betrayed me– she had the helplessness and fearful innocence of madness–in that condition I could not have hurt a hair of her head. I stepped hastily forward–I resolved to take her out of the vault–after all I would not leave her thus–but as I approached, she withdrew from me, and with an angry stamp of her foot motioned me backward, while a dark frown knitted her fair brows.

"Who are you?" she cried, imperiously. "You are dead, quite dead! How dare you come out of your grave!"

And she stared at me defiantly–then suddenly clasping her hands as though in ecstasy, and seeming to address some invisible being at her side, she said, in low, delighted tones:

"He is dead, Guido! Are you not glad?" She paused, apparently expecting some reply, for she looked about her wonderingly, and continued–"You did not answer me–are you afraid? Why are you so pale and stern? Have you just come back from Rome? What have you heard? That I am false?–oh, no! I will love you still–Ah! I forgot! you also are dead, Guido! I remember now–you cannot hurt me anymore–I am free–and quite happy!"

Smiling, she continued her song:

"Ti saluto, Sol di Maggio Col two raggio ti saluto! Sei l'Apollo del passato Sei l'amore incoronato!"

Again–again!–that hollow rumbling and crackling sound overhead. What could it be?

"L'amore incoronato!" hummed Nina fitfully, as she plunged her round, jeweled arm down again into the chest of treasure. *"Si, si! Che morendo si fa sposa–che morendo si fa sposa–ah!"*

This last was an exclamation of pleasure; she had found some toy that charmed her–it was the old mirror set in its frame of pearls. The possession of this object seemed to fill her with extraordinary joy, and she evidently retained no consciousness of where she was, for she sat down on the upturned coffin, which had held my living body, with absolute indifference. Still singing softly to herself, she gazed lovingly at her own reflection, and fingered the jewels she wore, arranging and rearranging them in various patterns with one hand, while in the other she raised the looking-glass in the flare of the candles which lighted up its quaint setting. A strange and awful picture she made there–gazing with such lingering tenderness on the portrait of her own beauty–while surrounded by the moldering coffins that silently announced how little such beauty was worth–playing with jewels, the foolish trinkets of life, in the abode of skeletons, where the password is death! Thinking thus, I gazed at her, as one might gaze at a dead body–not loathingly anymore, but only mournfully. My vengeance was satiated. I could not wage war against this vacantly smiling mad creature, out of whom the spirit of a devilish intelligence and cunning had been torn, and who therefore was no longer the same woman. Her loss of wit should compensate for my loss of love. I determined to try and attract her attention again. I opened my lips to speak–but before the words could form themselves, that odd rumbling noise again broke on my ears–this time with a loud reverberation that rolled overhead like the thunder of artillery. Before I could imagine the reason of it– before I could advance one step toward my wife, who still sat on the upturned coffin, smiling at herself in the mirror–before I could utter a word or move an inch, a tremendous crash resounded through the vault, followed by a stinging shower of stones, dust, and pulverized mortar! I stepped backward amazed, bewildered– speechless–instinctively shutting my eyes–when I opened them again all was darkness–all was silence! Only the wind howled outside more frantically than ever–a sweeping gust whirled through the vault, blowing some dead leaves against my face, and I heard the boughs of trees creaking noisily in the fury of the storm. Hush!–was that a faint moan? Quivering in every limb, and sick with a nameless dread, I sought in my pocket for matches–I found them. Then with an effort, mastering the shuddering revulsion of my nerves, I struck a light. The flame was so dim that for an instant I could see nothing. I called loudly:

"Nina!" There was no answer.

One of the extinguished candles was near me; I lighted it with trembling hands and held it aloft–then I uttered a wild shriek of horror! Oh, God of inexorable justice, surely Thy vengeance was greater than mine! An enormous block of stone, dislodged by the violence of the storm, had fallen from the roof of the vault; fallen sheer down over the very place where SHE had sat a minute or two before, fantastically smiling! Crushed under the huge mass–crushed into the very splinters of my own empty coffin, she lay–and yet– and yet–I could see nothing, save one white hand protruding–the hand on which the marriage-ring glittered mockingly! Even as I looked, that hand quivered violently–beat the ground–and then–was still! It was horrible. In dreams I see that quivering white hand now, the jewels on it sparkling with derisive luster. It appeals, it calls, it threatens, it prays! and when my time comes to die, it will beckon me to my grave! A portion of her costly dress was visible–my eyes lighted on this–and I saw a slow stream of blood oozing thickly from beneath the stone–the ponderous stone that no man could have moved an inch–the stone that sealed her awful sepulcher! Great Heaven! how fast the crimson stream of life trickled!–staining the snowy lace of her garment with a dark and dreadful hue! Staggering feebly like a drunken man–half delirious with anguish–I approached and touched that small white hand that lay stiffly on the ground–I bent my head–I almost kissed it, but some strange revulsion rose in my soul and forbade the act!

In a stupor of dull agony I sought and found the crucifix of the monk Cipriano that had fallen to the floor–I closed the yet warm finger-tips around it and left it thus; an unnatural, terrible calmness froze the excitement of my strained nerves.

"'Tis all I can do for thee!" I muttered, incoherently. "May Christ forgive thee, though I cannot!"

And covering my eyes to shut out the sight before me I

turned away. I hurried in a sort of frenzy toward the stairway–on reaching the lowest step I extinguished the torch I carried. Some impulse made me glance back–and I saw what I see now–what I shall always see till I die! An aperture had been made through the roof of the vault by the fall of the great stone, and through this the fitful moon poured down a long ghostly ray. The green glimmer, like a spectral lamp, deepened the surrounding darkness, only showing up with fell distinctness one object–that slender protruding wrist and hand, whiter than Alpine snow! I gazed at it wildly–the gleam of the jewels down there hurt my eyes–the shine of the silver crucifix clasped in those little waxen fingers dazzled my brain-and with a frantic cry of unreasoning terror, I rushed up the steps with a maniac speed–opened the iron gate through which SHE would pass no more, and stood at liberty in the free air, face to face with a wind as tempestuous as my own passions. With what furious haste I shut the entrance to the vault! with what fierce precaution I locked and doubled-locked it! Nay, so little did I realize that she was actually dead, that I caught myself saying aloud–"Safe–safe at last! She cannot escape–I have closed the secret passage–no one will hear her cries–she will struggle a little, but it will soon be over–she will never laugh any more–never kiss–never love–never tell lies for the fooling of men!–she is buried as I was–buried alive!"

Muttering thus to myself with a sort of sobbing incoherence, I turned to meet the snarl of the savage blast of the night, with my brain reeling, my limbs weak and trembling–with the heavens and earth rocking before me like a wild sea–with the flying moon staring aghast through the driving clouds–with all the universe, as it were, in a broken and shapeless chaos about me; even so I went forth to meet my fate–and left her!

* * *

Unrecognized, untracked, I departed from Naples.

Wrapped in my cloak, and stretched in a sort of heavy stupor on the deck of the "Rondinella," my appearance apparently excited no suspicion in the mind of the skipper, old Antonio Bardi, with whom my friend Andrea had made terms for my voyage, little aware of the real identity of the passenger he recommended.

The morning was radiantly beautiful–the sparkling waves rose high on tiptoe to kiss the still boisterous wind–the sunlight broke in a wide smile of springtide glory over the world! With the burden of my agony upon me–with the utter exhaustion of my overwrought nerves, I beheld all things as in a feverish dream–the laughing light, the azure ripple of waters–the receding line of my native shores– everything was blurred, indistinct, and unreal to me, though my soul, Argus-eyed, incessantly peered down, down into those darksome depths where SHE lay, silent forever. For now I knew she was dead. Fate had killed her–not I. All unrepentant as she was, triumphing in her treachery to the last, even in her madness, still I would have saved her, though she strove to murder me.

Yet it was well the stone had fallen–who knows!–if she had lived– I strove not to think of her, and drawing the key of the vault from my pocket, I let it drop with a sudden splash into the waves. All was over–no one pursued me–no one inquired whither I went. I arrived at Civita Vecchia unquestioned; from thence I travelled to Leghorn, where I embarked on board a merchant trading vessel bound for South America. Thus I lost myself to the world; thus I became, as it were, buried alive for the second time. I am safely sepulchered in these wild woods, and I seek no escape.

Wearing the guise of a rough settler, one who works in common with others, hewing down tough parasites and poisonous undergrowths in order to effect a clearing through these pathless solitudes, none can trace in the strong stern man, with the care-worn face and white hair, any resemblance to the once popular and wealthy Count Oliva, whose disappearance, so strange and sudden, was for a time the talk of all Italy. For, on one occasion when visiting the nearest town, I saw an article in a newspaper, headed "Mysterious Occurrence in Naples," and I read every word of it with a sensation of dull amusement.

From it I learned that the Count Oliva was advertised for. His abrupt departure, together with that of his newly married wife, formerly Contessa Romani, on the very night of their wedding, had created the utmost excitement in the city. The landlord of the hotel where he stayed was prosecuting inquiries–so was the count's former valet, one Vincenzo Flamma. Any information would be gratefully received by the police authorities. If within twelve months no news were obtained, the immense properties of the Romani family, in default of existing kindred, would be handed over to the crown.

There was much more to the same effect, and I read it with the utmost indifference. Why do they not search the Romani vault?–I thought gloomily–they would find some authentic information there! But I know the Neapolitans well; they are timorous and superstitious; they would as soon hug a pestilence as explore a charnel house. One thing gladdened me; it was the projected disposal of my fortune. The crown, the Kingdom of Italy, was surely as noble an heir as a man could have! I returned to my woodland hut with a strange peace on my soul.

As I told you at first, I am a dead man–the world, with its busy life and aims, has naught to do with me. The tall trees, the birds, the whispering grasses are my friends and my companions–they, and they only, are sometimes the silent witnesses of the torturing fits of agony that every now and then overwhelm me with bitterness. For I suffer always. That is natural. Revenge is sweet!–but who shall paint the horrors of memory? My vengeance now recoils upon my own head. I do not complain of this–it is the law of compensation–it is just. I blame no one–save Her, the woman who wrought my wrong. Dead as she is I do not forgive her; I have tried to, but I cannot! Do men ever truly forgive the women who ruin their lives? I doubt it. As for me, I feel that the end is not yet–that when my soul is released from its earthly prison, I shall still be doomed in some drear dim way to pursue her treacherous flitting spirit over the black chasms of a hell darker than Dante's–she in the likeness of a wandering flame–I as her haunting shadow; she, flying before me in coward fear–I, hasting after her in relentless wrath–and this forever and ever!

But I ask no pity–I need none. I punished the guilty, and in doing so suffered more than they–that is as it must always be. I have no regret and no remorse; only one thing troubles me– one little thing–a mere foolish fancy! It conies upon me in the night, when the large-faced moon looks at me from heaven. For the moon is grand in this climate; she is like a golden-robed empress of all the worlds as she sweeps in lustrous magnificence through the dense violet skies. I shut out her radiance as much as I can; I close the blind at the narrow window of my solitary forest cabin; and yet do what I will, one wide ray creeps in always–one ray that eludes all my efforts to expel it. Under the door it comes, or through some unguessed cranny in the wood-work. I have in vain tried to find the place of its entrance.

The color of the moonlight in this climate is of a mellow amber–so I cannot understand why that pallid ray that visits me so often, should be green–a livid, cold, watery green; and in it, like a lily in an emerald pool, I see a little white hand on which the jewels cluster thick like drops of dew! The hand moves–it lifts itself– the small fingers point at me threateningly–they quiver–and then– they beckon me slowly, solemnly, commandingly onward!–onward!–to some infinite land of awful mysteries where Light and Love shall dawn for me no more.

ABOUT THE AUTHOR

Marie Corelli (1 May 1855 – 21 April 1924) was a British novelist. She enjoyed a period of great literary success from the publication of her first novel in 1886 until World War I. Corelli's novels sold more copies than the combined sales of popular contemporaries, including Arthur Conan Doyle, H. G. Wells, and Rudyard Kipling, although critics often derided her work as "the favourite of the common multitude."

Mackay began her career as a musician, adopting the name Marie Corelli for her billing. Eventually she turned to writing and published her first novel, A Romance of Two Worlds, in 1886. In her time, she was the most widely read author of fiction. Her works were collected by Winston Churchill, Randolph Churchill, and members of the British Royal Family, among others.

Wikipedia, May 2014

Other Books from Villainous Press

The Adventures of Dr. Bird	Sterner St. Paul Meek
Giants on the Earth	Sterner St. Paul Meek
The Heaviside Layer	Sterner St. Paul Meek
Ancient Terrors 1	Guy Anthony De Marco
Ancient Terrors 2	Guy Anthony De Marco
Ancient Terrors 3	Guy Anthony De Marco
Life & Everything Too	Guy Anthony De Marco
Odd Places	Guy Anthony De Marco
Tales from the Fleet	Guy Anthony De Marco
Golden Girl of Munan	Harl Vincent
Barton's Island	Harl Vincent
Purple & Gray	Harl Vincent
Vagabonds	Harl Vincent
Drylands of Mars	Harl Vincent
Subterrania	Harl Vincent
Air Wonder Stories	Harl Vincent
Copper-Clad World	Harl Vincent
A Princess of Mars	Edgar Rice Burroughs
Warlord of Mars	Edgar Rice Burroughs
The Gods of Mars	Edgar Rice Burroughs
Thuvia, Maid of Mars	Edgar Rice Burroughs
The Chessmen of Mars	Edgar Rice Burroughs
House on the Borderland	William Hope Hodgson
Grey Shapes	E. Charles Vivian
Pharos the Egyptian	Guy Boothby
The Gates Ajar	Elizabeth Stuart Phelps
Sorceress of the Strand	L.T. Meade & R. Eustace
The Thing from the Lake	Eleanor M. Ingram
Watcher by the Threshold	John Buchan
Steampunk: The Other Worlds	Sam Knight

Available at VillainousPress.com